CAR

D0588520

TO

DIE

TIME

TO

DIE

CAROLINE MITCHELL

bookouture

Published by Bookouture

An imprint of StoryFire Ltd.
23 Sussex Road, Ickenham, UB10 8PN
United Kingdom

www.bookouture.com

ISBN: 978-1-909490-43-5
eBook ISBN: 978-1-909490-42-8

ACKNOWLEDGMENTS

I am hugely grateful to the people who have helped bring this book, the second in the DC Knight series to fruition.

To Oliver Rhodes, Claire Bord, Kim Nash, Keshini Naidoo, and my wonderful tribe of Bookouture authors – Thank you, your support has been phenomenal.

To Tracy Fenton, who tirelessly brings authors, readers and reviewers together in THE Book Club on Facebook. Your sense of humour, passion for books and support for new authors is commendable.

To the band of dedicated book reviewers and readers who have championed DC Jennifer Knight from the beginning – You know who you are! Thank you just doesn't cut it, here's a huge virtual hug from me.

To my family, friends and JDATT colleagues, thank you for putting up with my writing obsession over the last year. It's been a pleasure to share this leg of my journey with you.

To my lovely husband Neil, I wouldn't be writing this acknowledgement if it weren't for your support. I'd also like to give a special thanks to your mum and dad, Valerie and Patrick Coughlan, for being my surrogate parents since our move to the UK. I could not have wished for nicer in-laws.

To my children. Thank you for understanding all the days I have come home tired from work and locked myself away in a room to write. For all the times you've done the housework when I've been rushing to meet deadlines, and most of all, for all your hugs. Paul, Aoife, Jessica and Benjamin; remember, you can do anything if you set your mind to it.

To my readers, there wouldn't be any DC Knight books without you. I hope you enjoy her latest adventure. You never know where she's going to take you!

This book is dedicated to my father Niall Mitchell,
who taught me the value of hard work and determination.

CHAPTER ONE
Bert

'*Please don't hurt me.*' Mother's voice rang in his ears as Bert drove through the inky rain-drenched streets. The wipers of the rusty orange van whipped back and forth like a metronome, conducting his thoughts into a symphony of torment.

'*Please Bertram don't ...*'

Bert turned up the radio to drown out the memory. It blended in a mind crowded with dark thoughts, surfacing as the maddening itch that threatened the remains of his sanity. He swore as the Volkswagen hit a pothole and jolted him in his seat. The moonless sky did little to ease his journey, and he peered through the rain-streaked windscreen at the road sign ahead. *Haven*. Bert bared his teeth in a sharp smile. It was almost biblical.

The exhaust pipe of his van belched out a plume of smoke before shuddering into submission in the rear car park of The Cherry Tree pub. Bert threw off the seatbelt that had long since lost its elasticity and wrenched the handbrake as far as it would go. Giving himself one last glance in the rear view mirror, he nodded in silent affirmation before throwing open the van door. Clamping a hand over his black fedora hat, he ran to the pub as the rain beat into his back, his long black trench coat flapping open.

The sweet smell of damp logs rose from the open fire, and he shook his foot to dispel the water trickling through the hole in his shoe. At least the place was warm. The early spring evening had brought a biting chill to the air. He shoved the van keys deep into his pocket, shuddering at the thought of returning to the cold metal tomb. It was a poor comparison to his warm bed at home. But he couldn't go back. Not now.

His small flint eyes slid over the patrons in the low-beamed pub. A disinterested-looking couple sat beside the log fire, their fingers pecking at their iPhones in the absence of conversation. His gaze moved to the bar, where a well-padded man in a navy suit sat staring into his pint. A thought snaked into Bert's consciousness. *He's the one.* Shaking the rain from his hat, Bert dragged a metal comb through his damp wisps of silver hair. He rifled for change in his worn suit pocket and ordered a pint of Guinness, dropping an array of coins on the dusky wooden bar.

The barman curled his fat fingers over the five and ten pence pieces, his lips moving silently as he counted them into the till. But Bert was not interested in him. He was focused on the man at the bar. His heart cranked up a notch at the thought of what lay ahead, and he left his pint to rest. Five minutes. He needed five minutes to steady himself, and then he would begin. The stench of piss and cigarette stubs rose from the men's toilets, and he gripped the corners of the ceramic sink as he drew upon his reserves of strength. Staring in the mirror, he sought out his power. It lay in the darkness behind his eyes, sank deep in their sockets. It will be done, he whispered, a twisted smile playing on his lips.

He returned to find suit man half asleep, his fleshy cheeks pressing through open fingers as he leaned into his hands.

Bert sank back mouthfuls of Guinness, savouring the creamy black liquid as it hit the back of his throat. Satiated, he rifled in his pocket for his battered deck of tarot cards. An unlikely tool to initiate the death of another, but for Bert, therein lay the appeal.

'What you got there, buddy?' suit man said, the trace of an American accent on his lips.

Bert's lips narrowed in a smile as he patted the deck of cards in front of him. 'These, my friend, can predict your future.'

Suit man snickered before raising the whisky chaser to his lips and knocking it back. 'Scuse me, can I order another round and a Guinness for my compadre here?'

The barman cast a curious glance over the unlikely friendship before drying his glass with a tea towel and turning to dispense the drinks.

'Much appreciated,' Bert said, in his most amenable tone.

'That's OK. I'm feeling friendly. That barman is as much fun as a root canal.'

Bert laughed mechanically, narrowing his eyes at the barman returning with their drinks.

'Have you had your fortune told before?' Bert asked, scratching the itch behind his ear. It burned like fire into his skin. He hated small talk, but he did what he could to gain the trust of those chosen to receive their prophecy.

The man dropped his eyes as he picked at his beer mat. 'No I haven't. Lately I seem to spend all my time in the past.'

Bert understood the sentiment, but he truly didn't care. 'Give me a tenner and I'll tell you your future. What do you say?'

Suit man leaned to the left as he pulled out a wad of money from his back pocket. Dipping his fingers into the roll, he slipped ten pounds on the bar. 'Hit me.'

Bert wiped the bar clean with his sleeve as faint laughter echoed from within. Shuffling the cards, he felt the joy of release as he transferred his energies to the pack. He fanned out the deck, asking the man to choose three cards before placing them face down on the bar.

'These are past, present and future,' Bert said, turning the first card over. It had begun. Like the roll of a dice, the prophecy had been set into action and could not be halted. The reading was accurate and to the point. He told of suit man's success in business, and the sleep paralysis which terrorised his nights. A condition so debilitating he had forced himself to return to face a past best forgotten. His face was an expressionless mask as the words unfolded in Bert's gravelly drawl.

Bert took in the images only he could see, suit man's past delivered to his mind's eye in cine-camera pictures complete with sound, smells, and dark emotions.

Suit man was a good deal younger, his dark hair skimming the collar of his black leather jacket. His parents owned the pub in which they sat, and he was no stranger to driving his father's car after a belly full of cider. As he sped past the rows of trees, he did not see the six-year-old child chase her dog down the footpath. Blonde curls bouncing, she didn't have time to scream as he lost control and clipped the kerb. A screeching of brakes was followed by a sickening thud. She didn't stand a chance. Bile rose to his throat at the sight of the motionless body in his rear view mirror. Where was her mother? Why had nobody been watching her? Heart clamouring, he reached for the car door handle, and then paused. What was the point in stopping now? The damage had been done. Pumping the accelerator, he sped down the sun-streaked road. He must have imagined it. It must have been a dog not a child, and it was far too beautiful a day for such a horrific thing to occur.

Bert took a deep breath as the image passed. He did not feel disgust at the man's actions; it was too late for that now. No, he felt delight. For he was going to help the transgressor atone for his sins. After all, wasn't that what he was here for? A shot of death in the vein of this diseased soul. The fact that he would benefit from the demise of another simply told him it was meant to be.

'This is the last card,' Bert said, his throat dry. He wondered why he hadn't revealed the man's murky past, why he hadn't whispered those two words ... *I know*. But now it was time for the grand finale. The climax, and Bert could barely wait. 'You might not want to hear what I have to say but I'm going to complete the reading with a future prophecy.'

Suit man shrugged as his words curled in a slur. 'You've blown me away so far. Feel free.' Bert's eyes flickered to suit man's car keys, sat like an accusation on the bar. He licked his lips as he dealt his last hand.

'That rope in the boot of your car, the one you've been playing with, well tonight you're going to use it. Because it's the only way you can pay for what you've done.' Bert held back a chuckle as a frisson of excitement rose up inside him. Was there really a rope in the boot of his car? The crumpled expression on the man's face told him there was. He paused for breath and glanced around the pub. The couple had left and the dying embers of the fire faintly crackled in the background. A clock ticked on the wall, a reminder that time was running out for both of them. The tiniest of smiles tugged at Bert's lips as he slowly and deliberately delivered the final words. 'You came to face your demons but *you* are the monster of your nightmares. Finish it now and beg for forgiveness when you meet your maker. It's the only way to save your soul.'

The man's mask of friendship fell away to reveal eyes filled with torture and anguish. It was as if someone had let the air out of his face, and the age-ripened lines and grooves deepened in his distress. Slowly he nodded, before finishing his drink and sliding off the leather barstool. 'It's time,' suit man said, in a hollow voice.

'Yes,' Bert agreed, his voice dropping to a whisper. 'Time to die.' He did not try to stop the man as he left the pub, his shoulders slouched under the burden of guilt. The ker-thunk sound of the double doors announced he had exited the building.

Snapping into action, Bert gathered together his cards. The shake in his hands was not from fear, but from the adrenalin coursing through his veins. It would not be long now. Giving the cards a quick shuffle, he slipped them back into the red velvet pouch before tugging the frayed gold drawstrings. It was a suitable punishment for the wicked, and a blessed release for him. Tonight suit man would take the rope to the dingy bedroom he was renting, and throw it over the strongest beam. With Bert's words echoing in his mind, he would climb up onto a chair and place the noose over his head. Suit man's final thoughts would be of the little girl he mowed down all those years ago.

Bert swigged the leftover whisky chaser in one gulp. As he slid off the barstool something on the floor caught his eye. Could it be? He ran his fingers through his hair, purposely knocking off his hat. Bending down to pick it up, he placed it over the wad of notes that had fallen from suit man's pocket onto the floor. *There must be a few hundred quid there.* Sliding them into the inner lip of his hat, he walked out to his van. The prediction had served him well, and the man would not need it any more. He smiled at the prospect of his next kill. Sin was all around. He would not be found wanting.

CHAPTER TWO

'Stop, police!' DC Jennifer Knight yelled at the young woman, who appeared to have gained the ability of a gazelle through the streets of Haven. 'Why do I always get the runners?' she said between breaths. 'Emily, stop, I just need to talk to you.'

'Bog off!' the girl yelled, her long auburn hair streaming behind her as she clattered down the narrow alleyway, dodging puddles and overstuffed rubbish bins.

Jennifer began to lose ground and wondered where her partner DC Will Dunston had gotten to. He appeared at the end of the alleyway and took the girl's legs in a swift rugby tackle. Not one to lose face, Jennifer pulled the girl out of the gutter by the scruff of her neck.

'When I say stop, I mean stop,' she said, pulling Emily's wrists behind her as Will locked the cuffs in place. Jennifer recited the caution before arresting her for theft. A quick search under her puffa jacket produced the stash of jewellery freshly stolen from the counter of the jewellers on the high street. Shouts of police brutality drowned out her words as the insolent teen dragged her heels to the unmarked police car.

'You want me to drive?' Will asked, a smug grin creeping behind his beard. 'You look all done in.'

Jennifer fingered a loose tendril of brown wavy hair back into her hairclip. 'I was just giving you a head start. You drive, I'll sit in the back with our friend here.' She clicked Emily's seatbelt in its holster before sliding in beside her, muttering under her breath as her puddle-stained trousers seeped through to her skin.

The best thing about working for Operation Moonlight was the steady stream of unusual cases hitting their office on a daily basis. Emily Clarke was a particular person of interest, and unfortunately for her, was being monitored by Will and Jennifer as she made an impromptu visit to the jewellers. Loath to blow her cover, Jennifer allowed uniformed officers to deal with the aftermath of Emily's shoplifting of make-up and clothes, but expensive jewellery? As Will said, that was taking the piss. The elevation of her crime confirmed Jennifer's suspicions. Emily was getting desperate.

Back at the station, Jennifer filled her sergeant in on Emily's arrest, and together they wrote up interview tactics, which were far more about extracting intelligence than theft of jewellery. Emily was a member of a cult that was spreading to every county in the UK. Weekly meetings resulted in chants, meditation, and the so-called rebirthing process, which gave the group its name: 'The Reborners'. Hailed as a second chance at life, they had no shortage of followers. But intelligence on drug use and suicides within neighbouring groups suggested all was not what it seemed. Nicknamed 'The God Drug', DMT, was the cheaply made psychedelic used to initiate powerful 'spiritual experiences'. With high joining fees and low production costs, The Reborners was a profitable money making machine.

Tasked to shut the Haven branch down, Op Moonlight were under pressure to locate the clandestine gatherings.

'Are you happy with that?' DS Claire Gilmour asked, as Jennifer finished making her notes. 'Will deals with the theft offence, and hopefully persuades her to speak to you about the cult. If we can't convince her to speak, then remind her that social services will be all over this like a rash, if she ends up inside.'

'It's all for the greater good,' Jennifer said, glad they were on the same wavelength. Using Emily's misfortune as leverage for gaining quality intelligence may have seemed distasteful to some, but her cooperation could secure a suspended sentence, which meant keeping her out of prison as long as she kept her nose clean. It was a case of one back scratching the other, and worth pursuing, if it meant cleaning up the streets.

Jennifer had been thrilled to discover Claire was supervising Op Moonlight. An old friend from her joining-up days, her psychic talents had led to her being offered a place supervising the team. Claire's office was clean and efficient, apart from the scent of dog that sometimes lingered on her clothes.

'What do you think? Does it look like me? I bought it in Wilko's,' Claire said, holding a small spiky cactus decorated with two plastic eyes and a tuft of black curly hair.

'I can see a passing resemblance,' Jennifer laughed, enjoying the contrast between Claire and her previous sergeant, whose default mode was permanently stressed.

'Can you do me a favour?' Claire asked, as Jennifer rose to leave.

'Of course,' Jennifer said, sitting back down on the worn swivel chair.

'We have a new starter this afternoon. Her name is Zoe. She's only twenty-six. I'd like you to take her under your wing, help her settle in.'

'Sure,' Jennifer smiled, still feeling like the newbie herself. The four months since she had joined had flown by. It wasn't as if she had gone very far from her old office in Haven CID. Still on the same floor, she accessed her office through a security coded interconnecting door.

'And if she asks about the operation name, tell her she can thank DI Cole. I think our boss fancies himself as a black James Bond.'

'It's better than the "Supernatural Homicide Investigation Team", as suggested by Will.' Jennifer chuckled at the acronym. 'It's funny; when I tell people I'm working under Operation Moonlight, most coppers just nod their head and pretend they know what it is.'

Claire nodded. 'Men in black we ain't. We're still coppers and a crime is a crime, regardless of who's doing the mopping up.'

DI Ethan Cole poked his head through the door, making Claire jump. A well-dressed and classically handsome young man, he didn't have any psychic skills that Jennifer was aware of, but his enthusiasm for his job was palpable. Whether he was recruiting new staff or organising dawn raids, he gave the team one hundred and ten percent. While Claire was involved in the day to day running of the team, Ethan made all the major decisions, and bore the brunt of responsibility when things went wrong.

'Sorry to interrupt,' he said, addressing them both. 'I was wondering if Jennifer has time to attend The Cherry Tree pub with me. It's a sudden death, sounds like it's right up our street.'

Jennifer's eyes lit up at the prospect of another case involving the supernatural. She quickly did the maths. A sudden death shouldn't take too long, and the pub wasn't too far away. There was plenty of time for Will to interview Emily for theft then release her to assist Jennifer with her enquiries on The Reborners cult.

'Sure thing, boss,' Jennifer nodded, a tingle of anticipation making her giddy inside.

She pushed open the back doors to the outside yard, welcoming the crisp, fresh air into her lungs. Spring was finally in bloom, and the weak afternoon sun battled its way through the clouds that had not long since shed a fine mist of rain.

'Is this the hanging they were talking about earlier?' Jennifer asked. Nowadays her police radio was always on, and attached to the slim-fitting waistband of her designer trousers. Since the incident with Frank Foster, she did not want to miss a thing. A serial killer more dead than alive, he had left his mark deep in her psyche, and she knew that it would not be long before someone like Frank found her again. But right now, her thoughts were with Ethan, and she was keen to hear what he made of the sudden death they were tagged to attend.

'Yes, it's another suicide by the sound of it,' Ethan said, pushing back the car passenger seat to accommodate his long legs. 'The victim isn't even from around here. I wish people would kill themselves in their hometowns, and save me the paperwork.'

'You should be a spokesperson for the Samaritans, boss,' Jennifer said with a grin.

The right side of Ethan's mouth jerked upwards in his signature half smile. He was looking a lot happier now he and his father had put their differences behind them. Heading Operation Moonlight was something he embraced, and Jennifer was proud to be part of his team.

'The victim was found hung in his room,' Ethan said. 'There was no note, no sign of a struggle, and no forced entry. The informant mentioned a man posing as a fortune teller acting suspiciously the night before.'

As Ethan took the point-to-point call from the officer on scene, Jennifer began to feel a sense of unease creeping up on her. She drove in silence, straining to tune into the frequency of whatever was trying to warn her.

'Steady, you'll miss the turning,' Ethan said, pressing his foot on an imaginary brake.

'Oops, sorry, I was miles away,' she said, hastily skidding the unmarked Ford Focus into the car park of The Cherry Tree pub.

Ethan introduced himself to the landlord, who was carrying a tray of tea and slightly curled sandwiches to an elderly couple at the far end of the bar.

'I'll be with you in a minute,' the thickset man said in a slow, tired drone.

'Bit of a dive, isn't it?' Jennifer whispered to Ethan, as she leaned back on her elbows against the bar.

'Yeah. I heard this place reopened, doesn't look like he's done much with it.' Ethan lowered his voice as the barman returned and picked up a tea towel.

The landlord was surprisingly candid. 'I'll have to be quick. I've been running this place single-handed since the missus ran off.' He began to methodically polish each glass before holding them up to the light and placing them on a weathered brown tray.

Ethan cast his eyes downwards, giving a curt nod. It was as close as he could get to offering sympathy. 'You mentioned suspicious activity?'

He jabbed his thumb over his shoulder to the pensioners picking at their lunch. 'Old people and day trippers, that's all we usually get in here. They like the specials. Mr Price and the bloke last night stuck out like sore thumbs.'

Jennifer frowned. Price. The name rang a bell. But she had dealt with so many people in the last few months that she would need more to go on.

The barman finished his last glass and slung the tea towel over his shoulder.

'Price was over here from America. His parents used to own this place so he'd been renting a room for old time's sake, or so he said. Most nights he sat there, downing pints and chasers at the bar. Then this scruffy-looking bloke came in. He latched onto Price soon enough, blooming sponger. Are you getting all this down?' he asked, watching Jennifer scribble in her pocket notebook.

Jennifer flashed him a smile as she nodded and a pink tinge lit up his cheeks in return.

'He didn't seem to have much money but I pulled him a pint of Guinness and he drank it after he used the gents.'

'How long was he here?'

'Long enough to spread some cards across my bar and read Price his future. I only heard bits, but he said Price was going to hang himself. I thought it was some kind of wind-up until I found him dead.'

'Do you think they knew each other?' Jennifer asked.

'I doubt it. Can I get you a drink? A coffee maybe?' The landlord looked at her hopefully.

Jennifer shook her head. 'No thanks. Do you think there was foul play with Mr Price?'

The man shrugged his shoulders, 'I can't say for sure, but he was as creepy as hell. I've worked behind bars long enough to be a good judge of character, and I didn't like him one little bit.'

The landlord's overheads did not stretch to CCTV, and Jennifer took a quick description of the man before joining her DI, who had gone to check out the body.

By the time Jennifer joined him, the corpse of Mr Price had been zipped into a stiff black body bag by the undertakers, who were trying to work out how they were going to get such a large man down the narrow winding staircase.

Ethan looked at his watch, keen to get away before he was roped into some strange manoeuvres with the corpse.

The outdated bedroom looked more like something from an episode of *Most Haunted* than a room guests would pay to sleep in. Discoloured woodchip paper hung limply on the walls, decorated by wisps of spider webs clinging to each corner of the room. A worn hemp rope hung from the thick beam overhead, and beneath it, a toppled wooden chair. In the corner of the room was an unmade single bed, beside a tightly shuttered Georgian window. The musty smell suggested it hadn't been opened for some time. The smell also relayed the victim had soiled himself at the time of death, which made the cramped space unbearable. But Jennifer was not ready to leave just yet.

'Hang on,' she said, approaching them. 'Can I have a quick look? I've got a feeling I know him.'

Jennifer stared down at the cold bloated face as the zip of the body bag was pulled back. His twisted features were far from at peace. She searched her memory for a living version of the corpse before her, and something clicked into place. 'Of course, he came to see me the other day.'

Ethan left the undertakers scratching their heads on the landing as he made his escape down the narrow winding staircase. 'There's nothing on PNC for him,' he said to Jennifer as she followed him down. Attending officers had already checked the police national computer, which would highlight any offending history.

Jennifer clutched the handrail for support. 'I know. I checked him out too. He came to make an enquiry for *a friend*. He asked for me specifically because he knew me growing up.'

'Were you close?'

'Oh not at all. His parents owned this pub years ago. I used to come in to collect dad after he'd been drinking. Price must have looked me up.'

Ethan's face set in a grim line at the mention of her father. 'So what did Price want?'

'He asked about past offences and how people were treated if they confessed to historic crimes. I gave him some strong advice and told him it was best to come clean, especially with advances in forensics. He thanked me and left. I made a note to do some digging on offences around the time he mentioned. It's in my "to do" pile.'

'Looks like he found another way of dealing with it. Did you pick anything up at the scene?'

'Not a thing. But it all seems a bit weird with that other guy telling him to go for it.'

Ethan blew out his cheeks in exhalation. 'I'm not convinced there's anything paranormal connected with this, but do a bit of digging on Price and submit a report on the tarot card reader just the same.' An intelligence report submitted under the Operation Moonlight banner would trigger a confidential information sharing process between the other hubs, located in London, Wales, and Scotland.

'You're teaching your grandma how to suck eggs,' Jennifer said absentmindedly, rooting in her bag for the car keys. She reddened as she pulled the keys out of her bag, reminding herself she was with Ethan, not Will, and his tolerance for banter had not yet been tested.

'Point taken,' Ethan said, holding out his hand for the keys. 'I'll drive if that's OK with you.'

After an uneventful journey back to the station, Jennifer sat at her desk and stared at the files in various colour binders. As much as she loved Op Moonlight, finding a genuine case involving the paranormal meant wading through police incidents full of fanciful accusations and unlikely events. A unit in the control centre filtered reports of interest to their team, allocating the steady flow of incidents involving the paranormal from across the county, with Haven and Lexton being the main hotspots of activity. They were then emailed to her sergeant, who printed and collated files of the reports, colour coding them as they were disseminated for further investigation within the team. Red was urgent, amber was important, and green was non-priority – or a crock of shit as Will so delicately put it. Jennifer sighed as she counted the number of green folders. At least she didn't have to travel for those ones. Most of the time she could deal with them over the phone.

She cast an eye over Will's wrinkled suit as he came purposefully striding over, hiding one hand behind his back. She wished he would take more pride in his appearance, but her efforts to bring him into step never lasted very long. Perhaps it was time she accepted him for who he was. Jennifer sighed as he stood before her, an expectant look on his face.

'Please tell me there haven't been any more nickings while I've been out. I've got to speak to Emily yet, and all these jobs have magically landed on my desk.'

'Emily's been bailed. Childcare issues. She's promised to come in tomorrow and tell all.'

'She'd better,' Jennifer said, jabbing a thumb towards Will's spotless workspace. 'I cleaned your desk while you were out. The least you can do is take some of these green files off me.'

'Not my fault you keep swanning off with the DI,' Will said, holding out a letter. 'Here. It was dropped into front counter after you left.'

Jennifer frowned as she stared at her name scrawled on the white bonded envelope. It felt cold to the touch, as if it had been stored in a fridge.

'Maybe it's a thank you letter,' Will said before snickering, 'oh sorry, I forgot, you don't get those, do you?'

Jennifer narrowed her eyes at Will in mock disgust. Her computer pinged with twelve new emails to add to her already neglected inbox. He was right. She needed to stay in the office and get on top of things. A decent case was hiding somewhere in the deluge of enquiries. Lifting the envelope to her nose, she closed her eyes and inhaled. She was rewarded with a faint musty smell. 'Huh,' she said, opening her eyes to see Will regarding her comically.

Ignoring his funny looks, she opened the stiff white envelope and pulled out a folded piece of bonded notepaper between the tips of her fingers. Laying it on her desk, she flicked it back with her pen and stared at the faded print of the newspaper clipping attached. It revealed a story of a hit and run back in the ninetics in Haven. Jennifer vaguely remembered that the case had never been solved. She shook the envelope, raising her eyebrows as a small black feather floated onto her desk.

CHAPTER THREE

There was little time for Jennifer to contemplate the letter as Ethan walked into the room, with a young woman by his side. The slight flush creeping up her throat suggested she was not as comfortable in the limelight as he was. The tapping of keyboards and ringing of phones silenced as Ethan cleared his throat to speak.

'I'm glad I've got you all together, I'd like you to join me in welcoming the newest member of our team, DC Zoe Fox.'

A petite girl with a nose stud, Zoe looked much younger than her twenty-six years. She was dressed in a loosely fitting black shift dress and matching pumps that spoke of comfort rather than money. Zoe's kohl-lined eyes flicked up from under her jagged black fringe and a faint smile crossed her lips as she caught Jennifer's stare.

Jennifer returned her smile, feeling Zoe's dark eyes delve into her psyche. It was as if a freezing cold hand had been shoved down her back. She shuddered, switching her gaze back to Ethan, who had launched into a speech praising them for all their hard work. Jennifer loved his zest for life, and rousing talks on teamwork. Will, on the other hand, was less impressed, describing his talks as the 'Ethan Cole Roadshow'. She kicked him under the table as he stifled a yawn. Will was there at her insistence, because Jennifer wouldn't accept the role without him. But as time went on, Ethan had come to value his skeptical nature and analytic mind. It helped keep them grounded, and Will had gained enough convictions to prove his worth on the team. It was voiced in his speech, as he praised them in turn.

'You all form an integral part of Op Moonlight, and I'd like to take this opportunity to thank you for your hard work and commitment, both now and in the future. Now please, don't let me hold you up with your work any longer.'

As Ethan finished talking, Jennifer felt as if she should clap, but Will had already turned back to his computer and Claire had skulked into her office, as she often did, to avoid being roped in. Ethan rocked on his heels for a couple of seconds, before introducing Zoe to Jennifer and loping out the door.

'That was some speech,' Zoe said, in a strong Essex accent. 'I hope I can live up to his expectations.'

'He wouldn't have picked you if you couldn't,' Jennifer replied, catching sight of a scar running from the top of Zoe's cheekbone, to the edge of her jaw. It was camouflaged in the palest of foundation, and Jennifer felt a rush of inexplicable sorrow. She drew her glance away and swept a hand towards her desk. 'I've got a load of work to get through, you're welcome to join me.'

Zoe's eyes darted towards her sergeant's office. 'I've got some admin to go through with Claire, computer access, lockers, boring stuff like that. Thanks for the offer though.'

'Can I get you a coffee?' Will said, as Jennifer introduced him.

'Nah, I don't touch the stuff. It's great to meet you both, Ethan's told me a lot about you.'

Will raised an eyebrow in response. 'Don't believe a word. What about you? What's brought you to Haven?'

Zoe glanced around before speaking. Jennifer recognised the habit; it was something she used to do when discussing anything out of the ordinary. It would take a while for Zoe to accept she was in a safe environment in the Op Moonlight office.

'I'm a demonologist,' Zoe said, her voice a whisper.

'Blimey,' Will said, 'like on those *Most Haunted* programmes?'

Jennifer rolled her eyes. 'I'm sorry, my colleague isn't renowned for his sensitivity.'

Zoe's face lit up as she laughed, and her shoulders dropped as she visibly relaxed in their company. 'Nothing as glamorous as that. It just means I'm trained to conduct exorcisms. I can also recognise when someone's faking it, or has been possessed in the past.'

'I could have done with you a few months ago, when I dealt with a bad possession,' Jennifer said.

'Ah. That explains it then.'

Jennifer shot Zoe a puzzled look, feeling Will's body tense beside her. 'Explains what?'

'I picked up that you'd been possessed in the past. I'm glad you got it sorted.' Zoe swivelled her head to respond to Claire beckoning her into her office. 'Looks like I've been summoned. I'll chat to you later, yeah?'

Jennifer frowned as she returned to her desk. What did Zoe mean, she'd been possessed in the past? It was news to her. She looked to Will, waiting for him to crack a joke, but instead caught a flicker of uncertainty in his eyes.

'What was that about?' Jennifer said, as a trickle of dread seeped into her consciousness. It was as if something far away had been left unresolved, like leaving the gas on, but much, much worse.

'Mmmm?' Will replied, engrossed in his paperwork for the first time that day.

She leaned in, her words slow and deliberate. It was the voice she used with suspects, when she wasn't to be messed with. 'You heard me.'

'Oh, that? Demonology isn't an exact science. But I wouldn't say anything, you don't want to dent her confidence on her first day.'

Putting her reservations behind her, she returned her attention to her paperwork as Will answered the phone. It seemed heavy in his hand as he hung up the call.

'It's bad news, I'm afraid,' he said.

'Don't tell me, the eighties called. George Michael wants his beard back.' Jennifer smiled.

'You won't be laughing when you hear your star witness for your Reborners case has pulled out.'

'Who, Emily? You're joking.'

'As if I'd joke about that.' Will said. 'She said she felt pressured into agreeing to help, and she's changed her mind. I've told her there'll be implications but she said she's not talking and that's it.'

'Whoever's behind this must have got to her. Witness intimidation, that's what it is,' Jennifer said, pulling out her files for the number.

'Calm down, she's gone out now. I think she was scared of telling you herself.'

Jennifer snapped her file shut. 'She promised she'd give me a statement tonight. It took me weeks to trace her to that cult, and now it's all gone down the pan.' What had been her crowning moment was now falling apart.

'She seemed to believe that if she gave names, she would prevent herself getting time. I soon put her straight. As if things work that way,' Will said.

Jennifer flushed as she recalled her advice: *the more helpful you are, the better chance you have of a suspended sentence.* It was often true, but she had leaned on Emily too hard. She ground her teeth in annoyance. She had really messed up this time.

Will was still talking. 'Looks like we're back to square one.'

Jennifer drummed her fingers on the table. Deep inside she knew he was right, but it was too soon for I told you so.

A bar of chocolate was shoved under her nose, and she nodded in thanks as she broke off a square of fruit and nut. 'How's your workload?' she said, swirling the chocolate in her mouth. It really did make everything feel better.

Will took a seat beside her. 'I'm living the dream. I have a burglar who blames his crimes on an organ transplant, a grave robber who hears the voice of God, and a woman who says it's OK for her husband to beat her up because he's possessed. If he is, it must be by the spirit of Stella Artois as he's raving drunk every bleeding time he does it.'

Jennifer pushed away the gnawing doubt as she pressed the doorbell of Emily Clarke's front door. She couldn't end her working day without knowing why she had changed her mind about providing a statement against the group leader. She pressed down on the doorbell, wishing Emily would hurry up. Located on the deprived side of Haven, Crescent Avenue always seemed dank and depressing. Perhaps it was the combined energies of the residents within that made it that way. It was the children that Jennifer felt the most sorry for, and their faces haunted her long after she'd left. Most of the time they stood with palms pressed against the windows as they stared down at a world that had long since forgotten them. Once a retirement village for the elderly, its residents had relocated to the other side of the bridge where the more affluent homes offered them the protection that the more deprived end of Haven could not.

The door opened suddenly, and Emily's face fell. 'Oh. I thought you were someone else.'

'Clearly,' Jennifer said, nudging forward. 'Can I come in?'

Emily chewed the candy pink lipstick from her bottom lip. 'Am I in trouble?'

'No, not at all. I just want to ask you about your statement.'

'OK,' she said, sliding a phone from her tracksuit bottoms and quickly speeding through a text.

'Where's your little boy?'

Emily's finger froze mid-text. 'Asleep. Why?'

'No reason,' Jennifer said, as she was hit with the stale smell of cigarette smoke, which hung in the air. One glance around the dank room was enough to justify her assumptions about Emily's chaotic lifestyle. Faded tie-dye material hung from curtain wire on the window, more to block out the gaze of unwanted visitors rather than the light that cast a stream onto the linoleum floor. An old tea towel hung over a shabby porcelain lamp and the fringed throw on the sofa had seen better days. Jennifer navigated her feet among the broken toys and sticky plates of uneaten food. Every inch of space seemed to be covered with something. Her eyes fell on the empty wine bottles on the coffee table next to a one-legged Action Man.

'I haven't had a chance to clean up yet,' Emily said, her arms folded tightly across her chest.

Jennifer shrugged. There was no law against it, but her visit would be followed up by a social services referral. Emily had often cropped up as a victim of domestic abuse, hooking up with unsuitable men in the hope of finding someone who would save her from her miserable existence. Jennifer wondered how long it would be before social services took her child into care.

Jennifer moved a half-eaten jam sandwich from the sofa to the coffee table. 'Mind if I sit down? I'm dead on my feet today.'

'As long as you're quick.'

Jennifer clasped her hands together on her lap. 'I want to know why you've changed your mind about helping us with our enquiries.'

Emily jutted her chin defiantly. 'I lied.'

'Why?'

'You said that if I helped then I could stay out of prison, you didn't say it had to be the truth,' Emily said.

Jennifer stared in disbelief. 'I took it for granted you'd know I meant the truth. I certainly didn't tell you to lie. That's perverting the course of justice. It carries a prison sentence all of its own.'

'I wish I never spoke to you, all I get is grief, and for what?' Emily said, sweeping the messy room with her arm. 'Look around you, do I look like I've made from this?'

'Do you know what I think? You've gotten yourself involved in The Reborners and you're in way over your head. Why did you join them? Is life so bad that you have to resort to drugs?'

'The best gift in life is a second chance ...' Emily mumbled, her voice tailing away. She plopped onto the chair, as if the life had left her legs.

Jennifer's voice softened as she tried to coax out the truth. 'Do they really help you forget your past? Become reborn?'

'Things happened when I was a kid ... stuff no amount of soap can scrub clean. If I could forget ... maybe I could be like the mothers on the telly. I want that, really I do,' Emily said, her gaze turned inwards.

'So why are you so scared? Why have they put the frighteners on you?'

Emily fell back into silence as her defences rose.

'Tell me who they are,' Jennifer said. 'This is your chance to do what's best.'

Emily stabbed her finger to her chest, but the anger in her voice could not disguise the worry behind her eyes. 'I'll do what's best for me.'

Jennifer didn't normally put words into her witnesses' mouths but she had to know. 'Is the coven a front for drug use?' Mike Stone controlled the network of drug dealers in Haven, and Jennifer would not have put it past him to intimidate Emily into keeping quiet.

Emily rubbed the back of her neck and choked a dry, bitter laugh. 'You really have no clue, do you? This thing ... it's bigger than both of us. I want you to leave. It's not doing me any good talking to the cops. It makes people nervous around here.'

Jennifer frowned. 'If you're being intimidated you've got to tell us.'

'And what are you gonna do about it? Put a guard on my door twenty-four-seven?' Emily caught her glance. 'No. I thought not. Now piss off and leave me alone. I can manage this by myself.'

'Well don't do what you did today and open the door without checking who's there first.'

'Don't worry. Next time you come calling I won't answer,' Emily said petulantly.

Jennifer shook her head, her patience wearing thin. She thought of Emily's son, brought up with the stench of booze and cigarette smoke in the air. Bitter memories of her upbringing unleashed a flare of anger. 'Why don't you sort yourself out and maybe there won't be a next time? Look at this place. It's not fit to raise a child in.'

'You think it's so easy, don't you? With your well-paid job and fancy house. Have a nice husband at home, do you?' Emily curled her lip in disgust, 'People like you just don't understand the real world.'

Jennifer walked towards the front door. 'I understand all right, but you can't use what's happened to you in the past as an excuse to stop moving forward. Just keep yourself safe. Call us if you need us, and don't go out alone at night, at least until all this calms down.'

Emily turned the latch to let her out. 'I'm able to look after myself.'

Jennifer recognised the defiance in Emily's eyes because she owned it herself once. If she had been placed in a children's home instead of the care of her aunt then things would have turned out very differently. She pulled out her wallet from her jacket pocket and slid out a twenty-pound note. 'Here. Use it to buy some food for your son.'

Emily's mouth turned upwards in a half smile. 'Is this a bribe? Because if it is I want more ...'

The colour drained from Jennifer's face, as Emily tried to tug the cash from her hand. 'Christ no! I'm not bent. If I thought you believed that ...'

Emily snatched the money. 'All right, keep your hair on, I'm only saying. You don't get nothing for nothing in my world.'

Jennifer sighed as she stepped over the broken concrete path to her car. There was no helping some people and for Emily it was too little too late. It was a sentiment echoed by the row of sharp-eyed ravens perched on the roof of Emily's home.

CHAPTER FOUR
Bert

The tinny clunk of beer barrels stirred Bert from his sleep as they rolled from the lorry to the pub where he'd abandoned his van the night before. He scratched his beaky nose as he found his bearings. He was used to waking up confused and disjointed. Squinting at the large round face of his watch, he tapped the glass to check it was still working. Nine o'clock? He should have been up by now, boiling the kettle on the gas stove in the back of his van. He rubbed his face as memories from the night before replayed in his mind. Running his fingers through the rim of his hat, he plucked out the wad of cash and smiled as he planned what to do with it. It was not just the money that made him smile. The itching had eased and he felt better than he had in weeks. He imagined suit man's dead weight stretching the hemp rope as it hung taut over the timber beam. He spared himself another smile. Death by proxy was not as powerful as murder, but it had granted him respite from his ills, at least for today.

He headed for breakfast and a shower in 'The Truck-Stoppers Cafe' and then went shopping for a cheap suit. After all, nobody would want their prophecy told by an old man smelling of last week's refuse. Bert traipsed around the shops for a while, but the young assistant's stony glare made his hackles rise. As his annoyance grew, he sensed a stirring within. Calm down,

Bert reminded himself, for an unguarded thought was a dangerous one. He quashed his temper and counted out the crumpled
notes to pay for his off-the-peg suit. Today was a good day. He
was out in public, had stayed in control, and everything was on
track. Walking down the busy windswept street, he clamped his
hand over his hat as the wind tried to whip it away. He hated
being out in the open among so many people. If it were not for
his plan, he would live alone, somewhere remote. Somewhere
like home.

His morning breakfast of a bacon sandwich had earned Bert
a serious thirst, and he welcomed the trip to the country pub to
quench it. Squeals from a group of females made him pause at
the double doors. She's here, Bert thought as he drove himself
onwards to the busy bar, where he laid his cards face down.

Right on cue, the lanky blonde tottered over to the bar. She
waved her folded twenty-pound note like a wand at the staff,
who were busy serving a coachload of pensioners.

'Felicity, love, just get me a coffee, it's too early for booze,' a
croaky voice shouted over the din.

Felicity guffawed, a loud hoarse laugh. 'You're having a proper drink, babe, I don't care what time it is.'

Bert bristled at the sight of the girl, her Prada sunglasses
perched precariously on her head. His eyes trailed over the various designer brands draped over her body. Handbag, jewellery,
shoes, clothes, not to mention the overinflated breasts on par
with her chin. Felicity guffawed again and Bert ground his to-
bacco-stained teeth. You know what you have to do, he thought
as he forced himself to strike up conversation. Painting on a
smile, he pointed to the plastic L-plate gaudily hanging from
her low-cut pink angora sweater. 'Getting married?' he said, the
overpowering smell of Chanel No. 5 wafting up his nose.

Felicity cast her eyes over his cheap black suit, the shoulders peppered with white flakes. Her fresh exuberance dismissed any reservations at speaking to the icky old man. 'Yeah, we're going to Brighton for my hen weekend. We're staying over, so I can drink when we get up there,' she said, flashing a toothy smile.

'Ah, well good luck.' Bert wondered if he could persuade her to take a reading and realised her gums were still flapping.

'My fiancé offered to pay for us to fly abroad, but I said, like, babe, I don't want nowhere but Brighton. He's a celebrity you know. Such a doll, he bought me a BMW to drive up in,' she squeaked, hunching her shoulders and wrinkling her nose. 'Are these your cards?' she asked, leaning across the bar in the hope of being served.

Bert tapped the deck. 'Yes. I predict the future,' he found himself saying.

'Ohhh. My fiancé's a psychic, but he doesn't like reading for family. Can *you* give me a reading?'

'The going rate is forty pounds.'

Hesitation flickered in Felicity's eyes.

Bert shrugged his oh-go-on-you've-twisted-my-arm look. 'I can give you a quick reading for twenty, seeing as you're getting married.'

Another shriek of delight as Felicity clapped her hands together, the note flapping between her fingers.

Bert attuned himself to her high-pitched frequency. It wasn't too bad once you got used to it. As long as she didn't try to touch him. He couldn't bear that. He hated the huggers, and people like Felicity were everything that was wrong with the world. Her equally deplorable friends gathered around as Bert cleared a table in the corner.

'This is a private reading,' he said bluntly, as the beast awoke from within. From early childhood, Bert's anger felt like a separate entity deep within his soul. He tried hard to keep it under control. Most of the time, he won.

Drink in hand, Felicity took a seat and dismissed her friends to the other side of the bar. Rifling in her purse, she paid the fee and dropped her designer bag under the table. It gaped open, revealing all the things you would expect of a woman whose only interests were designer brands and her weekly edition of *Heat* magazine.

Bert worked the cards as Felicity leaned over, her heaving chest resting on the table. He spoke of how she had been let down in the past. He disclosed that her fiancé was older than her, her one true love. Tears sprang in Felicity's doe eyes, acknowledging his words as truth. 'You have so many plans, and you want everything to be right for your special day.'

Felicity gave a watery smile as she played with a length of hair extension. 'Oh my God that's amazing. Tell me, how many babies are we gonna have?'

Bert waved his hands theatrically over the cards. 'You're not going to have any children.'

Felicity scowled, no doubt mourning the loss of dressing her newborn toy in Armani Baby designer wear. 'Why not?' she said.

'Have you ever heard of karma?' Bert said, relishing the words spilling out of his lips.

Felicity's scowl transformed into painful concentration as she searched her mind for answers. 'Karma? Yeah, you get what you give.'

Bert gave her a knowing look. 'You've got a secret, haven't you?' It was all becoming clear as the cards plucked her shameful secrets and laid them bare.

'I ... I don't know what you're talking about. What secret?'

Bert pointed at the card. 'I'm seeing college. So many friends, grateful to be in your company.'

'I've always been popular,' Felicity said, staring at the image on the card and not seeing any such thing.

Bert continued to glance down, feeling his heartbeat quicken as the scene unfolded before him. 'Yes. I'm seeing one schoolgirl in particular. Cara. With her cheap clothes and fake jewellery.'

The colour drained from Felicity's face. It was all the validation Bert needed.

He licked his dry cracked lips as he leaned in towards Felicity to deliver his condemnation. 'You hated that girl. The phone calls, the bullying, and then the night of the party, when you held her down, so those boys could familiarise themselves with her.'

'Nothing happened,' Felicity said, as the truth came back to haunt her. 'I let go before they did anything.'

Bert narrowed his eyes. 'She killed herself while your bruises were still fresh on her wrists.'

'Keep your voice down. I've done everything in my power to forget that girl. Why are you bringing it up now?' she whispered sharply. 'Just who are you?'

'My name is Raven. You asked for a reading,' Bert said as he turned the final card. There was no denying the enjoyment of wiping the smile off the bimbo's face, but the pub was filling up and discomfort began to creep up his spine as he leaned in to be heard. 'Now for your future.'

Felicity's bottom lip jutted outwards in a pout, making her look four years old.

'You're not going to make it to your wedding. You're going to die in the woods,' Bert said, waiting for the dramatics to unfold.

Sure enough they did. Felicity clasped a hand to her mouth, stemming the sharp intake of breath. 'Oh my God! You're telling me … I'm gonna die?'

Felicity's shrieks drew the attention of her friends, who were pointing in their direction. Bert felt his chest tighten as both dread and excitement coursed through him. He needed to get out before she made a scene. An agonising combination of emotions relayed on his contorted face.

'Yes. In the woods,' he said to Felicity, who was opening and closing her mouth like a goldfish about to be dropped into the toilet.

Felicity's chest heaved dramatically as she took great gulps of air. 'How dare you … How dare you say such a thing! I don't even know of any woods. You're nuts, that's what you are! Nuts!'

Bert hurriedly slid the cards together and tapped them on the table before returning them to the pouch. The last thing he wanted was to be mobbed by a group of hysterical women. Scurrying out of the building, he peered over his shoulder to see Felicity's friends click clacking towards her in their high heels as they rushed in response to her evident distress.

A sneer grew on his lips. She was as good as dead. Within forty-eight hours, her nail–varnished big toe would bear the mortician's tag.

The black BMW gleamed at the far end of the car park. Stupid girl, Bert thought as he strode past the empty bus that provided good cover from curious eyes. He tutted as he stopped to light a cigarette, gently puffing as the roll-up ignited into life. Anyone could vandalise it there. Anyone at all. He pressed the fob of the keys he had taken from her bag. The car lights flashed in response. He had learned all about cars when he was young, and how to loosen the wheel nuts just enough so they wouldn't come off straight away. Minutes later he threw the keys on the ground. The mysteries of fate were all well and good, but sometimes fate needed a helping hand. The corners of his mouth turned upwards in a taut smile and he tipped his hat to avoid the accusing glare of the sun.

That night he decided to leave his cards in his pocket. The urge to use them had dissipated, his inner self was positively purring after recent events. Death was a happy bedfellow and he would sleep easy tonight. He settled into the low-backed chair at the piano bar, his foot nodding in time to the music. His double brandy clawed at the back of his throat as it slid down, warming his senses.

He tapped the bar mat against the smooth mahogany table. The music tinkling in the background was far preferable to the rumble of his engine, and he was in no hurry to return to his cot bed in the back of the van. He could return to mother. He pushed away the thought but the unease lingered. He would return. But not before he finished what he set out to do.

CHAPTER FIVE

Jennifer pressed her failing pen against the paper as she took notes. It felt peculiar, taking a statement from her old school mate. She had hoped to spare her blushes by racing through their discussion, but Christian Bowe's playful mood meant he was not going to allow her off the hook that easily. Jennifer folded a victim pamphlet and shoved it under the leg of the table before returning to her paperwork. Her handwriting was bad enough, but the wonky table had made it look as if a spider had crawled all over the page.

Christian looked immaculate, even after ten hours of filming. He had come straight from the London studio, still wearing his usual black jeans and crisp white shirt, his rolled-up sleeves complementing his tanned skin. The open neck of his shirt revealed a small silver cross resting just beneath his collarbone. Jennifer inhaled the elegant scent of Paco Rabanne as it lingered in the air. It was a vast improvement on the usual smells in the poky witness interview room.

Christian tilted his blond head to one side and smiled; the same expression on the TV shows that had made him the housewife's favourite. 'Jenny Knight, I just can't believe it's you. It's so good to see you again.'

Jennifer nodded as another wave of embarrassment washed over her. Christian had always been tactile, and had hugged her tightly when he realised who she was. She was pleased she had chosen to wear her new black suit to work. It had been an impulse buy when she was checking out the new designer store on the posh side of Haven. The strappy black heels were also crying out to be taken home, but at least now she could justify the dent in her credit card. Her adolescent crush for Christian had long since evaporated, but there was nothing worse than seeing a blast from the past when you looked like crap.

'You haven't changed much since our schooldays,' she said, preferring to get back to the task in hand.

'Thanks. And what about you? I would never have guessed you'd turn out to be a detective. I mean, you were always playing truant at school,' Christian smiled.

Jennifer grinned at the memory. She hated high school because it separated her from Amy. She used to bunk off to watch her in the primary school playground at lunchtime, jumping the fence if anyone dared utter a cross word in her sister's direction.

'Yeah. I managed to sort myself out in the end. You seem to have done pretty well.'

Christian nodded. 'I was lucky, I fell in with the right people who accepted me for who I was.'

Jennifer had heard about his engagement to Felicity Baron, newly fledged reality TV star. The publicity had rocketed his stardom even further, and a week rarely passed without the pair of them featuring in celebrity gossip magazines.

Jennifer cleared her throat, concentrating on the task in hand. The statement complete, she had one more question to go before completing the victim personal statement, a series of questions involving the impact of the crime on his personal life. Such statements were useful in court, and proved to convey the far-reaching consequences of crime.

'I just have one more question for you, how has this made you feel, being a victim of harassment by your cousin?'

The smile slid from Christian's face and he threaded his fingers together. 'I feel terrible for reporting this, but I'm worried what he's going to do next. He's hurt people, I know he has, and I can't help but feel responsible.' He sighed, his eyes filled with an apology that was not his to make.

'If you don't mind me saying, there's quite an age gap between you and your cousin.'

'Bert's mum was a lot older than mine. Auntie Grace had her twins in her teens, while I was a late in life surprise,' Christian smiled.

Jennifer rested her pen on the desk. 'Families come in all shapes and sizes. Well, normally harassments would be dealt with by uniformed officers, but you mentioned a premonition of a murder, and I happen to be one of the few people in Haven nick who takes these things seriously. I'm not going to include it in your statement, but I will record it in my pocket notebook. Is that OK with you?'

Christian nodded. 'Of course. I'm just happy someone's willing to listen to me.'

Jennifer flicked open her notebook, dating the top of the page and recording the time using the twenty-four-hour clock. The leather-bound cover bore the Op Moonlight logo, and was stamped confidential.

'What can you tell me?' Jennifer said.

Christian gesticulated as he spoke, his fingers composing his words. 'Firstly I want to impart just how bad I feel about all of this. I heard the institution was releasing my cousin into the community, and I didn't want to know. Since his release, I've been getting these frightening visions. He's plotting to murder people.'

Jennifer raised an eyebrow. 'You've already mentioned the strange phone calls, but they're non-threatening. What makes you think he's capable of murder?'

'Like I said, he rambles on about the past when he calls me. But he's mentally ill. I don't care what the hospital says – they shouldn't have released him.' Christian looked at her pleadingly, his eyes wide with anxiety. 'I trust my premonitions, Jennifer, it's a warning, I know it.'

This was a side of Christian that was not shown on the TV screens. She had watched as his career took hold, long after they lost touch, and tried to imagine what it must have felt like to be in his shoes. He always seemed so happy in the public eye, but as Jennifer was quickly learning, people revealed a different side to themselves when the cameras were turned off.

'Can you be a bit more specific?' she said. 'I want to help, but we don't have a lot to go on. The harassment offence barely warrants me giving him a warning, and murderous thoughts aren't a crime.'

Christian closed his eyes and drew slow, soothing breaths in through his nostrils and out through his mouth. Resting his hands on his lap, his voice became thick and drawn as he entered a trance-like state. 'He's in a dark space. It's enclosed, and it's cold. Almost like a tomb.' Christian raised his hand and raked his nails across the back of his neck. 'The itching. It's driving him insane. Driving him to the point of …'

Jennifer soundlessly scribbled in her notebook, recording his comments word for word. Christian stiffened in his chair, and his voice invoked a sense of urgency. 'He's planning to kill … he has clear intentions. He believes he's gaining from their deaths.' A long pause followed and Christian's eyes fluttered open. 'I can't … I can't make anything else out. I'm sorry.'

Jennifer sighed, frustrated by the lack of information. A small part of her was glad Op Moonlight's remit was hidden from the public, otherwise half her working day would be dealing with incidents she was unable to resolve. Haven kept her busy enough as it was. On one side were the wealthy residents who lived in luxury townhouses and commuted to their high-powered jobs. The other side was aptly nicknamed the old town. Forgotten and dilapidated, the land harboured a darkness borne from historic battles and ferocious witch hunts. Superstitious practices were passed down from one generation to another, and strangers were regarded with narrow-eyed mistrust.

'I need details. Locations, times, method. Have you a photo of your cousin? An address?'

'I'd describe him as a tall, thin, gaunt-looking man with grey hair. But I haven't seen him in years. The institution said he was being released to a hostel. They asked me to take him, but I declined. I just don't have the time to give him what he needs.'

Jennifer tapped her bottom lip thoughtfully. No doubt, his fiancée wasn't too keen on the idea either. 'Your cousin, does he read the tarot cards? Possess any psychic gifts?'

'Not that I know of,' Christian said.

'Does he drive?'

'He's been sectioned for half of his life, I doubt he'd have a driver's licence. Why?'

'It's just a case I'm working on. I wondered if there was a connection.' She pulled a business card from the inside of her jacket pocket and slid it across the table. 'If anything else comes to you, call me on this number. It doesn't matter what time it is. I know you're against changing your number, but I strongly advise you do.'

'He might come to the house if he can't get through on the phone. My kids stay weekends. I can't risk it.'

She passed over the statement, pointing to the signature block at the end. 'The allegation of harassment will give us an excuse to bring him in, and I'll make enquiries with the institution as to his whereabouts.'

'Thank you. I hope you find him soon,' he said, signing the statement and passing it back.

'Try not to worry. I'm sure it's not as bad as it seems,' she said, shuffling her papers.

Christian pushed his chair back as he stood up. 'We should go out for coffee, talk about the old days.'

Jennifer tucked her paperwork under her arm and walked towards the door. 'I'd like that.'

'Oh, and Jennifer, be careful with my cousin.' Christian's voice became slow and deliberate. 'He appears harmless on the outside ... but he harbours something dark. I felt it during my premonition.'

Jennifer gave him a wry smile as she showed him out. 'Congratulations. You've just described most of the people I deal with.'

Christian's warning played on her mind that night as she flicked through the pages of her paperback. It was one of the rare occasions that she finished work on time, and the evening seemed to stretch on forever. The institution that dealt with his cousin was called The Rivers, and had promised to get back to her the next day. She hadn't ruled out the possibility of him being the pub tarot card reader, but without CCTV, she didn't have much to go on.

Despite the soft music playing in the background, Jennifer found it impossible to relax. Two hours of cleaning her immaculate kitchen had left her with wrinkled fingers and stiff limbs. Coming from a childhood entrenched in neglect and disorder, cleaning was the only way she could stay in control. Her anxiety dictated the length she spent on it, and today's regime had managed to exhaust her. She massaged her shoulder blades, pinching her skin between forefinger and thumb in an effort to ease the tension. She thought about visiting her sister, but Amy had been very cagey lately. Jennifer's bond with her nephew Joshua was growing even stronger, and his attachment to her got on her sister's nerves.

Jennifer shut the book and allowed her mind to wander. The usual whispers floated through, disembodied voices seeking an audience. Some were connected to the house she lived in, but others were there simply because they tuned into her frequencies, like a scratchy radio channel, whispering words she could barely understand. Allowing them to pass through was easier than trying to shut them off. *Take the path of least resistance*, she had been advised, and it was working well.

A thump from her front door jolted her from her trance and she shook the sleep from her legs as she uncurled from the warmth of the sofa. Who's calling at this hour? she thought, flicking on the hall light. A cold breeze tickled the back of her neck as she approached the door, peering through the shadowless stained glass.

'Who's there?' she asked, holding her breath for a reply. Squeezing her left eye closed, she squinted through the peephole out to the orange glow of the streets beyond. Nothing. Jennifer twisted the latch, peeping out through the slant in the door. Her senses told her to be on her guard, senses that both frustrated and guided her. If those damned whispers made any sense then maybe they would be of use, she thought, shuddering as the cool night air curled around the legs of her satin pyjamas.

'Hello?' she said, holding tightly to the doorframe as she opened it wider. Her eyes dropped to the cement step onto a black bundle of feathers at her feet. Crouching down, she tentatively prodded the iridescent plume, her eyes darting upwards to the car-lined street then back to the black feathered bundle before her. The raven was still and warm, but the life had left its eyes. Jennifer stood up and scratched her head. Dead creatures didn't bother her in the slightest, having spent years in the country with her aunt Laura after her mother died. But anything deceased on her doorstep at night sent warning signals.

Scooping up the limp body into a black bin bag, she tried to make sense of its presence. It must have flown into the door, she thought, carrying it out to the bin. But why would a raven be flying in the dark? She hesitated as she lifted the dustbin lid. It didn't seem right to put the poor dishevelled creature out with the rubbish. Sighing heavily, she tied the bag and rested it gently outside the back door. She would bury it in the garden tomorrow.

Jennifer froze as a whisper carried on a breeze, and a feeling of unreality raised goose bumps on her flesh. *Bert Bishop ... look no further.* Jennifer peered out into the moonlit garden. Did the voice come from outside or the recesses of her mind? She didn't know. She searched her memory for recognition of a name that would come to mean a great deal. Bert Bishop was the name of Christian Bowe's cousin. She recalled the description of the creepy old man in the bar who had spoken to Alan Price. Stepping inside, she locked the back door as a feeling of unease crept up her spine. Staring out into the stillness of her garden, the affirmation grew stronger in her mind. She couldn't explain it but somehow she knew. Bertram Bishop had delivered the fatal prophecy to Alan Price in the bar – and he wasn't stopping there.

CHAPTER SIX
Bert

A hot shower, a brandy from the minibar, the feel of carpet under bare feet. In the comfort of his room, the simple things in life were bliss. But Bert's nightcap could not blot out the irritation from the perfumed soap seeping into the cracks in his skin. Dragging his nails over the inflammation, he groaned in short-lived gratification before blistering pain sliced through every nerve. Bert unzipped his toiletry bag and pulled out a small wrinkled tube. The steroid cream did little to ease the skin condition that fed off his tormented mind. *Hypocrite*, his conscience whispered, and Bert flapped his hands to the side of his head, dismissing the thoughts like a swarm of bees.

The mattress bounced gently as Bert tested the bed. He ran his hand over the crisp white duvet cover. He was looking forward to sleeping in fresh linen. It reminded him of when he was a boy. Each night mother dutifully slathered him in creams before bandaging his broken skin, humming a tune under her breath to avoid conversation. It was all done with all the love and attentiveness of someone gutting a fish.

She had little else to do, with one child in the family. But it was not always that way. The second of identical twins, Bert arrived to the world as an afterthought. His parents would have been content with Callum. His dimpled cherubic face and soft blond hair made him the perfect child. His beauty was enhanced even further by the arrival of his brother.

At half the weight, Bert came into the world a wizened creature, eyes squeezing hot tears as he rasped a starving cry. There was little known about twin-to-twin transfusion, and the doctor had explained it as simply as he could. Callum had taken the share of nutrition in the womb, leaving little for Bert, who was not expected to survive the night. His parents, who had only been expecting one baby anyway, took the sensible option of not getting attached to him. Besides, they had Callum, what more did they need?

Bert was a shrink-wrapped version of his twin; his face thin and scrawny, with blond hair drained to a brittle white. He bunched his fists as he screamed, his scaly pink scalp visible underneath the wisps of his listless hair. It was his anger, his fury at the world that ensured his survival.

His mother hid Bert away from visitors, producing Callum for their adoration. But the benefit of having a 'sickly child' gave Grace the excuse she needed to stay cocooned in her three-bedroom home. She ventured only to church on a Sunday, her lips moving in silent prayer as she drove the three miles into town for the nine o'clock sermon. Praying distracted her anxious mind from open spaces, and the rosary beads swinging from the mirror of their Ford car amused Callum as he accompanied her on these visits. Bert knew all this because of the cards. These dips into the past gave him answers to questions that swarmed in his mind. And it made him feel better about what happened with mother.

Bert pushed aside the thoughts. Throwing the cushions off the bed, he slid between the sheets, reaching for the well-thumbed newspaper on the bedside table. He smiled as he re-read the headlines on the second page. 'Celebrity Psychic's Tragic Fiancée Crash'. Bert picked up his glasses and scanned through the article again. The young blonde woman smiled at him from the page.

A TV reality star bride to be was involved in a one-car crash on the M25 on Thursday evening when the victim's car, 23-year-old Felicity Baron, veered off the M25 and plummeted down an embankment. After leaving the road, the vehicle dropped approximately 30ft down a steep slope and crashed into some trees on the border of a woodland reservation.

Baron, star of The Beauty Salon, *was on her way to Brighton with friends to celebrate her hen party when the accident occurred. While it is believed the members of her group had been drinking, friends report that Baron had been sober when her car veered out of control. She received a head injury and was airlifted to hospital where she later died. The other four passengers escaped with minor injuries.*

The accident happened one week before Baron's planned wedding to celebrity psychic Christian Bowes. In a further twist, her stunned friends stated that Baron had been upset that morning after receiving a tarot card reading from an unknown man predicting her death.

Police say excessive speed may have been a factor in the crash. Investigators are yet to determine if faulty mechanics played a role.

'If you go down to the woods tonight you're in for a big surprise,' Bert sang, dropping the paper. A guttural laugh rose from the pit of his stomach, as a sense of accomplishment surged through him. He did it again. He chuckled as he fell asleep. He couldn't wait to give another prediction, and with the help of the cards, he had just the person in mind.

CHAPTER SEVEN

A two-bar heater warmed Jennifer's trouser legs as she sat in her sergeant's office. The smell of freshly brewed coffee was a welcome one, and bleary eyed from a lack of sleep, Jennifer was on her second cup.

Claire took a sip of her sugarless brew. The 'World's Okayest Boss' mug was a secret Santa present she had received at Christmas, and it never failed to put a smile on her face. She turned to Jennifer, her fingers teasing her mop of hair. A tangle of curls, it suited her quirky personality. 'I need to discuss your tarot card man. I've been hoping to speak to Ethan but he's been called away to another meeting.'

Jennifer felt the coffee travel to the pit of her stomach, and relaxed into the worn leather swivel chair. 'The DI told me to close the case. But I felt it tied in with Christian Bowe's cousin, so I'm running it as a joint investigation unless I'm told otherwise.'

Claire nodded. 'Good. Have you got found him yet?'

'I've contacted The Rivers, but they're running on skeleton staff due to some flu bug, and it's taking some time to get the information.'

'Then I need you to chase them up. I take it you haven't seen the news.'

Jennifer's grip tightened on the armrests of the chair. 'No, why?'

'The next time you speak to Christian Bowes you might want to handle him sensitively …' Claire said, pausing as Jennifer hastily interrupted her.

'I'm not treating him any differently just because he's a celebrity.'

The phone emitted a shrill ring. Silencing the call, Claire turned back around. 'It's nothing to do with that. It's his fiancée. She crashed her car yesterday. She's dead.'

'Oh,' Jennifer said, suddenly at a loss for words. Her forehead creased in a frown as she tried to comprehend the news. 'Was it an accident?'

'Forensics are examining the car. But get this. Her friends stated she was read her fortune by an old man when they stopped off for a drink.'

'And you think it's the same man that prophesied Alan Price's death?'

'It's too much of a coincidence not to be. Lexton CID have got a hold of the case and are refusing to relinquish it to us as it's on their patch ...'

'But ... No, they can't ...' Jennifer said, the words tumbling out of her mouth.

Claire ignored her protest and carried on. 'We've come to a compromise and it's been agreed you can work together on the case. Obviously if there is any paranormal element you keep that information within our team. It's very early days, but if Christian Bowe's cousin *is* responsible then you need to liaise with them so they can effect an arrest early doors.'

Jennifer felt like she was twelve years old again, back at school being cheated out of an award by Sydney Jenkins, the headmaster's son. 'But it's my case. I don't want to hand it over.'

'You have no choice. If this turns out to be a murder, we won't have the manpower to investigate it by ourselves. Does it matter who does the nicking as long as the case is solved?'

It did to Jennifer. It mattered a lot. Dark thoughts clambered over each other, bumping shoulders as she figured out her next move. The Raven. The words clicked in her mind, slotting in like a piece of the puzzle with so many more pieces to find. The clipping with the black feather and the dead raven at her door: Christian's cousin was goading her into action. The afterglow of her coffee dissipated into thin air, and Jennifer licked her lips, keeping a lid on the simmering frustration within. She felt let down by her sergeant, who should have fought harder to keep the case.

'You're right,' Jennifer lied. She would attend briefing and do as she was told. But if the Raven wanted her, then he would get her – and nothing would stand in her way.

Given the mood she was in, Jennifer preferred to spend her shift with Will than some idiot from Lexton MIT. Her opinions of Lexton's Murder Investigation Team were forged from rumours and entirely justified in her mind. She abhorred bullying, and up until recently, the sharks in the MIT had made a meal out of anyone who deviated from the norm. Her sergeant was a prime example, and the memory of their treatment was most likely the reason for her backing down on the case. Claire had reported the team for bullying when she worked there as a DC, and being offered the role of sergeant over Operation Moonlight must have seemed like a good way of shutting her up. Her words rang in Jennifer's ears as she entered the office. *We have to integrate well with the other teams if we've any hope of surviving. Don't rock the boat.* The words sent a shiver down Jennifer's spine. Their team was new, she had never considered they could be disbanded. But like every team, they had to produce results to justify their existence.

Heads popped up from computers like meerkats in the gloomy office, and Jennifer scanned the room to see an overweight thirty-something man click his fingers in her direction. The office was half the size of theirs but appeared to have double the amount of officers. Overstuffed bins, dirty cups, and the stale aroma of body odour hung in the room. She was not going to outstay her welcome.

'DC Knight, I take it? Over here,' he said in a nasally voice.

What does he think I am? A dog? Jennifer steadied her breathing as she strode to the corner of the room.

'I'm DC Hardwick. I take it you're here to cast your eyes over *my* case,' the man said.

How precious, Jennifer thought, looking down her nose at the officer, now picking the remnants of his bacon baguette from between his teeth.

'I'm here to liaise with you over the Felicity Baron case, and I've been told you're happy to cooperate.'

He pulled over a swivel chair, his fingers leaving grease marks in their wake. 'Why don't you sit down? I'm always happy to help your little team,' he said, spitting specks of bread. 'So how is your sergeant, still as wibble as ever?'

A sharp intake of breath was heard as fingers froze on keyboards. Jennifer gave the officer a cramped smile. 'She sends her love, wanted to know if you're still as obnoxious as ever.'

Despite Claire's warning, Jennifer had only been in the office for five minutes and already insulted the one person willing to work with her. But she couldn't let him get away with calling her sergeant mad. A chorus of laughter ensued.

'You deserved that, Hardwick,' a middle-aged man said, his sleeves rolled up to the elbow. His loosened grey tie swung around his neck like a noose. 'This officer has come here to help. It'll be good to have another pair of eyes on the case.' He turned to Jennifer with an apologetic smile. 'If this reprobate gives you any more trouble you just let me know. I'm Sergeant Duncan, by the way.'

A firm handshake passed between them. Jennifer noted the camaraderie between the pair and decided to behave herself from thereon.

Armed with a copy of the case file, she returned to Haven to continue her investigations. Zoe's clipped tones echoed through the room as she took a call from a very disgruntled father. Jennifer threw Zoe a sympathetic glance as she tried to deflect the complaint coming her way.

'Mr Lynch, if you would let me speak ... yes I know your daughter's upset ... but it's very difficult for us to charge her partner if she refuses to provide us with a statement ... if you would stop swearing at me and listen ...' A bright pink rash spread from Zoe's pale chest up to her neck, reminding Jennifer of a kettle about to boil over.

'Oh dear,' Jennifer whispered as she sat beside Will, 'has she been like that for long?'

Will shook his head. 'About five minutes. How was the lion's den?'

'Full of testosterone. I was the only woman in briefing. Normally I wouldn't notice, but it was like they were just humouring me, when they eventually let me speak.'

Will shook his head. 'Yeah. I heard they were a bunch of dicks.'

'Dicks or not, they're flavour of the month with the command team,' Jennifer said. 'The tarot card reader that spoke to James Price matches the description of the one that forecast Felicity Baron's death. I've given them the clipping and the feather that was sent to me, but they're determined that Christian's ex-wife is the suspect.'

'Fill me in, I'd like to know a bit more in case I get roped in to help.'

'We believe he uses the name Raven. He's a person of interest, but their focus is on Christian's ex-wife. She was unhappy about the divorce settlement apparently.'

'A woman scorned,' Will said.

'Yeah, I know. As soon as the divorce came through, the younger model was announcing the wedding.'

'That's a kick in the gut. So what makes you think this Raven bloke has anything to do with it?'

'Felicity's friends said she lost her keys. They were in her bag in the pub, and after her reading, they were found near the car. They announced in briefing that tests show the car's been tampered with. Somebody opened the boot, took out the wheel nut thingy, and loosened the tyres. Not enough to notice straight away. Ex-wife has no alibi, and tarot guy has no motivation. But it's worth having a chat with him, don't you think?'

'Lug wrench,' Will said, taking a green file from his in-tray and opening it.

'What?'

'The thing for loosening wheel nuts, it's called a lug wrench. An obvious question but have they checked for fingerprints?'

Jennifer stifled a yawn with the back of her hand. 'Yeah, they've been wiped clean. No forensics.'

Will shook his head as he flicked through the paperwork before him. 'Y'know, I don't get this filing system. Don't you think it would be better if green meant important, yellow meant non-priority, and brown meant ...'

'I can guess what brown means, and I can't see the DI going for it,' Jennifer said.

'All the same, I think it might be worthy of another entry into the suggestion box,' Will grinned. 'Is there any previous police history on Raven?'

Jennifer shrugged. 'I can't tell you that because we don't know who he is. Raven could be his name or just a calling card. But if I'm proved right and Raven *is* Bertram Bishop, there's nothing on the system apart from a life in and out of mental institutions.'

Will frowned as he speed-read the contents of his file, closed it, then swapped it for a different one. 'At least you've got a quality job to get your teeth into. What's your next plan of action?'

'I've spoken to The Rivers mental health unit where Bert's been an in-patient. They've reported him as missing because he's no longer at the hostel. I'm not sure he ever stayed there. There's a psychic fair on in the town hall tomorrow. I'm driving over there for a look.'

Will groaned. He had two bail backs and a statement to take that day. 'I don't like you going single-crewed, what if you bump into this guy?'

'That's the whole point, isn't it?' Jennifer laughed. 'Don't look so worried. What's he going to do, batter me with his crystal ball?'

Will squeezed her hand, his brown eyes searching hers. 'Don't underestimate him. This sort of work is different than normal police work, nothing is what it seems.'

The warmth in his eyes followed by the sudden contact took Jennifer by surprise, and her face flushed in response.

'Fancy coming around to mine some night for a meal?' Will said. 'It gets a bit boring, going home to an empty flat every night.'

'I'm not sure if I'm brave enough. For the meal that is, I've seen your kitchen,' Jennifer said. As soon as the words were out she wanted to kick herself.

Will harrumphed. 'I've redecorated the flat, but if it's not good enough for you ...'

'I'm joking. Why don't I bring over a takeaway, save you having to cook. You can show me around.'

Will opened his mouth to reply, but was interrupted by Ethan, as he walked into the office.

'That's what I like to see, a happy workforce,' Ethan said.

Jennifer admired his new Hugo Boss suit, which was complemented by his steel grey tie. He oozed professionalism, from his polished leather shoes, to the clean lines of his haircut.

'You're looking very smart, boss, going somewhere?'

Ethan beamed a smile. 'I have a meeting with the command team, to justify our existence. A government representative is attending, and we intend on putting them in their place.'

'I'd like to be a fly on the wall for that,' Jennifer said.

'It should be interesting,' Ethan said, a hint of a smile tugging his lips. 'I hear you've been doing some good work with MIT on the Raven case.'

Jennifer made a face, which suggested that wasn't strictly true. 'It's going OK, I've come away with some taskings from briefing.'

Ethan's phone buzzed in his pocket and he glanced at the screen. 'Sorry, I have to take this. I'll catch up with you soon.' He turned on his heel and left.

Will locked the screen on his computer and rose to leave.

'Where are you going?' she asked, looking at her watch.

'The toilet. Now why don't you put the kettle on while I shake hands with the old chap?'

Jennifer grimaced. 'Too much information, Will, too much information.'

'Is that the kettle going on?' Zoe said. 'You couldn't make me a herbal tea, could you? I haven't stopped this morning ... talk about hitting the ground running.' Easing her feet out of her kitten heels, she walked barefoot to Jennifer's desk.

Jennifer found the box of teabags and plonked them beside the kettle. 'Sure, although I think you'll get more mileage out of coffee than nettle and mint.'

'You'd be surprised what herbs can do,' Zoe winked, tugging open the top button of her shirt. 'The DI is looking very smart today, does he always dress like he's going to the Academy Awards?'

Jennifer spooned out the coffee, warming to Zoe's sense of humour. 'He's got a meeting with the command team, very secret squirrel.'

'Well he's outside, deep in conversation with Will, maybe he's letting him in on the secret.'

'Maybe,' Jennifer said. She was going to say that Will was in the toilet, but stopped herself, not wanting to look a fool in front of the new starter. She squeezed out the teabag and walked over to the bin near the door, opening it enough so she could peep through the glass double doors in the hall, which led to the rear yard. She poked her head out to see Ethan and Will crossing the yard out of sight. There was something about it that made her uneasy. The last thing she wanted was to fall into the throes of paranoia, but Will was hiding something from her, and she couldn't bring herself to ask what it was. She handed the cup over to Zoe, who had taken off her ill-fitting jacket and rested it on a chair.

'Zoe,' Jennifer said, sidling up to her. 'Do you remember when we were introduced, you said that you could see I'd been possessed before? What did you mean by that?'

Zoe clicked her mouse, suddenly becoming very interested in her emails. 'Really? I don't remember.'

'Well it's kinda bothered me. I had some encounters before Christmas with an entity, but it didn't go that far. The thing is, I can't remember very much about what happened. Can you take a look, see if you pick up anything?'

Zoe's eyes flickered to Jennifer before returning her gaze to the computer screen. 'Sorry, babe, I can't. I'm not allowed to use my skills on colleagues, only suspects.'

'Really? Oh sorry, I must have misunderstood,' Jennifer said, not believing a word.

CHAPTER EIGHT

Will straightened his jacket as he walked out into the sunshine, relieved to see Ethan still talking on his phone. He caught a glimpse of him and ended the call.

'Sorry ... er, guv, but have you got a minute?' Will said, squinting against the sudden glare of the sun.

Ethan cracked a smile. 'You don't want to call me guv any more than I want to hear it. I've told you before. First name terms are fine. Now what can I do for you?'

'It's about Jennifer. I didn't want to say anything in the office in case she might hear.'

Ethan nodded. 'Sure. Walk with me.'

They crossed the rear yard as Will measured his words. 'I'm a bit worried about this investigation Jennifer's following. There's a suspicion this guy could be dangerous, and after what happened the last time ...'

Ethan clamped a hand on Will's shoulder; making him wish he had more of the tall gene. 'I understand your concerns but, as I said before, Jennifer's a capable woman, we can't mollycoddle her.'

Will balled his hands in his pockets. 'I know that, but aren't you worried it's a bit soon?'

'Frankly no, and you should give her more credit. I've been working with people like Jennifer for years. She's a strong woman and I want to explore every inch of her potential.'

I bet you do, you cheesy bastard, Will thought, as he politely bade his inspector goodbye. Will had played down the importance of the letter to Jennifer, not wanting to worry her. The raven feather was enough for him to link the sender to the recent deaths of Alan Price and Felicity Baron. The fact it was addressed directly to Jennifer brought his protectiveness galloping in. He decided to make his own enquiries. It was not difficult to view the CCTV and see young Charlie Sutton, Haven's most petty criminal, dropping in the envelope to front counter. Will knew exactly where he lived. The once splendorous Victorian homes in Florence Road had now been sold off to the housing authorities for the welfare families too large to accommodate elsewhere. Now decorated with outdoor sofas and rubbish bins, the overgrown gardens did little to showcase the dilapidated houses, neglected by the listless tenants within.

From an early age, Charlie Sutton's parents were hoisting him into buildings and through cat flaps to assist with their burglaries. But his career as a cat burglar was short-lived as he hit his teens and grew into a sturdy block of a boy. Luckily for Charlie, there were several younger brothers willing to step into the role. Will rapped on the frosted glass door of the two-storey home, and the family's Stafford Bull Terriers clawed against the inside of the glass, smudging it with an array of brown paw prints.

'Shat uuuuuuppp! Rocky! Spike! Shaaat upppp!' Ma Sutton's voice thundered from inside, her considerable bulk shadowing the glass as she opened the door. 'What do you want?' she said, struggling to keep hold of the dogs' thick black studded collars as their paws padded the air.

Will flashed his warrant card, his eyes on the dogs' bared teeth as they fought for release. 'I want a word with Charlie. He's not in any trouble.'

A formidable woman, Ma Sutton flicked her beady eyes upstairs and back to Will. 'It's the filth,' she shouted in the direction of the stairs. Footsteps scurried across the landing, like a nest of rats being poked with a stick.

Ma Sutton reluctantly allowed him inside, shoving the barking animals into a side room. 'He's in the kitchen,' she sniffed. 'And don't go snooping around or I'll have the dogs on ya.'

Will put his hands in the air in a gesture of defeat, and gave what he hoped was a reassuring smile. He squeezed past the bikes in the hall, their handlebars ripping into what was left of the wallpaper. A mixture of aromas greeted him and the windows steamed from the meat boiling on a gas cooker. It intermingled with the stench of oil from the remnants of a motorbike engine on the newspaper-clad kitchen table.

Charlie fingered the metal parts with thick greasy hands. 'See here, dad?' he said, poking at a cog. 'It's loose, that's what's wrong.'

Charlie's father rarely spoke. He just sat there with a dour expression, pinching tobacco into the thin cigarette papers with a well-practised hand.

'Will-I-am. What are you doing here?' Charlie said, staining his sweat-glistened forehead as he wiped it with the back of his hand. He swivelled in his chair, elbowing the small boy at the side of him. 'Alfie, open the back door, it's fucking boiling in here.'

Alfie scuttled from behind Charlie, and giving Will a cautious glance, opened the back door wide. A welcome gust of air blew in, scooping up the overpowering smells of bacon and oil and carrying them outside.

It was a short-lived respite as Charlie's father stood up and, his eyes never leaving Will, slammed the door shut and locked it.

Will's throat suddenly felt very dry and he swallowed hard. Mr Sutton was very protective of his family, and had assaulted officers previously with little warning. '

'It's OK, Charlie, you're not in any trouble,' Will said. 'I just need to speak to you about a letter you dropped into the nick yesterday.'

Charlie frowned, his grease-stained forehead gathering too many wrinkles for his age. With his cropped brown hair and jaunty expression, he had a look of Wayne Rooney about him, although that was as far as the resemblance went.

'Ah that. It weren't from me. I was paid to deliver it. No crime in that is there?'

Will rubbed his beard. 'No, none at all. Who gave it to you?'

'I'd like to help, but I can't remember very well. They gave me a tenner and asked me to drop it in, seems to be the going rate for favours. I've been trying to save up for a new engine for my motorbike, see? Every little helps ... as they say in Tesco's.' Charlie grinned.

Will frowned as he looked into his wallet. Thank God it was payday Friday, he thought, as he pulled out a ten-pound note and rested it on a small clean patch of newspaper.

'Who?' he said, feeling Mr Sutton's eyes boring down on him. Mr Sutton was also sitting near the block of carving knives. He had little tolerance for the police, and had been a bit of a nutter in his day.

Charlie rested his hand on the tenner and it disappeared from view. 'I thought it was a bit weird. I thought why wouldn't they just deliver it themselves? They offered me a tenner and I thought I may as well cash in. It was just a letter. I figured it couldn't be anything dodgy or owt.'

'Go on,' Will said to Charlie, as Ma Sutton came in and brushed past him to turn off the bubbling pot of meat.

'I'm no grass, you see, and giving info to coppers doesn't rest easy with me …' Charlie said as his little brother crept back behind him, giggling with a gap-toothed smile.

'I'm stony broke, Charlie, I haven't got any more cash. Look, I just want to know who gave you the letter. I'm not asking you to serve up the Mafia or anything.'

Charlie chuckled. 'Fair enough, Will-I-am. It was some old bloke; he must have been in his sixties at least. I ain't seen him around Haven before. He was driving an old VW van. Sounded like it had holes in the exhaust pipe, it was as rattly as fuck.'

'Can you remember anything else? What he was wearing? The colour of the van?'

Charlie shrugged. 'Nah. I was too busy looking at the colour of his money. Now I've gotta clear the table before me mam gives me hell.'

'Too right I'll give you hell, look at the state of it!' Ma Sutton screamed, piercing Will's eardrum. 'The dinner's almost ready.'

Will watched as she pounded the lumpy potatoes into submission with the masher, beads of sweat dripping from her forehead and dangling over the saucepan. It was all too much for Will, who thanked Charlie and left.

Will mulled it over as he walked back to the station. Did some old bloke in a van put Charlie up to delivering the letter? God knows that lying was as natural as breathing to the Suttons. What was the old joke? *How do you know a Sutton's lying? – Their lips are moving.* But why would someone pay to have a letter delivered to the nick? And why address it specifically to Jennifer?

CHAPTER NINE

The damp wooden bench outside the police station provided little shelter to George Butler as he tightened the tattered blanket around the terrier on his lap.

Jennifer scooted up beside him, trying to ignore the musty smell emitting from his direction. 'Here, I got you a sandwich and a cappuccino. It's gone a bit cold I'm afraid.'

'Ohh, very continental,' he said, removing the lid and gulping the coffee. He wiped the froth from his whiskers and turned to Jennifer, the lilt of his Irish accent music to her ears. 'You know, a little nip of something would keep out the harshness of the cold,' George said, wrapping his fingerless gloves around the warmth of his cup.

Jennifer gave him a withering look. 'I wouldn't dare ruin a good Costa with alcohol.'

The twinkle in George's eyes suggested he was willing to give it a try. 'Perhaps you're right. You know, Sergeant Claire was kind enough to take in Tinker for me yesterday while I spoke with the benefits lady.'

It wasn't the first time the scruffy terrier had been smuggled into the sergeant's office. A sucker for sad cases, Claire had done everything she could to help George and his dog. Jennifer had given up trying to get George into the homeless shelter. They didn't allow dogs, and George simply wouldn't leave him.

'Can I ask you a random question?' she said, shifting on the bench as the damp seeped through her trousers.

'Ask away,' George said, carefully disposing of his empty cup in a plastic bag.

'What are your thoughts on tarot cards?'

George took his glance to the sky as he recited the words. 'Let there not be found among you one who practises witchcraft, who interprets omens, a sorcerer, conjurer, medium, spiritist, or one who calls up from the dead. For all who do these things are an abomination to the Lord.'

He blinked before returning his attention to Jennifer, to answer her questioning gaze. 'It's a bible quote. Deuteronomy chapter eighteen, verses ten to twelve ... or as much of it as I can remember.'

'I didn't know you were religious,' Jennifer said, wondering what he would say if he knew of her history.

'There's a lot of things you don't know about me, *a leanabh*. Now aren't you meant to be getting to work?'

Jennifer said her goodbyes and walked the short distance to the police station to start her late shift. If someone had told her she would become friends with the skinny, grey-haired homeless man, she would never have believed them. Her, the clean freak, chatting with someone who made his bed on a public bench. But George had a way of getting under your skin, and was liked by everyone except the front office staff, who regularly badgered him to move on.

Jennifer glanced up at the row of ravens dotted on the telephone wire; lately they seemed to follow her everywhere she went. The hairs at the back of her neck prickled upwards as she counted ten, fifteen, twenty ravens staring intently with black glittering eyes. *Look no further*. The whisper penetrated her mind in a sudden gust of icy air. A loud knock from the office window above made her jump, and she quickly stepped inside, telling herself to focus. She was here to work, and could not afford to be distracted by birds, the weather, or any strange whispers nesting in her mind.

'Talking to your boyfriend again?' Will said, backing away from the office window.

'I've got a soft spot for the Irish, try not to be too jealous.' Jennifer grinned, hanging up her coat.

'Oh fff … fiddlesticks!' Zoe winced as the computer rejected her password for the third time. She looked at the pair of them apologetically. 'Sorry. I'm trying to stop swearing.'

'Here, let me,' Will said, leaning over her desk to guide her back onto the login page.

Jennifer peered out the window at the bare telephone line. Evening light was fading, and there was no sign of the black-cloaked birds that had flanked her entrance. Was her imagination creating havoc, or was she being issued with a warning? Christian's premonition, the presence of the ravens, it was like something out of a cheap horror movie. Her emotions played seesaw with her sensibilities; she was either falling into the hands of paranoia, or disregarding a very real threat. But there was one thing she had learned about the supernatural: if there *was* a message it would open itself up to her in time. She strode to her desk. It was time to focus on the living, at least until the dead were ready to give up their secrets.

Jennifer pulled a tissue from her pocket and sneezed. She had cleaned her desk already, but it was no good, she would have to do it again. She opened her drawer, settled her pens and pencils back into order, and pulled out three sterile wipes from a packet.

Rolling his chair back, Will allowed Jennifer to continue cleaning until the wipes ran dry. 'Did you mention the letter to Claire?' he said, slipping a soft mint from the shared bag on his desk.

Jennifer eyed the open bag and took one for herself, carefully disposing of the wrappers. 'Ethan's told me to close the Price case as non-suspicious.' Her words were betrayed by the lack of conviction in her voice. She glanced around the room. 'But he's all over the Christian Bowes case like a rash. I don't think it's fair that celebrities should get priority treatment over anyone else, do you?'

'Pfft,' Will said, blowing out his disgust. 'You already know my feelings on that.'

Jennifer lowered her voice to a whisper. 'The command team have been poking their nose in too. They don't want the publicity if it all goes wrong.'

'If it's a straightforward harassment then it won't.' Will rolled his sweet to the other side of his mouth. 'Our DI can say what he likes about the paranormal element of investigations, the CPS will only ever accept cold, hard facts.'

'I don't recall Ethan saying otherwise.' Plucking out another wipe, Jennifer ran it over the telephone handset. 'Do you think we could have our refs together tonight? Maybe go into Costa coffee before they close?' Lately refreshment breaks had been a luxury. They ate over their computer keyboards while working through their files, scattering crumbs which would clog their keys later.

Will grinned. 'You want quality time with me? That's a relief. I was worried I might have to join old George on the bench out there.'

'Well you're half way there. You've got the scruffy clothes and the beard,' Jennifer said, her dimples softening her smile.

'I got this in Topman, I'll have you know,' Will said, pulling the lapels of his charcoal suit. Jennifer cast her eyes appreciatively over the broadness of his shoulders. Despite his love of food, he had always been well proportioned. But their office banter didn't include compliments, and it was a lot easier taking the mickey out of his badly ironed shirt than admitting he had grown on her.

'Anyway we can't go out tonight, Claire's ordered Chinese takeaway, seeing as we've all been working so hard. Will you come with me to pick it up?' Will said.

'I'm hardly going to sit here eating sandwiches while the whole place is stinking of curry, am I? Count me in.'

The ping of an email brought her attention to her computer screen, and she swore under her breath.

'Everything alright?' Will said, tapping a wad of freshly printed papers against his desk.

Jennifer drummed her fingers on the table. It's DC Hardwick. He's arrested Christian Bowe's ex-missus for the Felicity Bowes case. We're meant to be working together and he didn't even consult me.'

'Are you heading over there?' Will said.

Jennifer shook her head. 'Why should I? Besides, it's obvious he doesn't want me. I like Christian, but he's a media whore. If his ex-wife gets charged there'll be hell to pay'

'Well in that case, you won't mind giving me a hand with some enquiries.'

After clearing it with her sergeant, Jennifer pulled out her copy of the file, and the enquiries to date. It was as if the Raven was a ghost. Nothing was returned on intelligence, and the ANPR had failed to pick up the licence plate of his van entering or leaving Haven. He wasn't registered for benefits, and didn't appear to have a bank account. But he did seem to know the area. Jennifer was left with the conclusion that he either lived in Haven, or was entering through the narrow country lanes, which were poorly marked and unknown to strangers. It wouldn't have come as much of a surprise to discover the Raven was homemade. If local legends were correct, the mystical lands of Haven occasionally sprouted homegrown terror, such darkness often finding a home in the breath of a newborn baby.

It made Jennifer's enquiries all the more urgent, but after finally obtaining the name of Bert's psychiatrist, she was told he was away on holidays. She slammed the phone down in frustration at being met with a dead end at every turn.

Will placed a mug of steaming coffee on her desk, sliding her paperwork aside as he did so. 'Your desk will be like mine if you don't watch out,' he said, amused at the uncharacteristic mess.

Jennifer pushed the statements around, like pieces of a puzzle. 'Where's the connection? Why would a tarot card reader encourage the deaths of two completely unrelated people? The answer is in here somewhere. I can feel it. If we find the connection, we find the Raven.'

'Unfortunately, the dead can't speak,' Will said as he took a seat.

'Their families can,' Jennifer said, picking up the phone and searching for the country code for America.

'Well that was interesting,' Jennifer replaced the handset after a lengthy phone call.

Will raised an eyebrow questioningly. After getting through some of his own work, he had begun reading the statements, lending a pair of fresh eyes to the investigation.

'Marcy – that's Alan Price's ex-wife – was spoken to by DC Hardwick after he died, but he only made notes that Alan was suffering from depression.'

'To be fair, he didn't have to document it at all, given his death was suicide,' Will said.

'If you're going to do a job then at least do it right.' Jennifer jabbed at the copies of the statements. 'Marcy said Alan's depression began after their daughter was born, and by the time their little girl had started school, they were divorced. Despite their differences, they messaged each other regularly on Facebook. She still has records of their conversations.'

'So what's unusual about that?' Will said.

'Alan told Marcy that he moved back to England for the gift of a second chance. When she asked what it meant, he said he was getting therapy for past issues. At first, it seemed to be going well, but then something changed. He said he'd been putting his trust in the wrong people, and she'd hear about it soon enough. That was a few days before his death.'

'Bloody hell.'

'I know. I was tempted to ask her about the hit and run, but she's grieving. It wouldn't have been fair to pile that on her as well. She's going to screenshot the conversations and email them over. What do you think Alan meant when he said she would hear about it soon enough?'

'Perhaps he meant he was planning his suicide.'

'Maybe. Or perhaps there's more to it than that. When I visited Emily she said a similar thing ... oh what was it?' She snapped her fingers. 'That's it! "The best gift in life is a second chance."'

'What does it mean?' Will said, rubbing his whiskers.

A slow smile spread across Jennifer's lips as realisation dawned. 'It means we have a connection.'

CHAPTER TEN

'Hey everyone, what better tune to celebrate Friday night than one from the queen of pop herself? That's right, iiiiiiit's Madonna!' the disc jockey said before playing 'Celebrate'. It was one of Will's little jokes; changing her car radio to the eighties channel when she wasn't looking. Jennifer reached for the off button as Will jumped in with the takeaway bags. It didn't take two of them to pick up the Chinese, but it was good to get away from the office, if only for a few minutes.

'Who's been in here while I was gone, one of Santa's elves?' Will said, bumping his knees against the glove box.

Jennifer bit back a smile. The seat shoved forward was payback for making her listen to the eighties channel. 'Elves? I think you'll find it was you.' She turned the ignition. 'I'm gonna trade it in soon, I'm thinking of getting myself a nice Audi A4 or something like that.'

'Well, all right for some,' Will said, pushing his hand against the glove box to shut it. A glimpse of white caught his eye and he dropped the door, allowing it to gape open.

'You didn't tell me you got another letter,' he said, pulling out the white bonded envelope.

'I haven't …' Jennifer's words were cut short as she stared at the envelope. 'Where did that come from?'

Will frowned. 'Here, in your glove box. Do you want me to open it?' he said, fishing in his jacket pocket for some PVC gloves. He shook the envelope. It was weighted at the bottom.

Jennifer turned off the car engine. She wasn't going anywhere until she figured out what to do. 'We should give it straight to forensics,' she said, biting the corner of her lip. She knew the suspense would eat away at her, and she wasn't in a hurry to hand the information over to DC Hardwick, given he'd been so flippant with her findings to date. 'Oh go on then, open it,' she heard herself say.

Will carefully opened the end, and watched as a round gold keyring fell into his lap. He reached for a pen from the glove box and poked it through the metal loop.

'Why would anyone send you a designer keyring?'

The letters D and G were intertwined in gold, with tiny studded diamonds twinkling under the interior car light. Will drew his attention to the envelope and gently teased it open. Just like the last one, it contained a small black feather.

'What the hell? How did that get into my car?' Jennifer said, her hands itching with the need to be scrubbed clean.

Will's brow furrowed. 'Someone has gone to a lot of trouble to send you this.'

'I can see that,' she said, annoyed by the idea of someone being in her car.

Will popped the keyring back inside the envelope and carefully folded it over. 'Are you sure this is the first you've seen of this?'

'What's that supposed to mean?' Jennifer said, drumming her fingers against the steering wheel. She welcomed the clues, but the invasion into her personal space had tapped into her compulsion to clean. The feeling of contamination grew, bringing with it a swell of apprehension, and it buzzed like a swarm of angry wasps in her chest.

Will sidestepped her question. 'Have you left your car unlocked? Lost any spare keys?'

'No … but I might have forgotten to lock it. I've been so busy lately …' Her voice trailed away.

Will gnawed his lip, staring into the distance.

'What's wrong?' she said, touching his arm to stir him from his thoughts.

Will took a deep breath but avoided her gaze. 'Nothing. I just don't like the thought of anyone being in your car.' His eyes flickered to hers then quickly back onto the streets. 'I can come over after work if you like, check your house out.'

Jennifer frowned. 'My house? Do you think that's necessary?'

The concern etched on Will's face conveyed he did. 'Best not to take any chances. I know you want to go this alone, but this is getting personal. You're better off handing everything over to DC Hardwick and assisting him with the enquiries.'

Jennifer's eyes crept to the ravens perched on the guttering of the buildings outside. Their heads bowed under the glow of the streetlamps as they bunched together conspiratorially, their beady eyes focused on her movements below.

'Will,' she said, her words delivered in a spoken sigh. 'This got personal a long time ago.'

'Oh.' Will went quiet. 'What makes you say that?'

She pointed up through the windscreen of her car. 'See those ravens up there? They're everywhere I go. I found one dead on my doorstep the other night. Ravens are said to carry powers of divination, and some believe they are omens of death.'

'Do you think they're connected to your suspect? It's a tenuous link,' Will said, gently reeling her back into the real world. He was met with silence, broken by his growling stomach.

'It's early days and I might have it all wrong. But there's more to it than that, isn't there?' Jennifer said, forcing him to look at her.

Will dropped his eyes again. He never was any good at lying. 'I was going to tell you … but I was going to speak to Claire first, see if she could put some safety measures in place.'

'I knew you were holding out. What were you going to tell me?' she said, starting the ignition and pulling away from the kerb. The smell of chow mein and curry wafting from the back seat reminded Jennifer they should be getting back. She was keen to leave the ravens behind, but Will's behaviour was niggling her.

'I know who delivered the first letter. It was Charlie Sutton,' Will said, clicking his seatbelt into place.

She glanced at her partner in disbelief. 'Sutton? Why would the little scroat do that?'

'He said an old fella paid him to drop it in. He was driving a van. I was going to tell you, I've only just found out myself.'

Jennifer lowered the car window, which had fogged in a fine mist of condensation.

'You should have told me the second you found out. We're meant to be a team.'

'We *are* a team. I literally just found out today. Can we have this argument after we've eaten? I'm bloody starving.'

Jennifer broke into an involuntary smile. Nothing could come between Will and his food, and she used the rest of the journey to iron out the case so far. They had come to the conclusion that the Raven, or Bert Bishop as she now presumed, was connected to The Reborners cult. He seemed no stranger to mystical practices, given his use of the tarot cards, and what better stomping ground than a mysterious cult, offering the promise of rebirth to tortured souls? But Bert was a stranger to Alan when they met in the pub, and she was yet to work out a motivation to kill car crash victim Felicity Bowes. Her efforts to warn Emily had drawn a blank, and she had fulfilled her promise of refusing to answer the door. All she could do was to flag Emily's address as a concern, and submit further intelligence. DC Hardwick was blinkered in his investigation. Although MIT were now actively seeking out Bert Bishop, she could tell he still held the belief that Bert was a mentally disturbed individual, responsible for nothing more than giving tarot card readings for money.

She promised to go inside as soon as she made a quick call. But she didn't have any phone call to make. As soon as Will had left, she took the letter from the glove box and held it up under her nose. She sniffed, as if smelling a milk bottle to see if the contents had soured. Jennifer wrinkled her nose. It was the same musty smell as before. Closing her eyes, she breathed in its essence before laying it back on her lap. Like the sun clearing through the clouds, her thought buds extended beyond herself, into another plane. Her breathing deepened as mental images were formed and the blurry image of a metal bed came into view. She touched her face, seeing what he saw, from the inside. Instead of her own smooth skin she felt a man's stubble, and winced as her fingers pressed on the soft pad of a swollen cheekbone. Tentatively, fingers reached to the back of his head and examined the dry blood matting through his hair. Everything hurt, throbbed, pinched and stung. In the distance a beep of a machine, soft shoes padding by. A hand curled around a thin blue curtain. Jennifer drew a sharp breath as probing eyes turned back on her. The black beady eyes of the raven stared back, taunting her. Jennifer gave a sharp gasp as a loud knock on her car window brought her abruptly back to reality.

'Oh!' Jennifer jumped out of her seat.

'The food's all laid out, are you coming in or what?' Will stood with his head cocked to one side, wearing his usual grin.

'You frightened the life out of me,' she said, her heart pounding as she grounded herself.

He tapped the car window. 'What? I can't hear you. Are you OK?'

'It's … It's nothing. It's just a headache,' she said, undoing her seatbelt and opening the door.

'I hope so,' he said, as he pressed his fob against the door to allow them entry into the back of the station. 'I can't take on your workload, I've enough of my own.'

As she ate her chow mein, Jennifer's mind kept wandering back to what she had seen. She couldn't shake off the feeling that it was a premonition of something to come. The face in her vision felt weathered and gaunt, and there was no mistaking the injuries. But what did it mean? Had she picked up the embodiment of the man known as Raven? And if so, what was the connection to the keyring found in her car? The obvious answer was that it belonged to Felicity Baron, who died as prophesied. The witness statements mentioned her losing her car keys and finding them again, but nothing about the absence of a D&G keyring specifically. It had to be connected.

Question after question spun in her mind. Why would someone go out of their way to kill an innocent young woman? The fact that Jennifer knew each of the victims in some way did not escape her attention. Alan Price, whose parents owned the pub where her father spent most of his time. Christian Bowes, her old school friend whose Fiancee was tragically murdered. Just who was next? She glanced up from her plate to catch Will staring at her, his unwavering protectiveness evident by the concern shadowing his face. He winked, and she smiled in return. She took a chip from her plate, returning her thoughts to the case. There was only one person who could answer her question about the keyring. And that was Christian Bowes.

CHAPTER ELEVEN
Bert

Bert sneezed as the tickle of incense wafted through the draughty hall at the psychic fair. He could not bear the smell, and he longed for the mossy scent of the forest. He glared at the empty plastic chair opposite his makeshift table. People preferred the showier mediums to his humble stall. The ironic thing was, he knew more than all of them put together. He siphoned the dregs from his plastic coffee cup, and crumpled it up before throwing it in the bin. Felicity's death had already lost its impact, and the urge to make another prophecy drove him onwards. The bones of his backside seemed to grate on the hard plastic chair. The itching had returned, making every fold and joint of his skin feel as if it was on fire. Oh for blessed release, he thought, wishing she would hurry up. He flicked his tongue to the cracked corners of his lips, tasting his bitter rough skin. The action was devoid of comfort, and he longed to drag his nails over the torturous itch. But he had to remain focused. Relief would come. He rifled in his pocket for a tissue, not noticing the woman and child approach until they were in front of him.

A child was not part of the plan, he thought, expecting her to be alone. The resemblance between them was striking. They shared the same blue eyes, their skin peppered with freckles. Bert did not need the cards to tell him the boy would have been teased for his flaming red hair – if he were old enough to attend school, that was. Bert had the measure of the young woman in seconds. His eyes trailed over the thin material of her blue dress, dotted with white swallows. It was something she kept for 'good wear' along with the matching blue shoes, which gaped at the heels, too big for her feet. Her long auburn hair was hastily tied into a bun, because that was how a good mother dressed. Bert allowed a soft groan to pass his lips. She was definitely the one. But he hadn't known about the kid. Why the hell did she have to bring him with her? He rose from his chair, gasping as the fresh cracks in his skin sent daggers of pain through his nerve endings. That was when he knew; it was too late to back out now.

'Excuse me.' Bert cracked his most inoffensive smile. 'Would you like a free five-minute reading?'

The woman nodded sharply, unable to believe her luck. Her son never took his eyes off her as he followed, holding her tightly by the hand.

Bert gestured to the empty chair. 'Are you happy to have the boy present during the reading?' Bert said, his thoughts racing. She was a thief. Yet the image before him showed a young woman trying to pull her life together.

The woman whispered what sounded like a well-rehearsed line. 'Don't mind him. He doesn't know what's going on half the time.'

Bert sat across from them, his eyes flicking back to the boy. She was right. His face had a vacant look, as if whatever was in there had upped and left one day. As Bert touched the deck of cards, he began to have second thoughts. Perhaps the death prediction would not come. A nice reading, that's what she wanted. He could see it in her face. She wanted a tall dark stranger to come and save the day. She would go away happy and the kid would get a couple of smiles from his mother before she realised it was all a dream. But as he shuffled the cards, fresh feelings of dread began to take root. He crossed his legs underneath the chair, scratching his calf muscle with his shoe. The discomfort helped him focus on his purpose, as he watched the images unfold.

'I see you've had a tough time since your son was born,' he said solemnly. 'His dad didn't hang around after the diagnosis.'

Wide-eyed in wonder, the blue dress woman nodded, pulling her chair in closer for a better listen.

'You've had to make many sacrifices. It's hard being so isolated since you gave up working.'

'Yes,' she said in a quiet voice. 'I didn't want to give up my job, but the child minder wanted more money than I could earn.'

Bert wanted to say she would be fine, because that's what she wanted to hear. He wanted to say that she would meet her tall handsome stranger on either the eleventh day or the eleventh month or the eleventh hour. Then Bert saw something that took the words away. He spoke in measured tones. 'I can see it's hard but it's not the kid's fault.'

'What do you mean by that?' she said, a flush creeping up her face. 'I manage just fine.'

Bert shook his head. 'Your life is going down the pan. The drugs, the shoplifting, then leaving him alone when you go out. There's no excuse for it.'

The blue dress woman shrank from him, shame reflected in her eyes. 'Who are you, the social services? I asked for a reading, not judgment.'

Bert spoke in soothing tones. 'I just say what comes to me. Give me a second and I'll predict your future.'

She sat back expectantly. The boy stared with a wilted expression, slightly swaying on his feet. He reminded Bert of one of those inflatables in front of car showrooms after the air has started seeping out. He couldn't feel anger towards them. They had nothing, and clearly loved each other.

'You ...' The words rolled to his throat like boulders, but he could not bring himself to utter them. But the fatal prediction flashed in vivid colour, even behind his closed eyes. *A dog's barks echo in an alleyway, and cars skid into puddles from the main road. Quickening footsteps as a leering pock-faced man looms into view. His dirty-gloved hands tug the woman's dress as he catches up with her on her way back from the shops. She didn't want to take the shortcut, but she needs to get back because her son is all alone. She clutches her bag to her chest as pock-faced man jostles her for money. Throwing the empty purse to the ground, he tugs the woman by the hips, and his face is met by a stinging slap. Her screams are silenced as the man punches her face and her head hits the broken cement of the footpath. Her last thought is for her son.*

Bert's eyes flickered to the child, who returned his haunted gaze. Looking into the kid's eyes was like looking into his own. Unable to understand why the world couldn't accept him, he clung to his mother like a raft on choppy seas. But soon he would be cast adrift. A pang of guilt struck deep into his psyche, and he barely recognised the emotion. He was just a kid. Despite what his mother did, Bert couldn't afford him that pain. He tripped on the words, and began to stutter as he tried desperately to hold them back.

'You ... willaaargh.' Bubbles of saliva formed in the corners of his lips as he rejected the prediction. His tongue rolled to form the words and he bit down hard, causing a stream of blood to trickle through his fingers.

'Are you, OK, mister?' the woman said.

Bert stumbled away from the table, his blood-stained mouth still fighting to speak as the words backed up in his throat.

Heart pounding, he gulped in mouthfuls of fresh air as he burst through the swing doors. His tongue throbbed as he leaned against the wall, hastily spitting blood into a tissue. A bird's caws echoed in the distance.

The woman rushed out, dragging the boy behind her. 'Are you OK?'

Bert swallowed hard, and a burning sensation slid down his throat and settled in his belly. 'Yes,' he gasped, 'thank you for asking.'

'Good. I thought you were having a stroke,' she said, her voice lowering to a whisper before glancing either side. 'What you said about my boy … I'm trying to get help. It won't happen again.'

'Lots of people struggle,' Bert said, relieved to have control of his voice. 'You have to be strong.' He turned to spit into his hanky. Silence passed between them. He fixed his black fedora as the woman turned to go back inside.

'Oh and miss? Don't go out on your own at night. It's not safe where you live.'

'How do you know …?'

'I don't. I'm just passing on the message. I advise you listen.' A cawing from above alerted him to the high-heeled footsteps crunching up the gravel drive. Bert flattened against the wall, peeking around the corner to see the slim, well-dressed detective push through the double doors.

Bert's uncharacteristic act of compassion baffled him as he sat at the bar of the Hare and Hound pub, downing his fifth pint. His triumph at dodging DC Knight was short-lived, as he counted the last of his money. If he had delivered the prophecy he would have been rewarded in so many ways. He would have awoken in the morning feeling rejuvenated and pain free, at least for a while. Money would have found its way into his hands, leaving him free to continue his mission. *Why did I do that? I disobeyed the prophecy.* His scaly fingers touched the swollen bite mark on his tongue, regretting his moment of weakness. *What will happen now?* The prediction would have to be fulfilled. He knew that from sorry experience. But now he had messed everything up by warning her. She wouldn't go out alone tonight. His skin crawled with agitation, and he scratched the back of his neck. His fingernails returned hooked with blood. Alcohol had anaesthetised his nerve endings, but it was a temporary solution to an endless affliction.

A pair of eyes bored into his back as he shoved the folded-up cash into the crevice of his hat. He stumbled down the path into the night, cursing under his breath as car tyres splashed puddles and drenched his clothes. Lost in his anger, he did not hear the lone figure approach. A dog barked in the distance, as the clouds blotted the moon, but Bert was alerted to the familiar scene too late. His eyes bulged as a gloved hand clamped over his mouth, his captor spitting angry threats. Bert gagged, the smell of vomit and cigarettes overpowering as the gloved hand dragged him backwards into an alleyway. Staring but not seeing, Bert tripped over the broken concrete, desperately trying to gather his thoughts. An icy wind cut through the alley as the moon cleared the clouds, bringing a familiarity to the scene. It hit him with frightening clarity – this was the scene of Emily's prediction. His heart hammered in his ribcage as he fought for breath. Was he taking the punishment in Emily's place? A strike of terror drove through his heart as the pock-faced man bore down on him.

CHAPTER TWELVE
Bert

Searing white pain greeted Bert as he awoke with a groan in the narrow metal bed. 'Mother?' came out as a muffled 'Muffah?' through blood-crusted lips, and the world began to sway as he struggled to focus with swollen eyes. Panic rose in his throat as he clawed the bed, trying to find his bearings.

'Steady now.' A soft voice approached and a hand touched his bare arm.

Bert shrivelled from the contact. This was not mother.

'You're in hospital. Just try to relax,' the nurse said, smoothing his blankets with soft, gentle hands. She was so close he could smell her perfume, which was flowery and sweet, somewhat like her.

Bert drew soothing breaths and his vision began to clear. 'What happened?' He touched his temples and winced. His head felt like it had been stuffed with bricks.

'You've had a beating and concussion, but nothing that won't heal. Here, have a drink.'

With trembling hands, Bert gripped the plastic tumbler and gulped down tepid water.

'There's an officer here very keen to speak to you. I'll go and get her.'

Police involvement was the last thing Bert wanted, at least not yet. But by the time he sat up to argue, the nurse was gone.

He gave a weary sigh as a broad woman in a very tight police uniform plodded through the curtain surrounding his bed. Her black bobbed hair hung limply as if it were attached to the inside of her police hat.

Bert looked past his unwelcome visitor and through the gap in the hospital curtain. A yellowed semblance of a man slept in the bed across from him, his toothless mouth drawing in the hospital air that could soon be his last. Bert shuddered. The thoughts of sleeping in a shared ward gave him a sudden impulse to grab his things and leave.

A deep voice broke into his thoughts. 'I'm Officer Wallace, the neighbourhood constable for this area. Can I have a minute of your time?'

Bert stared, mesmerised by the woman's facial hair.

She did not wait for a reply. 'You were found in an alleyway by a man looking for his dog. We've had several reports of robberies in this area. Can you tell me what happened?'

'I can't remember,' Bert croaked, wishing the flowery nurse would return.

The woman bit the top of her pen as she shuffled closer to the side of his bed. For one horrifying moment, Bert thought she was going to sit on it.

'Can you start by giving me your details? You didn't have any ID when they brought you in.'

'My cards. They've taken my cards?' Bert whispered, more to himself than anyone else.

She nodded sympathetically, completely missing the point. 'You'll have to report any missing cards to the bank. Now if you'd like to provide me with your details we can find out who's done this to you.'

'No. I don't know anything. Just leave me alone.' Bert flapped his hands. *Why wouldn't she go away instead of mooing in his ear?*

The officer slapped her pocket notebook shut and backed away. 'I'm sorry, sir, I didn't mean to upset you. I'll come back tomorrow when you're feeling better.'

'Have a shave first,' Bert felt like saying. He was not feeling charitable. If there was one thing he hated it was hospitals. He always left feeling like he had been taken apart and put back together the wrong way. Bert tried to remember the last time he was in hospital but the memories were behind doors that would not open.

He lay back on the bed and closed his eyes, too tired to stop the voices flooding his mind. *The dog barking, the broken concrete, the pock-faced man. They're all from the premonition.* Bert replayed the reading at the psychic fair, and biting his tongue to stop the words, which felt so unnatural in his mouth. Once a premonition was invoked, it was almost impossible to halt. What goes around comes around. It was the law of the universe.

Bert relived the attack, trying to make sense of it all. Lying in a piss-stained alleyway as the pock-faced man pummelled him with feet and fists. Curling up in a ball as the final kick came, shielding his head from the gut-wrenching blows.

He should have been relieved he saved the young woman and her son the consequences of such a terrible fate. After all, she was a young mother with a special needs child. But in the cold light of day he was wishing, more than anything, that it had been her, even if it had left her on a mortuary slab. A trolley rattled past and Bert waved away the offer of tea. I can't stay here. I'll get dressed and leave, Bert thought. His eyes grew heavy and despite the background noise, he succumbed to sleep. The closed-in feeling and antiseptic smell transported him to his bedroom and his earliest memory.

As soon as he learned to walk, he wanted to be outside. The whistle of the wind was far more enticing than his pull-along toys.

While Callum sang nursery rhymes with mother, Bert remained silent, animated by the whispers of the forest that only he could hear. To him there was nothing more powerful than nature, the crashing thunder and the rolling clouds laced with rain that stabbed the galvanised roof of their home. Nature was a powerful call, and as he stared through the window, his painted wooden blocks and balding teddy bears paled in comparison.

Bert's unwillingness to speak did not reflect a lack of intelligence, which was sharp beyond his years. His insight was not afforded to others. To his family, midnight was a time to turn their back on the beauty of the moon, the numbness of sleep blocking out the night cries of the nocturnal. But to Bert, the most enlivening time was between midnight and three am, when the veil between his reality and the world beyond was at its thinnest.

That night he stroked the long inky tail feather that had fluttered through his open window. Bert did not feel the cold as he stared out to the fields beyond. He gasped as a raven cut through the diamond-studded night, flapping, cawing, swooping through the air, the gap in its tail feathers reflected by the sombre moon. Holding the feather tight in his grasp, he pulled on his red wellingtons and duffle coat, his small bony fingers struggling to thread the thick buttons through the frayed loops. Pulling back his blanket, he positioned the pillow underneath. It was unlikely anyone would check, but it made him feel better about leaving. Grasping the window ledge, he stepped onto his toy chest and slipped through the open window to the back yard. He had often snuck out unseen during the day, splintering his palms as he gripped the rough wooden ledge. But this was his first night excursion, and a tremble of excitement rose as his heart tick tocked like the drum of his wind-up toy solider.

The frost sparkling on the gravel path seemed magical, and glinted invitingly as it stretched to the forest beyond. He glanced behind only once, before chasing the black feathered watchman down the track, deep into the purple shadows of the woodlands. A rasping caw of approval sliced through the air, and Bert's heart clattered in his chest, as the exhilaration of freedom pumped blood through his veins like never before. He was running wild, and the night welcomed him. As he stretched out his arms either side, he imagined his flight, his clumsy red wellington boots replaced by powerful scaly claws, tucked under his body as he sped through the woodlands with ease. Eyes streaming, his hot breath puffed plumes of white smoke from his mouth, and for the first time in his short existence, he felt capable of anything. He ran until his lungs burned and the thorny-edged brambles tugged at his clothes, slowing his flight. Exhilarated, he dropped to the twitching forest floor, and a living carpet of tiny creatures scuttled away from their human invader. Bert smiled in wonder, breathing in the smell of frosted pinecones sweetening the air. He was lying in the birthplace of something dark and powerful, but he was not afraid. Whispers grew and branches crackled as he laid his weary body against a majestic tree – a silent witness of dark rituals and sacrifices decades before. The malevolence that seeped through the earth could not serve to hurt him now. It made the soil rich with an energy that promised strength, as long as he knew how to use it. His eyelids became heavy as the faint trace of icy fingertips touched his skin.

Bert drew in a sharp breath as he realised he was no longer a four-year-old child in the depths of the forest, but a sixty-five-year-old man in a hospital. Yet as he blinked in awakening, the fingers continued to touch his senses; glacial messengers sent through a psychic link, seeping curious thoughts into his presence. It was the detective. She was looking for him.

She was a person of flesh and blood like him, but with abilities beyond her understanding. He had been waiting for her, each victim a breadcrumb trail for her to follow. Their destinies were intertwined, but it was not yet their time. Bert swung his legs out of the bed and fumbled for his clothes, relieved to find his cards in his jacket pocket. Time was passing at a merciless rate, and more prophecies had to be delivered before the ritual came to its climax. His mouth cranked upwards at the promise of rejuvenation. A storm was coming for Jennifer Knight ... but her death would not be in vain.

CHAPTER THIRTEEN

'I don't believe it!' Jennifer threw her hands in the air. 'We've missed him by minutes.' The smokers outside Haven Hospital gave Jennifer a bemused look as she paced the pavement.

'In which case he can't have gone far,' Will said. 'Come on, get in the car, we'll have a scout around.'

Jennifer cursed her stupidity as she wrestled with the car seatbelt. She should have gone straight to the hospital after her premonition. She had seen a bruised man in a metal bed, but didn't know what it meant. The beeping machines, a hand drawn over a curtain … it all made sense now. But it wasn't until she received the call from the neighbourhood police officer in response to her missing persons report that everything clicked into place. PC Wallace had informed her that she visited an elderly man matching Bert Bishop's description in hospital. Unfortunately, he had just left, after being treated for concussion and bruising. The nurse described him as pleasant enough, somewhat bewildered, a little evasive, and suffering from acute eczema. Apart from that, he seemed no different to the many patients that discharged themselves without so much as a by-your-leave.

The car jerked forward as Will pulled out of the car park, the wipers working to dispel the fat droplets of rain beginning to plop on the windscreen. 'What's the latest description?'

Jennifer swallowed. Her throat felt like a sandpit and she really needed a coffee. 'He's tall and thin with short grey hair, wearing a long black coat and hat. He has facial injuries and bruising to his cheekbone. They think he discharged himself within the last thirty minutes. Their CCTV is under maintenance so I can't even get a copy of that.'

'How do we know it's our Raven? There must be plenty of old men that fall around drunk and end up in the hospital.'

Jennifer recalled her premonition and shuddered. 'Take my word for it, I know.'

The streets of Haven were not ready to give up the Raven, and Jennifer attended afternoon briefing with the Lexton Murder Investigation Team, offering up what information she had of value. Returning to Haven with notes and tasks, her eyes were drawn to the yellow Post-it note alerting her to a missed call. She peeled it from her computer screen as she automatically dialled the number and introduced herself. It took her several seconds to recognise the voice on the other side.

'My girl is dead. My beautiful Felicity is dead,' Christian cried, the words erupting into sobs.

Jennifer cradled the phone against her ear, cursing herself for failing to recognise his number. She wondered if he felt more comfortable with her than his shallow showbiz friends.

'I know. I'm very sorry for your loss.' Jennifer bit her tongue. She hated those words, having heard them over and over at her mother's funeral when she was just ten years old. *Sorry for your loss, sorry for your loss*, accompanied by firm handshakes from smartly dressed police officers conveying their sympathies. Wearing full dress uniform, with shiny buttons and squeaky polished boots, they extended their hands in sympathy. She had grasped each one until her fingers ached, while her father's shoulders shook, tears running in rivulets down his unshaven face. She could smell the alcohol on his breath even then. The office door slammed, and Jennifer snapped out of her memory, returning her attention to Christian.

His slow deliberate tones could not disguise the slur in his voice. 'Why have the police arrested my ex-wife?' A bottle clinked against glass in the background.

'I'm sorry, you need to speak to DC Hardwick,' Jennifer said. Her knowledge of the arrest was that Christian's ex-wife had denied all offences and been bailed for further enquiries while they checked out her alibi. Her reluctance to provide one was because she had been with another man, something she had wanted to keep to herself.

Christian's thick breathing intermingled with old reruns of the reality TV programme, *The Beauty Salon*, as it played in the background. She caught the unmistakable laugh of his dead fiancée as it blared through his speaker system.

'I've lost everything.' Christian cried, great big heaving sobs down the phone.

'I'm sorry, but ...'

Lost in his grief, Christian just kept talking. 'I told you there was something dark on the horizon and you wouldn't listen. Now Felicity's dead.'

Jennifer's jaw clenched as his words hit close to the mark. She had forgotten all about his warning, but there was little point discussing it when Christian was off his face. 'I'm at work now, but how about we meet for a coffee? I'll text you when I've worked something out, how about that?'

But Christian wasn't listening, and another sob erupted as he blurted out the words, 'She's dead. My beautiful girl is dead.'

Jennifer took a deep breath. She had been meaning to ask the question and now was as good a time as any. 'Did Felicity have a keyring on her car keys?'

Christian sniffled loudly before replying. 'A keyring? Well ... yes. It was a diamond-studded D and G. I bought it for her when I gave her the car. I wish I'd never bought her that car ...'

Jennifer sighed. At least she had clarification of the owner of the keyring. MIT would surely listen to her now. It had already been booked into the property system, a request on its way for forensics to check for fingerprints. She would also need a statement from Christian outlining what he had just said. But now was not the time. 'You sound worn out. Is anyone staying with you?'

'My ... mum ... and the children. What if the police charge my ex-wife? You should be speaking to my cousin, not her. What if she goes to prison? What about them?'

Jennifer extricated her fingers from the tightly wound phone cord as she prepared to end the call. 'She may just be helping them with their questioning. Have you heard from your cousin at all?'

'No ... Why? You think he did it, don't you?'

Jennifer paused, choosing her words carefully. 'There are often several persons of interest in investigations. But if you hear from him, you must contact us immediately. I've put a flag on your address and phone line, so any calls will be treated as a priority. Now why don't you get some rest, it sounds like you need it.'

Christian exhaled slowly, as if he had been deflated and was slowly coming to ground. 'I'm sorry. I didn't mean to have a go at you. I comfort people about life after death, but I've never experienced loss before. I don't know what to do with myself.'

Jennifer's voice softened. 'You've had a lot to endure. Get some rest, you need to stay strong for your children.'

The phone call left Jennifer feeling emotionally drained. It wasn't the right time to go into details of his cousin's involvement. It was all so horrendous.

It was time to bring her sergeant up to date with the briefing on the Raven case, and inform her about the letter found in the glove box of her car. Admitting her discovery of a dead raven outside her home could have her removed from the case for her own safety, and she had warned Will to keep that snippet of information to himself.

Claire opened the door a couple of inches before swiftly pulling Jennifer inside.

'Is everything all right?' Jennifer said, wondering why the sudden need for secrecy.

Claire gave an apologetic smile. 'Yeah, sorry. I've a guest with me and I didn't want anyone else seeing.'

'A guest?' Jennifer looked around the empty room, and then heard a drumming noise under Claire's desk. She bent down to see a small wiry dog lying on his back with his tail pounding a beat against the carpeted floor. 'Hello boy,' Jennifer said, his back leg twitching as she reached down and scratched his stomach. 'Is that George's dog?'

Claire smiled, 'Yes. The old codger persuaded me to take him in while he sorted out his benefits. It's the second time this week.'

'Hasn't anyone noticed?'

'No, and don't tell Will, because he'll be mooning over him instead of getting on with his work.'

'Hmm, pongs a bit though,' Jennifer said, sniffing her hands.

Claire shrugged. 'Ah well, that's dogs for you. How are you finding Zoe?'

Jennifer peered out the window to see her new colleague chatting to Will, toying with her stationery, as she sat in her chair. 'She's a nice girl, although she didn't need much babysitting from me, she seems happier working alone.'

'We'll have to organise a works night out soon, once we get on top of our workload. You and Will have quite a double act going on at the moment. You're like yin and yang but I like it.'

'It works for me. I feel like we're on the verge of something big with this Raven case, but it's frustrating not having full control of the investigation. I've got some fresh evidence, and it pains me to have to hand it over to MIT.' Jennifer passed her report to Claire, which was typed up and ready to pass over.

Her sergeant scanned the pages, making 'mmm' sounds as she absorbed herself in the updates.

Jennifer glanced through the window again to see Will tidying her desk, straightening the pens and stationery that Zoe had inadvertently moved. A warm glow spread through her, and seconds passed before her sergeant cleared her throat.

'Will found evidence in your car?' Claire raised an eyebrow as she finished reading the report. 'I'll need to speak to the DI about this.'

The fact Claire had called him the DI and not Ethan set alarm bells ringing in Jennifer's head. She hadn't considered the option that she herself could become a person of interest in the Felicity Baron case. 'Should I be worried?'

'No, I just think he should be aware before you update them.' Claire slipped off her pumps and scratched Tinker's belly with her feet. The dog emitted a low satisfied moan, underneath her desk.

Jennifer gave a short-lived smile at her sergeant's quirkiness. 'Perhaps I *am* responsible for all this. Sometimes I feel like I'm attracting bad energies and the people of Haven are paying for it.'

Claire shook her head. 'Don't be silly. I just want you to hold off while I make sure we're supporting you as best we can. Eventually the Raven will give a little more of himself, but for now, be careful. Don't put yourself in a position where you're vulnerable.'

Jennifer mulled over their meeting as she returned to her desk. Flipping back the cap from her anti-bacterial gel, she squirted a blob on the palm of her hand. Fresh dust particles on her computer monitor glittered accusingly under the light of the fluorescent tubes, feeding her growing apprehension. She itched to march outside and scrub the inside of her car, but she wouldn't be able to touch it until crime scene investigators had checked for fingerprints. Her senses told her they would not be forthcoming. Something dark was on the horizon, and she could not shake off the feeling that another prediction was on its way.

CHAPTER FOURTEEN

The news that her sister was visiting that evening sent Jennifer in a tailspin of emotions. Amy had not visited her home in over a year, and there was something about the edge in her voice that left her uneasy. Her phone call had been short, not because Jennifer was driving home, but due to the way she grilled her like a suspect in custody. She had gleaned enough information to find out that Amy's sudden attendance had nothing to do with the children. Jennifer took out her trepidation on the wooden hall floor as she gripped the scrubbing brush. She swirled the soapy water over the knots, then dropped the brush in favour of a toothbrush, working her way into the grooves until her arms weakened and her back ached. The carpet was the only surface she could not disinfect, and it never felt truly clean. She had been in far worse places, where her shoes stuck to the floor and she wiped her feet on the way out. But this was her home, and she had learned to cope with other people's low standards of hygiene as long as *her* living space was clean and ordered. She sat back on her legs, pushing strings of hair off her sweaty face. Her prune fingers gave comfort as her need for order grew. When it came to her sister, the old feelings of protectiveness and control often came back into play. It had been tough for Jennifer to let go when Amy got married, and although David was as straight-laced as they came, he always made sure she had everything she wanted.

Jennifer didn't want anything to rock the boat now, not when things were going so well.

She had just enough time to shower and change before the doorbell rang. Anxious thoughts rebounded from one corner of her brain to the next as she searched the ceiling for invisible cobwebs. Amy would never call around like this, not unless she had a reason. It had always been up to Jennifer to visit her. Perhaps she was moving away, or there was something wrong with Josh. Perhaps ...

The doorbell rang again as an impatient finger leaned on the buzzer. Taking a deep, calming breath, Jennifer opened it wide, her face breaking out into a smile as she welcomed her sister inside. Her hug was stiff and awkward, so unlike the warm squeezes her little sister would give her when she tucked her up in bed at night. She shook the beads of rain from Amy's coat and hung it on the hanger, anxiously glancing at her muddied shoes. Amy opened the door to the living room and paused teasingly in the doorway.

'I'd better take these off before you have kittens,' she said, easing her feet out of her flat Mary Jane shoes.

She wasn't far wrong. Jennifer felt she was expecting a bunch of lively felines already. She scratched the back of her hand, anything to keep her grounded.

'Wow,' Amy said, running her hands over the expensive furniture. 'This place is even nicer than I remember. Can you imagine Josh in here? He'd have a field day with your cream carpet.'

Jennifer cleared her throat. 'The kids are welcome here any time. Can I get you anything?'

Amy waved her offer away. 'No thanks, I can't stay long. I just wanted to pop in ...' Amy hesitated, swallowing hard. She stared at her stocking feet, unable to meet her sister's eyes.

'If you've come here to tell me something, it's best you just get on with it.' Jennifer stood at the fireplace, too nervy to sit.

Amy clasped her fingers tightly over her knee. 'Straight to the point, as always, sis.' She exhaled a short-lived laugh. I came because I didn't want to tell you on the phone. But you've got to promise not to blow your top.'

Jennifer frowned. If it wasn't anything to do with the kids, the other thing that could provoke such a reaction was … Her eyes opened wide. 'Please tell me you've not been speaking to dad.'

Amy's lips turned downwards as she squirmed in her seat. It was the same pouty frown she wore as a child when she didn't get her own way. 'How do you do that?'

'Do what?' Jennifer asked, wishing her sister would get on with it and tell her what was wrong.

'Steal my thoughts. It's the same with Josh. I only have to think something and he knows what it is.'

Jennifer felt a ripple of anger. 'So you *have* been speaking to dad then?'

'Yes as it happens. He wants to see his grandchildren,' she said, her voice carrying an air of defiance.

Jennifer rubbed her hands against the back of her jeans. She had an uncanny urge to dip them in bleach and inhale the reassuring smell as they found her cuts and scratches. Disbelief, anger, and jealousy mixed in a sickening cocktail as it churned her stomach and raised her voice. 'I don't believe this. Why are you allowing that drunk back into our lives?'

Amy stood, pulling the thick strap of her handbag over her shoulder. 'David said I didn't have to justify my actions to you, and he was right.'

The comment inflamed Jennifer's irritation. 'Oh so what David says goes, is that it? What about us? Don't you remember what dad was like?'

'He's not drinking any more. He's changed.'

Jennifer rolled her eyes at the line. *He's changed. He's sorry. He'll never do it again.* These were words she had heard victims recount countless times before. 'And you believe that?'

Amy blew out an exaggerated sigh. 'I can't deprive the children of a grandfather. Aunt Laura thinks it's a good idea.'

Jennifer's fists clenched as she paced the airy room, wishing she could shake some sense into her sister. 'Laura? That's a joke,' she said with a bitter laugh. 'She's carried a torch for dad for years. No wonder *she* wants him back.'

Amy took a step forward, jabbing her finger in her sister's direction. 'It's all right for you, with your exciting job and designer clothes. For some of us, family is all we have.'

Silence descended as Jennifer digested the words. If family meant everything to her sister then why was she pushing her away? Fighting with Amy was the last thing she wanted, but she wasn't going to allow her to slate everything she had worked so hard to build.

'Oh, I get it. You're speaking to dad to spite me, because you're jealous of my lifestyle.'

'Why would I be jealous of you?' Amy retorted. 'I mean, look around this place. It's soulless. You don't have one family photo on the walls. Where's all the pictures Joshua drew you? Filed away in a cabinet under J?'

'That's not fair. Just because I don't like clutter doesn't mean I don't treasure everything he's given me. And speaking of Josh, don't you think it's time you put him first? Letting dad meet the kids is selfish and irresponsible.' As soon as the words left her lips, Jennifer knew she had pulled the trigger on the grenade. If anything pressed her sister's buttons, it was being accused of being a bad mother. Amy lived for her children, but Jennifer had had enough of bearing the brunt of her moods when her sister could not get her own way.

Amy's face flared, red blotches staining on her cheeks. 'You call me irresponsible? Perhaps if you hadn't spun so many tales when we were kids, dad would have been allowed to see us.'

Anger rose in every cell of Jennifer's body. Her sister may as well have slapped her in the face. Her fists curled as the heat spread from her fingertips to the flush in her throat.

'Told tales? Told tales? I knew you were living in a dreamland, but you really don't have a clue! Don't you remember his three-day benders? Or the days I had to get you ready for school, while he was still wearing his vomit from the night before? Or what about the times his scummy friends tried to come into our bedroom while our precious dad was comatose on the sofa downstairs?'

Amy's eyes darted around the room at the sight of her sister so incensed. 'I knew you'd blow your top,' she glowered, her words trailing behind her as she slipped her feet into her shoes in the hall. 'Why do you think I didn't want tea? I knew I'd be fucking wearing it.'

The front door slammed in her wake, and Jennifer let her go. She should have been shocked to hear her homely sister swear, but she was lost in the pain of her betrayal. With shaking hands she rummaged in her bag for anti-bacterial gel, her fury overtaking her as she fiddled with the cap. The memory of her father flashed before her, his breath tainted with the sour smell of beer and cigarettes.

She fumbled with the lid, feeling as if she was going to explode. 'Argh!' Releasing a scream, she sent the plastic bottle rebounding against the wooden floor, skidding to a halt at her front door. Her legs weakening, Jennifer plopped heavily onto the stairs. The thought of her father being welcomed into the fold while she was kept at arm's length was more than she could bear. The betrayal in her sister's words hit hard, and she guessed what happened to make Amy turn on her so savagely. Her sister had always been a daddy's girl, and would believe anything if it softened her vision of days gone by. Her father was the master of denial, and lies came as easily to him as breathing. It would not have taken long for him to weave a new fabric of the past. One that involved him being the misunderstood father, grieving for his dead wife while his eldest daughter schemed against him. It was a romantic notion that would fit into the well-stacked bookshelf in Amy's bedroom.

Jennifer threaded her fingers through her hair as she took stock. Her argument with Amy would soon blow over, but the words would not be forgotten. She felt a pang in her chest as she thought of her mother. If she were alive, she would stand up for Jennifer, and tell Amy to see sense. It seemed so unfair, that she would lose her mother at such a young age, especially when she had so much to cope with. Jennifer stared at the front door, wishing she could erase the last twenty minutes from her life. She would have to weather the storm, allow Amy to meet her father, then be waiting in the sidelines when he let her down all over again. But as Jennifer took the stairs to get ready for work, she knew things may never be the same again.

CHAPTER FIFTEEN
Bert

As Bert pushed through the fire exit doors of the hospital, he was resolute. Every step he took from the looming grey building helped clear the fog of confusion in his brain. Time did not travel in a straight line. For him it was curved, a free flow of squiggles, returning to the past, and occasionally darting to places he had long since forgotten. Some places were a dead end. Routine served to confuse him further, and slinking away unnoticed from his hospital bed was the safest thing to do. The feeling of incarceration was not unfamiliar, and not something his jumbled mind wanted to explore. But he was clear about one thing. He had to set things right. He had interfered with a prediction, and that was interfering with time itself.

The blue dress woman was named Emily Clarke. It was neatly printed on the bills piling up behind the narrow door of her two-bedroom bungalow. Gaining access through the bedroom window was easy. When the cards directed him, anything was possible. It was a sign he was on the right path, and as he scooted under the unmade double bed, his conviction grew strong. Emily was out thieving again, shoving food into her child's pushchair as she strode through the aisles of the local One Stop, the only supermarket not to have installed CCTV. High-value items like batteries or meat could be traded for a drink and a packet of cigarettes if she was lucky. The extra few quid would help take the edge off when the bills mounted, bold red letters demanding her attention. All she wanted was a nice man, but she was not going to meet him down the Spread Eagle public house, where sawdust lined the floor and the landlord turned a blind eye. Bert had seen it all in the cards. Even if she had survived the prediction, she was destined to hook up with abusers who would shred her of every last ounce of dignity. And who would suffer? The poor kid with the haunted eyes. He was doing her a favour and saving the child a lifetime of pain. He would deliver a quick death for her sins. It seemed a fair exchange that her expiring life would replenish his.

His musings were cut short as the front door rattled open, rebounding off the front tyre of the pushchair as it squeezed through the narrow hall. Bert's breathing grew shallow in the confines of her streetlit tumbledown room. His vision was blinkered by his narrow viewpoint, and for a fraction of a second he forgot where he was. His mind had wandered again, but returned as quickly as it left. He turned his head to the sliver of light under the bedroom door, watching the shadow of Emily's footsteps pace back and forth, unburdening the pushchair her son had long since grown out of. A long-legged spider scuttled across the dusty bedroom carpet. Bert was not afraid of spiders, he had spent long hours with the creatures of the leafy forest floor. Thoughts of the forest enforced his determination further, and any doubts about killing Emily evaporated as he heard her telling the child to go to bed and not to answer the door to anyone. Minutes later, her instruction was followed by the front door slamming, then a rattling of keys on the other side.

The little boy pottered around the flat for a while, and the muffled sound of the television carried through the crack in the door. The bedside clock ticked incessantly as seconds and minutes dragged by. The television abruptly silenced, and Bert felt his heart freeze in his chest as the little boy entered the bedroom. He held his breath as the child's bare feet padded to the bedroom window. Staring out into the darkness, he made little mewing sobs for his mummy. It felt like a well-practised routine. Anger ignited inside Bert, spreading until it reached every fibre of his body. He clenched his fists until his sharp fingernails pierced his woollen gloves into his palms. Dark wings stretched inside him, rising upwards with every hiccupped sob that left the child's lips. With narrowed eyes, Bert watched the boy leave the room, sniffling and hiccupping. The thin blue striped pyjamas stretched only to the top of his ankles, doing little to protect him from the chill in the air.

The clock ticked onwards, marching to midnight when the streetlights were extinguished, plunging the bedroom into a murky gloom. The council's money-saving efforts were of great value to him, as it guaranteed him an escape under the cover of darkness. The clatter of the front door announced Emily was home. Bert flexed his fingers and toes, bringing back life to his stiffened limbs.

Emily tiptoed to her son's room, then returned to her own, swaying slightly as she opened the door, her shadow cast long in the light flooding from the hall. Kicking off her shoes, she stepped out of her denim skirt and left it in a puddle on the floor. The bed bounced as she climbed in, the sagging mattress almost touching Bert's long nose, and his heartbeat thundered in his ears. As he inhaled the shifting dust, a tickle formed in his throat, and he clamped his gloved hands over his mouth as he fought the urge to cough. His Adam's apple bobbed as he swallowed it back, and he reined in his accelerating breath. He could not afford to mess this up again. Every second seemed like an eternity as he waited, his body spiked with adrenalin to prepare for what lay ahead. Soon the air was filled with soft drunken snores. Gathering his nerve, he rolled out from under the bed. He stood over the sleeping woman, his long black coat encased in a layer of dust. He should not have interfered in the prophecy. He could see that now. He could never move forward until it was done. Summoning the darkness from within to assist with the kill, he clenched his fists as he felt the power surge through his body. Releasing the salivating monster, he reached for her tights on the floor.

The next morning Bert tentatively touched his face. It had returned to normal size. He rolled off his low cot bed, rubbing the crusts from his eyes. Slouched in the cramped space, he picked up his mirror and gasped at his reflection. It was as if his beating had never taken place.

'And so shall her passing soul nourish mine,' he whispered, as his stomach rumbled. 'But I need money,' he said. Like a chick in a nest, he cast his face upwards, waiting for sustenance, but all he could see was the yellowed roof lining of his dingy van. Bert cast his mind back to Emily Clarke. He staged the body, as if she were sleeping, her red hair framing her face, her mouth pursed in a silent 'O' of surprise. Locking the bedroom door from the inside, he had wandered around her poky room. The blue dress had hung limply in her wardrobe. It was a testament to her efforts to get her life back on track. But it had not been enough. She, like many, had laid their secrets bare and did not deserve to live. He picked up the phone handset and lay it on the table, the curled cord recoiling like a snake as he jabbed 999. He didn't need to speak. Police were obliged to respond to abandoned calls regardless of whether they heard a voice or not. He had been careful to cover his tracks. The tights were too embedded in her neck to bring with him, but he knew enough of police investigations to ensure he had left no sign of his presence.

Bert scratched the back of his neck as he felt his skin flare. He continued with the raking, scratching his arms, and then, pulling up his trouser legs, he dug his nails into his flesh and moaned in short-lived relief. The loss of Emily's life had healed his injuries, but only eased the skin condition that drove him to the edge. It would take the death of a very special person to provide him with such power. Jennifer Knight. She carried an aura that drew him in like a magnet. He imagined her visiting the scene of Emily's murder, her slim graceful fingers touching the places he had been. She would not be able to resist the shadow of his presence, even if she did not understand why.

'*Please, Bertram, don't …*' Mother's voice echoed faintly in the recesses of his mind. He rubbed his forehead as his thoughts became jumbled. It felt as if there was too much packed behind the small space, and his skull was unable to accommodate it. But soon it would clear. Soon everything would be better. So much of his life was spent in the past, and there was no getting away from the memories that weighed heavily on his mind. He climbed into the front of the van. He would have to visit mother, if only to silence her pleading and get on with the task in hand. Sighing heavily, he climbed onto the driver's seat to make the journey home.

CHAPTER SIXTEEN
Bert

As Bert grew, so did his love of the outdoors, which was sorely stifled by his mother in daylight hours. A cold virus left him unable to leave his room in the unguarded night, and too weak to chase the raven that cawed outside his window. Globules of Vicks smothered his chest, and screwed-up tissues dotted the old comics. Callum had read them to him until he knew the stories off by heart. The stifling room smelt of cleaning fluid and watered-down chicken soup, and mother hummed a nursery rhyme as she pottered around the kitchen.

Callum did everything he could to ease Bert's confinement, and his latest visit was accompanied with gifts. As he laid the shiny conkers on the bed, Bert masked his resentment with snuffled 'thanks', and raised them to his nose. He breathed in the woodland smell. It tainted him. Just like every breath Callum took.

Bert didn't choose to hate his brother. Hate got him all angry and stirred the black nest of creatures inside. They told him to do things his body didn't have the strength to facilitate. He knew Callum kept things from him because he didn't want him to feel bad. It didn't make any difference; his mother had a knack of announcing it on the front porch as Callum left.

Good luck at the football today, score one for me! Be careful on those rides now, sweetheart! *And Bert's favourite:* Have a great time at the party, dear, shame I've got to stay at home and look after your brother.

It was always followed by that little sigh, her martyrdom a touching sight. But it was all a lie. She loved the attention from her church friends when they came to visit, speaking in sympathetic whispers as they peeped in on her bedridden child. He was called such because nobody knew what was wrong with him, and nobody had the heart to ask. Sitting around her kitchen table with their gifts of freshly made scones, his devoted mother was almost nominated for sainthood. And when the sympathy waned, she'd cut his hair into a concentration camp style, restricting his food to complete the look. Clutching their hands to their chest, the women promised a mention in every mass before returning to town to spread the word.

It would have been enough to drive him to the edge of his sanity, had it not been for his moonlit excursions. School had interfered with his sleeping pattern, but it was easy to feign sickness then sleep all day and wake at midnight to visit his special place. The forest felt like another world, a place where he belonged and his presence was welcomed. The only birds that lived in the forest were the magnificent black ravens that nested in the branches of the tall domineering trees. They were attracted by the energy of the land, just as he was, and while it bolstered their spirit, to others it created a feeling of unease. His special raven was always at his side, his blue-purple iridescent feathers cloaking his body and bringing colour to the night. Bert set traps in the forest, and then hung the corpses of the gutted rodents from tree branches as offerings. The raven repaid him in loyalty and guardianship, something his life had been lacking up until now.

CHAPTER SEVENTEEN

Jennifer had taken on the role of mature adult long before she reached her teens. The stress of losing her mother at such an early age, combined with taking responsibility for her sister, had left its mark. She was fully aware of her failings, and they took up many pages of the journals kept neatly hidden in her bedside locker. Having little knowledge of a normal loving relationship, she usually hoped for the best and expected the worst. Such thinking had lived up to her expectations so far. That was, until she met Will. Although he held a rugged charm, he was the complete flip side to everything she went for in a man. Her usual boyfriends were self-assured, selfish and often unpredictable men, not dissimilar to her DI, Ethan Cole. But there was something about Will that warmed her, a caring, protective nature that told her this was the way it was *meant* to be. Slowly he had grown on her, and in recent months she found herself looking at him in a different light. She even found herself welcoming Will's company, since the discovery of the envelope in her car.

It was fortunate their rest days coincided. Jennifer knew of married police officers working opposite shifts, who crossed over in the night, barely seeing each other. It was another promising spring day, and Jennifer had decided to wear one of her summer dresses to celebrate the arrival of the sun. The pub breakfast had been delicious, and she had enjoyed the view of the river as the fresh morning sunlight danced on the water. Will sat across from her, looking relaxed in his white t-shirt and faded Diesel jeans. She wanted to tell him he looked good, but she couldn't find the words.

Nervousness bubbled up inside her as he followed her into her home. It was no secret that they liked each other, but they had been friends for so long, taking things to the next level was a welcome but daunting prospect.

She groaned as she picked up the yellow padded envelope nestling under a fresh crop of junk mail. 'I wish they'd stop sending this crap through the post. Last week I got a pack about a retirement home.'

'Hang on, that's not junk mail,' Will said, securing the door behind them.

Jennifer gave Will a wilted look as she walked through to the kitchen, ripping the envelope open.

If it *were* anything suspicious she would risk a telling-off from forensics to find out what it was.

'It's very light …' She paused, dipping her hand inside. Peering into the envelope, her fingers found a thin-strapped satin camisole top. 'What the…?' she said, passing the envelope to Will as she held it up by its straps. For a fleeting second she wondered if it was some sort of joke Will had orchestrated, until she realised one side was slightly heavier than the other. She spun it around to see a plastic security tag attached. 'It's still got the tag on.'

Will took a corner of the envelope and turned it upside down. A shiny black feather lightly touched the black granite counter.

'It's from him,' Jennifer whispered, dropping the camisole on the counter like it was hot.

'I'm not having this,' Will growled, tense and muscled as he headed for the stairs.

'Wait, where are you going?'

'To check upstairs. This joker's playing with us.'

Jennifer groaned. Three objects sent to taunt her. How many more were there to come? And if each one represented a death, then who was connected to the camisole? Or was it meant for her? She shuddered. They had to catch the killer before he moved on to someone else. Opening her handbag, she pulled out a clear evidence bag and popped the letter in one. A supply of PVC gloves and evidence bags may have seemed like an unusual assortment among her lipstick, antiseptic wipes and car keys, but Jennifer was detective through and through, and always prepared. As she opened the bag for the camisole, Jennifer's heart quickened. She had been given her first proper clue.

'I recognise this label,' she said, before dropping the cami inside. She sighed. Their alone time would have to wait.

She grabbed her car keys and shouted up the stairs to Will. 'Fancy a trip into town?'

'Good morning, my lovely, what can I do for you?' the tall blonde woman behind the smooth backlit counter said.

'Hi Jacqui, I'm here on police business I'm afraid.'

Jennifer had known Jacqui since school. After her modelling career failed, she set up a lingerie shop in Haven, which had since grown to a chain. Jacqui divided her time between each store, but always returned to her hometown. The spacious store was a shoplifter's dream, and it would have been easy to get lost in the rows of padded hangers displaying various brands of elegant lingerie, nightwear, and dressing gowns.

Jennifer pulled out the camisole top, still in its clear plastic bag. 'I was wondering if you could trace this. It appears to have come from your store.'

Jacqui pulled the glasses from the top of her blonde bouffant and pushed them onto the bridge of her nose. Her heavily made-up eyes widened as she peered through the bag.

'Ah yes, I recognise that label.' She scanned the item into her till software. 'There it is. That's a brand new line. We only put it on display a couple of days ago. Damn thieves, they always go for the most expensive products.'

Jennifer felt a flicker of excitement. 'A couple of days ago? That narrows it down.' Her face tilted up as she looked for cameras. 'Do you have CCTV?'

Jacqui nodded. 'Of course, for all the good it does. And as for these tags … I spent a fortune installing them, but they always find new ways of getting past the scanners. I should shut this store down and concentrate on the others, but I like being in Haven.' Jacqui pushed her glasses back onto her head and handed back the evidence bag.

Jennifer completely understood the hold Haven had over its inhabitants. 'Could I have a look at the CCTV?'

'Babe, I'd like nothing better, but I'm a technophobe. I'll get one of the staff to download it and call you when it's ready.'

Jennifer pushed the object back into her black leather bag. 'Thanks. I'll submit this for fingerprint testing, they use a special oil to test the material. I'm afraid it won't be any use to you afterwards.'

Jacqui grimaced. 'I wouldn't want it back anyway, now someone's mucky paws have been all over it. Anyway, my lovely, what about you? Any men on the scene? All those hot cops in your station, there must be someone.'

Jennifer shrugged, relieved that she had asked Will to wait outside. Jacqui would have eaten him alive. 'No, they're in short supply and I'm too busy with work for all that.'

Jacqui raised her finger in the air, the nail painted her signature siren red. 'I have just the thing. Why don't you come to mine next weekend? I'm having a Botox party. I'll give you the first jab on the house.'

The first one? How many do I need? Jennifer thought, the prospect filling her with horror. 'Sorry, I'm working, some other time maybe. Oh, can I get you to sign this disclaimer form before I go?' She swiftly changed the subject, remembering why she did not spend much time with her old friend.

A tall hazelnut latte awaited Jennifer as she joined Will at Costa Coffee three doors down. Closing her eyes, she savoured the long, slow mouthful.

'I fancied something sweet, do you want some?' he said, shoving an almond croissant towards her.

Jennifer smiled, before sliding out a mirror from her bag. 'Do I need Botox?' she asked, frowning at her reflection in the compact mirror.

'Botox? Don't be daft,' Will said. 'Where's that come from?'

Snapping the mirror shut, she threw it in her bag and shook her head. 'Nothing, it's just Jacqui being her normal self.' It had only been a couple of hours since breakfast, but the smell of fresh pastry wafted towards her and she tore off a corner.

'Any joy with the camisole?'

Jennifer covered her mouth to shield any offending pastry flakes. 'It's been nicked in the last forty-eight hours. She's going to burn off the CCTV.'

Will rubbed his soft blond whiskers. 'It has to be Raven. He could be watching us right now.' He glanced around at the passers-by.

Jennifer took a sip of her coffee. 'Or that could be a smoke-screen. But why send stuff to me?'

'Why not? You're a police officer. He *wants* us sitting here trying to work it out. Otherwise why bother sending clues to the same person every time?'

'I'd just like to know their end game,' Jennifer said. 'I thought I was getting a connection with Alan Price's death and The Reborners cult, but Felicity Baron? It makes no sense.'

Will tilted his head to one side as he considered the prospect. 'Unless they're random killings. I mean, does there have to be an end game?'

'There's always an end game. It's our job to find out what it is, before anyone else gets hurt,' Jennifer said. But it did not appear to comfort Will, whose face was still knotted in a frown.

'My main concern is that they've been in your car and know where you live.'

'I know. But the important thing for now is to work out the connections then try to predict what he's going to do next,' Jennifer said. 'Ethan has spoken to the DI on the Murder Investigation Team and presented them with our evidence. Don't be surprised if you get a call to check your statement about finding the evidence in my car. They've got teams of people swarming all over this guy, and yet there's no trace. Another predicted death is on its way. I can feel it.'

Will laid his hand over hers, his honey brown eyes full of concern. 'I know we're in Operation Moonlight, but it's important to look at this rationally. The way I see it, this Raven guy is some loon making up predictions and following them through. *He* probably believes they're real but they're all in his head. That's what makes him dangerous. He's on some kind of mission, and for some reason it involves you.'

Jennifer knew Will's scepticism was healthy, and tried not to feel let down. 'But he accurately predicted Felicity dying in the woods. He may have tampered with the car but how would he have known that? It could have happened anywhere.'

Will gave a non-committal shrug. 'Coincidence. First he got Price to unburden himself over a drink. He watched you visit his sudden death and that's where he came up with the idea to send you a letter. Then he saw you deal with Christian and when he couldn't get near him, he targeted his girlfriend Felicity. He's probably after infamy, or revenge for the fact Christian blanked him. Who knows, maybe it was Felicity who said he couldn't stay at their house.'

'Mmm.' Jennifer dropped her gaze. It was a tired and worn-out argument that got her nowhere. She didn't tell Will her sense of foreboding was growing, as black as the wings of the ravens now perched on the rooftops of her home. She steadied her breath to push down the worry fluttering inside her. This man wanted more than infamy. He wanted people to die.

She painted a smile on her face. 'This is meant to be our day off. Why don't I book this into the property system and we can talk about it back at mine? I've got beer.'

Will's face lit up like the sun breaking through the clouds. 'That's the best thing I've heard all day.'

It took Jennifer just an hour to book the camisole into the property system and write up a quick statement before speaking to the DI on duty.

Her phone buzzed in her pocket and she picked it up, expecting to see Will's name flash up on screen. But the voice on the other end belonged to Jacqui, the shop owner.

'Hi babes, I just wanted to let you know one of my staff has come in and helped me view the CCTV on fast forward. We've found the shoplifter. One of our usuals I'm afraid.'

Jennifer sat bolt upright as she clung to her phone for the answer. Could she be closing in on the suspect?

'Really? You know them?'

'Oh yes, she's been arrested before. She's banned from the shop but I had new staff working for me that day and the little cow came in and robbed me blind.'

'It's a girl? Who is it?' Jennifer said, hastily barging out of the cubicle while balancing the phone to her ear.

'Emily Clarke. She came in with her little boy and shoved things in his buggy. You can't miss her, with her long auburn hair.'

CHAPTER EIGHTEEN
Bert

Driving down the sharp winding road on the edge of the forest had sent a surge of mixed emotions through Bert. He had avoided it up until now for this very reason. To allow his mind to wander would put his plan at risk, but he needed to rid himself of his mother's cries in order to focus on what lay ahead. The memory haunted him; her begging for mercy, clawing his wrists as he wrapped his fingers around her throat. The memory was sharp but when did it happen? Last week, last month or beyond? A cold sense of dread enveloped him as his mind refused to provide answers. The hardwood peaks of his family home came into view as his van chugged up the steep gravel hill.

Bert drove through the rusted gates barely clinging to their hinges. A mist descended on the house, threatening a rain yet to come. He climbed out of the van, his limbs feeling fragile and old, much older than when he was last under the shadow of the imposing house. The damp breeze carried the smell of dead leaves, and he listened for the raven through air that returned only silence. The bird that called from his bedroom window had gone, and even through his confusion, Bert did not believe he would see him again. He searched the building for life, but all he could see were various stages of decay. The slumped roof threatened to buckle the windows below, and vine leaves snaked up the walls, strangling the once beautiful roses that lived there.

Bert walked forward, inhaling the damp musky smell from the rotten cavities gnawing through the bricks. He fingered his van keys as he dragged his feet to the front door. It creaked a greeting as he pushed it open, sending an empty milk bottle rolling through the leaf-swept hall.

'Mother?' he called, a brooding fear urging him to leave. He pushed the cobwebbed door to the right, leading to the living room where he had left her. The air felt cold and neglected as he poked his head through the gap. Surely she's not living like this? he thought. But as the door fell ajar, Bert's mouth gaped open, and for a few seconds he forgot to breathe.

Grace was rocking in front of the old stone fireplace. Her grey hair framed her fragile face, lined from a lifetime of grief and misfortune. The flickering fire did little to heat the dismal room, and nothing to dispel the musty spores climbing the walls.

'Mother,' he whispered, the words catching in his throat.

She looked up, her eyebrows raised. 'Bertram, is that you?' she said, staring right through him. Grasping the wooden arms of the rocking chair, she cocked her head to one side for a response. It was as if she was speaking from very far away.

Bert took two steps forward and stood in a shaft of dying sunlight. 'Yes it's me. So you're all right then?'

Her voice sounded faint, and she leaned forward as if she was going to stand, then relaxed in the chair and set it back in motion. 'Do I look all right?'

It was not a sarcastic question. A simple woman, she never understood complicated humour.

'Yes you look fine,' Bert said, shifting uncomfortably on the balls of his feet.

His mother nodded matter of factly. 'Then yes, I am all right.'

For a moment, Bert felt sympathy, but it was fleeting and left before it had a chance to take hold. He glanced at the picture of the crying boy hanging over the mantelpiece, yellowed with age and as forlorn as the room that contained it. He waited for mother to shout at him, ask what he had been thinking strangling her like that, but she just rocked gently, staring into the fire.

'It's cold in here,' Bert said, rubbing his arms. 'Do you want me to get some wood for the fire?'

'No,' she replied softly, almost without breath. 'I have everything I need. And you? Are you all right, son?'

Son. He couldn't remember the last time she called him that. 'Just a bit tired. I ... I've not been very well.'

She pursed her lips together and glanced in his direction. 'You've *never* been well. Why have you come?'

Bert took in his mother's vacant expression and the dilapidated house. His eyes fell to the hem of her long black skirt, which touched the floor each time the old chair creaked forward. It was the skirt she had worn when Callum died. The pieces fell into place.

'You're not real, are you?' he said, his voice husky. A vice-like band wrapped around his head and tightened with the realisation. It was taking him away. To the other place.

Mother narrowed her eyes, her voice full of steely hatred. Her skin paled, before becoming translucent. 'I'm waiting for Callum.'

Bert took a step backwards as clarity descended. It was a mistake coming back to this place. If he stayed here he would never get better, he would return to the darkness, which brought the rage that ended his mother's life. Perhaps it was already with him.

Memories of his childhood soured sympathy into disdain. He pushed his hands into his coat pockets and wrapped his bony fingers around the cold hard metal of his van keys. Creak,

creak, creak, the rocking chair groaned, the infernal noise making him grip the keys tighter until they pierced his skin. The room fell into darkness, lit only by the shafts of light through the broken shuttered window.

Bert retreated to the door, as the final threads of clarity evaporated. He backed away, his leaden feet bringing him to his bedroom one last time. Clasping his hand over the wrought iron bedpost, he stared through the white timbered window as his fragile mind transported him back to the most significant day of his life. The day his brother died.

CHAPTER NINETEEN

Jennifer's eyes swept up to the cool, clear sky to search for ravens. Mumbling under her breath, she told herself to stop being melodramatic. She had done all she could, and most likely Emily would live to steal another day.

Jennifer pulled the handbrake of her car and peered at the houses to the left of Will's vision. 'It's one of these bungalows over here,' she said, pointing across the way. Doors slammed and blinds twitched as they walked towards Emily's front door. These were people who could smell police a mile away. The fresh morning air did little to ease the sense of desolation. The residents were nocturnal creatures, rarely surfacing before the afternoon. Emily Clarke would not appreciate her visit, but being arrested for a minor theft may well keep her safe in custody for a few hours. God knew what Jennifer was going to do with her son if there was nobody there to look after him.

'Here it is,' Jennifer said, pressing the doorbell. No answer. Jennifer knelt down, lifting the scratched silver letterbox to peer inside. 'Hello,' she shouted, checking the listless property for signs of life.

'I'll go around the back,' Will said, opening the stiff wooden gate to the side alley, which led to the rear of the house.

Jennifer nodded before turning her attention back to the letterbox. She poked her fingers through the stiff bristles of the draught excluder blocking her vision. The last time she did that a dog nearly had her fingers off, but she already knew that there were no pets in Emily Clarke's home. 'Hello. It's the police. Can you open the door?'

Her ears pricked to hear the pitter patter of bare feet against lino. 'Hello?' Jennifer repeated in a gentle voice. 'Is there anybody home?'

A flash of red hair bobbed from what looked like the kitchen at the end of the corridor, just long enough for Jennifer to get a glimpse of a little boy. Please don't tell me she's gone off and left him all alone, Jennifer thought. She patted her pockets and was relieved to find a packet of Maltesers in her jacket. 'My name is Jennifer. I've got chocolate,' she said. 'Would you like some?'

The rustle of the bag drew out the boy, and he ran to the letterbox, extending his dirty hands to the open hatch. 'Can you open the door?' Jennifer asked, pushing back the bristles to get a better look.

He shook his tear-streaked face, his eyes wide and hungry. Jennifer pushed the bag through the gap and he snatched it with a gasp. His small, skinny fingers tore open the packet and shoved handfuls of chocolate into his mouth, enlarging his cheeks and sending a dribble of brown saliva down his freckled chin. Having devoured the chocolate, the little boy wobbled to one side as he scampered into a side room and slammed the door.

Jennifer reached for her radio to call for social services, and was joined by Will, his mouth set in a grim line.

She had seen that look before, and she knew exactly what it meant.

'Please tell me you haven't found a body.'

Will nodded. 'Her bedroom window is open. Her body is on the bed. I don't know how long she's been there but I'm guessing over twenty-four hours.'

Jennifer felt as if she was sinking in quicksand. Was there anything she could have done to stop this? What sort of a person would kill a young girl with her son present? A look of horror crossed her face as the enormity of the situation fell upon her. 'Her son's in there. We've got to get him out.'

'He's inside? Shit,' Will said, turning up the radio clipped to his shoulder harness. 'I've notified control of the body. Backup isn't far away.'

Jennifer shielded her face with her hand, blotting out the intrusive sun. 'Are you mad? The killer could still be inside. I'm not waiting a second longer. Keep the boy talking while I climb in through the bedroom window.'

'I don't think it's a good idea …' Will's voice tailed off as Jennifer disappeared down the side alley of the house.

Jennifer rooted in her jacket pockets, relieved to find a single glove. It was better than nothing. She unclipped her baton from her shoulder harness, gripping the padded handle. With a flick of her wrist, she extended the cold hard metal, using it to cast aside the heavy maroon curtains in the bedroom window. Jennifer eased herself over the chipped wooden frame, cursing the tremor in her legs as adrenalin pumped through her body. The fact she might be using the same point of entry as the killer heightened the sense of menace, and she scoped the small, cluttered bedroom, holding her baton tightly in defence. Her gaze rested on Emily, partially concealed under the flower-patterned duvet. She shook her head in sorrow for the woman who would not see her little boy grow up. Jennifer pushed back the feelings of self-reprobation, leaning hard on her police training as she gazed upon Emily's waxen face. The burst blood vessels in her eyes combined with the tightly bound ligature suggested a brutal suffocation. Jennifer's eyes flickered towards the closed bedroom door, hearing Will's comforting tones speak to the child through the letterbox. She quickly updated control of her position at the scene, her mind racing between horror at Emily's death, and the urgent need for forensic evidence. Emily's expression was one of frozen shock, yet the attack had been followed by a period of calm as her hair was gracefully positioned over the pillow, and her arms lay neatly by her sides. That was, unless her son had tucked her in. Jennifer shuddered. It did not bear thinking about.

Her baton still extended, she took in her surroundings. A pair of knee-length leather boots lay on their side next to a denim skirt and a hastily strewn sweatshirt. The glint of a mobile phone spilling out from the skirt pocket caught her attention. Jennifer moved it with her baton. It was a smartphone, which meant it had access to Facebook, and of course, text messages and phone calls. She *should* leave it in situ. Attending officers would seize it and download any data, which would later be shared with her. But this was *her* case. *She* wanted to be the one to bring the Raven in, not for the glory, but for Emily's son. The hollowed scream of sirens snapped her out of her indecision. There was no time to spare. Hastily grabbing a plastic carrier bag from the floor, she threw it over the phone and slipped it into her jacket pocket. She grasped the door handle with her gloved hand, and exhaled in relief as it refused to open. Emily's son had not been able to gain access to his mother's broken body, because the door had been locked from the inside. She quickly turned the key in the latch and entered the narrow hall.

Will's coaxing murmurs echoed from the other side of the door, and she opened it wide, the sound of sirens filtering through as they drew near. 'You'd better stay here. I'll get the boy.'

She tentatively knocked on what was the living room door before pushing it open. 'Hey there,' she said, looking around. 'Want to come out to the car and see if we can find you some more chocolate?'

A tuft of red hair popped up from over the brown fabric sofa – followed by a pair of eyes and a freckled nose. Slowly he walked out, nodding in agreement.

Jennifer looked at his dirt-streaked feet. 'You've no shoes on. Would you like me to carry you?' Jennifer said, curling her fingers around his hand.

The little boy nodded, staring up at her with round liquid eyes full of sadness and knowing. Somehow, he knew his mother wasn't coming back, and it broke Jennifer's heart. She was no stranger to neglect, and for the second time she swallowed back a tide of emotions, her throat clicking dryly in response. Pulling a throw from the sofa, she placed it around the little boy's shoulders. His thin body clung to her like a limpet and she carried him from the house. She whispered words of reassurance, rubbing his back to ease the shivering vibrating through his tiny frame. *It's OK, shhh … you're safe now. We're going to get you somewhere nice and warm.* Police cars silenced their sirens as they drew up on the pavement in front of the house. She recognised the social worker as she stepped out of the car, flanked by a police officer. Jennifer gave her a watery smile as she joined them. The boy's small, stiff fingers clung tightly to the back of her neck, and Jennifer's heart ached. It was not the first time had she felt like bringing a child home. Out of all the horrific incidents she had to attend, child abuse was the one that she struggled with the most. But she had a job to do, and gently she handed him to the woman from social care. The little boy gave Jennifer a look of regret before being taken away.

Jennifer stood, unconsciously wringing her hands as she watched the car drive away. Will gently touched her forearm, bringing her back to the task in hand. 'He's safe now. We have to concentrate on finding this guy before he kills again.'

She could see from his worried expression that any doubts he had about the seriousness of the killer were now cast from his mind. 'He must have taken the camisole from her room and posted it through my letterbox,' she said, her voice sounding a million miles away.

'Hello,' a voice said from behind, accompanied by the lingering smell of cigarettes. Jennifer swivelled around to see Ethan, and hoped he wouldn't tell her off for entering the scene.

'I'm glad to see you, boss. I'm afraid I've had to enter the scene to remove the child.'

'Your sergeant has filled me in. As for entering the scene, you would have been severely criticised if you'd left the child in there alone. You did the right thing.'

Jennifer exhaled in relief, and left Ethan to liaise with the pathologist. Briefing was in Lexton that afternoon, and she had to get back to the station to examine the phone. She fully intended to book in Emily's phone as evidence, but not before she'd had a chance to examine her texts and social media for herself.

She couldn't leave without speaking to the next-door neighbour, who would make up part of the house-to-house enquiries. The man was named Mr Marshall. At least that's what he told her when she asked him for his details. He seemed affronted by Jennifer's presence and refused to invite her inside, despite the small crowd gathering on Emily's front lawn. It was only a matter of time before the local news turned up, and Jennifer prayed she would be long gone when they did. Working where she lived only became a problem when her face was broadcast in the local media, and like most of her colleagues, she preferred to remain anonymous.

Mr Marshall leaned against the chipped doorframe, staring at her with apathy. It was most likely the same apathy that earned him his considerable girth bulging over his faded blue jeans. His lumberjack checked shirt gave off a pungent odour of sweat and tobacco, making Jennifer grateful for the warm spring air.

'So you're telling me you didn't hear anything suspicious last night? Anything at all?' Jennifer asked, her mouth set in a grim line. She was still reeling from Emily's death, and could not get the image of the little boy's wide moon eyes out of her mind. Recriminations wormed their way into her mind as she glanced over at the police tape surrounding Emily's house. She should have kept a better eye out for the young mother. If she had, maybe she'd still be alive.

Mr Marshall spoke with half-closed eyes, like someone who had just woken up, but Jennifer guessed that was his default setting. 'That kid was always up against the window, crying and whining, just like he was last night. This used to be a nice neighbourhood, until they moved all the social welfare cases in.'

Jennifer resisted the urge to ask the slovenly man what contribution he had made to the world. 'So you're telling me you saw the little boy crying? Was there anyone looking after him?'

He waved his hand in front of him, as if he was swatting away a fly. 'Nah, she was too busy going out to worry about him. She was always bringing back fellas, you'd hear them kicking off in the middle of the night. Then your lot would turn up, and that would be the last you'd see of them. It's the kid, you see, not right in the head. What bloke would want to be involved with *that*?' He emphasised his point by tapping the side of his greasy forehead.

Jennifer clenched her jaw as hot fury built inside her. She swallowed back the bitter taste invading her mouth. Her words came in a low growl. 'You mean to tell me you *knew* the child was left alone and you didn't report it to anyone?'

Mr Marshall shifted his slippered feet. 'Not my business. Besides, you get a brick through your window for reporting things around here. Now if you don't mind, I'm watching the footie.'

Jennifer shoved her foot in the doorway. 'Mr Marshall, this is a murder investigation, so I can assure you it takes precedence over a game of football. If you're withholding evidence we can discuss this matter down the police station.'

Marshall's eyebrows shot up; the blubber on his chin wobbling as he vehemently shook his head. 'There's no need for that. Come inside if you want, but I've told you everything I know.'

Jennifer followed him inside. It was amazing how the hint of arrest opened doors.

Apart from giving Jennifer the opportunity to voice her disgust, her meeting with Mr Marshall did little more than confirm Emily's son was sadly neglected. Such information compounded her regret, but did not bring her any closer to resolution. But there was more than one way to catch a killer. Emily's mobile phone burned in her pocket with the need to examine it.

CHAPTER TWENTY
Bert

Bert eyed up the large oak tree that skirted the empty fields at the end of their house. Lately he had been feeling sicker than ever, and wondered if the special concoctions his mother brought him to drink contained more than just vitamins. Sleepy all the time, his legs no longer afforded him the strength to escape to the forest. Instead, he focused on the oak tree, staring at the raven housed in its branches, waiting for him to come. As he hitched up his dungarees, his mother's voice echoed throughout the house in song. She was busy making preserves, and the last thing he wanted was attention being drawn to the fact he was doing something she perceived as dangerous. But he had gotten away with disposing of his special tonic, and was going to make the most of the time he felt well enough to go outside. Bert swung his leg through the open window. He was eight years old now, and didn't need his toy box to reach it any more. He ambled down the field, swearing under his breath as Callum called after him from the shed. He swore a lot in his head, they were words he picked up from his father, used only when mother was not around. He liked how they made him feel. Callum would never swear. The very mention of a swearword made his face crumple, as if someone had kicked him in the stomach.

Bert kept walking, his head bowed against the wind as he kept the oak tree in sight. Tiny spikes of drizzle jabbed his face as he strode down the damp gravel path. Callum scampered after him, his heavy footsteps kicking up stones in their wake. Dad used to say that Callum had footballer's legs. They were far removed from Bert's spindly limbs, which had spent too long resting to build any muscle.

'Bert, you shouldn't be out here, if mum …' Callum panted.

'If mum nuthin,' Bert said, scowling at his red-cheeked brother. 'I'm just getting some air, and she don't have to know about it.'

Callum's face screwed up in frustration. He knew better than to argue with his brother. 'Well, just a few minutes, then you'd better head back in before she comes looking.'

'Yeah, yeah,' Bert said, infuriated by his brother's attention. He was such a pain, why did he have to be around him all the time? Callum the annoying shadow, who had to be prised away to attend football games and the occasional birthday party. Mother's ray of sunshine. Well he'd show them. He'd be the one to blot out the sun. Bert stared up at the oak tree, wondering if his scrawny muscles would find the strength to climb it. The branches bowed and shook as the wind whooped around them. Bert kicked off his shoes and began his ascent, clutching the knobbly tree bark as he panted in his efforts to reach the top. He could do it, he knew he could do it.

'Come down,' Callum shouted, clenching his fists and stamping his foot against the ground. It was a habit he had picked up from mother when she didn't get her own way. 'It's too windy, come down right now.'

Bert climbed upwards, the howling wind whipping his brother's words away. His shirt flapped and the hard, cold branches bit into the soles of his feet, but he kept climbing until his muscles trembled and he was too tired to go on.

'Bert you get down … you hear? Mum's gonna …'

As Bert clung to the branches and looked at the view across the fields, he didn't feel free at all. His skinny limbs were frozen like icicles, and just as rigid. 'I can't,' he said feebly, too scared to shake his head. His mother's calls echoed in the distance as she called for them. He was really going to get it now.

'It's OK, I'll come get you,' Callum said, wrestling his way up in half the time. Their mother was still looking for them when Callum reached the branch beside him, red-faced and out of breath. 'I've never been this high up before,' Callum panted, looking down at the fields below. 'Are you trying to get yourself killed?'

If only you would get yourself killed, Bert thought, wiping his streaming nose on his shirtsleeves. 'You're the same age as me, Callum, it don't give you the right to boss me around.' The cold was really biting into him now, and his teeth chattered as his body shivered involuntarily.

'It's my neck on the line too, if mum finds us up here she'll go spare,' Callum said.

'Not to you she won't. She won't say nothing to you,' Bert said bitterly, knowing his escape would cost him dearly. A raven flew past, its caws slicing through the air. Bert wished he were more like the black-feathered bird, strong, independent, free.

Callum frowned, and spoke through chattering teeth. 'Follow me down, OK?'

'I can't,' Bert said, his fingers sliding into the moss-lined grooves of the tree.

'Hold onto me if it makes you feel better.' Callum glanced down. 'Oh hell, she's seen us. We'd better hurry up before she calls dad.'

Fuck it, Bert thought, a familiar anger rising within. It's all his fault. Mum wouldn't have come looking if Callum hadn't followed. Why does he have to get involved in everything? Bert's heart began to pound, fury boiling his blood and drawing out his darkest thoughts.

Callum shifted position to climb down the tree, and beckoned at him to follow.

Grabbing the back of Callum's shirt, Bert stepped onto another branch. The sudden movement jerked his brother forward, causing him to lose his footing. He could have pulled Callum back, helped him steady himself on the tree. In that split second, he held Callum's life in his hands. Bertram simply smiled. And released his grip.

A sharp howl rose up between them as Callum slipped off the branch, his arms flapping as if he was trying to fly. He fell like a stone, screaming and grasping for a hold of something, anything which would slow the plummet to the unforgiving ground rising up to meet him. Bert squeezed his eyes shut but could not block out the noise of his brother thudding to the ground below. Reluctantly he opened them to see his mother dropping to her knees beside Callum, patting his face in an effort to bring him back to life.

'Nooooo,' she wailed, as the pool of blood spread through the mud, soaking the hem of her long black skirt.

Her head snapped upwards at Bert, who was still embracing the tree. Her face was contorted in fear and rage as she screamed the words 'What have you done?'

The wind whipped and billowed Bert's clothes as it howled in an angry roar. Bert panted in cold breaths as he edged along. Something warm greased the branch and he looked down to see a small blood trail leaking from the sole of his foot. He was so engrossed, he had not even felt the tree branch slice his skin. Slowly he clambered down, clamping his arms around the branches as they swayed, toes and fingers stiffly bent over and gripping with the conviction that he would do what his brother was unable to do. The thought warmed him. He was better than Callum. He could reach the bottom without falling. By the time his bare feet touched the ground, his mother had driven Callum's body to the hospital. But it was the mortuary she needed.

Bert rested his weary limbs, hugging his knees as he tried to figure out what to do now Callum was gone. It wasn't at all as he imagined, and he had not counted on having a witness. All the years Bert had prayed to be an only child, fate had decided to give

him his wish just as his mother was watching. But he was gone just
the same and that was a good thing. Turning his head to the rolling
clouds, he watched the black knights of the sky circle overhead. As
always, he marvelled at their freedom, wishing he had been granted
such power and grace. His eyes crept over to the pool of blood now
thickening as it soaked into the soil. It reminded him of mother's
preserves. She had shown him how to test a spoonful, hot from the
bubbling pot. First, you cooled it by blowing on the spoon, then
you jabbed the thickening liquid with the tip of your finger. If it
wrinkled, then the jam was done. He shuffled over to the blood
and nudged it with his big toe. Small bubbles were forming as it
congealed – as if taking a few final breaths before leaving for good.
Fuckarooney, he muttered. Mum and dad were going to be really
pissed off at him.

The raven took his thoughts as it swooped down. Bert gasped
as the bird opened its long black claws and expertly grasped the
branch. He had never seen his friend of the night so close in the
daylight before. 'Auugh! Auugh!' the raven said, his beady black eyes
swivelling towards the blood and back to Bert again.

Bert embraced the moment; the smell of the wind, the coldness
slapping his cheeks. The creaking branches fighting to stay in position as the wind tried to bend them to its will. The feel of the cold
earth beneath his feet and the heady desire to touch the blood. His
brother was dead. It was time to reclaim what was his. Shaking its
long sleek feathers, the raven opened his beak and gave a hearty cry.
'Augh! Augh Augh!' he screamed as his magnificent throat feathers
expanded in a flurry.

'Caw! Caw!' Bert replied, and smiled as the bird hopped closer.
Bert lay down. Stretching out his arms as far as they would go he
moved them up, then down, flapping against the cold hard earth.

The raven cawed overhead as if to say, 'That's right! That's how
you do it!'

'Caw caw,' Bert said loudly, 'caw! I'm a raven!' Bert closed his eyes and imagined soaring through the skies, slicing through the wind and the rain, tearing up his prey without a moment's thought. Spots of rain landing on his nose and eyes halted the exhilaration.

Sitting up, he turned to stare at the blood-soaked ground behind him. The length of his body patterned the cold earth, with dark wings either side. A beautiful blood angel. Sober thoughts returned in aid of self-preservation. He would take himself home and hide his clothes. He would have a bath and wait for his parents to return. He would cry all night if he had to, so he didn't get the blame. None of that mattered right now because he had passed his initiation. Dark grey clouds rolled overhead, laden with rain. The downpour would wash the blood away, but he was an honorary raven, bold and wild and free, with no need to answer to anyone.

CHAPTER TWENTY-ONE

It was a common occurrence to be called into work on your days off, have them cancelled, or sometimes, be forcibly ordered to work overtime. Members of the police were not allowed to join a union for a reason, but spending more time at work than at home didn't bother Jennifer, because for her, work *was* her home, and her colleagues were her family. She would lay her life on the line to protect them, and the people of Haven, whom she served. She always maintained a professional distance with her cases, and never came close to compromising an investigation. So why was she holding onto a dead girl's phone? The high tech crime unit could examine the handset at an advanced level, tracking phone calls, texts, pictures, emails, and even maps and GPS location. In the case of a murder investigation, they could even recover deleted items. Jennifer consoled herself that all she was doing was looking through the evidence bag and pressing a few buttons. She already knew the password, having watched Emily type in four zeros to access her texts the last time they spoke.

With one percent of battery left, Jennifer accessed Emily's call history. It did not turn up the treasure trove of evidence she had hoped for. Emily appeared to have been deleting her texts and pictures as she went along. Jennifer chewed the inside of her lip as she trawled through the phone. No internet history, no call history, and no pictures … she threw her head back in exasperation.

'Everything all right?' Zoe said, bobbing her head up over her computer screen.

Jennifer's palm clasped her chest. 'Oh! You frightened the life out of me.'

Zoe stood, looking a lot more comfortable in her casual clothes of baggy jeans and vest top. 'I left my phone charger in my desk. You look guilty, whatcha up to?'

Jennifer trusted her new colleague enough to confess, and Zoe's eyes lit up with interest as she relayed the series of events.

'Flipping hell, girl, if delaying booking in evidence is the most dishonest thing you've done in your career then you've nothing to worry about. Now give it here.'

Jennifer handed the phone over. 'The battery's almost dead. I may as well book it in for the tech team.'

Zoe checked the bottom of the phone and gave Jennifer a knowing smile. 'This ...' she said, walking over to a plug '... may just be your lucky day.'

Jennifer was about to point out that it was unlikely, given a young girl had been murdered, but silenced her words as Zoe plugged in her charger and pierced the other end through the bottom of the bag. It clicked neatly into the phone socket. 'Look at that, fits perfectly. Now, let's have a little lookie ...'

'I didn't know you were a technical whizz,' Jennifer said, watching Zoe's fingers run nimbly through the various apps on the phone. 'What department did you work on before you came here?'

'I was a TP for six years for another force. Great job.'

'Oh I see,' Jennifer said. Suddenly it all made sense. Zoe's discomfort in formal wear, her habit of swearing, and her discomfort at being in the limelight; test purchasers were used to go deep undercover, integrating themselves in communities of drug users and pushers. Chameleons of sorts, they had to think on their feet and have the ability to reinvent themselves to suit any situation. Invaluable to the drug squad, their covert cameras delivered damning footage at court, which secured major convictions. Jennifer was about to ask why she had left, when Zoe exclaimed.

'Bingo! We're in.'

Jennifer looked over her shoulder to see Zoe trawling Facebook, scrolling through the pictures of Emily during various nights out with what looked like a string of random men. None of them matched the description of the Raven, but she hadn't expected to see him there anyway. She flicked to the side setting, finding the groups. They consisted of the usual free ads groups such as *Things For Sale in Haven* and *Second Hand Goods*. Then she caught sight of it, nestled among the other titles. *Second Chance Group*. Jennifer's gasp caught in her throat. No wonder her internet searches had drawn a blank. She had been searching for every variation of The Reborners online. Unlike the other groups, access to the Second Chance Group was by invitation only.

Jennifer stood with her hands on her hips, painfully conscious of the time. 'What do we do now? I have to go to Lexton for briefing. What will I tell them?'

Zoe tapped a black polished nail against her teeth. 'Say nothing. We'll book it in later.'

'But what value is keeping it if you can't get into the group?' Jennifer said.

'There's always a way. I have a fake Facebook account from my old TP days. I'll friend Emily through her account, then she'll invite me in. I'm not saying they'll give it up straight away, but leave it with me.'

'But won't the time of the request show up? Word will soon get around that she's dead.'

Zoe's eyes flicked up from the screen, alight with devilry. 'Ways and means, babe … ways and means.'

Jennifer mulled it over. The Facebook account would have been authorised by the police and been above board, and if anything, their involvement may speed things along. 'I'll book it in as seized property and tell them I'll drop it over to the tech team when briefing is over. Will that give you enough time?'

'Yeah, for sure,' Zoe said, logging onto the computer to open her corresponding Facebook account.

Jennifer was a small spoke in a very big wheel of officers investigating the murder, but she was grateful to be at briefing at all. Op Moonlight was limited and could not facilitate a complete murder investigation, but they provided invaluable advice and leads when it came to the investigative element of the case. She had access to the investigation without the burden of all the paperwork – or at least that's what Jennifer told herself as she entered the briefing room. The truth was, she wanted everything. Her need for control had always been there, but she managed it by keeping a professional distance. Now all of that was forgotten, as the Raven crept under her skin. The briefing location was a stifling windowless room without the luxury of air conditioning, but the whiteboard that took up one full wall left Jennifer in no doubt that no stone would be left unturned in the hunt for Bert Bishop.

Those who could not find a seat had to stand, and Jennifer was pleased to see a seat reserved in her name. Her position in the team had been elevated, and for once, people were interested in what she had to say. Officers hastily scribbled notes, as tasks and handouts were passed among them. Lexton's DCI Jamieson talked through the investigation to date. He was a thickset Scottish man, who took no bullshit but had a reputation for being fair. Jennifer was relieved to hear him announce that Christian Bowe's ex-wife was off the hook. As outlined on the board, their prime suspect was now a killer who created self-fulfilling death prophecies. Jennifer may have been tempted to shoot a smug grin across to DC Hardwick, if she had not been furious at the needless deaths of Emily Clarke and her predecessors. Her anger was fuelled by the discovery of a scrunched-up flyer from a recent psychic fair, found in the bin in Emily Clarke's bedroom. Jennifer's eyes widened as the evidence bag was passed around the room.

'I don't believe this,' she said, re-reading the same line of the flyer over and over again, through the transparent bag. 'I was there that day, I must have just missed him.'

DCI Jamieson unbuttoned his suit jacket and hung it on the chair. 'Probably. So far, this man has passed through Haven unnoticed. But to quote Doctor Locard, "every contact leaves a trace".' As if to assure himself more than anyone else, he added, 'It won't be long before we catch up with him.'

But Jennifer wasn't so sure. She believed that the best way to find Raven would be through The Reborners. While she relayed everything she knew in briefing, she fell short at giving them the name of the Facebook group. She justified her actions by telling herself it was the right thing to do. Operation Moonlight would investigate the Second Chance Group, and she'd infiltrate it herself if she had to.

CHAPTER TWENTY-TWO

Jennifer did not normally telephone her sister before calling over, but her gut told her not to drop by without checking first. She was grateful for Will's invitation of a late supper, and would have just enough time to drop over the kids' Easter eggs if she left soon. Having to work a rest day on such a harrowing case had heightened her stress levels, and she needed some normality to ground her, before going to see Will.

She switched on the house lamps as the dark closed in, and clicked up the heating dial a couple of notches. It may have been spring, but a chill was still capable of descending, and the high ceilings in her Victorian semi devoured the heat. The underfloor heating warmed the soles of her feet as she waited for her sister to pick up the phone. She was about to hang up when Amy answered, and Jennifer detected a slight edge in her voice in her greeting.

'Hey sis, I was thinking of popping over with Josh's Easter egg, will you be in?'

Silence descended on the other side. Jennifer was about to speak when her sister piped up.

'Em, sorry, could you leave it until tomorrow? I'm ... not free this evening.'

Jennifer's fingers wrapped tightly around the phone as her stomach clenched. 'It's dad, isn't it, you're meeting up with him.'

Amy spoke in a flat voice. 'I don't want to argue with you, just come tomorrow instead, all right?'

Jennifer bit her bottom lip, holding back the words that would only hurt her later. 'OK. I've ... I've got a toy for Lily, I didn't think you'd want her eating chocolate yet.'

The relief in her sister's voice was audible. 'I'm sure she'll love it. I'll see you tomorrow, yeah?'

Jennifer rested the house phone back into its cradle. Pulling the clips from her hair, she allowed the glossy strands to tumble down her back. She threaded her fingers through to her scalp, massaging where the clips had dug in too tightly. She needed a day in a spa, or somewhere nice, where she could relax and forget all about family, work, or the Raven. But who was she kidding? Having to sit and relax for hours at a time would drive her crazy. It was just like now, when she was trying to think of anything except her father. Yet the more she tried to drive him from her mind, the more space he occupied.

Jennifer eyed the children's presents. The purple and yellow Easter egg packaging looked out of place in her minimalistic home. She could put it in the boot of the car, in preparation for her visit tomorrow night. She stroked the fur of the soft bunny rabbit she had bought for Lily. Thumper was becoming her favourite Disney character, and she could imagine her niece's chubby little fingers enveloping the toy in a hug.

Jennifer grabbed her car keys and locked her front door behind her. The street lights flicked on and a cool breeze played with her hair as she shoved the presents in the boot of her car. She toyed with the car keys. Dad was probably at Amy's right now, having made the journey from wino city or wherever he lived. She snorted. Just what business had he, going around to her sister's and breaking up a happy home? She found herself climbing into the front seat, and placing her keys in the ignition. Clicking her safety belt she adjusted the mirror, catching sight of her harassed reflection staring back accusingly at her. *Just what the hell are you thinking? Going to see your father when you tore a strip off your sister for doing the same thing.*

'It's not as if I'm going to talk to him,' Jennifer mumbled to the mirror. 'If he turns up pissed, I'll call for backup and have him taken away.'

Jennifer parked her car behind a van next door from her sister's. Amy was unlikely to be looking out for her, and the housing estate streetlights offered a certain camouflage as they tinged the parked cars in the same orange hue. It reminded her of some of the covert jobs she had been on, camping out in some old dear's home to watch the neighbours from their bedroom window. They had been so obliging, laying on ham sandwiches and a pot of tea before making themselves scarce. Jennifer was not so sure she'd be as accommodating if a couple of police officers wanted to intrude on her privacy. The blinds were closed in Amy's home, with the usual flash of blue and white filtering through the curtains as their television entertained the children. She turned off the car radio as the seven o'clock news ended. Joshua would be in bed soon, and she longed to give him a goodnight cuddle.

She checked her phone for the tenth time. She had not heard anything since Zoe's call earlier in the day. Pleased she had gained access to the group, she was spending her evening scrolling through old discussions. There was lots of talk of second chances and starting again, but members were warned not to give away the location of their meetings online. Such activity would result in an instant ban, and Zoe mused that much of the information was exchanged through private messaging. For now, she was integrating herself as a troubled teen seeking help.

Jennifer slid her phone back into her pocket, returning her attention to Amy's house as the minutes ticked by. Twiddling with the ends of her hair, she wondered if she had it wrong. Perhaps Amy had just arranged to telephone her father, or Skype him with the kids. They certainly wouldn't have wanted Jennifer's face popping up during that conversation. She grasped the keys to turn over the ignition when a sporty-looking BMW drove past, with a recently registered plate. Jennifer narrowed her eyes as it braked, then parked next to the kerb outside Amy's home.

Jennifer scooted down in her seat, her stomach doing somersaults. She watched as Amy's front door opened, and she walked out to greet her visitors, wearing what looked like a new dress. Her sister's hair was tied up in a ponytail, and she beamed as the car doors opened. A tall blonde woman stepped out onto the pavement, closely followed by the driver, who took her sister in a tight embrace, kissing the top of her head as they broke apart.

Jennifer clasped her hand in front of her mouth as bile clawed its way up her throat. Seeing her father again brought all the old feelings flooding back, the anxiety she had fought so hard to control was now sending her thoughts into a whirlwind of confusion. His blonde companion kissed Amy on the cheek, and it was clear this was not their first meeting.

He looked well, more than well, he looked handsome. His dark wavy hair was now cropped neatly at the sides. His moustache had disappeared, and his clean-shaven face revealed a strong, square jawline. No longer was he walking with shoulders hunched over, hands gripped around a can of beer. Smartly dressed in a black jacket and trousers, he carried himself with a self-assured walk, and as his hand found his companion's waist, Jennifer guessed they were a couple. She was wearing a blue tie dress with matching heels, and carried herself with an air of sophistication.

'Crafty cow,' Jennifer muttered under her breath as Amy waved them inside. Anger, sadness, and dejection sank their teeth into her being in equal measure. The timing could not have been worse. The front door closed behind them, and Jennifer was left alone. She inhaled a ragged breath, wiping away her involuntary tears. She had seen everything she needed to see. Amy had welcomed their father and was happy to forget their past in order to do so. But the past also included her. Perhaps this was the way it was going to be: if Jennifer didn't come on board then Amy would slowly push her out of her life, sacrificing their relationship in preference for their father. Jennifer turned her car as fat raindrops began to dapple her windscreen. If she couldn't help her family then she could at least help others. It was time to make contact with the Raven.

CHAPTER TWENTY-THREE

The recent spring weather seemed a dim memory as the wind threatened the newly formed buds of the elm trees lining the path into the park. Jennifer huddled under her umbrella, the rain bouncing hard against the pavement. The legs of her trousers were already soaked through, and she hoped her attempts at communicating with the Raven would be fruitful. She could not risk invoking anything in her home, and on such a foul evening, the park would be deserted. Shaking her umbrella, she took refuge inside the small wooden shelter overlooking the children's playground. Black clouds rumbled forth, casting the gloomy space into a monochrome grey. She hoped George had gotten himself down to the local homeless shelter. Even he had noticed the ravens watching her from the trees as they spoke earlier in the day.

She couldn't leave it a minute longer. She had to try to make contact in whatever way she could.

As the wind howled through the chain-linked swings it felt as if she was the only person alive. Jennifer sat on the damp wooden bench, preparing to send feelers out into the darkness. It was a practice she had finely tuned in the last few months. Her unearthly communication was not just for speaking to the dead. If a living person was of a strong psychic nature and attuned to her frequency, she may be able to gently ease herself into their senses. But doing so was fraught with danger, used only as a last resort. She rested her hands on her lap and closed her eyes. Asking for protection, her breathing settled into a slow, steady flow. She sent her thoughts to the Raven. Her plan was to seek out his location then withdraw.

Her eyes fluttered shut, and she relaxed her limbs, searching the darkness for a face. She blinked, pushing visions of Will to the back of her mind, wishing he wasn't such a distraction. Her breathing grew shallow as she focused on what appeared to be a fuzzy tunnel. No, it was a bridge. A set of rosary beads swung from side to side from a windscreen mirror. A country and western singer crooned in the background about standing by your man, and a gruff voice chuckled to himself. The vehicle rattled, making a whistling noise where the air filtered through the windows, and the car seat bounced with every bump in the road. She tried to look out for signs. Where was he? She tentatively pushed on, trying to focus on his face. The driver scratched behind his ear but the itch crawled to the back of his neck, and then his right arm. Jennifer gritted her teeth as the itch spread through her, crawling under her skin. He licked his furred teeth and she felt the slime on her tongue. It was almost too much to bear.

While I nodded, gently napping, suddenly there came a tapping, as of someone gently rapping, rapping at my chamber door, his voice whispered in the darkness.

'Who are you?' Jennifer whispered the thoughts in her mind, gently coaxing. Psychic communication was not like being in a police interview room. Demanding answers would not get her anywhere.

The thought returned felt razor sharp. *You come knocking on my door and you ask me who I am?*

'You have made yourself known to me prior to this, so I would argue it is you knocking on my door,' Jennifer said, unable to resist the dig. She sensed his amusement as he delivered the answer.

Why I'm Raven of course.

Jennifer swallowed, feeling like she was falling into the abyss of his mind. But she could not withdraw now, not yet. 'Did you kill Emily Clarke?' her thoughts whispered seductively. There was no place for anger in this world, and she sent her words like silken messengers rubbing against his rugged skin.

Maybe, maybe not, a faint echo of laughter, carried with a layer of dark intent.

'What do you want, Raven? Tell me, perhaps I can help ...'

You'll find out soon enough. But do not come to me uninvited again ...

Jennifer ignored his warning and probed further for clues, snaking through his energy. The vehicle came to an abrupt halt as the driver gathered strength. An earthy scent found her, not the fresh smell of the rain-sodden leaves in the park, but the smell of rotting tree roots, its bark infested with insects. By the time she felt the Raven's energy build, it was too late to recoil. A raspy voice sent daggered shockwaves through her brain. The sound was deafening. *GET OUT little pig! I said, GET OUT!* Raven screamed, the painful impact throwing a stunned Jennifer back to reality. Clasping her hands over her ears, she bent over until the shockwaves ebbed. She groaned as her senses returned to the physical world, but the transition had been too quick. It felt like squeezing sweaty feet into a pair of ill-fitting shoes, and she sucked in cooling breaths, focusing on the rain tapping on the roof of the shelter, a hundred tiny nails drawing her attention. She ran her tongue over her teeth, relieved to find them clean, and free of the taint of tobacco she had tasted minutes before. But she desperately needed to shower, and scrub away the feeling of being in another man's skin.

Jennifer reflected upon the contact on her way home. The rosary beads could give a connection to religious undertones and he seemed to be driving a car. Anxiety had begun to nest as the crawling sensation under her skin refused to leave. She inhaled deeply and breathed out slowly, releasing the rising tension. The dark voice carried a sense of urgency that worried her. *You'll find out soon enough.* He wasn't giving up. She scratched the back of her neck, focusing on the shower waiting for her at home. Will had invited her around and she was grateful for the distraction. She had spent too long in the Raven's energy, and would be darkly rewarded by the feel of the old man's body for several hours to come.

Jennifer glanced at the light in Will's living room window. It was nice to be looked after, and all the old anxieties about their relationship slowly loosened their grip. Life was too short, and she had decided to allow things to take their natural course, whatever it may be. The smell of chopped onions and garlic met her in the hall as he opened the door. Will looked relaxed and happy in his tracksuit bottoms and a white t-shirt. It complemented his broad shoulders, and she threw him a smile as she handed him a bottle of red wine.

Will squinted at the label, although she knew he hadn't a clue about wine. 'Thanks. This … er … looks good. I hope you're hungry. Don't worry about the mess, I'll clean up in a minute.'

'Don't be daft, you don't need to apologise to me,' Jennifer said, averting her eyes from the dirty saucepans and dishes littering the counter. Will gave her a look that said he knew better, and she gladly took a glass of wine from his outstretched hand.

'Thanks, it smells delicious,' she said, sniffing the curry and jasmine rice bubbling on the stove. 'Do you want to talk about the case, or is this a work-free zone?'

'Feel free,' Will said, tasting the curry before washing the spoon and laying it on the side. Jennifer smiled. No doubt he was tempted to plunge it straight back in the pot, and was doing his best to appease her.

'I tried to make contact but I didn't get very far. He knew I was on to him.' Jennifer shuddered at the memory.

Frowning, Will turned off the gas. 'I can't even imagine what it's like trying to communicate like that, but for God's sake be careful. The person stalking you is a killer.'

'If he wanted to hurt me he would have made a move by now.'

'Yes well, keep your distance, and let the MIT get on with the investigation,' Will said, taking two warmed plates out of the oven.

Jennifer drained her glass. 'I'm a copper, Will. I'll do exactly what *you* would do in my shoes.' That said, she did not relish the thought of further communication. Memories of the Raven's scaly neck and fur-lined teeth had made her scrub her skin until it was bright red. It was only after brushing her teeth and slathering her skin in oils and body lotions that she had begun to feel herself again. The Raven's voice had dark roots, and although human, he was no stranger to the supernatural. Whatever the man was carrying within, there would be no reasoning with it.

'From what I can see the only hope they have of stopping this guy is finding him in the area or if he slips up the next time he does it.'

'Mmmm,' Jennifer said, keeping details of the online group to herself. She breathed in the delicious aroma of spices as Will filled her plate. She owed it to herself to try to enjoy what was left of the evening. Since the advent of Op Moonlight, she felt she had turned a corner, gaining in strength and accepting herself for who she was. She couldn't allow the Raven to drive her back to the dark, lonely place she once frequented.

She knew she shone like a beacon when it came to psychic energies, and questions came faster than she could answer them. She could have drawn the killer right to Haven. Was he really predicting their futures or just making it happen? And if every incident preceded a reading then surely all people had to do was to keep away from tarot readers.

'Do me a favour,' Jennifer said to Will as they finished their desserts. 'Ring your family and tell them not to accept any card readings, no matter how charming the person offering. I've told my sister to do the same.'

Will gave a chuckle, then realised she was serious. 'I'll do it but they'll think I've lost my marbles.'

The words stung and Jennifer refilled her wine glass. 'Best you warn them just the same.' It was not difficult to see where Will inherited his scepticism.

Jennifer listened as Will spoke to his mother on the phone. She envied their closeness, drawing in a soft breath as a wave of sadness overcame her. What she would give for such warmth, for her mother to hug her and tell her everything would be all right. But her childhood hugs were a faded memory.

She scratched the back of her neck as she recalled her earlier contact. The Raven was still in Haven. Shadows drew in around her and warned caution. But as she recalled the menace in his words, she knew it might already be too late.

CHAPTER TWENTY-FOUR
Bert

The house was steeped in a grief as thick as treacle. His mother became 'that unfortunate woman'. So unfortunate in fact that her church friends stopped visiting, for fear of catching her grief. The air that once held his mother's song now returned only muffled wails from the rocking chair in which she reclined. Threads of silvery grey hair bloomed from her centre parting, exacerbated by the deepening lines on her once pretty face. She no longer pottered in the kitchen or made preserves, and the family dynamic changed beyond recognition. Mother did not need Bert to be sick any more, and apart from occasional bouts of eczema, a rapid recovery ensued. Father made half-hearted attempts to take him out, but Bert knew by their dagger glances that both parents blamed him for the death of their golden boy. Bert played the grieving brother for as long as was convincing and waited expectantly for things to improve. He was free to attend school again, but had fallen so far behind, the teasing from his school companions did nothing but fuel the flames of hatred within. His time with the raven was the only thing that eased the frustration gnawing at his insides.

He sat cross-legged under the branches of the large oak tree and fingered the petals of the roses placed under its shadow. The branches were laden with coloured leaves, awaiting the autumn winds to unburden their treasures. It was the first anniversary of Callum's death, and it felt a lot warmer than last year, when the leaves had been forcefully shed with wind so cold it watered his eyes and reddened his nose. Bert groaned as he opened his fingers, realising he had plucked the flowers bare.

'Aw shit,' he said, scattering the petals so an animal could take the blame. It was the first time he'd sworn aloud since Callum died. After all, who was left to swear to? Not his mother or father that was for sure.

Father withered to nothing after the funeral. He didn't need to speak; the pain was evident from the deep grooves on his face. His eyes sunk deep in his skull, motionless and unthinking. Every night he sat on the porch, staring out at the tree, mumbling to himself about cutting it down. But mother wouldn't let him, saying it was a memorial of the only child she had ever loved. Mother lost all interest in Bert and he was free to roam the land as he pleased.

Sometimes he caught his parents' thoughts. If Bert had died in infancy, Callum would still be alive. They infested his brain, hardening his heart and darkening his soul. They didn't know he could hear them. The darkest thoughts sprang to his attention like poison darts, and there was nothing he could do but allow them inside.

Bert jumped as a twig snapped behind him, and rustling footsteps made him spring to attention.

'It's me,' his mother's soft voice whispered, flat and emotionless.

'I was just …' But Bert couldn't finish because he couldn't think what he was doing there.

'You don't need to explain. Now come home, I need to lock up and you've got school in the morning.'

It was the first time mother had spoken directly to him, other than one-syllable responses. Bert searched for something to say. Something that would make her stay. Sometimes, when mother was near, his emotions felt all jumbled inside, all going in different directions, making him feel sick. A big part of him was eaten by the darkness, but sometimes he wanted her to stroke his hair, just like she did with Callum. When he was little, mother would loosely throw her arm around his shoulder, and it made him feel all happy inside, like butterflies dancing in the sunlight.

'He's not gone, mum, not really,' he said. Perhaps his words would help her forgive him if she thought her loss was not quite so great.

Mother froze, the moonlight throwing her face into a patchy light, blotted by the rustling leaves overhead. Her eyes were puffy from crying and her words delivered by a voice tinged with urgency. 'What did you say?'

Bert dug his fingers into the soft brown soil in front of him. It smelt earthy and rich. 'I ... I said he's not gone. He talks to me. I don't think he ever really left.'

Mother rushed over in two long strides and dropped down, grasping him by the shoulders. 'Is this some kind of joke, Bert, because if it is ...'

Bert flinched, expecting a slap for suggesting such a thing, but all he found were the whites of his mother's eyes, searching his face for signs of hope. 'No joke, mum, I swear. He spoke to me just today.' Bert bit his lip, choosing his words carefully. 'A girl in school was mean to me and he was angry about it.'

Grace stiffened as her cold fingers dug into his shoulder. 'Callum never got angry.'

'He always stuck up for me, mum, you know that.'

Mother considered it. Her head should have told her it couldn't be true, but her heart, raw and aching, won out. 'I've heard about things like this, when twins have a telepathic bond. Can you hear him now?'

Bert screwed up his face. He needed to think this one over. 'Not right now, but he's always there, I can feel him, inside me.' He shook the earth from his fingers and pointed to his chest. It was a half truth. There was certainly something in there.

Mother blurted out a convulsive sob, so sudden that it made him jerk back, for fear he had gone too far. Letting go of his shoulders, she wiped her eyes then pulled him to her, wrapping her arms so tightly around him he could barely breathe. The smell of coconut shampoo arose from her wavy blonde hair, and he closed his eyes as he breathed in the precious moment.

'Callum,' she whispered, 'Callum, if you can hear me, daddy and I love you so much.'

Bert closed his eyes and pretended she was talking to him. His mother's body shuddered and she released her grip, swallowing back her tears and fixing the loose strands of hair that were taken by the light breeze. 'Bert, if you ever get a message then you've got to tell me, but say nothing to your father, OK?'

Message? Bert thought. The only messages he got were from the voice in his head telling him to hurt people. Mother sighed as she spotted the rose petals scattered on the ground. Her attempts at growing flowers around the ill-fated oak tree had failed as the pansies and daffodils withered and died. Bert allowed himself a secret smile. He could have told her – nothing would grow in soil soaked in blood.

TWENTY-FIVE

Bert sucked what was left of his roll-up cigarette. Taking his mother's car was a wise move. The police were bound to be looking for him now, and they had all sorts of gadgets to check number plates and such. He used to watch a lot of police programmes on the television. His mother didn't allow a television in the house. He shrugged. It didn't matter where he watched it. The past did not matter to him any more. When he was well, everything would slot together like pieces of a puzzle. He would be himself again, and the clouds would clear to bring days filled with hope and lucidity. He had enjoyed watching Jennifer leave work, stopping to talk to the ragged old man. Mother's binoculars were proving quite useful. He had cracked a smile as a lone raven swooped over their heads, stopping to perch in the spindly tree overlooking the bench. They were part of him, the ravens. They were as capable of carrying his presence as much as if he walked up behind her and whispered in her ear.

He watched as Jennifer glanced up at the raven overhead and brought her hand to the back of her neck, caressing the skin before shooing the raven away. But the bird stared fixedly at them both, and as her hand returned to scratch her neck once more, he allowed a smugness to wash over him. This would be easier than he thought. But all in good time. He was enjoying playing with her too much to cut it short now.

That evening he drove back to the forest where he abandoned his van. It was quite safe there because nobody ventured far into

Raven's woods any more. Turning on the radio, he began to warble as he drove down the bumpy unused track. His mother's rosary beads swung back and forth from the mirror as he did so, and he forgot all his worries as he filled his thoughts with future plans.

It wasn't until he drove over the narrow bridge that he noticed somebody poking around in his mind. The thoughts felt icy cold, frozen sparks shooting through his brain. He did not appreciate their attempts to see through his eyes. He knew exactly who it was. Bert stopped singing and clenched his teeth at the audacity. He scratched behind his ear. Who did she think she was, nothing but a girl poking around in his private thoughts? Worse still, she was trying to catch him off guard when he was driving. He ground his teeth. *He* instructed *her*, not the other way around. An angry itch spread over his raised skin like a coat of wasps and he dug his nails into his right arm. He would give her something to worry about. She was not playing fair, using her power to catch an old man off guard. He drew back his lips at the prospect of the pain he was going to make her endure, blocking her probing with his favourite poem. *While I nodded, nearly napping, suddenly there came a tapping, as of someone gently rapping, rapping at my chamber door*, his voice whispered in the darkness.

'Who are you?' Jennifer whispered.

Bert laughed at the audacity. *You come knocking on my door and you ask me who I am?*

'You have made yourself known to me prior to this, so I would argue it is you knocking on my door,' the self-assured response came forth.

Bert's cracked lips twitched in a smile. Perhaps she was more of a challenge than he thought. He liked that. He granted her an answer. *Why I'm Raven of course.*

'Did you kill Emily?'

Maybe, maybe not. A faint echo of laughter.

'What do you want, Raven? Tell me, perhaps I can help ...'

You'll find out soon enough. But do not come to me uninvited again ...

But Jennifer probed further, reaching out for clues.

Bert climbed out of his van in his secret place in the forest, gathering every ounce of energy to deliver his warning. Dropping to his knees, he dug his bony fingers into the soft soil of the earth, summoning the eager darkness. The trees echoed with flapping wings, working with the clouds to blot out the dying sun. The air filled with cries of abandon. Bert took a deep breath and held it. *GET OUT little pig! I said, GET OUT!* he screamed internally, the shockwaves sending the unwanted intruder back to reality. Spent, Bert leaned against a tree as he sat, the birds coming to nest all around him. He took what he could from the land to replenish his energy. Jennifer Knight was drawing near. He touched the cards in his jacket pocket. It was time for another prediction.

CHAPTER TWENTY-FIVE

Her brief contact with the Raven left Jennifer uneasy in her skin. Despite the wine, she could still taste the tobacco in his mouth and feel the dull throb of the veins in his temple. Parting the curtains in Will's flat, she peered out to the grey-blue slate rooftops of the houses across the road. A couple walked down the deserted street, arms interlinked as their footsteps echoed through the night. A blast of cold night air sliced through the gap in the window, and Jennifer strained to listen for the flap of black feathered wings. Thoughts loomed cold and dark as goose bumps rose on her skin. What if they were waiting for her at home? she thought, sitting on the rooftops and chimney pot as she pushed the key into the door. What then? She rubbed her arms. Ravens didn't usually come out at night but she was living in a world where anything could happen. Speaking seductively to the murderous man had made her flesh crawl, and she could not bear the thought of sleeping alone. The ten o'clock news rang out on the television. Will shook the half-empty bottle of wine and placed it back on the table. 'You're not in a hurry to go, are you?'

Jennifer shook her head, a little frisson of nerves bubbling inside her as the words formed in her mouth. 'I was wondering …' she said, taking a deep breath to finish her sentence. 'Do you think I could stay over? It's just with everything going on, I don't want to be on my own.'

Will's face broke into a smile. 'Of course. You can sleep in my bed. I'll kip on the sofa.'

'Thanks,' Jennifer said, half-heartedly. She was not ready to let him go just yet. 'Do you think we can stay up for a while? Watch some movies?' Jennifer kicked off her heels, wishing she'd worn something more comfortable than a shirt and trousers.

'Your encounter's really shaken you, hasn't it? We can stay up all night if you like, it's not as if we have to get up for work in the morning.'

'I'd like that,' she said, picking up her empty wine glass for replenishment.

Will turned on the old portable television, jabbing at the plastic buttons as a hazy picture came up on the screen. 'Sorry,' he said. 'I moved the flatscreen into my bedroom. It seemed like a good idea at the time.'

'Well, what are we waiting for? You bring the sofa cushions. I'll bring the booze,' Jennifer said.

'I didn't want you to think ...' Will's voice tapered off as he reddened.

Jennifer flashed a smile. 'I don't,' she lied. Will was only taking it slow because she asked him to. But lately any romance between them had come to a grinding halt. Her heart fluttered in her chest and she felt sixteen all over again.

The bedroom was bigger than Jennifer's but came with a more lived-in feel. A kingsize bed graced the middle of the room, and it was a typical bachelor pad, reasonably clean, comfortable, with shelves filled with the latest PlayStation and Xbox games. Will apologised as he tidied, picking up clothes and shutting wardrobe doors, removing empty coffee cups from his bedside table, and switching off the harsh overhead light in exchange for the soft bedside lamps. Jennifer smiled as she came from the bathroom wearing a pair of tracksuit bottoms borrowed from Will, and a freshly washed t-shirt. For once her mind was not on cleaning, and she plumped the cushions as she lay on the bed, patting a space beside her. 'Leave it, Will, just come and sit beside me. It's fine.'

Will gave her a curious glance before leaning back on the cushions and pillows, locking his hands behind his head. They settled back into easy conversation as the movie played, berating the actors, and the weak plot about a superhero disguised as a homeless man.

Will leaned his head on his hand and turned to her as the end credits rolled.

'Do you think George is like that?' he said. 'To us he's some harmless old dude, shuffling around, but in reality he's biding his time, waiting to save us with a flap of his cape.'

'If he's got a costume on under his clothes it must be pretty stinky by now,' Jennifer said.

Will flattened his pillow as he turned to look at her. 'I don't get it, how come you've taken such a liking to him?'

Jennifer smiled, her eyes dreamy. 'You probably think I'm mad but …'

'Go on,' Will said gently, coaxing out her inner thoughts.

'Since the incident last year with Frank, I feel like there's been a weight lifted. It's hard to explain, but I feel better in myself, less selfish.' She gave an uncomfortable laugh.

They rarely spoke about the incident in the boathouse, and it all felt like it happened so long ago. A fleeting look of concern crossed Will's face. It was gone so quick she wondered if she imagined it.

'Anyway, you know all about me. What about you? You must have some skeletons in your closet,' Jennifer said.

Will stifled a yawn with his hand. The white mark from the absence of his wedding ring had gone, and Jennifer found herself feeling pleased about it.

'There's nothing exciting to share,' he said, glancing over at the digital alarm clock by the side of the bed, which glowed '02:00' in red flashing lights.

But Jennifer didn't want to go to sleep yet. Sleep would bring the nightmares. Her face buried in the pillow, she turned to face him, inhaling the scent of fabric softener.

'Aw c'mon, there must be something about you that nobody else knows, or at least nobody from work. I don't mean bad habits or anything like that, you must have something to share.'

Will tilted his head to one side and a spark of inspiration brought a smile to his face. 'There is actually, but you're not to take the piss out of me in work for this.'

Jennifer crossed her chest with her finger. 'I won't, I promise, what happens in Will's manor stays in Will's manor.'

'OK.' Will turned down the TV as an advert for toilet cleaner flashed on the screen. 'Have you ever wanted a tattoo?'

Jennifer's eyes twinkled. Did Will have a tattoo? It was possible, she had never seen him naked. 'I've thought about it.'

'Where would you have it?'

'On my side, say here,' she said, pointing to the bra strap visible under her white t-shirt, 'down my side to below my hip bone.'

Will gave a wry smile. 'No anchors or love and hate on your knuckles?'

'No, definitely not,' Jennifer said.

'Maybe something pretty, and trailing, like a vine, or dark flowers?' Will said.

'Yes, I'd say you've got it. So what's your secret? Have you a tattoo?'

Will's eyes glinted in the warmth of the bedside light. 'I do as it happens but my surprise is something else. Stay where you are and I'll show you.'

The bed bounced as Will jumped off and padded to the wardrobe in his stocking feet. 'Ah, here it is,' he said, pulling out a brown leather bag which was buried in the back. Rolling open the flap, an array of art supplies fanned on the bed.

Jennifer took one look at the pens and gave a nervous giggle. 'Oh my God, you're not going to tattoo me, are you?'

'Yes. No. Kind of. It's temporary ink. Want to give it a go?'

'I'd love to,' Jennifer said, mellowed by the wine, and warmed by his presence. 'Have you ever done this before?'

'My brother bought his own tattoo parlour a couple of years ago, he gave me a tattoo and showed me how to do it. He's a brilliant artist.'

Jennifer thought of Will's doodles in interview, and all the scraps of paper buried in his drawers at work. 'So you've done this before?'

'I've given tattoos, yes. You'll have to stay still, mind. I don't want you to see this until I'm done.'

Jennifer lay on her side, leaning on her elbow as she supported her head with her hand.

'You'll have to lift up your t-shirt. I can't draw over it.'

A giggle erupted from Jennifer's lips. 'Of course, all in the name of art of course.'

'I assure you it is, Miss Knight. If you'd rather have a butterfly on your ankle…'

Jennifer thought of Will giving tattoos to female customers and felt a small pang of jealousy. 'Work away.'

Her heart began to flutter as she pulled off the t-shirt, revealing her white lacy bra underneath. In the flickering light of the television Will's face was one of concentration.

'Um, where do you want me to start?' Will said, the warmth of his hand sending tingles through her skin as he touched her side.

'Here,' Jennifer pointed above her bra strap, until she realised she would have to undo her bra for him to get underneath. Swallowing hard, she grabbed a pillow and pulled it towards her. Resting her chest in the softness, she slightly reached around and allowed the straps to fall off her shoulders. 'There you go, free access.'

'OK, just lean on the pillow slightly on your side, that's right, it will be worth it, I promise.'

It was already worth it. Every time Will touched her skin was soothing, and instead of being nervous, she felt entranced by the warmth of his hands. His honeyed voice removed any traces of anxiety from her contact with the Raven earlier in the day.

'Now stay still, this may tickle but you mustn't move or you'll ruin it.'

Gentle fingertips touched her skin, as they planned the pen strokes to come. Jennifer felt her breathing deepen as he brushed past the side of her breast and moved downwards. Swirls, pen strokes light and hard worked efficiently, as she stared at the wall, resisting the urge to bring her hand back and touch the man examining her body with such intensity. As Will moved closer for the tinier strokes of his pen, Jennifer could feel the heat of his body, and closed her eyes, enjoying the sensations of touch alone. She raised her hand to caress him and he reprimanded her instantly, lost in his creation.

'Don't move an inch,' he said, dominating the moment.

'You're very serious,' she giggled, biting her lip as the pen tickled her skin.

'Shh, I'm concentrating.'

Dropping her hand, she felt like a living piece of art, as he worked, creating goose bumps, blowing the ink dry before dotting her skin with coloured pens. The pen dipped before reaching the curve of her hip, and quickened as it reached the end.

Will's breathing had also deepened, and as he reached her hip, he coughed to clear his throat. 'Do you want me to stop here?'

'No,' Jennifer said, her voice husky. 'Where I showed you, hang on.' Taking another deep breath as she dropped the pillow from her breasts, she slipped off the tracksuit bottoms with her underwear. Lying back down, she allowed him to finish his creation. But the artist paused, and as Jennifer looked from the corner of her eye, she could see the tremble in his hand.

'You're killing me, Jennifer,' he murmured.

She turned to face him, the cool breeze of the night on her naked body. She could almost feel Will's heart pound against her as she pulled him towards her. There was no point in trying to fight it any more, and as Will's lips found hers, she wrapped her limbs around his. His tongue flickered and he pulled away, his eyes unsure, questioning. Face flushed, Jennifer could barely find her voice to whisper, 'It's OK.'

Afterwards they lay in silence until Jennifer spoke, her face resting on Will's chest. 'I hope I didn't spoil the picture for you.'

Will stroked her tousled hair. 'I think you'll like it.'

Jennifer grabbed a sheet as she rose from the bed and walked to the full-length mirror in the bathroom. 'It's beautiful,' she gasped. Looking at the intricacies of the black roses climbing up the length of her body. The jagged leaves were bowed with dewy blood red drops. Tiny yellow stars twinkled around the vine snaking up her side and it was there, in the detail of the drawing, that she saw his love.

Overwhelmed, she could hardly breathe. 'It's beautiful. I wish it was permanent.'

'Sorry we didn't get to finish it,' he grinned, clasping his hands behind his head.

'Where's your tattoo? Or was it all a ploy?'

'No ploy, I guess you're going to have to look for it.'

It was then that she saw the words, in the inner creases of his elbows. 'Heart' was underlined in the creases of his inner left arm, and underneath it, the word 'mind' and on his right, 'courage' underlined over the word 'fear' tattooed underneath.

'Wow, that's quite profound. I never knew you had so many hidden depths, Mr Dunston,' Jennifer said, tracing the words with her finger. She felt strengthened by their developing relationship, and any reservations were long forgotten. Sliding under the duvet, she wrapped her arms around him, absorbing his strength and falling into the best sleep she'd had all year.

CHAPTER TWENTY-SIX
Bert

Bert had come home from school to find mother asleep in bed. His senses dictated that napping was just another means of avoidance. He gobbled down the cold sausage sandwich on the table along with a glass of milk. The cupboard hinges whined in indignation as he gingerly searched for food. There was little point, because homemade pies or cakes were only baked for good boys like Callum. But Callum wasn't here any more and Bert was not a good boy. Kicking off his worn leather shoes, he strode to his room. With the promise of a full moon, he needed to get some sleep, otherwise he wouldn't be able to get up to visit the woods later on.

His eyes lit on the package on his bed. He ran his fingers over the smooth brown paper, slowly picking at the Sellotape with his bitten-down nails. It wasn't his birthday, and even if it was, that day had been dedicated to Callum. Mother's candles had burned brightly next to the framed photo on the dresser, and nothing was allowed to interfere with her mourning.

He dragged the heavy box from the top of the bed and sat on the floor with it between his legs. It was postmarked and addressed to his mother. But it must have been for him otherwise she wouldn't have left it there. Chewing the corner of his lip, he tore back another strip of paper, enjoying the tingly feeling of receiving a gift of his very own. He hardly noticed his mother's slim frame leaning against the door as he eagerly cast away the packaging. The gift was mail order by the look of it, and it was no coincidence it had arrived the week his father left for a fishing trip to the coast. He spent more and more time away from home now, and mother had a suspicion he was getting comfort elsewhere. At least, that's what Bert heard her say when she mumbled to herself during the day. After Callum died, her singing was replaced by the hum of prayer. When the pain and anger became too much, she ditched prayer and began talking to herself. Sometimes she became so animated in her conversations she would stamp her feet against the wooden floor, or hammer her fists on the table as she ate. Any attempt to interrupt her would be met with clenched fists and a steely glare.

She had been a lot kinder to him since he lied about communicating with Callum. Bert surmised that such contact may have been possible, but there was no way he was going to try. He had not wanted to hear from his brother when he was alive, much less after he had sent him to his death.

Bert unwrapped the globular-shaped package first. At first he thought it was a world globe, but as he tore off the rest of the paper, he revealed a glass ball on a black plastic plinth. It was hard and heavy, and he looked at his mother quizzically. She nodded at him to open the other packages. The second was a flat wooden board, all letters and numbers, with a small wooden plinth on a roller ball. He had heard about ouija boards at school, but the ones the kids spoke about were homemade, nothing as sophisticated as this. Smiling, he opened the third and last package. It was small, square, and heavy in his palm. Ripping open the paper he stared at the red velvet pouch, and after a cursory glance at his mother, eased the gold strings open to reveal a strange-looking deck of cards.

'They're tarot cards,' she said, smiling. The expression looked alien on her face, and lasted only a second before falling back into her customary anxious frown. 'They're all for you, Bert, so you can talk to Callum. But only when your father's not around. Do you think it will help you speak to him?'

Bert shrugged. He didn't feel like being kind to her today. But then he caught the edge of a doubtful thought and sprang from the floor to hug her.

'Don't be sad, mummy, I'll speak to him tonight, I promise.'

Grace nodded unconvincingly, as she tried to extricate herself from his hug. 'In that case I'll leave you to it. I'm going back to bed.'

The house was eerily quiet in the absence of mother's singing. In the olden days, she would be doing something productive, baking, painting, or chatting with father. Now the house was as bleak as the light behind her eyes, and Bert could barely stand it. The barbed thoughts, the pity of his school classmates … if it weren't for his ally the raven, he would have felt very alone.

Bert sat on the floor until his bottom went numb. The crystal ball was cheap rubbish, and he wiped away his fingerprints before returning it to the box. Mother would send the presents back when the whim suited her anyway. He didn't like the ouija board. The second he placed the plinth on the wood he knew it was a doorway into something too dark for him to handle. What if his brother started talking to him through it? What if Callum said that he was going to hell for making him fall from that tree? His mother told him about hell once, a long time ago, when she used to go to church, but Bert's harsh life lessons demonstrated that the darkness of hell was not reserved for the afterlife. It was with him every minute of every day.

He turned his attention back to the cards, feeling a tingle shoot up his finger as he touched the deck. It brought with it a hint of the power lying behind the shop-coated smell. A flutter of excitement rose, as he clumsily thumbed the pictures. Death, temperance, and judgment, the meaning of each card whispered softly into his senses. Bert smiled as he brought them to his nose, inhaling their power. The empty feeling he had been carrying evaporated as he basked in their potency.

CHAPTER TWENTY-SEVEN

The itch. The damned itch! Jennifer squirmed as she raked her skin with long yellow nails, leaving ragged blood-seeped tracks in their wake. She looked down at her shaking hands, scaly and withered, gasping as they touched her bristled face.

'No,' she said, 'get away from me, no!'

A light flickered on and Jennifer recoiled from the hand on her shoulder.

'Hey, hey, it's me, Will. You're dreaming.'

She blinked, looking left to right. 'Mmm? Where am I?'

Will murmured softly. 'Shhh, it's OK, it's just a bad dream.'

Jennifer mumbled something incoherent before lying back down. Slowly her heartbeat returned to a normal rhythm as she surrendered to sleep.

Will pressed his lips against her forehead before turning to face the wall.

Easing herself into the warmth of his back, Jennifer snaked her hand around his waist, and he drew it up into the groove of his chest, drawing her close to banish the nightmares.

'You're late, I didn't think you were coming,' Amy said, pulling open the door. Her usual weekly visit had been delayed by a late afternoon lie-in at Will's, and a shared shower after dinner. Jennifer grinned sheepishly as she followed her sister inside, hopping on one of the barstools next to the compact breakfast bar. The sense of betrayal diminished since her father's visit, and a night spent with Will had eased the loneliness nesting in her heart. Her sister seemed buoyant, which suggested it had gone well. Nevertheless, Jennifer was not going to mention her father unless Amy brought him up first.

Six sterilised baby bottles were lined up in a row next to an open tin of milk powder, and Amy completed the routine of mixing, shaking and storing the feeds before wiping down the counter and making two cups of tea. Jennifer watched with admiration as Amy worked, cleaning the kitchen, listening to the baby monitor, and telling Joshua to go to bed. She thought of their own childhood; when they were free to do what they wanted until the pubs closed. Then their father came home stinking of beer, and Jennifer would creep down in her nightie to lock the front door behind him. On a good night, he'd be lying comatose on the sofa, and Jennifer would prise the empty beer can from his grasp before covering him with a blanket. On a bad night, he'd bring back company. Narrow-eyed drunks who would raid her food supplies and leer as she darted back upstairs and locked her bedroom door.

Jennifer pulled herself away from the past and drew her attention back to her sister. Her home was full of comforting things, a smaller version of their aunt Laura's, the woman who saved them from a life in care. Wicker love hearts hanging from cupboard handles, wall art advocating love, life, and laughter, knitted tea cosies shaped like owls, with the smell of freshly baked cookies wafting from the oven. It transported her sister to a better place, a time of love and security. Jennifer thought of her bleached black and white home and wondered what it said about her.

Soon the pair of them were chatting about the kids, family life, and a censored version of life in the police force. Jennifer laughed as Joshua ran up the stairs in his Spider-Man pyjamas, expending his limitless amounts of energy before bed.

'I got his test results back today,' Amy said, lightly stirring the tea before pushing it across the marble counter.

Jennifer took the cup, patterned with purple and yellow splodges. She had a similar one, which looked so out of place in her sterile kitchen cupboard – a gift from Joshua after one of his nursery craft sessions. Her eyes flickered over the fridge door, adorned with colourful magnets holding up his various paintings and star-emblazoned awards. There was nothing wrong with her beloved nephew, but in a world obsessed with labels he would be pressured to shed his identity and conform.

'What did they come up with?'

Amy shrugged. 'He's perfectly healthy. No ADHD, no autism, nothing. Just a busy boy with an overactive imagination.'

'Good,' Jennifer said, trying hard not to interfere. Her sister began to ramble on about her recent membership to the Women's Institute, and Jennifer's thoughts drifted to Will as she stared dreamily into her cup of tea.

'You seem different tonight, sis, any news?' Amy said, delivering the words with a knowing smile.

Jennifer shrugged innocently. 'No, same old, same old, lots of work, you know how it is.'

Amy leaned forward, her chin resting on the palm of her hand. 'So you've not been shagging anyone? It's just that you stink of sex.'

Jennifer's eyes widened at the accusation. 'Amy! What sort of a thing is that to say?'

'The sort of thing you say when your sister's been holding out. Now spill. I know you've been seeing someone.'

'I've not ...'

Amy chuckled, sliding her mobile phone across the counter and pressing the button to display a text. 'Then why did you send this text an hour before you got here?'

Jennifer flushed as her eyes crept over the text. *See you later sexy xxx.* Amy was her last phone contact, so the text must have been sent to her instead of Will. Seconds passed, and Jennifer's mouth gaped open with very little coming out. There was no point in trying to wriggle out of it; Amy could read her like a book.

'It's early days, I wasn't going to say anything yet.'

Amy wagged her finger. 'I'm your sister, you shouldn't be holding out on me. It's the guy that stayed over when you were in hospital, isn't it?'

Jennifer nodded. 'We've only just got together this weekend. It's a bit awkward with work so we weren't going to let on just yet.'

'Hmm,' Amy said, raising her cup to finish her tea. 'He's a bit scruffy, but you like them rough and ready, don't you?'

Jennifer was about to leap to Will's defence, when her sister tittered from behind her cup. 'Relax, I'm only joking. You *have* got it bad, haven't you?'

Jennifer's dimples came into life as she beamed a smile. Talking about boyfriends with her sister gave her a warm glow inside. 'He's lovely. He comes from a very close family.'

'Does he know about our band of misfits?' Amy said.

Jennifer's smile faltered, but not long enough for Amy to notice. 'Yep, and he still wants to know me. Who'd believe it?'

'Well I wouldn't kick him out of bed for farting,' Amy grinned.

Jennifer swallowed the last of her tea, the tang of unstirred sugar hitting the back of her throat. She felt more like a mother to her sister, and sex wasn't something she was comfortable discussing with her.

'I'd best be off. Mind if I say goodnight to Josh before I go?'

'He'll go mad if you don't. Can you get him to brush his teeth while you're up there? He's going through a defiant stage, it takes forever to get him to bed.'

Jennifer convinced Josh that if he brushed his teeth he'd get more money from the tooth fairy when they fell out. It seemed a perfectly plausible explanation to the four-year-old child, and five minutes later, he was tucked up under his Spider-Man duvet. Jennifer was not one to push the subject of Josh's psychic powers. She would have been just as happy if they disappeared overnight, like a passing phase. But the wordless thoughts that passed between them seemed too powerful to simply dissipate. His energy was bright and happy, and she felt a pang of guilt as she chatted to her favourite little boy, hoping she had not inadvertently brought danger to his door. Thoughts of her father streamed back into her consciousness, and she itched to ask about their meeting. But she had dealt with enough domestic incidents in the police to vow she would never use a child as a pawn, and the last thing she wanted was to involve him in her and Amy's dispute. She had barely closed his bedroom door when his footsteps thumped across the carpet and the light switch clicked on. Poking her head around, she caught him jumping into bed.

'Everything all right, sweetie? Are you scared to sleep with the light off?'

'Nope,' Josh said, sitting up as he pulled a comic from under his pillow. 'I'm reading.' He flipped the pages of the comic book with the same stance as his father reading the *Financial Times*.

'Oh I see. Well don't stay up too late eh, you need your sleep.'

Jennifer turned to leave. She would let his mother argue it out with him.

'Jenny?' Josh said. 'Stay away from the woods.'

Jennifer froze. 'What woods?'

'The dark woods. With the blackbirds. It's a bad place.'

She crept back to her nephew, keeping her voice low. 'I don't understand. Where did you get this from?'

Josh shrugged, and giggled as he pointed to a character in the *Beano* magazine. 'He's called Pongo, he's farty. Can you read it to me?'

'Only if you promise to go to sleep when I'm done.' Jennifer nudged him up on the bed and relayed the rest of the comic story. She knew not to push him for answers. Sometimes insights came in flashes, and were gone as quickly as they came. She closed the comic book and laid it on the floor.

'Everything all right now?' she said, an open invitation to disclose more.

'Uh-huh. I love you,' Josh said before snuggling into his pillow and closing his eyes.

Jennifer kissed his warm forehead and pulled the duvet to his shoulder. 'I love you too, goodnight sweetie.'

She activated the soft round nightlight and switched off the bulb on the wall, casting the room into a bluish glow. Joshua looked so small under the Spider-Man duvet cover, his vulnerability raising her emotions until they formed as a lump in her throat. She clicked the door behind her and tried to decipher the message. It had to be related to the Raven, but how? Stay away from the woods? The woods where Felicity Baron was killed was miles away. Unless he meant the woods around the boathouse? No. These were fresh concerns. A new warning for her ears only. Chances were he didn't even understand it himself, hence his inability to elaborate. It was as if someone had whispered in his ear and the words came from his mouth. Jennifer wondered if it was her mother at play. Sometimes it was easier for spirits to come through children than adults. Adults simply added their own perceptions to messages, whereas children told it as it was.

Jennifer's happiness melted away as she drove home. She had made a quick call to Will to cancel their meeting. He was still at his parents', and informed Jennifer they had invited her around for dinner. The thought of being introduced to his perfect mother and father made her squirm. It was doubtful they would approve, and according to Will, they had made no secret of the fact they wanted a grandchild – that was until his wife had an affair and split their marriage into two. Jennifer grunted to herself. They had better not set their hopes upon her. She had enough to contend with, without throwing a baby into the mix. Police careers did not support family life, least of all ones dealing with the supernatural. It was hard enough to protect Joshua.

Would they start on her family next? Thoughts loomed heavy and daunting in her mind. Joshua had told her not to enter the woods, but as she parked the car outside her home, she knew that was exactly where she needed to go.

CHAPTER TWENTY-EIGHT
Bert

Mother was even more unbearable after she bought Bert the cards. Each evening she leaned against his bedroom door, her long black skirt casting shadows in his room, on his things. They were the same clothes she'd worn the day Callum died. Bert remembered the heavy material of her skirt dragging a crimson trail of blood as she carried Callum's body to the car. The skirt was far too big for her now, and the slim buckled belt had tightened several notches around her waist. Perhaps it made her feel closer to Callum. Or maybe she was trying to remind him of what she had lost. Either way Bert didn't care.

'Bert,' she rasped, through a pinched mouth, delivering shrill utterances that made him wince. Her once pretty features were locked in a scowl, her colourless skin stretched over jutting cheekbones, exasperated by the tightly wound bun in her hair.

Bert ignored his mother in the hope she would go away. At first he had appeased her, making up sickly sweet words of love, the kind Callum would be likely to say. I love you mummy. I'm always with you mummy. One day we will be together and you can read to me again. *But after a while, the words ran dry. The very sight of her made him angry, and he was fed up with her constant need for reassurance. He wanted to slap her, to stare into those misty eyes and tell her that he was her son and he needed her here, looking after him, making him feel his existence meant something. But she was just a shell, filled to the brim with bitterness and pain. She coughed. Bert carried on with his sketch of the woods. He was trying to figure out a way he could make them private. He didn't know who owned them, but as far as he was concerned, they were his. If he sowed enough thorny bushes, dug enough ravines, it would keep out the campers who sometimes came to explore.*

'Bert. Do you have a message for me, Bert?' mother said, in rapid bursts of staccato. She crossed her arms, her elbows pointing sharply either side as she waited for her message from beyond the grave.

Bert grimaced. It wasn't as if he got any special treatment for passing them on. As soon as he'd given her the message, she would snatch away the words, repeating them over as she sobbed to her unseen ghost.

'Bert. Are you listening to me?'

Anger rose with each syllable his mother uttered. He pushed his pencil into the paper, growling as the leaden point snapped in half. 'Leave me alone,' he said, pushing past her to the back door. 'Just fuck off and leave me alone!'

Mother's tightly laced leather shoes clip clopped against the bare floorboards as she chased him to the door. 'How dare you!' she thundered, her words laced with disgust. 'How dare you speak to your mother like that!'

Bert laughed wildly as he flung the door open, sending it rebounding against the wall. Still laughing, he mocked her inability to leave the house. She could no longer visit Callum's grave. Even her steps to the oak tree were unsure and faltering, and always after dark.

'Callum's dead!' Bert screamed as he ran towards the oak tree. 'And I wish you were dead too!'

But Bert underestimated his mother, and the fire of her fury propelled her out of the house, skeletal fingers extended as she hunted him down the path. Bert's ear burned as she pinched it hard, swinging him off his bare feet.

'Don't you ever speak to me like that again,' she spat, pulling back her hand to slap him across the face.

'Ca … caw,' Bert stammered. *'Caw, caw!'*

His mother froze, her right hand mid-air. *'What? … What's wrong with you?'*

The words had barely left her lips when the raven drew down on her, slicing the back of her hand with dagger-sharp claws. Mother screamed, thrown off balance as the raven bore down again, slicing and tearing, its cries piercing the evening air.

Bert's eyes sparkled as his black winged guardian defended him from the sharp sting of the slap that was to come. But as much as his mother annoyed him, he needed her to sustain him. He flapped his feeble arms as he called the raven off.

'Come away, come away,' he shouted, and the raven took flight, cutting through the air with long graceful wings as Bert's mother lay bleeding on the ground.

CHAPTER TWENTY-NINE

Jennifer could not hold back any longer. Enquiries with the Facebook group were taking too long. She had to visit the woods, if only to get answers for the questions relentlessly invading her thoughts. Her visit with Joshua reminded her what was at stake. She couldn't wait for the Raven to make contact, and a quick internet search pulled up exactly what she needed. Haven was a historic town, and many of the original names given during times of folklore had long since been forgotten. The river, once named as 'Black Water', had been renamed Blakewater, and Haven was originally called Heaven, many years ago. Jennifer knew that, having lived there all her life. But she was surprised to discover an extended patch of woodlands behind the boathouses, named Raven Woods. She dug deeper, becoming drawn into an internet forum on local history, featuring the little known forest.

User *frightgirl95* described camping with a couple of her friends. Stories of witchcraft had drawn them to Raven Woods, where she described the stale air carrying the sour scent of decay. She spoke of their sleep being disturbed by gut-wrenching screams, and their torch beams picking up nothing but bark-stripped trees housing beady-eyed ravens overhead. Stumbling back to their tent, they were horrified to discover the heavy-duty material ripped to shreds. It was all the persuasion they needed to leave.

Jennifer traced the location of Raven Woods to the rear of the river, down a narrow weather-beaten dirt track. Tourists preferred to camp beside the riverside forest, with its picnic benches and BMX tracks. But there were no such paths where she was going, and the only things bordering the long stiff trees were strands of horned barbed wire, flanked by deep ditches and a keep out sign. The fact it was dented with buckshot gave a double-edged meaning. Keep – out – or else. Jennifer took one last glance before driving past. Someone just took a random shot, she thought, trying to keep the tide of dread at bay. She pressed her brakes as she caught sight of fresh tyre tracks in the mud. They veered off to the left and disappeared down a valley between the trees. Pulling her handbrake as far as it would go, she parked on a mound of grass. She had lived in Haven all her life but with acres of dense unexplored woodlands, she was a stranger to these parts. Swinging her legs out of the car, she plodded down the grassy bank, sidestepping the pebbles of rabbit droppings as she followed the tyre tracks. She checked her mobile phone. No signal. A cold breeze touched her skin and her internal warning system piped up as her nephew's words replayed in her mind. *Stay away from the woods.* But she had to find answers, before it was too late.

She approached the leafy vegetation, her eyes narrowing as she took in the horizontal branches. Trees with no trunks … Jennifer shielded her arms over her face as she pushed through the undergrowth, nothing more than camouflage for the gap that lay behind it. Enough for a car to pass through, judging by the tyre tracks. She bit her lip as her apprehension grew. The forest held a presence all of its own. If she got into trouble nobody would see her in here, much less hear her screams … Giving one last glance back at her car, Jennifer allowed the dead branches to whip her limbs as she pushed through the makeshift gate, keeping her wits on high alert. Her breath felt warm against her lips, cooled by the drop in temperature. Casting her face to the tree tops, she searched the air for ravens as she made a three hundred and sixty degree circle. The forest was a kaleidoscope of mist and branches. Greasy leaves lined her path when they should have been shooting from fresh spring buds. She wrinkled her nose. This was not a pleasant woodland smell. It smelt meaty, decaying, and anyone venturing this far would be turning back now if they had any sense. She strode onwards in grim determination, her boots rustling through the insect-infested undergrowth. Her eyes shot back up to the trees disappearing into the misted sky. *Where are the buds and shoots? Where are the finches and the robins, the squirrels and the foxes? Not even a raven in sight.* The only signs of life were the spiders threading thick dewy cobwebs, ready to bait the flies trailing in her wake. The hairs prickled on the back of her neck as she felt the stare of hooded eyes, all holding dark intentions.

'Come out, come out, wherever you are …' Jennifer whispered, steeling herself for confrontation. Her heart froze as a sudden scream echoed throughout the forest.

'Help me! Someone, help me!'

She ran through the thickening mist, following the screams to a copse in the distance. Her heart began to pound in her ribcage, and every fibre in her being demanded she turn back. A sense of evil intent emanated from the copse, but Jennifer drove onwards, feeling a hundred sets of eyes on her back. The sour smell was overpowering, and brought with it the tang of freshly spilt blood. Were the screams real or echoes from the past? Was she walking into a trap? She couldn't leave now.

Swearing under her breath, her eyes searched for a weapon, and her fingers wrapped around a splintered piece of wood. Flapping black wings swooped through the sky as the ravens flew from their hiding places, but Jennifer's attention was swift-ly drawn back to an army of tiny legs marching up her arm. Screaming, she dropped the branch and furiously shook her hand to rid herself of the millipedes that claimed it. She thought of Will, and pulled her phone from her pocket. Groaning, she realised the newly charged battery was now completely drained. She couldn't call for help even if she wanted to. She wrapped her fingers around her car keys, keeping the sharp edge exposed through her bent fingers. It was an old trick, but enough to gouge someone's face if she had to. Her heart beating hard, she pushed through the prickly bushes, shielding her face as sharp-edged thorns scratched softly at the seams of her jacket and trousers.

Bert squinted at the sky as the raven's caws filled the air. There was someone in the forest. His forest. He raised his nose to the air and closed his eyes, inhaling deeply. Could it be? His senses strained to reach the outskirts of the woods, and he fingered the knife in his pocket. It was a shame he didn't have his shotgun. But there was something very impersonal about guns, whereas knives … A rush of excitement flowed through his veins. The madness had returned, and he would do whatever it took to protect the forest. His thoughts went to Jennifer Knight. Could she be looking for him? After all, their futures were intertwined. She would not stay long in a forest filled with anguish, but she was strong. She would fight against her instincts if it meant leading her to the person who threatened her the most.

A rat jumped through the undergrowth, startled by Jennifer's urgent footsteps. The screams had stopped, but the silence that lay in its place was heavy and menacing. Jennifer slowly edged around an imposing oak tree. It was different to the others. The surrounding air carried a thickness that made it hard to breathe. Tracing the scarred bark with her fingers, Jennifer knew she had reached the beating heart of Raven Woods. She pushed her tousled hair off her face, determined to keep her emotions in check. But she was deep in the forest – and she was not alone. Pressing her hands against the bark, her eyelids fluttered shut in a last-ditch attempt at communication. Her senses blocked her attempts, screaming a warning; she was in danger, and she had to leave now. Sense finally prevailed, and shielding her face with her hands, she pushed her way back through the briars to leave the way she came. But it seemed the forest was not ready to release her, and the thorns that gently scratched her upon entrance now held her firmly in their grip. She pushed through the copse, gasping as thorny cables tore through her clothes and into her flesh. Blood beaded on her thighs and legs, as black flapping wings drummed a beat overhead. Jennifer's legs weakened as her own vulnerability became evident. They were coming. The ravens were coming. The sight of the birds circling the pearly grey sky sent a dagger of fear through her heart.

Jennifer clambered through the dense forest, trying to find her bearings as the birds settled in the branches just above her head. Their stares were icy cold, and the noise of her backward steps in the still air seemed magnified a hundredfold. Jennifer swallowed, trying to calm her pounding heart. More and more birds roosted on the branches overhead, until they were thick and black, bearing feathers instead of the rotting leaves underfoot. Lost and disorientated in the dead, soulless forest, Jennifer whispered a silent prayer.

Bert was close to the forest now, he watched as a cloud of black ravens descended in the woodlands and held their prey. His tongue darted from his lips and he moistened them in expectation. Just a few more minutes and he would be there.

Disorientated, Jennifer forced one leg in front of the other. If the ravens beat her down now, they would tear her to shreds.

'Get the hell off me,' she growled as the first raven swooped overhead. Jennifer batted the bird away, staggering through the woodland as another took its place. 'Help me! Someone, help me!' her screams echoed through the forest as she pulled up her hood to protect her face. Warm blood trickled down her hand as a raven tore flesh from the back of her hand, its screams intermingling with hers in the fight for control. Jennifer spun around, lost and disorientated as she batted off countless birds while clinging desperately to her hood.

Suddenly a flash of white cut through the air. Jennifer instinctively followed the fluttering wings as they swooped to avoid the predators overhead. Her arms aching, she batted off the birds as she found her way through the forest. The ravens held back as she left, and the leaves underfoot were replaced by fresh, untainted soil.

'Wait!' Jennifer cried, reaching out with a bloodied hand. Relief flooded through her as the clearing came into view, and she scrambled up the grassy bank to her parked car, which was pimpled in a dewy mist. Peeling the keys from her sweaty palm, she jumped inside and activated the central locking. The car veered onto the dirt path, the ding ding of the car alarm protesting until she clicked in her seatbelt. It was not until the forest was out of sight that she pulled over, her stomach lurching from the adrenalin come-down. Taking in lungfuls of air, she leaned

through the open window. Jennifer spat the sour taste from her mouth and lifted her hand to wipe it, sticky with a mixture of dirt and blood. Tears prickled the backs of her eyes as the pain from her injuries cut through her nerve endings. Who was she to think she could overcome such darkness? She grabbed her bag from under the seat, and tentatively dabbed her hand before allowing the tears to roll down her cheeks. Her wound needed dressing, and she was in no state to do it alone. But where should she go? Will would give her a telling-off for going to the woods alone. Amy would ask too many questions, and turning up in such a state would upset her nephew, who had told her not to go. Her eyes blurred as she stared at her trembling hands, trying to muster the strength to drive to casualty. A flash of black darted in her rear view mirror as she turned the ignition key. Jennifer drove away, the ravens' cries echoing in her ears.

CHAPTER THIRTY
Bert

Bert blew his nose in disgust. The forest smelt contaminated, as if someone had poured bleach, making it shrivel in its wake. He gripped the knife, his wheezing echoing in his ears. His eyes flickered to the ravens huddled on the bare branches. Their heads hung low as he glared at them for the late warning. All apart from the one with the missing tail feather and bloodied beak. Bert tried to count the years since he had seen his feathered companion. There was no mistaking the same glossy blue and purple coated bird. His guardian. Against all odds it had come back to see him finish the job. Bert lifted his arm high as he held his breath and beckoned the bird towards him.

The raven ruffled its feathers before spreading his wings wide and propelling himself from the branch to the ragged man below. With regal magnificence, it swooped through the thickening air.

Bert's heart pounded as the bird got closer, giving no signs of stopping. Its wingspan was wide and strong, and it was the largest raven Bert had ever seen. He held his stance to welcome his old friend. The bird's claws opened, grasping Bert's skinny bicep, making it shudder under his weight.

'Augh, Augh!' the raven screamed, his cries slicing through Bert like a blunt razor. Bert hunched his shoulders, conscious of

the strength in his domed beak. As the bird settled on his arm, Bert gave a humble sideways glance at the raven he had known since childhood. How was this possible? It was breaking all the boundaries. Bert's eyes found the blood flecks on the bird's beak. It was her blood. The raven had started what he had yet to end. Bowing his head, he scraped his beak on Bert's sleeve before launching high into the sky. Just like all those years ago, he had laid down the gauntlet. And Bert would not let him down.

Bert had many voices in his head, but there was only one worth listening to. The one which gave him instruction to kill, and provided him with the tools to do so. It was the raven. Each predicted death brought a rich reward, but none would be so rich as ending the detective who tried to halt his mission. There was strength to be gained from killing those on his list, but the detective … she possessed enough psychic energy not just to replenish his body, but also to extend his life for years. The fact she was tormented by the recent deaths brought pleasure to his day. Bert said goodbye to the forest, a giggle rising in his throat. He had a prediction to make, and he couldn't wait to see Jennifer's reaction when she found out who it was.

CHAPTER THIRTY-ONE

Jennifer apologised to the nurse as she fought to stem the blood dripping from her shaking hand. The sterile wipe had blossomed a bright red as the blood seeped through, dripping onto the counter and earning her a disapproving look. She took the wad of paper towels offered to her and sat in the hard plastic chair as she waited to be seen. Jennifer tried to think rationally. It was the shock that made her want to cry, nothing else. She was in the wrong place at the wrong time and was attacked by a territorial flock of birds. She could hear Will's words now. That's what happens when you go into something with blinkered vision, embellished with an overactive imagination. She gulped back the lump in her throat as she avoided the stares of the other patients, their sideways glances confirming that she looked a state. She thought about what she would say if someone like her turned up at the police station, shredded clothes, bloodied skin, and a wild look in her eyes. She'd be thinking mental health issues before they even got the chance to speak.

She stared forlornly at the floor and a pair of blue Crocs came into her vision. The skinny young man smiled apologetically at the other people in the queue and signalled her into a cubicle ahead of them.

Jennifer sucked in a breath as he peeled off the layers of blood-soaked tissues from her right hand. She was grateful for his kindly face. His dark eyes were tinged with shadows, and he

looked as overworked as the rest of the staff she had seen that night. She knew the feeling. Thoughts of work made her heart flicker as she remembered the real reason behind her woodland excursion. The man responsible for the murders was still out there, and she had to get back to the investigation. The doctor's voice broke into her thoughts as he looked up from under his thick wavy fringe.

'This looks nasty, what happened?'

'I was attacked,' Jennifer blurted out the words. Her voice sounded strangled, and she took a deep breath to steady herself.

'Attacked? Have you reported this to the police?'

'No. It was a flock of birds. I was in the woods, I must have stumbled upon a nest or something.'

The young man frowned as he tenderly examined both her hands. 'It's unusual to see birds cause so much damage.'

Jennifer sighed. The last thing she needed was the well-meaning doctor reporting her injuries to the police.

'Well, I'm a police officer, you see, I was investigating a case in the area. I was lost and slid down a ravine in the woods. I guess some of the injuries were caused when I fell over.'

'Ah, I thought I'd seen you around. Well, this is going to need a couple of stitches, it's quite deep I'm afraid. You're lucky you don't have tendon damage.'

Jennifer sat back as the doctor examined then dressed her wounds. Her right hand was gouged, and her legs and arms were scratched from the brambles. A nurse poked her fingers through the hole in the hood of her coat in amazement. Jennifer shuddered as the ravens crept into her memory.

'Is there anyone you can call to pick you up?' The doctor said. 'You need to rest this hand.'

Jennifer nodded. She would have to call Will. She thanked the doctor and went to the bathroom to clean up, gasping at her reflection. No wonder those people had stared. If this is what she looked like after treatment, what had she seemed like before it?

Will got a taxi to the hospital. It made sense to drive her car back rather than leave it in the car park. He paled as he approached her, his face set in a worried scowl. She had to dilute the truth to save them both grief.

'I'm OK,' she smiled. 'I went to the woods to see if I could find the van and fell down a ravine. I must have disturbed a nest of birds because they started attacking me. It looks a lot worse than it is.'

'You're not to go off like that on your own again. Honestly Jennifer, it's like you have a death wish. There's a serial killer on the loose and you're just putting yourself in the line of fire.' Will winced as he turned over her bandaged hand. 'And what's happened to your hand?'

Jennifer hunched over, wishing she had just called a cab and gone home alone. But she was still feeling woozy and upset. She needed a warm set of arms, even if it did come with frantic nagging.

'They're just scratches. The doctor gave me couple of steri strips where I gouged my hand on a dead tree branch when I slipped over on the leaves.'

'Leaves? You must be a bit concussed, there's no leaves on the ground yet.'

'Mud, I meant mud. Can we just go home? I'm really tired and I need coffee.'

They went back to her place at her insistence. Her rising anxiety levels meant the clutter she overlooked in Will's flat would now grate on her nerves. Will left her soaking in a hot bath as he went out to buy food, promising he would leave her kitchen as clean as he found it.

She closed her eyes as she tried to decipher her visit, picking through her experience in an effort to take something positive from her ordeal. This figure, the Raven, he was like her, of flesh and bone, but heavily influenced by something in the forest. She had felt his presence near, so he couldn't have lived very far away. But with the ravens on his side, he was a lot stronger than she gave him credit for. She had sensed dark sacrifices from long ago, and the land was soaked with blood. Thick with dark energy, it could easily envelop the young or the vulnerable. *Help me, Someone, help me*, the words that drew her into the forest rebounded in her head. The same words she screamed when the ravens were attacking her. Had the forest echoed her words long before she uttered them? How was that possible?

Jennifer groaned, easing further into the bathwater until it touched her chin. Too exhausted to process any more, she rested her bandaged hand on the side, the sharp aroma of disinfectant filling her nostrils as it stung every scratch and open wound. The pain was comforting as it purged the woodlands from her body, and she allowed her mind to wander while the tea lights flickered on the edge of the bath. The smell of antiseptic brought her to another place, a little boy in bed, staring out at the forest … the picture changed to the same boy, bigger now, digging up a pack of tarot cards from the earthen forest…

Jennifer abruptly snapped out of her vision to banging on her bathroom door. The water was freezing cold, and all but one of the tea lights had extinguished. Will was hammering on the other side.

'Jennifer, are you in there? If you don't answer me soon I'll have to force open the door.'

Jennifer blinked as she grounded herself, her pruned fingers reaching for a nearby towel. 'I'm fine … I must have dozed off. I'm getting out now.'

She pulled the plug and watched ribbons of blood-tinged water swirl away. Her mind raced as she patted the goose bumps on her skin dry. Her vision provided her with more than an insight into a little boy's past. It brought her deep inside the mind of a killer.

CHAPTER THIRTY-TWO
Bert

Bert scratched the new scrub of beard forming on his chin as he stared through the grimy window of the derelict room. He would be here soon, his next pawn in the game. Emitting a little chuckle, he thought of his next victim. Officer Knight was sure to shed a few tears over this one. She would blame herself, and she would be right. His targets didn't deserve their so-called second chance, and the fact the interfering detective knew them gave them even higher priority on his list.

His thoughts were interrupted by a scuffling noise down-stairs. His heart thumped a dull throb in his chest. What if it's the police? He placed the open can of beans on the floor and cautiously walked out of the room to investigate. The police don't normally hum, he thought, and peered out over the stair-well on the landing. A small skinny man sung to himself as he rifled through his bag, picking out scraps of food to eat and talking to his dog.

'Look at this, Tinker, we're going to dine well tonight. Ham sandwiches.'

Bert's yellow teeth glistened as he drew back his lips in a sneer. He shoved his hand into his pocket and sharply drew back his finger as static electricity snapped from his tarot cards in response. His instincts had been proven right.

Bert snuck back into the bedroom and waited. Sliding out a half-empty bottle of whisky, he placed it on the bare floorboards and resumed eating his cold beans. The stage set, he waited for his prey to come.

Soft footsteps pressed against the stairs, followed by a hoarse bark. 'Oh jaysus, mister, ya frightened the life out of me. I thought we had ghosts up here.'

Bert smiled, raising one wiry eyebrow in mock surprise. 'Don't mind me. Anyway, looks like you're at an advantage with your guard dog there.'

'Tinker? He just looks out for me, that's all. I was planning to stay the night here, it's a bit rough outside, and I don't have anywhere to take me dog. Is that OK with you, mister?'

'Sure. Care to share a drink?' Bert raised the bottle and George shuffled over, keeping a tight hold of Tinker, whose hackles rose in spiked formation. Head lowered, he emitted a low rumbling growl before stopping to lick his paws.

The atmosphere between George and Bert warmed as they siphoned the whisky. The bottle drained and George looked sorrowfully at the empty tumbler before placing it back on the flask that Jennifer had loaned him. Sitting back against the wall, he interlinked his fingers as he placed them behind his head, wondering what she would bring him tomorrow. The shuffle of cards made him open his eyes and glance in Bert's direction.

Sitting up, George rubbed his fingerless gloved hands to-gether.

'I love a game of cards. Do ya play poker?'

Bert shuffled the cards from hand to hand in expert fashion. They were large and feathered, but comfortable in his grasp. 'They aren't playing cards, they're tarot.'

George shuffled nearer on his bottom, giving Bert a look of caution. 'You should be careful with those, the dark arts aren't to be messed with.'

'It's only a bit of fun. Haven't you ever had your fortune told?' Bert said.

Inebriated from the whisky, George gave a little chuckle. 'When I was thirteen, I had me tealeaves read by a traveller on the common. A big fat lady named Ruby. Sure I was too busy looking at her ample chest to take in what she was saying. God, they could have suffocated me but what a way to go, I would have loved it.'

'Would you like me to read for you?' Bert said, forcing a smile.

George gave a little chuckle, the image of Ruby still alive in his memory. 'Sure, why not.'

Bert laid out the cards in the usual manner and waved his hands over them as the images came into play.

'What do ya see?' George said, his eyes flickering from the cards to Bert.

'I see you started off very differently to what you are now. You were well educated, but left home at an early age.'

George opened his eyes wide in amazement. 'Well would ya credit it, you're right, but it's nothing I like to dwell on now.'

'You're very alone: apart from a few kind faces, it's just you and your dog.'

'I'm happy on my own. It's exactly how I want it.'

'It won't always be. One day you're going to return to your past. It hasn't left you and it never will,' Bert said.

George frowned. 'I've put all that behind me.'

The candlelight exposed the doubt on Bert's face as he spoke. 'But you haven't, have you? The truth is you have a lot to answer for. You think you're punishing yourself now, but deep down you know it's nothing in comparison to the act you've committed all those years ago. I can see it, here in the cards.'

'I only agreed to this to be sociable. I don't want to *talk* about it or *think* about it any more. So if you don't mind I'm going to sleep.'

Bert turned over the last card. 'I'm sorry, friend, I can't stop a prediction once it's started. You can close your eyes if you wish, but I'm going to finish.'

George folded his arms and shuffled back against the wall.

Bert revelled in the little man's discomfort. The wind howled mercilessly outside as the rain beat against the path, and he knew George couldn't bring Tinker out in that. He carried on, ignoring the fact that George had closed his eyes. He didn't need him to be awake for the reading. Hell, now he had started he didn't need him there at all. But it was always more fun revealing the ugly truth with the participant present. Bert snickered to himself as he watched his past open up in front of him. Officer Knight would not have been so charitable had she known of his history. It was distasteful to say the least, and he did not need to repeat it aloud. Bert read out his future like he was reading out the news.

'You will return to your past by seeking out the highest point in Haven. From that point you will jump from the roof as an act of penance.'

George frowned as he opened his eyes. 'You've lost the plot, mister. I'd never leave me little Tinker to fend for himself.' He rolled the idea around in his head before commenting further. 'And I don't agree with suicide. Every day of life is a gift, and it's a slap in the face to your creator if you bail out without very good reason.' George gave an imperceivable nod as he agreed with himself. 'Lots of people are lonely. It's not a good reason.'

Bert regarded him comically. The reactions were always the same. They ask for the truth then get mad when it's delivered to them.

'I read what I see,' he said, picking up his cards and sliding them into his pocket.

'Well I wished I never asked now, you're after putting me in bad form.'

Bert smiled and handed him what was left in his mug. 'Here, I'm done with this. You want it?'

George nodded gratefully and outstretched his hand to grasp the neck of the bottle.

'I'll leave it with you. I'm heading off now, places to go, people to see.'

'You don't have to go, mister, I'm not vexed really. I can stay downstairs if you like.'

'No, it's not that, this was just a stopgap until the rain eased. I really do have somewhere to go.'

George raised the bottle, 'In that case, *sláinte*, and no hard feelings.'

Bert tipped his hat and gathered up his belongings. 'We'll meet again I'm sure.'

CHAPTER THIRTY-THREE

Jennifer could tell by the way her sergeant was drumming her pen on her table that Claire did not believe her in the slightest. She had meant to tell the truth but she was too embarrassed when under scrutiny, and the last thing she wanted was to be told off for taking stupid risks.

'Are you sure nothing else happened?' Claire asked, lifting the pen and clicking on the head in the most irritating fashion. The clicking seemed to permeate Jennifer's brain. If it weren't for the murder enquiry, she would have taken some time off work to clear her head.

'No, honestly,' Jennifer said in her most convincing voice. 'It was a stupid accident. I don't know what I was thinking, going snooping in the woods when it was so muddy.'

'Perhaps if you wore some suitable footwear?' Claire said, pointing at her heels. 'Although they've certainly reduced in height. Seeing someone new?'

Jennifer spluttered on her coffee. 'How do you relate my heels to being in a relationship?'

Claire stopped clicking her pen and rested it on the table. 'Experience. My first husband wasn't much taller than me. He hated being overshadowed. The day after he left, I went out and bought a five-inch pair of red killer heels. They're still in the back of my wardrobe somewhere.'

Jennifer crossed her legs. She had worn her navy kitten heels because they matched her pinstripe trouser suit. Skirts were off for the next few days, at least until the bramble scratches faded from her legs. 'I'm afraid you're off kilter on this one. I'm just being kinder to my feet.'

'Of course, because you'd be the first person to fill me in, wouldn't you? Remember, I have no life, I have to get my kicks through you.'

You wouldn't want to live through me, Jennifer thought, before giving her sergeant a half smile and rising from her chair.

She jiggled her mouse as she powered up her computer. The Rivers mental health institution had finally sent her a picture of Bert Bishop. She clicked the link and gasped as the face of a bristly faced old man stared back at her. His wiry grey eyebrows jutted out over black beady eyes in an intense gaze. The pouches under his eyes combined with the weather-beaten face fitted the witness descriptions exactly. Jennifer put her hand to her cheek, recalling the contours of his bristled jawline when she made contact. There was no doubt about it. This was the face of the killer.

She chewed the lipstick from her bottom lip as she clicked on the confidential report accompanying the email. Her eyes greedily scanned the computer screen as it flickered into life. Bert had been assessed several times for making continuous calls to Christian Bowes. The source of the phone was unknown, although, like prisons, patients were known to smuggle items through visitors and use them as currency. Jennifer flipped open her journal, scribbling times, dates and the name of the doctor listed. A dart of pain from her bandaged hand reminded her of the urgency of the enquiry. Dr Lionel Carter. After further digging, she found his number and punched it into her phone.

'Hey you,' Will said, dropping a thick file onto his newly cleaned desk.

Jennifer swivelled her chair to greet him, opening her top drawer and rolling a Cadbury's Creme Egg across the desk. 'Here you go. I've cleaned your desk and given you chocolate, what more could a bloke want?'

The look in Will's eyes relayed he could come up with several suggestions. 'How are you feeling?' he said, pushing aside the paperwork to unwrap the chocolate egg.

'Fine. My hand's a little stiff and I can't do much typing but it's better than it was.'

Will frowned, but Jennifer had already told him what to do with his suggestion that she should be at home resting.

'You'll never guess what I've found out about Claire,' Will said, keeping his voice low.

'As long as it's not gossip,' Jennifer said. 'I like Claire, and she's had enough mud slung in her direction over the years.'

Will looked affronted. 'What do you take me for? It's about her abilities. Haven't you ever wondered what they are?'

Jennifer wondered all the time, but Claire didn't seem comfortable talking about it so she figured she'd find out for herself. This seemed as good a time as any.

'Go on then, what is it?'

'Zoe said she can read auras, you know, the coloured energies people have around them. They change according to your moods. She can even tell if you're lying. I wish someone had warned me, I'll be on my guard from now on.'

Jennifer clasped her hand to her mouth, her earlier chat with her sergeant coming back to haunt her. 'You're joking me.'

'Afraid not,' Will said. As he chatted animatedly about his discussion with Zoe, two things crossed Jennifer's mind. One was that she could understand why Claire would be cagey. Everybody lied, and people were bound to treat her differently once they knew. The second thing Jennifer noticed was how quickly Will accepted Zoe's explanation. There was no mention of rational thought or not getting carried away; Zoe's word was taken as fact.

'Are you all right? You're looking very miffed,' Will said, throwing his chocolate wrapper into the bin.

Jennifer reddened, relieved that Will couldn't read her thoughts. 'Huh? Um no ... I just need to have a chat with Claire. I wasn't entirely truthful this morning and I think it's time I came clean.'

'Sounds ominous,' Will said. 'Nothing bad, I hope?'

'I've had a breakthrough with the Raven case. Zoe and I have accessed the Facebook group Emily Clarke was using before her death.'

Claire did not look surprised to see Jennifer return to her door. Jennifer began with an apology, followed by admissions of what happened in the woods, her relationship with Will, and her progress on the Raven.

'I take it someone has told you, then,' Claire said, folding her arms.

Jennifer opened her mouth to speak then paused, measuring her words. 'It just came up in conversation. Apparently you know when people are lying.'

Claire smiled. 'That's one way of putting it. I'm an empath. I can read people's energies, see their auras, and take on other people's emotions. Sometimes I can determine if they're telling the truth or not. Just like with you earlier today. I knew you were hiding something, but I trusted it was for a good reason, and if it were important, you'd tell me. Everyone is entitled to their privacy, Jennifer, and as thrilled as I am that you've got it together with Will, who you see in your own time is none of my business.'

Jennifer nodded, keen to change the subject. 'I take it your abilities don't stand up in court.'

'No. Think of it as a copper's intuition. Evidentially you can't use it, but it can point us in the right direction.'

'It's a cool trait. Remind me to bring you into interview.'

Claire smirked. 'It's not foolproof, so I don't rely on it too heavily. I mean, it's not like a lie detector test. But let's put all that aside for now, I'm more concerned about your investigation. It's time we called the DI in here, and work out a plan of action for the Raven.'

Claire was impressed to see Jennifer had made good headway into the investigation, having arranged an informal appointment with Bert's psychiatrist the next day. Ethan, her DI, had taken the decision to bring Lexton MIT fully up to date on their investigation. Although unhappy at being kept in the dark, progression of an undercover officer in the Facebook group was welcomed, and Zoe's activity was being closely monitored.

Officers would be briefed and kept on standby for any forthcoming raids, and although Ethan had given her a telling-off for withholding information, Jennifer felt she was finally making some progress in the investigation. She was painfully aware of the lack of physical forensic evidence, but she was closing in on the killer, and if anyone could help her, his psychiatrist could.

An evening call from her sister was the last thing she expected, and Jennifer cradled the phone as she whipped together some eggs.

'Hi, how are you?' Amy asked.

Jennifer gave a wry smile. She always recognised when her sister's calls were leading up to something. 'Fine, just making an omelette for supper. Is everything OK?'

'Mmm? Oh yeah, fine ... Josh stop that ... no, Lily isn't allowed Lego ...'

Jennifer diced a spring onion and plopped it into the egg mix, imagining her nephew presenting his little sister with his latest Lego creation.

'Sorry,' Amy said, 'I was wondering if you'd be free to babysit Josh and Lily some night? Just for a couple of hours. I haven't been out with David for ages, thought it would do us good.'

Jennifer stood open-mouthed as thin blue smoke began to rise from the frying pan. Amy rarely asked her to babysit Josh, and always brought Lily with her.

'Yeah, sure, I'd love to ... oh crap, hang on, my pan is burning.' She turned off the pan and pushed it to the side. A thought occurred to her. Jennifer wondered if the offer was a thinly veiled peace offering. Amy was the only person she knew who looked upon the offer of babysitting as a treat. 'So how did it go? With dad, I mean. It's OK to talk about him, I won't snap your head off, I promise.'

'It was all right,' Amy said flatly.

'Just all right?' Jennifer said, trying to remember that she wasn't supposed to have seen him. 'Is he still off the booze?'

'Oh yeah, he's been off it for some time now. He goes to AA, or so he tells me. He's got a girlfriend, she's American.'

Jennifer pretended to sound surprised. 'Really? I take it she's an improvement on mad Peggy from Hackney then?'

Amy snorted. 'Anything's an improvement on that silly woman. Dominique, this one's called, very glam. She was his hypnotherapist.'

Silence passed and Jennifer gave in to her curiosity. 'Dad has a therapist? Go on then, spill the beans.'

Amy whispered conspiratorially down the mouthpiece of the phone. 'She's very wealthy. I liked her at first but now …' A door closed in the background and Amy's voice drew closer to the phone. '… She's a bit pushy, and she doesn't like kids.'

Jennifer smiled. Not liking children was a hanging offence in her sister's eyes.

'And dad's no better, he didn't even bring them a bag of sweets! And I know I'm always telling you off for buying chocolate but they could have brought Josh something, the tight gits.'

'Mmm,' Jennifer said, not entirely surprised. Their father had never even sent her a birthday card.

'And that's not all. I went to a real effort, baking a Victoria sponge and those nice little jam tarts that you like.'

Jennifer's mouth watered at the prospect. Her sister was the best cook she knew.

'David took the kids into the sitting room and I brought dad and Dominique into the kitchen for a chat. She started looking around the place saying how quaint everything was. Quaint. I'll give her blooming quaint …'

Jennifer giggled into her hand, reluctant to interrupt her sister's flow.

'So I gave them tea and cake using my best china, and … well, you'd think I'd given her poison. She started going on about how bad carbs were for you, and wouldn't allow dad to have any either. Then it just went from bad to worse.'

'Worse? How could it get any worse?' Jennifer said, abandoning her unmade omelette as she pulled out a chair to sit down.

'She started saying that dad had to sort out his *issues* before he could move forward, and it wasn't long before I realised that we were the *issues* she was talking about.'

'Bloody cheek. What did he say?'

'He couldn't get a word in. Then she said that in order for him come to terms with things, we would have to set up a family meeting so we could all move forward. I said "What things?" and she said – wait 'til you hear this – she said that when dad was regressed, he said *you* set fire to the boathouse on purpose. Have you ever heard anything so stupid?'

Jennifer held her breath, relieved her sister could not see the look on her face. A sick feeling of dread erupted in the pit of her stomach, the words filling her with shame.

'Hello? Are you there?' Amy said.

'Yeah, sorry, I'm just … astounded.'

'That's how I felt … for about two seconds. Then I told her that when we were living in the boathouse, dad was pissed most of the time, and then I told her that her theory was thoughtless and cruel. I've looked it up, she's filling his head with false memories through her hypnotherapy sessions.'

'Yeah … that's what it is.' Jennifer's hand caressed her throat as a red flush spread from her collarbone to her jawline.

'That's when I threw them out.'

Jennifer would have laughed if she were not feeling weak at the revelation. 'You didn't, did you?'

'Well, I politely asked them to leave. Dad was full of apologies but she wasn't. I don't think she liked me calling her a quack.'

This time Jennifer did laugh. 'Oh dear. She didn't do a very good job at impressing you, did she?'

'Honestly, I don't think she could have insulted me any more if she tried. First my kids, then my house, my baking, and finally you! Who does she think she is? Snooty cow.'

'So what now?'

'I've told dad we're not here to make him feel better about himself. If he just wants to rake over the past, I'm not interested. He's said he's sorry, but we'll see where it goes.'

Jennifer was not sorry things had worked out the way they did. At least now, Amy was back on her side. The comment about the fire made her feel sick to her stomach. The last thing she needed was being confronted about the past. Her sister's loyalty had proved itself to be fickle, and if the truth came out, Amy would never forgive her. Jennifer emptied the contents of the pan in the bin, having lost her appetite. Much of her life was spent raking over the bones of her past, and she wished she could wipe the slate clean. She shook her head at the irony. She was hunting down a group whose aim was the exact same thing.

She recalled how Zoe mocked her for being so straight-laced. If only she knew. The boathouse ... it was so long ago, but the memory was easily recalled, bringing with it a fresh dose of pain. That awful night, when her father came home drunk, calling her dead mother's name. His breath, soured from beer and cigarettes, was heavy on her face as he climbed into bed, clawing at her nightdress. She wriggled free that night, and he always acted as if he didn't remember a thing. But Jennifer knew. If he didn't take her innocence then one of his scummy friends would. She hoped the memory resurfaced in his regression sessions. She'd like to see how his girlfriend would cope with that little nugget of information. But as bad as he was, her father was right. She *had* set fire to the boathouse. Had she really wanted to kill him as she placed the candles under the curtains where he slept? Hatred had consumed her for the man that was meant to be her protector. It was him or them. She had to protect her sister. Or was that too easy an explanation for a woman who couldn't face her past? Jennifer rubbed her eyes, trying to push the memories back into their box. She couldn't face them. Not now. She would rather spend the rest of her days risking her life protecting others, than face her own fraught past.

CHAPTER THIRTY-FOUR
Bert

The cards were just tools, an extension of the woodlands in which they were hidden. Bert knew his mother would see sense and demand he return the gifts she lavished upon him, but he had hidden the cards far from her reach in the woodland soil.

That night his path was well lit, as he visited his haunt in the forest. The air felt different somehow, and the raven flew with a sense of purpose overhead. Swooping and cawing, it led him to the tall tree that was so alive he could almost feel it breathe. Bert sat at the mossy base, closing his eyes as he inhaled the dead leaf smell. Digging his fingers into the dirt, he enjoyed the tickle of creatures as they slithered through his fingers. Bert sat back on his knees, pulling handfuls of warm moist soil as he dug deeper.. He cleared the soil away from his special hiding place, squinting to see the small tin box nestled underneath the thick root, which had grown protectively over it. Nine months had passed since he had been given the cards, and he grunted as he pulled the small narrow tin box from its hiding place. The lid refused to give and he jammed his stubby dirt-lined nails under the tightly sealed lip. He had bided his time as they absorbed the energies of the land. His tongue poked out the corner of his mouth and he tugged until the lid popped off with a whoosh. Wiping his dirty hands on the back of his clothes, he tipped the contents of the box onto his hands. Now tantalisingly musty and discoloured, the pictures were printed in intricate patterns and colours, emitting an energy all of their own. Like everything in the forest they had a quality that would be negative to others, but felt like home to him.

As dawn streaked through the sky in purple and pink hues, he entered his window as quickly as his muscles would allow. Bert held the cards under his nose, breathing in the sour odour. It was beautiful in comparison to the smell of bleach that permeated the house. The cards felt alive as he laid them on his bed, and each one told a story. They had lain in the ground for a long time, and returned to hands that would make good use of them. Bert did not need instructions, and in the quietness of his room when everyone was asleep, he laid the cards out again and again until he understood their meanings. They worked with him as he flicked them over, getting to grips with each image. Their hypnotic quality made him lose hours of the night under their spell. Once mastered, Bert began to resume a normal sleeping pattern. He was keen to get out in the world to put them to good use. The fact the raven chose him simply reinforced the knowledge that they were interlinked with the forest. His research on ravens in the old school library told him they were highly intelligent, associated with witchcraft and powers of divination. Bert smiled. He was strong and he was not alone. And with the cards giving him the power of prophecy, he was Raven.

CHAPTER THIRTY-FIVE

Dr Carter's telephone voice made him sound like a giant, but in the flesh, he was shorter than Jennifer in his wrinkled off-white suit. His vice-like handshake left Jennifer in no doubt that what he lacked in height he made up for in strength of character.

His office was exactly how she imagined it to be. A spacious but cosy grandfatherly room, with a hint of cigar smoke, featuring wood-panelled walls and a well-stocked bookshelf. The wall facing the street had two windows, and crooked venetian blinds filtered the afternoon light. Jennifer itched to straighten them until they were both the same level.

Dr Carter gestured towards the buttoned leather chair. 'Please, have a seat.' He paused, his eyes returning to the windows. 'Would you like me to lower the other blind and switch on the lamp?'

'No, that's fine, thank you.' Jennifer tried to contain her smile. Only a doctor dealing in the complexities of the human mind would notice her discomfort and understand the reasons behind it. She wondered if it was some kind of test, or if the pleasant pink-faced man was just good at his job.

Dr Carter sat back in his leather chair, his cheerful face a direct contrast to the oil painting of men in battle, which was hung on the wall overhead. He reminded Jennifer of Colonel Sanders with his pointed white beard and thatch of grey hair, and she developed a sudden craving for KFC. She brought her mind back to the task in hand, and hoped to commit his every word to memory.

'Thank you for seeing me at such short notice,' she said, sitting on the edge of the leather sofa.

'I was happy to do so. Do you understand what I meant on the phone when I said I was grateful for the opportunity to repay a debt?'

Jennifer nodded. 'You mentioned my mother helped your family in the past.'

He steepled his fingers together, paling his lips as he pressed them against his teeth 'That, my dear, is an understatement.' Dr Carter reached for a framed photo on his desk and turned it to face her. A young blonde woman sat in her graduation cap and gown, clutching a ribboned certificate. She had the same small stature as Dr Carter, and her features encompassed the same determined expression.

'This is Amelia. My wife and I had almost given up when God blessed us with her.' Dr Carter's face clouded over as he stared at the photo, drifting back to another time. 'She was six years old when she disappeared. We thought she had been kidnapped while she played in the garden. My wife and I ... we were hysterical. Your mother arrived at our door, and the warmth and respect she conveyed is something I will always remember. She arranged for a team of officers to search the streets and beyond, but she felt drawn to our back garden. She couldn't explain it but she seemed to know that Amelia had not gone far. She squeezed through a gap in the fence to next door, and found a disused shed at the bottom of their garden. She found Amelia in an old chest freezer. She must have gone exploring and gotten trapped inside. She was blue and limp when your mother pulled her out. Elizabeth resuscitated her until the ambulance came. She could have died.' Dr Carter paused, as if to give the memory respect.

'My wife and I were very upset when we read of Elizabeth's passing, and I was always left with a sense of regret that I didn't thank her properly.'

'I'm sure my mother received enough reward in finding your daughter. But having said that, I'm very grateful for any information you can give me on Bertram Bishop.'

Dr Carter made the transition from father to professional as he straightened in his chair. 'I'm sure I don't need to tell you that until you process the correct documentation this remains between us.'

'That goes without saying. I'm nothing if not professional,' Jennifer said, unable to prevent her eyes flicking back to the blinds. They really were getting on her nerves.

'Bit too bright in here, don't you think?' Dr Carter said as he got up and walked to the half-drawn blind, releasing it to the bottom of the ledge. Switching on the lamp, he returned to his chair. 'So tell me, what are your concerns about Mr Bishop?'

Jennifer warmed to Dr Carter even more. 'I don't know if you've seen the newspapers, but we believe there may be a connection between Bertram and some recent deaths in the area. His whereabouts are unknown and frankly I'm at a loss as to what I'm dealing with, given his lack of history with the police.'

'And forensically? Sorry, I fancy myself as a bit of an armchair detective,' Dr Carter said.

Jennifer sighed. This wasn't meant to be a two-way exchange, but she would have to give something if she wanted to gain his trust.

'I can't really say. But it's only a matter of time until he slips up, and when he does I want to be ready for him.'

Dr Carter nodded as if to say he could read between the lines. The evidence was thin, and made his disclosure all the

more important. He took a deep breath and his voice slowed, as
if the words weighed heavy on his tongue.

'Where to start? Bert is a fascinating character, but highly
delusional. My colleagues believe his problems stem from the
death of his twin brother, but I think it goes back much further
than that.'

'How did his twin die?' Jennifer asked.

'A tragic accident. Bert and his brother … what was his name
now…?' Dr Carter took a manila folder from his desk drawer
and flicked through the paperwork. 'Here it is … Callum. They
were climbing a tree when Callum fell to his death. Unfortunately, Bert's mother spent the rest of her life blaming him.
Given what Bert has told me about her, it would seem she had
several undiagnosed mental health issues herself, anxiety, pos-
sibly Munchausen's … she was not a well woman.'

'The apple doesn't fall far from the tree.' Jennifer shrugged at
the doctor's raised brow. 'Armchair psychiatrist.'

Dr Carter's mouth twinged upwards in a smile. 'Quite.'

'Bert seems to have an affinity for ravens, can you tell me
anything about that?'

'Bert compensated for his parents' apathy by inventing a personal guardian in the form of a raven. It helped him when he
was growing up to feel there was someone out there, guiding
him. The meaning of his name hasn't helped. It has only enforced his conviction further.'

'His name? It's Bert Bishop, isn't it?'

'Yes it is, but the actual meaning of Bertram is raven. In contrast, his brother's name Callum meant dove. He once told me
his mother was surprised to hear the meanings, but I believe it
was just another way to enforce her favouritism. That woman
had a lot to answer for.'

Jennifer held back a gasp as the memory of the white bird in the forest returned. Was it the spirit of Callum coming back to save her? She rubbed her hand, tracing her finger over the scar that remained. Her eyes returned to the doctor. 'Has anyone traced the history of the land?'

He shook his head. 'Much like the police, we deal in fact. To encourage the delusions would only exacerbate his condition. My role was to assist him in coping with life in the *real* world.'

Just because it's *your* world doesn't make it the *real* world, Jennifer thought. She would have enjoyed debating the subject, but time was precious.

'True,' she said, 'but we always ensure we have the whole picture when dealing with something as serious as this. His mother is dead, isn't she? How did she die?'

Dr Carter flicked through the paperwork before pushing it back into the folder and returning it to his drawer. 'A heart attack,' he said, discreetly casting a glance over the clock on the wall.

Jennifer itched to take a copy of the folder, but their conversation would have to suffice until the official channels were adhered to.

Dr Carter clasped his fingers together and leaned over his desk. 'Mr Bishop was fit and well when he left us. People with mental health issues are often subject to discrimination. I'd hate for him to be treated in a way that would result in him spending the remainder of his days in an institution. The most important thing for him is to keep his life normal.'

'The problem is that he's been giving readings, and certain recipients have died. I believe he's responsible for their murders.'

'Well, DC Knight, I wouldn't tell you how to do your job no more than I would accept you telling me how to do mine. I'm afraid I'm going to leave the investigation in your hands. If you do arrest Bert I would be very grateful if you could make me aware.' Dr Carter slid a packet from his breast pocket and pulled out a thick cigar.

Jennifer sensed the doctor's impatience, but there was so much she needed to know. 'Do you know anything about his nephew, Christian Bowes? He's reported Bert for harassing him.'

'You know as much as I do when it comes to Mr Bowes. But I will ask you one thing. If Bert *has* relapsed, he may be confused and disorientated. He might have no recollection of his treatment, or indeed may be living in a completely different time. Mr Bowes may be his link to the past. If he turns up and Mr Bowes antagonises him ...' Dr Carter shook his head. 'Let's just say it's important Bert's returned to our care so we can offer him the help he needs.'

Jennifer nodded, finding it hard to muster sympathy for a man who had left a child motherless and a fiancé without a wife. 'Thank you, I appreciate your time.'

Dr Carter stood and extended his hand. 'And I appreciate the opportunity to pay back an overdue debt. If it weren't for your mother, my daughter wouldn't be alive today.'

Jennifer shook his hand, hoping to tease out one last nugget of information. 'So I take it that you're telling me Bert's not capable of murder.'

'Ah.' The doctor wagged his finger in the air. 'I didn't say that. I have no doubt he is capable of violence while in a delusional state. When in this state, with the validation of others, he could prove to be very dangerous indeed.'

CHAPTER THIRTY-SIX

It should have felt strange, sharing her bed with a man after being on her own for so long. Jennifer breathed in the scent of Will's pillow as she curled her legs around the warmth of his body. She had forgotten just how much she missed him, and Will's soft snores were a welcome distraction from the sounds of the branches tapping on her window in the night. As dawn broke through and filtered soft morning light into her bedroom, she wished that she could bask in the warmth emanating from his body, instead of having to face the prospect of a killer loose on the streets of Haven. The haunting figure of Emily's child replayed in her mind, lost and alone in the house with little food or water. Who would be next? She smoothed over her duvet, eyeing her clothes on the ground. She fought the sudden need to hang them in the wardrobe. Her relationship with Will would not be smooth sailing, she knew that. There would be times when she needed to be alone, and she couldn't foresee a time when they could ever live together. Will's messiness would get on her nerves, and he would resent having to constantly clean, once the first flush of their relationship had mellowed. They were the classic odd couple, but that was all right with her. Will stirred and Jennifer edged over to her side of the bed, wanting to be showered before he woke. She rubbed the sleep from her eyes and slid out from between the sheets.

'Where do you think you're going?' Will murmured, his muscles rippling as he stretched.

'Shower, then I'm going to make you breakfast. Is that to your satisfaction, Mr Dunston?'

'Come back to bed first. I've got something for you,' Will said sleepily.

'Not until I've brushed my teeth,' Jennifer said, pulling on a t-shirt. But Will was too quick, and in one steady movement he had her pinned on the bed.

'My mum's been asking about you,' he murmured, brushing aside her hair as he kissed her collarbone.

Jennifer wriggled under his grasp. 'I know you're an expert in pulling women, but talking about your mother in bed is not what I'd call a turn-on.'

Will paused long enough for her to slide free from his grasp. 'No, I don't suppose it is. Wouldn't you like to meet her?'

Jennifer's voice trailed behind her as she walked to the en suite. 'Early days, love. Early days.'

Jennifer relished the hot spikes of water cascading from her chrome showerhead, and used the time to organise her thoughts. Will had recently come out of a difficult marriage, and the last thing she wanted was to be his rebound lover. But recent events had shown her just how much he cared, and it was pointless spending any more time fretting about if it would work out between them or not. She had far bigger concerns. The extractor fan rattled as it tried to keep up with the level of steam in the bathroom. Will had described her shower as boiling hot needles of hell, preferring his own gentle showerhead attached to the wall over his bath. She squeezed out the shampoo and lathered it into her hair. Some people sang in the shower. She used the time to mull over her latest cases. It was surprising what came to you when you were hidden away, devoid of distractions of the outside world.

Her thoughts returned to Alan Price, Felicity Baron, and Emily Clarke. Alan's death seemed to involve minimal effort, and Felicity's death involved tinkering with her car. However, no effort was made to pass Emily Clarke's death off as an unfortunate accident. It was violent and brutal, and that's what worried her most. The Raven was gaining in confidence, each kill more daring than the one before. He was building up to something, his escape from the law strengthening his resolve. Her thoughts drifted to a serial rapist she had investigated in her old station. He started off small, speaking to random women to ask them the time, then moving on to handbag snatches down lonely paths. Once he had gotten away with that, he escalated to snatching the bag and giving the victim a push as he did so. The pushes became more violent and turned into punches. Yet he remained elusive to the police, varying his routes, changing his appearance, but all the while growing in confidence until he carried out first one rape, then two. It would have ended in murder had she not brought him to justice. To Jennifer, the Raven was just the same. He was testing the waters. He was testing her.

She turned off the tap and squeezed the excess water from her hair. Blotting her face against a towel, she tried to envisage what was coming next. Was it possible to escalate from murder? If he was willing to kill in a house with a child, just what was he capable of? But there was still a chink of humanity present, as he had locked the bedroom door to stop the boy witnessing the horror. Phone records had shown Emily's telephone was cut off the day before for non-payment. What if the killer hadn't known that? What if he'd dialled for help before he left? Perhaps he seen the state of the place and thought the boy was better off without her. There was no doubt in her mind that Emily had been involved in The Reborners group. Was the Raven picking them off because they didn't deserve a second chance? Did he think the same about her?

Jennifer patted her skin dry before winding the towel around her body and picking up her toothbrush. She wanted to grasp for hope anywhere she could find it. If there was some semblance of empathy in the killer then perhaps the answer lay in his past. There was just one person who could help her with that. She would need to visit Christian Bowes.

CHAPTER THIRTY-SEVEN
Bert

At thirteen, Bert looked forward to the day he could leave school. The kudos of being Callum's brother had long since worn off, and Bert could not wait until he was old enough to make his way in the world. His Saturday job in the mail sorting office was given to him as a tribute to his father, whose sudden passing fell like an axe onto their home. Callum's school friends had forgotten him, and to them, Bert was just plain creepy. It was a comment by Lucy Grimshaw that sparked him off.

Cycling beside him, she asked who he was going to dress up as for Halloween. Her two companions flanking her on either side emitted a chorus of shrill giggles.

Bert felt a blush rise to his pale cheekbones as she slowed her bike to a crawl, balancing the quivering handlebars to meet his steady gait. He thought it was cute, how she could cycle so slowly without having to put her feet to the ground. Bert was trying to think of an impressive reply when she broke into his thoughts, giggling between chews of gum.

'Only I was thinking we could go to the Halloween disco together.'

Bertram's heart gave a little flutter in his chest. It was such an alien feeling he gave a little gasp to accommodate it.

Lucy smiled. 'I'm gonna be the bride of Frankenstein ...'

She squeezed her brakes as his bike shot ahead, and steadied it before turning her sky blue eyes back on his face. 'Wanna know what the best part about it would be?'

Bert cleared his throat with a small cough, digging his hands into his pockets as a shy smile crossed his face. 'What?'

'You wouldn't even need an outfit!' An explosion of laughter followed the punchline as the girls leaned forward on their bikes and cycled down the road. 'So long, loser!' Lucy shouted, blonde ponytail bobbing, oblivious to the devastation in her wake.

It wouldn't have mattered if he hadn't liked her. He'd mistaken her glances for interest, when it was just morbid curiosity.

Bert clenched his fists as he gulped back the hot tears that threatened to flow. Walking home with his head bowed, his insides began to boil with indignation. A bird cawed in the distance. He felt a fluttering sensation, a stretching of wings, and steel grey eyes snapping open. The tarot cards. That night as he laid the cards on his bed, they produced a welcome image. It was like watching a television programme as Bert envisaged Lucy being knocked off her bike in front of an oncoming car. His breath quickened as the scene unravelled before him; Lucy, no longer mocking but a broken mess of matted hair. Rivulets of her blood decorating the black asphalt in his wake. Such thoughts both frightened and excited him. It was then that the raven within came into its own.

Bert jerked his rucksack forward as he walked home. Today was the day he had planned to carry out Lucy's prediction, but second thoughts had plunged the heat of his anger into ice, and turning his back on his school he cast his head down as he pushed his thumbs under the straps biting into his shoulders. The rucksack felt ten times heavier, as if large claws were yanking it backwards with each step he took. The more he hurried, the more he could feel the breath of his nightmares tickle the back of his neck. Yes, he wanted revenge on Lucy, but killing her?

Another jerk of his rucksack gained his attention and Bert pulled it back, spitting the words. 'I'm not killing anyone, now leave me alone!'

The reply was so low it was not audible, but he felt it just the same. 'You didn't mind killing Callum.'

The mention of his brother's name sent a chill down his spine. 'What? No … I didn't.'

The voice from within sneered. 'Want to hear what he has to say about it? I come from death, I can bring him to you.'

Bert sucked in great mouthfuls of air as he turned down their laneway and caught sight of home. He tried to tell himself the voice was inside his head. It couldn't hurt him if it was part of him, could it? His panic was coming in waves now, surging, and then ebbing just enough to allow him to suck in air before he was engulfed in the terror again. The thoughts of hearing Callum's voice were more than he could bear. He threw his rucksack on the porch and ran to his room.

He tried to broach the subject as mother treated his eczema, which had flared into angry red welts on his skin. The house was eerily quiet as he sat at the table, the only sound the ticking of the clock and the wind howling outside. He wished he had a television like other families. Books were fine, but they could not silence the voices intruding in his thoughts. Bert took a deep breath and blurted out what was troubling him.

'Mum, sometimes I hear voices telling me to do things.'

'It's just your imagination,' she said, as she slathered the cream up his arms.

'But sometimes it tells me to do things I don't wanna do,' Bert said, shivering in his vest.

His mother laughed, but her face was cold and hard. 'Poor Bert, you're so afraid of life. Not like Callum. He wasn't afraid of anything.'

Bert was taken back by his mother's intense stare. She rarely mentioned Callum any more.

Her desperate eyes stared into his, trying to see any trace of the boy she missed so much. Her grip sent sharp painful darts into his broken skin.

'You're hurting me,' Bert said, pulling back his arm with a gasp.

Mother lowered her eyes and handed him the roll of bandages. 'You're old enough to do this yourself now. You don't need me any more.'

Something shifted that night as Bert felt his passenger grow form. It wrestled with his inner conscience, the one that told him killing was bad. The raven reminded him he was summoned as his protector, and he could not lie dormant forever. Bert knew deep down it was what he wanted, and that night as he stared at the bare branches of the oak tree, a frost crept through his soul.

On Thursday evenings, Lucy Grimshaw went to book club after school and cycled home alone. Bert was waiting. The timing would have to be right, but the cards had guided him and wouldn't let him down. Bert hid in the bushes as her bicycle approached. Pulling the black balaclava over his head, he was grateful for the winter nights, which were drawing in. The noise of the lorries drowned out his heavy breathing as adrenalin coursed through his body. Perhaps she would just fall off and scuff her knees, he thought, picking up the pole, his heart hammering a warm beat in his chest. He crouched down into position. The plan was to ram the pole into the tyre of her bike and run like hell. Bert tried to ignore the steady stream of cars, and to stem that nagging feeling that being upended off your bike in heavy traffic seemed an excessive punishment for being a tease. But it wasn't just that. Bertram's eczema had become unbearable, and school was only going to get worse. Carrying out the raven's wishes may stem the voice hungry for blood. The doctor had told them his skin condition was stress related, and to Bert, his annoyance over Lucy was never going to dissipate unless he did something about it. Besides, a prediction had been made, and blood would be shed one way or another. A single bicycle headlight glared in the distance, flickering on, off, on, off in time with the dynamo that powered it. Oh shit and fuck, Bert thought, as a lorry came rumbling up behind her, trying to overtake but was hemmed in by the cars passing the other side. Bert prayed his black clothes would protect him from onlookers.

'Just be quick, a quick jab is all it needs, then take the pole and run,' the voice said, bubbling within him. Bert's heart pounded at twice its normal speed.

There was no time to dwell as the bicycle drew near. This stretch of the road was downhill and Lucy was travelling at speed. She was near enough now for him to hear her humming a tune. Bert tried to make it out. If someone was going to die, then the last song they sung should at least be noted. But it was too late for all that now. Rain began to pelt from the skies, and Bert thanked the skies for the blessing of what would cloak him into further obscurity. The voice whispered, reminding him of how he felt the day Lucy humiliated him in front of everyone. 'Are you going to let people walk over you all your life, Bert? It's time to be a man, take control. She won't disrespect you a second time.' His heart thundering in his ears, Bert jumped from the bushes. Lucy was so busy concentrating on the lorry beside her that she didn't see the pole catch the spokes of the front wheel of her bike. The motion jerked Bert forward, his arms rattling in their sockets. Clamping his hands on the rain-greased pole, he jerked it back, falling on his bottom onto the edge of the path. Lucy didn't have time to scream as the front wheel jammed, making the rear wheel of her bike come up. Dismounting its passenger, it threw her into the path of the impatient lorry driver. A horn shrilled and a ker-thunk noise followed as the brakes shrieked, too late for Lucy. Car brakes screeched amidst grinding metal. By the time the drivers got out of their vehicles, Bert was long gone, gasping for breath, snivelling and laughing at the same time and not understanding why.

When he got home and discarded his clothes he felt like he had been through an initiation of sorts. The voice, now satisfied, whispered in its slumber. 'You're a man now, Bert. You did good.'

His hometown was shocked, as apart from the bad luck his own family generated, there was not much in the way of deaths in their area. Newspapers reported that it had been raining heavily, visibility was bad as darkness fell, and the young girl just came off her bike into the path of the lorry, who was driving way too close in his impatience to deliver his goods on time. His arrest was little comfort to her parents. The thrill Bert felt at reaching manhood outweighed any doubts in his mind. It was there in black and white, the lorry driver was to blame. By the end of the day, he had relinquished all feelings of guilt. Bert was becoming a master at reconstructing past events to suit himself. A sense of empowerment overcame him as he stretched to full height before the mirror. His eczema had virtually cleared overnight, and he felt like the old days, unencumbered by pain, grief, or feelings of worthlessness.

Each initiation was Bert's strongest memory. The first was his earliest recollection, the night he was summoned to the woods. The second was when he lay in the blood of his brother and created a raven onto the soil. The third and final was in his adolescence when he killed Lucy Grimshaw. That was all it took to make him what he was. Many people had crossed his path since then, and with the help of the cards many had come to regret it. He often wondered how he could remember parts of his life so clearly when others were so hazy. He sometimes dreamt of a clinical room, speaking in groups, watching a large-screened television from a paint-chipped wall. The dreams were so vivid he could recall many programmes in his mind when he heard the theme tunes but not how or where he had watched them. Small flashes seeped into his consciousness; nametags waving on clothing, swallowing multi-coloured capsules with thin plastic cups of water that quivered in his hand. But the memories were foggy and the darkness inside him worked hard to keep them repressed. Those memories served only to weaken him. He would have to remain strong for what lay ahead.

CHAPTER THIRTY-EIGHT

The tall electric gates parted to allow Jennifer and Will's un-marked Ford Focus inside. Will gave a low whistle as they drove past the beautifully manicured garden bordering the long gravel driveway to Christian Bowe's impressive six-bedroom home.

'We're in the wrong jobs,' Will said as the three-storey house came into view. The large bay windows and solar panels fed from the generous morning sunlight, which beamed down on the English country home. Expansive green fields flanked the gravel driveway, maintaining the privacy of the residents within.

Jennifer glanced up at the old fashioned street lamps that disguised the CCTV domes discreetly hidden within. Several burglar alarms flashed on the outside of the building and all exits appeared to be securely fenced. Christian certainly wasn't taking any chances with security. Their old Ford Focus appeared sorely out of place next to the red Jaguar as they parked in the driveway. Jennifer ran her fingertips over the shiny paintwork as she walked to the door, knowing it was the nearest she'd ever come to having one.

She was half expecting a butler to answer the glossy red wooden door, but instead she got Christian, red-eyed and gaunt, a sharp contrast to the publicity images splashed across the tabloid magazines.

'Oh Jenny it's awful, isn't it,' Christian said, before wrapping his arms around her and dropping his head into her shoulder.

Although taken aback by the sudden display of affection, she reciprocated by rubbing his back, allowing him time to catch his breath before breaking away.

'I'm sorry,' he said, 'I'm a mess, I know. I … I just don't know what to do with myself. Please, come inside.'

Jennifer ran her eyes over his baggy clothes. He had lost weight, and his shoulders appeared to have dropped a couple of inches since she had seen him last. His slow lifeless feet dragged across the oak floor as he led her through the double doors to the vast living room. Jennifer wondered if their visit would make things better or worse.

The delicate fragrance of white lilies greeted them as they entered the bright but stuffy room, and Jennifer's eyes danced over the overflowing vases decorating the window ledge and mahogany sideboards. Her eyes drifted to a portrait hanging over the wide traditional fireplace. Felicity Baron looked stunning in a full-length white gown, her face framed by her wavy blonde hair. Christian was standing behind her, one hand around her slender waist, the other holding her left hand, which was showing off an engagement ring the queen mother would have been proud of.

'Beautiful, wasn't she,' Christian said, his eyes misting over. 'It was taken at our engagement party last year.'

'I'm so very sorry,' Jennifer said, usually one to shy from such acts of grandeur. 'Thank you for seeing me, I understand your need for privacy at this time.'

Christian waved a hand over the leather sofa. 'I could do with a friendly face. At the moment, all I get are paparazzi calling me day and night. I didn't need friends when I had Felicity. But now …' The words caught in his throat and he gestured towards the sofa. 'Please, take a seat. I take it this is police business?'

Jennifer nodded solemnly. She glanced around the room as Will tinkered with framed photographs on the sideboard. 'Are the children about?'

Christian stared into space for several seconds before responding. 'The children? Oh ... they're with their mother. She's been cleared by the police, but I expect you know that.'

Jennifer undid her jacket. The room was stifling, and she wondered when was the last time he had opened a window. 'Yes I was aware. Right now we're looking into every aspect of Felicity's case. Part of the investigation involves interviewing family members.'

'I was recording a live television show when Felicity ...'

'I know that, Christian, and this isn't about you, so please don't worry. I want to ask you about your cousin, Bert.'

Christian's head snapped up, and he hastily daubed away the tears welling in his eyes. 'Bert? Do you finally believe me that he had something to do with this?'

Jennifer squared her shoulders. 'I'm afraid that's a very distinct possibility, and he may be involved in a lot more.'

Christian gasped, cupping a hand to his mouth. 'There was a murder on the news ... a young woman, found dead in her bed. Was that him?'

'I can't say either way,' Jennifer said, leaning her notebook on her crossed legs. 'That's why it's important that we know everything there is about his background. The police are doing everything they can to find him. Teams of officers are scouring local areas, dog handlers are searching the woodlands, and the police helicopter has made several trips overhead to search for his van.'

Christian blew his nose and replaced his sodden tissue with a fresh one from the box on the coffee table. 'Bert's spent half his life in and out of mental institutions. Why do they keep letting him out? Don't they ever learn?'

'We've got your earlier statement, but can you tell me a bit more about the last time you saw him?' Jennifer said, trying to obtain the information before he broke down. She felt like a vulture, feeding off him for answers when he was in so much pain. But that was often the way in the police. You saw people at their worst, and all you could do to help was apprehend the people responsible for their pain. Her eyes flicked to Will, who was now staring out the window. He was in his comfort zone when he was on foot chases, or struggling with suspects as he locked his cuffs in place. Grief unsettled him, and he was happy to leave such interviews to her.

Christian took a sip of water from a glass on the table and coughed to clear his throat. 'Bert used to visit our house when I was young. He made mum nervous, so she told him to stay away. Then when I was on TV, he managed to get a hold of my mobile number and began calling me night and day. He even got to a phone when he was in the institution. It carried on long after he left. That's when I reported him for harassment.'

'Why the fascination with you?'

Christian shrugged. 'He's plagued me half my life. Mother thinks I remind him of his brother, the one that died when he was a child. Can I get you a drink?'

Will opened his mouth to respond but Jennifer cut him off. 'No thanks. What sort of things would he say or do when he came to visit? Did he give any readings?'

'Readings? No. Sometimes he'd talk about his mother as if she was still alive.' Christian sighed, recalling the memory. 'When I was young, he'd ramble on about his blackbirds and how he used to save them from traps. Sometimes the farmers would hang out dead jackdaws on their land to keep the birds from their crops. I remember Bert telling me that once he was up all night cutting them down. He'd save a few of their feathers as keepsakes then bury their bodies in the woods. In the early days, he used to tell me his stories. He'd sit there, scratching his arms and legs until they bled. He had terrible eczema, but I was young and I felt sorry for him. To me, he was a fragile old man.'

'Did you ever speak to his mother?' Jennifer said, scribbling his answers in her pocket notebook.

'Aunty Grace? God no. After her husband died she isolated herself from the world, wouldn't even allow mother to visit. God only knows what used to go on in that big old house, with just the two of them rattling around up there. She was dead for weeks before anyone found her.'

'How did she die?' Jennifer said, nodding at Will to join her on the sofa.

'They said it was her heart but her body wasn't discovered for several weeks. Bert had left, and was sleeping rough in his father's old van. You don't think he had anything to do with it, do you? I mean, Bert was creepy, but this all still seems a bit beyond him.'

Jennifer was non-committal. 'I'm just trying to get a feel for what your cousin is like, and your relationship with him.'

'What should I do if he comes back?'

'You've got excellent security. Be alert, and carry your phone with you at all times. If you hear from him, call us straight away.'

Christian pulled a tissue from his pocket and blew his nose. He glanced up at the picture one more time before speaking. 'Felicity would hate to see me like this. She loved the kids, you know, she'd tell me to be strong for them.'

The mention of Felicity's name brought a fresh question to Jennifer's mind. 'Can I ask ... did Felicity ever mention a group called "The Reborners" to you?'

'No. What's that?'

'It's like a self-help group for people who want to forget their past and begin again. Does that sound like something she could have been interested in at some point in her life?' Jennifer would have liked to mention the Facebook group they discovered, but Zoe had given her strict instructions not to breathe a word. Besides, she had already seen Felicity's very public Facebook profile and she wasn't a member of any groups.

Christian shook his head. 'Felicity told me everything. She was a very happy young lady, and had no regrets in life.' He stared back up at the picture as fresh tears began to fall. 'Oh Fliss, why did you have to leave me?'

Jennifer gave him the only crumb of hope she could think of. 'Christian, you know better than anyone that there's life after death. You have to take comfort in that.'

'I know. But I want her here with me, now. I miss her so much.' Christian's face crumpled and he folded his arms tightly around his stomach, leaning forward in the chair.

Jennifer's eyes met Will's, and he mouthed the words 'Let's go'. She felt uncomfortable invading Christian's grief when it was still so raw, but she was a professional, and finding the person who tampered with Felicity's car would at least provide him with a grain of comfort. 'It's very early days. Give yourself time.'

Will interjected as he stood behind them. 'Have you spoken to any of Felicity's friends since the funeral?'

Christian stared at him, as if he had only just realised he was there. 'No. I know it sounds selfish but I just don't have time for anyone else's grief right now.'

Jennifer understood the sentiment, and it made her all the more determined to get her hands on the Raven before he could kill again.

CHAPTER THIRTY-NINE
Bert

Bert wrapped his fingers around the chipped mug, slowly drain-ing the scotch and allowing it to warm the pit of his stomach. Branches tapped the roof of the van like long bony fingertips, tap tap tapping into his psyche, the pitch-black night causing him to awake disorientated and confused. But camping out in the depths of the forest was better than going home to mother, or whatever was left of her. He imagined her still sitting in her rocking chair, just as she did when he was a boy. He tried to recall a time when he felt kindness. There had been a woman ... Bert gasped as the name came to him through the mists of his mind. Rosa. That was her name.

Bert had celebrated his fortieth birthday. Rosa was older than he was, but he liked the way she cared for him because she wasn't afraid to touch his red itchy skin. He wasn't at home, although it smelt like home – antiseptic and clinical. Memories of a hospital building ... sometimes he would sit with the others and watch television, his tartan slipper dangling off one foot as he bobbed his leg in time to the theme tune. Crime programmes were his favourite, although it was hard to hear them over the spasmodic moans and shouts in the background. Rosa always made sure he had a seat at the front, and extra biscuits with his tea. Sometimes she would stand behind him and watch too, her hand resting on the back of his neck. She stretched onto her toes and kissed him on the cheek once, when no-

*body was looking. She said that everybody deserved a kiss on their
birthday. Bert had never had a girlfriend before, and wondered
what it would have been like. Rosa was small and podgy, with big
bosoms that moved when she walked. He liked that.*

*The minute Rosa entered his room he noticed the unshed tears
in her eyes.*

'What's the matter?' Bert asked.

*'I need some guidance,' Rosa said. 'I think my husband is having
an affair. I don't know how much more I can take.'*

*'Why don't you talk to him?' Bert said. It seemed pretty straight-
forward to him.*

*'I can't,' she whispered. 'I need some advice about what to do
first. I've been left a big inheritance and he wants me to put it in
our joint account. I need to know if he's just staying with me for the
money.'*

*Bert shrugged. He was the last person to give advice on affairs of
the heart. 'I wish I could help you.'*

*Rosa sat beside him on the bed and grasped his hand. 'You can.
You know how we talked about your gift of divination? Well, my
grandmother didn't just give me money … she left me these. They've
been in our family for years.'*

*Rosa undid the first two buttons of her tunic and plunged her
hand down her top.*

*Bert's eyes were drawn to the pinkness of her cleavage, hemmed
in by the taut white bra. He felt himself redden as she caught his
stare.*

*Rosa hunched her shoulders, screwing up her nose in mouse-like
fashion as she squeaked a giggle. 'Oops, sorry. This was the only
place I could think of hiding these.' She pressed the warm deck of
cards into his hands then quickly buttoned up her top. 'Don't let
anyone see them, will you? I'll be back tonight for my reading.' Rosa
straightened up her tunic and patted her hair before planting a kiss*

on his cheek. 'I know you won't let me down,' she whispered, leaving him heady in the wake of her perfume, and hotly aroused.

Shift changeover was a good time to meet as the staff had a half-hourly meeting to discuss events of the evening before going home. Rosa slid into the darkness of Bert's room, clicking on the side lamp as she pulled up a chair next to his bed. It was after nine pm and most of the patients were drugged and asleep. Bert had decided to forgo his medication to see Rosa, hoping if he played coy she would give him more than a peck on the cheek.

'Well?' Rosa said, pulling a chair to the side of his bed. 'Can you work with those cards?'

'I don't know,' Bert said. 'I'm not supposed to ...'

Rosa scowled, jumping up from her chair and extending a pudgy hand. 'Well in that case I'll have them back. I should have known you wouldn't do it.'

'No, wait,' Bert said, aghast. 'I didn't say I couldn't. Sit down. I can do a three card reading, past, present and future.'

Rosa threw her arms around him, pressing her bosoms into his chest. 'Oh thank you, Bert, I knew you wouldn't let me down.' She released her grip and relaxed back into her chair, her mouth upturned in a congenial smile.

Bert felt his pyjamas tighten with his arousal; relieved his modesty was preserved under the hospital blankets. Taking a few short breaths, he focused on the cards. Rosa had a short temper, and they did not have much time. He shuffled the deck before laying the three cards face down on the bed. Working with a different deck was like wearing someone else's clothes. He wondered how he had forgotten about his own deck of cards, buried underneath the roots of the tree. He scratched his neck, and turned over the first card.

'This is your past. Life has not been kind to you. I see a man, a uncle. He's much older than you. He is entering your room. You are pretending to be asleep but he doesn't care ...'

Rosa's eyes grew wide and she reached out to snatch the card. Bert batted her hand away. 'Don't be upset. It's over now. I'll move on to the present. You mustn't dwell on the past.'

Rosa glanced back at the room door and frowned. 'Can you hurry up? We haven't got much time.'

Bert turned over the card. 'I see a bald man, with a black mous-tache. He is kissing you goodbye and leaving your home.'

'Yes that's him,' Rosa said, leaning forward in her chair.

'I see him again, sitting in his car with a tall, thin, red-haired woman. They're planning what to do with your money. He's kissing her, telling her she's the only one he's ever loved.' Bert knew that each word was a dagger into Rosa's heart. But he had little sympathy for her when she treated him so abruptly.

'I knew it,' she whispered, her eyes narrowing as she spat the words. 'The bastard. He said he was visiting his father.'

But the reading had not finished, and Bert felt his blood boil as he watched images of Rosa stealing from her patients on a daily basis. The more disabled they were, the more she took. Trinkets from home, soap, jewellery, even socks. No wonder she waddled when she walked; her bra held a lot more than her breasts alone. Like a mag-pie she would fish through her trinkets, some of them never seeing the light of day. But it gave her a certain satisfaction, stealing from people who could not answer back.

Rosa blew her nose before standing up to leave. 'All this time I've been wondering what's going on and you gave it to me straight. Thank you.'

'The reading's not over yet. Wouldn't you like to know your fu-ture?'

Rosa sneered. 'I already know. I'm kicking that bastard out, then I'm going to book a cruise. That's the last you'll see of me.'

Bert set his mouth into a thin line. He could hear voices down the corridor as the meeting broke up. Rosa put out her hand for the cards. 'I've got to go. Give me back the cards. You'll have no use for them now.'

Bert quickly shoved the cards under his pillow. 'Wait, I have news of your future. It's very important. Meet me on the fourth floor tomorrow night at nine, room 113.'

'But that floor's taped off for renovation. You won't get in,' Rosa whispered.

'Leave it to me, I'm good at sneaking out. This is important, Rosa. I'll see you tomorrow.'

Rosa nodded before hastily making her way out the door.

It was just like the old days for Bert when he escaped outside under the cover of darkness. The floor had been cordoned off due to renovations so only pass holders could gain access. PVC was replacing the rotted sash windows, and room 113 was windowless, because they had ordered the wrong size. But Rosa didn't know that. She rubbed her arms as she entered, squinting in the darkness. The electricity for that part of the building had been turned off, and as Bert stepped out of the shadows, he relayed the rest of her reading. She was going to die after falling out of the fourth-floor window at three minutes past nine. Rose had barely enough time to scream before she realised what was going on. Bert's push sent her falling into the arms of the cold night air, screaming and flailing like a wingless bird.

As Rosa's bloodied corpse lay on the concrete ground below, Bert ran to the other end of the building and climbed down the piping into his own room. As he gripped the cold metal chutes, he was reminded of the old oak tree from which Callum fell. He would have loved to have seen Rosa fall for himself, but he had to make do with pretending to wake from his sleep, acting groggy and confused as he asked the other staff what was going on. A later search revealed many stolen items in her locker, and Bert played his audience as he told them how Rosa used to sneak into his room at night, desperate *to talk about her childhood abuse. Bert was lucid enough to explain how she had kissed him on the cheek and left, saying goodbye one last time. Like before, Bert had given a very good performance, and her death provided him with respite from his ills. His story was backed up by the CCTV, which only covered the inside of the building. All they could see was Rosa making her way through the corridor alone.*

Killing Rosa made him long for the forest, and he vowed to do whatever it took to be free. His cards awaited him, and they would afford him the power to do so much more.

CHAPTER FORTY

Briefing brought with it the usual workload of jobs that had trickled in from the night before. Jennifer's sergeant apologised as she handed the jobs out to her small team. She looked slightly harried, her curly black hair springing up from the crown of her head, reminding Jennifer of a jack-in-the-box toy she had as a child.

'I'm sorry, guys, but today we've got to mop up some plain old domestic incidents to help CID. They're quite nasty so don't rush, but if you happen to get any downtime I recommend sorting out whatever outstanding paperwork you have. Jennifer, you're down to attend briefing in Lexton MIT. See if there're any updates on the Raven case. Zoe's written up a report of her dealings with the Facebook group to date, you can bring that with you.'

Jennifer nodded. Zoe had been keeping Jennifer updated by text. She was slowly winning the group members' trust, particularly a member known as Geoff. She was playing the persona of a teenage girl who had turned to drugs because her parents fed her money instead of love. Each word she typed on the group's page was carefully constructed, and she expected to be invited to a meeting very soon. Jennifer sipped her coffee as her sergeant continued doling out jobs, and none of them were to her liking.

'Will, there's a domestic here for the Cravens. As usual, it's resulted in a counter allegation, and both parties are in custody.

You work with the husband and Zoe can interview the wife. Collate the paperwork and send it to CPS. They're one of our regulars so you should be able to get a decision today.'

Briefing in Lexton failed to turn up any new leads. The general consensus was that the Raven had abandoned his van in favour of other means of transport. He was not claiming benefits, and it wasn't possible to track his spending habits without bank account details. They were at a loss as to how he was sustaining himself. Jennifer wondered if his mother had been one of those mistrusting people who kept her money in a mattress instead of in a bank like everyone else. Her thoughts returned to Emily's little boy. Her nightmares were filled with his sorrow – she could not get him out of her mind. She turned to Will, his head bowed as he pored over his paperwork. The couple he was working on must have had the police on speed dial, as not a weekend passed without the police being called to their address.

'The Cravens, they've got kids haven't they?' Jennifer asked.

'Five, God help them, and a menagerie of animals.'

'Mmm,' Jennifer said, 'I take it you'll be giving social services a call to update them on the progress of the case. Would you like me to do that for you?'

'What are you up to? It sounds like you've enough work of your own to be getting on with.'

'No, that's OK, I'll do it. What's the number of that social worker you're friendly with, Sally something, isn't it?'

'Why are you so keen to call social care all of a sudden?' Will lifted his gaze from the page and his face broke into a smile. 'Hold on, you're after an update on Emily Clarke's kid, aren't you?'

'I might be,' Jennifer said. She had gotten used to never knowing the outcome of many of the jobs she attended. It was part of the job. You turned up when all hell was breaking loose, and if you were lucky, you found out how it went. Most of the time, you never heard anything, and you had to let it go. Being able to show empathy without becoming emotionally attached became a skill to master. But this time she had to know.

Will handed her a slip of paper. 'Here's her direct line. Don't abuse it.'

'Thanks,' Jennifer said, before punching in her number. 'Hi Sally, it's DC Jennifer Knight from Haven CID. Sorry to call on your direct line but Will and I are working on a case involving the Craven family and I just wanted to check if you've received a social services referral.'

Sally was a children's advisor, and all referrals in Haven passed through her. Will had gotten to know her over the years, and she was happy to update her that a social worker had already been assigned. Just as she was about to finish her call, Jennifer caught her attention.

'Oh Sally, before you go, do you have any updates on the little boy who was taken into care the other day? His mother was Emily Clarke. She was murdered.'

'Oh of course I know about that one, very sad wasn't it? Let me see ... why do you need this information again?'

Her fingers busily clacked on the keyboard as Sally typed in the background.

Jennifer twisted the phone cord between her fingers. Saying she felt a pang of guilt for his mother's death would not provide her with the information she needed. 'It's relevant to the case,' Jennifer heard herself say. 'We need to ascertain if the child has said anything about his mother's killer, if he's settling in, things like that.'

Jennifer could hear the thud of a cup being placed on a desk. 'Hmm, well it says here a DC Hardwick has already called with a view to interviewing him. Nothing's been arranged yet, but the key worker has said in her notes he is showing no adverse signs so far. I imagine it'll come out in his assessment but there doesn't appear to be any lasting damage.'

Jennifer warmed to the idea of that. 'That's good, so he's in care, I take it?'

'He's been fostered already. It's early days but he's doing really well, poor mite.'

It was the best news Jennifer had received all day. 'Great! Thanks for that, Sally, I should have checked with DC Hardwick first. Sounds like a case of the left hand not knowing what the right hand is doing.'

'Are you any nearer to catching the killer or are you not allowed to say?' Sally said.

Jennifer squirmed. She thought of the whiteboard in the MIT briefing room, and the wall covered with photos of the unfortunate victims, followed by pins dotting destinations, forensics, names, and places. She decided to go for the politician-style answer, and sidestepped the question completely. 'We're throwing everything at this case. I'm sure it's only a matter of time.'

'Aye, well good luck with it, and don't forget to give me the update on the Cravens.'

Jennifer would hand the responsibility for the updates over to Will and Zoe. They were welcome to them as far as she was concerned. One parent was as bad as the other, and neither thought of their children when they were tearing strips off each other during booze-fuelled arguments.

Jennifer was in the middle of Tesco's when she received the call from Ethan. The hum of a car told her he was going somewhere, and the urgency in his voice made her hurry as she scanned her sandwich through the self-service checkout. There was no time for small talk as he relayed the news.

'We've had word, there's a raid going ahead. They've found The Reborners' location.'

'Really? I'm just grabbing a sandwich. What time is kick-off?'

Ethan mumbled something about turning left and Jennifer guessed he was being driven. 'No, you don't understand. Lexton MIT have been hacking into Zoe's Facebook account and monitoring her conversations in the Second Chance group. While she was in interview, one of the group members invited her to a meeting.'

Jennifer swore under her breath. They were giving their full cooperation, there was no need for underhand tactics. 'So when is the meeting? Is it today?'

'It's now. They've planned the raid without us. Zoe and I are on our way. Get yourself down to the quarry now.'

CHAPTER FORTY-ONE

Jennifer found Ethan at the entrance to a disused warehouse at the south-facing end of the old chalk quarry. It had been closed off to the public several years ago, situated at the back of the industrial site, miles away from town. Barbed-wire fences and signs threatening prosecution were usually enough to see people off, but it was a desolate enough location to provide shelter for The Reborners group without being found. Police had searched it when the investigation began, and Jennifer wondered if the group was relying on lightning not striking twice in the same place. The warehouse was large and draughty, and someone had covered the chalky floor with numerous blankets and cushions, all laid in a circular pattern. The centre culminated in a collection of bungs, lighters, and pipes. Jennifer scanned the room for Bert Bishop, the man who called himself the Raven. It was obvious she was the last one to arrive, as the dregs of the occupants were questioned, some being led out in handcuffs. Ethan gave the scene a murderous glare as he waited to confront the head of the operation. Jennifer was not surprised to hear it was a fresh-out-of-the-box DCI. Underhand dealings went a long way to winning promotion, but would award him little respect from his colleagues.

'Why was the location messaged at such late notice?' Jennifer said, peering into the scene.

Ethan pulled an electronic cigarette from his inside jacket pocket and inhaled the vapour. He seemed too clean-cut to use them, but all coppers had their coping mechanisms, much like Jennifer with her swearing and office banter. He blew out the smoke, before turning to answer. 'That's how the group works. New members aren't trusted. They only receive notification once the sessions are in progress. Sometimes they get there for the tail end. The message came in just as Zoe was in interview with her domestic suspect. She knew something was up when she checked Facebook, because someone had replied on her behalf.'

'Sneaky bastards. How did they do that?'

'It's a police-authorised social media account. It wouldn't have been difficult to get the password, with the right authorisation.'

'I take it they haven't found him … the Raven,' Jennifer said; she had thought not, judging by her DI's disgruntled expression.

'Of course they haven't. We'd planned for Zoe to infiltrate the group slowly and put her undercover experience to good use, but they just went bowling in there.'

'So what now?' Jennifer said.

'You head back to the nick with Zoe while I speak to the DCI here. Zoe's waiting in the car, there's no point in compromising her identity,' Ethan said, his voice tinged with annoyance.

'But what about the interviews, boss? Shouldn't we head back to Lexton to get the ball rolling?'

'No. Take Zoe back to Haven and await further instruction,' Ethan said firmly.

Jennifer sighed. There was no reasoning with him when he was like this. He was too busy gearing up for turf wars, police style.

Zoe's black baseball hat sat low on her forehead during the drive back to the station, reminding Jennifer of a sullen teen. She was relieved she turned down Zoe's offer to drive. She seemed to be in a worse mood than Ethan, and that was saying something.

'They've made some drug arrests, and seized some DMT,' Jennifer said. 'Hopefully they'll be able to get some decent intel in interview.'

'Not with those bunch of clowns interviewing them,' Zoe said. 'They don't know what they're dealing with.'

'I don't get how people have kept quiet about it for so long. It's been going on for months now, I would have thought someone would have given their location away.'

Zoe slouched in her seat. 'There's no chance of that. They know what happens to people who squeal.'

'If they're so scared, why are so many people desperate to join? Is it for the drugs or the promise of redemption? DMT's not addictive, is it?'

'It's not about addiction. The people who join The Reborners have lived very troubled lives. The cult makes big promises, and it delivers. DMT is mindblowing. It can literally help people become born again.'

'Sounds like you're speaking from experience.'

Zoe lifted her cap, giving Jennifer a sly grin. 'If I had, I wouldn't admit it to a fellow copper. I like my job too much.'

Jennifer smiled. The more she talked to Zoe, the more intriguing she became. 'But the effects are hallucinatory. Aren't all drugs are like that?'

'They're not random trips, lots of people report visiting the same spiritual dimension. It's a process. Each time you do it, you progress further, receiving messages, communicating with higher realms. The drug doesn't stay in your system like others do, but the psychological effects are long term.'

'Why are people killing themselves, if it's so great?'

'DMT fucks up your head for one, and can give you flash-backs. Long-term users can disassociate themselves from real-ity, although it's beyond me how anyone can do DMT for very long. It's not like recreational drugs, it's heavy shit – and if you have a bad trip …' Zoe whistled. 'It's enough to make you lose your mind.'

'Hence the suicides. So what happened when you did it?' Jennifer asked.

Zoe smiled knowingly. 'Cheeky. We'd have to be on intimate terms for me to tell you that.'

Jennifer smiled as she pulled into the station car park, feeling very much like she was being flirted with. 'You know, I'd never take drugs, but if I was held at gunpoint and forced to choose one …'

'Then choose weed,' Zoe said. 'DMT's not for you. Believe me, babe, you don't want to go there.'

The first thing Jennifer did when she got back to the station was log on to the custody system to read the updates on the arrests. The updates were disappointing, with five people nicked, out of a group of over fifty members. Five people, in a drug-fuelled oblivion, who spoke of meeting mother earth and beings from another dimension. None of them stood out as having any prior dealings with the police, and one was ac-tually a vicar. Jennifer swivelled her chair around as Claire exited her office.

'Sarge, check this out. One of the suspects is a vicar! Hope-fully he'll have an attack of conscience and give us some names.'

'From what I've heard so far, not many people were privy to names,' Claire said, flatly. 'Their so-called leader wore a mask.'

Zoe piped up. 'Interesting, reminds me a bit of the Wizard of Oz. I wonder if Bert Bishop was the one behind the curtain?'

Claire folded her arms and sat on the edge of her desk. 'We'll be the last ones to know if he is. Ethan's just called in. He doesn't want us helping Lexton with the interviews.'

Jennifer frowned, her voice rising in her throat. 'What? He can't do that!'

'He has,' Claire said. 'He's had a bust-up with the DCI and threatened to cut all ties. He's told me to inform you that from now on we keep our own cases.'

'But what about this case?' Jennifer said. 'We need to speak to the suspects in custody.'

Claire emitted a sigh. 'I'm sorry. This is my fault. I should have insisted we kept ownership from the start. Ethan will be back later. He'll explain things then.'

Jennifer decided not to impart the response resting on her tongue, instead nodding in mock understanding. Lexton had been using them all along. She lowered her eyes to the floor, too annoyed to speak. She would go it alone if she had to. She had a connection with the Raven, something Lexton MIT couldn't comprehend. He would be hers, even if it meant risking her job.

CHAPTER FORTY-TWO

'Thanks for arranging to meet up, Jenny,' Christian said, as Jennifer rested the cappuccinos on the table. She took a seat in his booth, adjusting her ears to the chatter of a language she did not understand. The town had been flooded with foreign students during the Easter break, and Haven's coffee shops and eateries now came filled with noisy queues. She returned her attention to Christian. Clean-shaven and well-dressed, he appeared a lot more together than the last time they met. It felt like the old days, meeting up for a coffee in town.

She had forgotten many of her school friends to concentrate on her career, but her friendship with Christian was something she was happy to resurrect, particularly if she gleaned any new information about the Raven. Jennifer felt a pang of sympathy, wondering if Christian's showbiz friends had deserted him now he was in the throes of grief.

'Everyone calls me Jennifer now,' she said. 'I left Jenny behind after I finished school. How are you doing?'

Christian wrapped his hands around his mug. 'It comes in waves. I feel guilty for talking about Felicity all the time, because people must be getting sick of hearing me go on about her. The problem is, I can't think of anything else.'

'Well you can talk to me. I know what it's like to lose a loved one.' Jennifer stirred in her sugar, wishing they had arranged to meet somewhere quieter. She leaned forward, resisting the urge to rest her hand on his. 'I won't tell you that you'll get over it because you won't, but it will get easier as time goes by.'

Christian nodded slowly. 'My mother keeps telling me I should go for grief counselling, but I want to wait a few weeks, see how I feel then.'

'That sounds sensible. I remember when my mum died I didn't want to talk about her to anyone. Now … well, I'm moving forward with my life, and I think she'd be happy about that.'

Christian drew in a small intake of breath. 'How insensitive of me, waffling on about myself after you losing your mum at such an early age.'

'Don't be daft. I don't have the monopoly on grief,' Jennifer said, relieved to hear the cacophony of noise float out of the building as the foreign students disappeared with their takeaway cups.

Christian gave a faint smile. 'I can't tell you how good it is to meet up with someone from the old days. The showbiz scene is everything I ever wanted, but some of the people I work with are very jaded. That's what I liked about Felicity, she was so exuberant, so full of life. She loved being in the spotlight, but she never forgot her humble beginnings.'

Jennifer thought of the young girl, due to get married with her whole life ahead of her. 'I'm sorry, Christian. You know if there was anything I could have done to have stopped this …'

'Don't think that for a second, and I didn't mean what I said before about warning you something was going to happen. The only person to blame for this is my cousin. I'm convinced of it now. I haven't had one phone call from him since Felicity died. Killing Felicity was revenge for me refusing to take him in.' Christian paused to swallow his coffee. 'I've written down some things about my cousin that I didn't mention before; perhaps it might help with your enquiries.'

Christian spent the next twenty minutes filling Jennifer in on his cousin's strange behaviour: what he knew about his background, what his mother had told him about Bert's family, and his last contact. But it was nothing Jennifer had not already gleaned from Dr Carter.

Her phone began to vibrate on the table and she frowned at the unknown number. 'Sorry, Christian, do you mind if I take this?'

'Go ahead, I'll get us another coffee.'

Jennifer gave him the thumbs-up sign as she pressed the answer button. She really should be heading back, but Christian had brightened so much since coming out, she didn't have the heart to say goodbye.

'Hello?' Jennifer said as she answered her phone. There was silence on the other end. She strained her ears to hear breathing in the background. She was in no mood to deal with a prank caller. 'You have three seconds to speak or I'm hanging up. One … Two …'

'Wait, Jennifer, it's me.'

Jennifer frowned. 'Who?' The answer came as soon as she had uttered the words.

'It's me, dad.'

Her stomach flipped. It was her turn to remain silent, and it took several hellos before she spoke.

'How did you get my number?' she said, a trickle of fury rising within.

'I took it from Amy's phone.'

'You *took* it, not asked for it I presume.'

'I don't want to argue, Jenny, I just want to talk.'

Jennifer cringed at the sound of her name being shortened for the second time that day. It served as a reminder of a past she would rather forget. 'It's Jennifer. And I don't want to talk to you.'

'You seem to be carrying a lot of anger. I think it would be good for us to talk about things, move forward.'

You want to blame me for everything you mean, Jennifer thought. She glanced around the coffee shop. She wouldn't put it past him to be watching her, gauging her reaction. So she did what she always did when she was trying to conceal her fury. She put on her best telephone voice and responded the same way she did to the cold callers that plagued her home number. 'No thank you, I'm perfectly happy as I am. Now if you don't mind I'm in the middle of something. Please don't bother me again.'

Jennifer swiftly ended the call and switched her phone to silent. Closing her eyes, she took a deep breath, and opened them to find Christian sitting in front of her. His awkward smile displayed his discomfort. 'Sorry. Private call?'

She shrugged apologetically as she accepted another coffee. 'It's my dad. I haven't heard from him in a decade and suddenly he wants to be friends.'

'I take it that you don't want to?' Christian said.

Jennifer tore off the strips from two sugar sachets and poured their contents into the hot, frothy liquid. The chocolate powder design sank with the brown sugar, and she watched it all dissolve as she stirred it together.

'You don't know my father. He can't take responsibility for anything, including his own emotions. He'll always look for something, or someone, to fix things, because he can't do it himself. He tried it with the booze and now he's trying it with me. I'm not having it.'

'Sounds like you've given it a lot of thought.'

Jennifer gave a short laugh. 'You could say that. And I know people would say that life is short, and I should make up with him, but it's *because* life is short that I'm keeping well away. I don't want to waste my time with him.' She glanced up from her coffee, trying to read his expression. 'You probably think I'm a real cow.'

'Actually you're wrong. I remember what it was like for you growing up. From what I heard, your father was no help at all.'

'Oh yeah? You must have thought we were a right band of commoners,' Jennifer said, remembering her old school days. The darned tights, the second-hand uniforms. Christian was right. Her father was of no help at all.

'I wouldn't say that. I remember my parents talking about what a great police officer your mother was. Mum used to say that she made it her business to know everyone in Haven. Of course, the place was a lot smaller back then. But they were very sad when she died. I don't think your father was seen as a bad person, but it was no secret that he liked a drink. I think you've done very well with your life, considering all the upset you've been through.'

Jennifer may have taken offence if anyone else had dissected her home life like that, particularly people who had come from a privileged background themselves. But there was something about Christian's honeyed tones that made her feel better. Despite what he was going through himself, he still tried to provide comfort and reassurance to others. It just seemed to come naturally to him.

'Thanks. My days of dwelling on the past are behind me. I just want to move on,' Jennifer said, knowing that was not strictly true.

Christian displayed a smile full of warmth and empathy. 'I know it was the worst possible circumstances but I'm glad we were thrown together. In my line of work you just don't know who your real friends are.'

'I've enjoyed it. We'll have to do this again.' Jennifer looked at her watch then downed the rest of her coffee. 'I'm afraid I have to dash, but thanks for the coffees, my treat next time.'

Christian left with Jennifer as she pulled on her jacket. 'If you hear anything about Bert you'll let me know, won't you? I can't relax at night, knowing he's still out there. I told the kids' mum they can't stay over until he's caught. I couldn't bear it if anything happened to them.'

'Your home is like Fort Knox, and the police are all over this. As soon as he's apprehended I'll let you know.'

'He's here somewhere,' Christian said, as they entered the car park. 'Haven is such a rat run of lanes and hideaways, but he can't stay hidden forever.'

'Exactly. And as soon as he comes out, we'll be waiting. Just call me if you have any concerns, but in the meantime just take each day as it comes.'

Christian reached out his arms to give her a hug. It was one of the things she liked about him. He was never afraid to show his emotions.

Jennifer waved Christian off as he drove past, leaning against her car, mulling over her father's call. She took her phone out to delete the recent call history then paused. Perhaps it's better to keep his number, she thought, in case I need to get in touch. Her finger hovered over the delete button. Then again, I could save it under 'Twat' and then I'd know if he tried to call me again, she thought. She giggled to herself, and saved it under the letter 'D' for dad. It was as much as he deserved.

Her eyes flicked up to the sky and she was relieved to see an absence of ravens. Pinkish candy-floss clouds streaked the sky, intermingling with white smoky chemtrails as the sun went down. One of her mother's sayings repeated in her mind. 'Red sky at night, shepherd's delight.' Jennifer wondered what sort of worries her mum had at her age. Not serial killers and rabid ravens. As far as she knew, her mother dealt with only one killer in her lifetime. Jennifer shook her head. *Only one.* As if dealing with lots of serial killers was normal. For Jennifer, she knew terror would seek her out in every form. At least now she felt strong enough to know she would cope with whatever was thrown at her. Life had changed so much in the last year, yet she was feeling stronger now than ever. She was her own woman, had her own independence, and the strength to stand up to her father. Even the memories of the past could not hurt her any more. It was just as well. She would never truly be free of it.

CHAPTER FORTY-THREE
Bert

Bert peered through the car window down the quiet cul de sac. His time on the streets was severely restricted, now Haven was crawling with police. It wasn't the only thing that was crawling; the intense itching had returned like fire ants, boring tunnels under the surface of his skin. He had seen it in the cards. There would be another death before the homeless man's prediction came true.

It could not come quick enough as far as Bert was concerned. A mixture of torture and excitement heightened his senses. His cards had led him here, where all the houses looked the same, their low brick walls skirted by small neat flower gardens. All square, boring and functional. Not like the house he shared with mother. But mother was gone. He accepted that now. The cause of her death was murky. Had he really killed her? Or had he frightened her before he left, wrapping his fingers around her throat, only to release them as she cried out for mercy? Years of drug-taking had addled his brain. But it was not the recreational kind. The memories of The Rivers mental health facility had slowly returned, ebbing like the tide, bringing him nearer to lucidity. The closer he got to his end goal, the clearer his mind became.

He returned his attention to the task in hand. Net curtains twitched next door as a silver Mercedes pulled up on a driveway, the glint of the evening sun dazzling against the metallic paint.

A pair of long bronzed legs stepped out of the driver's side, attached to a pair of red high heels. Despite her short leather mini skirt and low-cut blouse, the woman alit with reasonable grace. Her long black hair contrasting against her sheer white blouse, she tottered to the boot of the car, wrapping her polished nails around the handles of the various pink glossy shopping bags. Bert squinted as she dropped her car keys, bending from the waist to pick them up. He tutted as he leaned forward for a better view. He could almost see her knickers as her skirt rode up her thighs. This woman clearly did not care about revealing her body to all and sundry. The next-door neighbour's curtains twitched a second time as the woman walked up her short drive with her purchases. Bert pulled his keys from the ignition and stepped out of the van. She was too wrapped up in her purchases to notice, and closed her front door behind her.

Bert felt a chill of unease. The bright spring weather left him exposed under the gaze of the surrounding houses, and he hesitated as he stepped onto the pavement. A crawling itch behind his right ear drove him onwards, and he tipped his hat over his forehead as he strode down the narrow alleyway. It acted as a cut-through between the house to his side and the one in front, affording him a clear view into the rear of the house with the twitching curtains. Bert peeped into the scrubby back garden, furnished with a homemade wooden tree house and glass house devoid of plants. The overgrown grass and lack of toys suggested the two-storey home was bereft of children. The tree house consisted of what appeared to be a hastily nailed together floor, supported by three rickety walls and a roof.

Bert ducked from view as a pot-bellied man exited the back door. His vest had seen better days, and even from over the fence, Bert could see it was stained with the remains of his lunch. The grey hairs running through his mop of sandy hair suggested he was at least late fifties. Peppered sideburns crept down his jaws, met by a patch of stubble. Pot-belly man waddled down the path humming happily. He hitched up his baggy jeans before beginning the ascent up the wooden steps of the dingy tree house. Bert cringed as the man's pants crept back down with every step he took, revealing the crack of his considerable backside. But it was of no concern to pot-belly man as he struggled to climb the ladder. His binoculars swung with each step, attached on a cord around his thick neck. Once inside, he pulled up a chair and stared expectantly through his binoculars. For a moment, Bert thought the man was bird watching, until it became apparent he was staring directly into the top window of the house next door. Bert rolled a cigarette, trying to look innocuous as he heard the hum of a car motor pulling up behind the Mercedes. As the car door slammed, pot-belly man beamed a smile, shifting in his chair as he leaned forward for a better view. What on earth? Bert thought, as the watcher's thick fingers single-handedly undid his belt buckle. Unable to see the focus of his excitement, Bert crept down the alley for a better view. But it was no use; although the room next door had no curtains or blinds, he was unable to see from his vantage point. Bert sucked the last of his cigarette and flicked it on the ground. He had other ways of finding out.

He returned to his mother's car, averting his eyes from the unsavoury activity in the tree house. Just how was he going to speak to him? It wasn't as if he could knock on his door and offer a reading. But like everything in Bert's life, the cards would guide him into finding a way.

The answer came the following morning as Bert ventured out with his van. He took the country lanes, rather than the main road that led him into town. They served not only as a useful short cut, but as excellent cover from the sharp-eyed locals on the lookout for suspicious activity. He tried to have confidence in his mission, but it was difficult to blend in when you were driving a rusted orange VW splodged with bird droppings.

He did not see the bicycle shoot out of the side road until it was too late. Bert stamped on the brakes, sending the van screeching to a halt, but the man he had watched the day before hit the panel with a thunk, before skidding off his bike onto the verge.

Bert clambered out of the van, wondering if this was a random accident or all part of a greater plan. 'Are you all right?' he asked, reluctant to offer his hand. He hesitated, and then remembered his gloves before pulling them on and reaching out to help.

'I ... I don't know what happened, I think my brakes failed.' Pot-belly man spoke in a scouse accent, groaning as he climbed to his feet. He brushed away the pebbles embedded in his face, each one blooming a pinprick of blood in its wake. He shook the dust from the knees of his baggy jeans, and then straightened up to inspect the damage to the van. Shaking his head, he stared at his mangled bike. 'That could have been me under there. Have I damaged your van?'

Bert looked at the gnarled metal of his bike partially lodged under the bumper. 'That's all right, it doesn't matter.' He tried to contain the tingle of excitement sparking inside him. The perfect opportunity had landed in his lap, and it would be worth a dent in the van to get the man alone. 'Just hold on while I pull it out,' he said, wrenching at the handlebars and pulling it free. The wheel was completely buckled, and he leaned what was left of the bike against the van, and turned to survey the man's injuries.

'Can I call you an ambulance?' Bert said, half-heartedly. 'Your elbow's bleeding.'

The man looked down at his elbow, the skin patterned with freshly forming blood patches. 'No, thanks mate, I don't need the ozzy. I'd better be getting back before it gets dark.' Taking the bike, he stifled a groan as he limped forwards.

Bert put his hands on the handlebars of the bent-up bike. 'Let me run you home, I insist.'

'That's proper kind of you. The name's Geoffrey by the way. I'd shake your hand but it's a bit sore like.'

Bert decided against offering his own name in return. 'No problem. Come in for a drink, you look like you're about to faint.'

Bert slid back the side door of the van and Geoffrey climbed inside, looking around in amazement as Bert flicked on the lights and showed him a seat.

Geoffrey squeezed in behind the jutting Formica table, resting his belly under the wood. Bowing his head, he clasped his hand to his jaw as he sat slumped with a sigh.

Bert handed Geoffrey a large brandy, mentally offsetting the costs against what was to come.

'Nice one, mate. I'm not holding you up, am I?' Geoffrey said, swirling the brandy in the chipped enamel cup.

'Not at all, I've finished my work for today,' Bert said, faking his cheeriest smile.

'Oh, I thought maybe you were retired. Things 'aven't been the same for me since I was made redundant.'

Bert nodded sympathetically. 'I'm a tarot card reader. I have clients up and down the country. Would you like me to read your cards?' Bert did not wait for a response as he plucked the musty deck of cards from his jacket pocket and placed them on the faded yellow Formica table.

Geoffrey frowned, but Bert knew that even if he did not believe in such things, he would not want to hurt his new friend's feelings while he was being so hospitable; particularly when he was willing to ignore the dent on the front of the van.

'Sure why not,' Geoffrey said, 'me sister's into all this, she goes to the spiritualist church and everything.'

'And what about you?' Bert said, licking his cracked lips as he shuffled the cards.

'No disrespect, mate, but I don't believe in all that stuff. Still, each to their own, eh?'

Bert laid down the cards and picked up the brandy bottle, clinking it against Geoffrey's ceramic cup. 'Here, have another drink.'

Bert felt the raven draw near as he rifled through Geoffrey's past. As cine-camera images flashed to the forefront of his mind, he recounted Geoffrey's early days as a mechanic in Liverpool, before he hurt his back and moved to Haven to be near his sister. He got a job as a factory packer and came close to marrying, but being made redundant caused his fiancée to break off the engagement. Geoffrey had since resigned himself to living alone.

Geoffrey shook his head in amazement. 'This is a wind-up. You've been speaking to my sister, haven't you?'

Bert raised an eyebrow in his direction. 'If that were the case I wouldn't be able to forecast what you've been up to of an evening now, would I?'

Geoffrey giggled, the brandy bringing a bloom to his cheeks. 'Oh yeah? And what would that be?'

Bert replied in a low voice, as he eyed the man with some disdain. 'I know that you like to spy on the woman next door.'

'Sexy Mandy? So would you if you'd seen her. Phwoar, she's dynamite!'

Bert was astounded. The man wasn't even ashamed of his actions.

'She's married,' Bert said. Even from a distance he had seen the flash of gold on her finger.

'I know, lucky bastard. I don't know what he did to deserve her. She's a right little goer,' Geoffrey chuckled, apparently none the wiser to his drinking buddy's disgust.

'It's voyeurism,' Bert said, his words measured. Now was not the time for anger.

But Geoffrey did not hear him. 'Last night she had on a black PVC bra, a fishnet vest and PVC pants. She goes shopping for all this gear then tries it on for her auld fella when he gets home from work. It's better than watching Television X!'

'It sounds like my predictions have been true. Let's look into your future.'

'Sure thing, mate, let me know if I score a night with that bird from next door.'

Bert steeled himself as he watched the last moments of Geoffrey's life unravel before him. Ironically, the sequence that led to his death occurred after another evening of watching Mandy perform for her husband. Bert tightened his lips, reining in his smile.

'You're going to break your neck climbing down from that tree house,' he said. Tipping off the man was the last thing he wanted to do, but giving the warning was all part of the reading and there was nothing he could do to stop it.

But Geoffrey burst out laughing, his large belly vibrating against the table. 'Thanks, mate, you've given me a right giggle there. Next thing you'll be telling me wanking makes me blind. I feel much better now, but I think it's time I made a move.'

Bert stared with his mouth open, speechless for the first time. He didn't believe him. He warned the fool and he didn't believe him.

Bert had learned from Geoffrey that he lived alone, and like many people living alone, he was a creature of habit. Every night at five he popped out to the chip shop for his tea. He was home by half five, and in the tree house by a quarter to six, to watch Mandy trying on her wares. Perhaps she knew what was happening, or perhaps she was not expecting someone to be watching her from that height. As the cards had shown, the tree house provided a direct view through the curtainless windows of her bedroom. But there was no excuse for Geoffrey's behaviour, and Bert would enjoy watching the fulfilling of the prophecy.

It was not difficult to slide into the unlocked back garden through the frail wooden gate. Geoffrey would be too busy waiting for Mandy to come home to notice Bert's intrusion. Bert positioned himself behind the mossy garden shed, smiling to himself as he cast his eyes over the ladder reaching up to the tree. The wooden steps were as rotten as he had envisaged, and would not hold Geoffrey's considerable bulk when he waddled down tonight. All he had to do was watch, if only to know his forthcoming reward was secure. Bert froze as he heard a rattling sound from the side of the house. The metallic rattling sound got closer and was followed by Geoffrey's whistle as he walked towards the tree house carrying a stepladder over his shoulder. Bert dug his nails into the palms of his hands. Damn him! He must have taken in some of the reading after all.

The steps creaked as Geoffrey climbed, muttering to himself as the binoculars swung from around his neck. 'C'mon girlie, let's see what you're wearing tonight … or rather not wearing,' he giggled.

As time went on, Bert edged closer to the tree house, his mind in turmoil. With a short push of the stepladder Geoffrey would end up dead. Bert's eyes followed the trajectory. It would come to rest on the glass house, which would make a hell of a crash as Geoffrey's body made impact. Bert dug his long nails into the back of his neck as he scratched the growing itch. The rampant next-door neighbours were sure to be alerted by the noise. Would he get away on time? He mulled it over. He could force Geoffrey into climbing down the wooden steps by taking away the metal stepladder, but that would put him on his guard, and he was a big man. Bert thought of Geoffrey's wide knuckles being slammed into his face, his gorilla hands wrapping around his neck, choking the life out of him.

'Fuck! What'll I do? What'll I do?' he rasped into the cool evening air, searching the skies for his beloved ravens. But the question was taken away as heavy footsteps creaked on the ladder above him.

'Who's there?' Geoffrey asked, his feet clanking against the metal steps as he made his descent.

'Shit shit shit!' Bert tore into the back of his neck, violently scratching in fear and frustration. He would not get away on time now. Another couple of steps and Geoffrey would be upon him. There was only one thing *to do*.

If Bert had been able to think clearly he would have seen the comical expression on Geoffrey's face as their eyes met. That in turn would have presented him with another option; one that suggested Bert himself had come for a viewing. Geoffrey's back gate held no lock and as he had already given him an invite, he may have laughed and waved him up. But he never got the chance, as Bert rushed forward and pushed the stepladder back with all his might. As he turned to run, a mighty yell and a crash splintered the air, and Bert craned his neck to see Geoffrey feverishly gripping the ladder as he crashed on his greenhouse below. The glass, now dripping with blood, served as an efficient executioner. As Bert ran to the safety of his van, his thoughts were not for the man bleeding his last among the splintered glass, but the benefits he would receive from fulfilling another prophecy.

CHAPTER FORTY-FOUR

As Jennifer hung her coat in the CID office her main priorities were firstly not to think about her father, and secondly to progress her case. Another body was going to turn up and it was going to be soon. She had felt it from the moment she woke up. The feeling of dread encompassed her, and though Will asked what was wrong, she found it impossible to put into words. Like a thick blanket of fog, it hung in the fibres of her clothes, in each strand of her hair. She scratched the nape of her neck with her pen as she read through her case file. It was hard to concentrate with the Raven in the back of her mind. Her case load was growing, but she had little time to dedicate to it. She was about to be dragged away from her paperwork yet again as Will grabbed the car keys from a hook on the wall and quickly scribbled his name on the log book to sign it out.

'Ethan's asked us to attend a sudden death,' Will said. 'MIT are already on scene.'

Jennifer raised one eyebrow. 'Lexton MIT? Why the sudden change of heart?'

'I think they're trying to build bridges. We may as well go over there and check it out. There's mention of a tarot card reader.'

Jennifer didn't need asking twice.

DC Hardwick took a bite from his Mars Bar and ambled over to Jennifer, giving Will a courteous nod. 'We meet again. Sounds like your spooky fortune teller is getting around, doesn't it?'

They were standing in the back garden of someone called Geoffrey Pike, and Jennifer was in no mood for jokes. 'Can you tell me what's going on?'

DC Hardwick scrunched up his wrapper and threw it on the ground. 'Seems pretty straightforward to me. Middle-aged man, lives on his own. He's got police history a mile long for sexual offences, flashing, and a regular peeping Tom. He seems to have been up in his tree house peeping on the new next-door neighbour.' DC Hardwick looked at Will. 'Oh man, if you'd seen her, you'd understand why. She is hot!' he said, squeezing a pair of imaginary breasts in front of him.

Jennifer folded her arms. 'How do you know he was spying on her?'

'It doesn't take a genius to work that out. Firstly he has a set of binoculars around his neck, secondly his trousers weren't done up all the way, and thirdly he has a stash of porn and tissues up there. I reckon he was coming down the ladder, his trousers came loose, he lost his grip and it tipped all the way from there,' he said, gesturing from the tree house to the greenhouse, 'over to there. Shard of glass in his windpipe, goodnight Vienna.'

Jennifer wanted to quip that his detective training did not go to waste given he was able to count to three, but she was at the scene of a possible murder, and that was no laughing matter.

'No signs of anyone else present, any foul play?' she said, pushing her hands into her jacket pockets.

'Nope. The back door of the house was unlocked, and there's cash, a laptop and other things lying around. The crime scene investigators are doing their bit but as far as I'm concerned it's non-suspicious.'

'I thought you said there was a fortune teller involved,' Will said.

DC Hardwick raised his eyebrows. 'Didn't you read the incident?'

'No, we came straight over.'

'His sister found the body. She told the call taker that Geoffrey had come off his bike last week, and some bloke in a van gave him a lift home. But before he did, he read his fortune, said he was going to break his neck or something.'

Jennifer interjected. 'Did his sister know what he was up to?'

'If she did she never let on.'

'What about the husband of this woman next door? Does he have an alibi?'

'Yeah, he was shagging his missus,' DC Hardwick broke into laughter.

Will joined in the laughter and Jennifer silenced him with a glare. This was the work of the Raven as far as Jennifer was concerned, but she had to explore all avenues. 'This husband, he could have seen what Geoffrey was up to and knocked him off the ladder.'

DC Hardwick shook his head. 'It's unlikely. His father's a super in the Met. They said they were in bed together when they heard a smash, but were so involved in what they were doing they didn't bother to check. They didn't seem to know they had a peeping Tom and we didn't enlighten them.'

'All the same ...'

Hardwick sighed, giving her a withered look. 'Look, the only reason I'm here and not at a proper job is because you've kicked up such a fuss with this Op Moonlight that I've got to attend all reports mentioning a tarot card reader. I've been here an hour now, and it's fifty-five minutes more than I need to be.'

'All right, mate, keep your hair on,' Will said, folding his arms. 'We're all trying to do our jobs here.'

'Yeah well you may be happy dealing with this crap but I'm not. I've missed out on a good suspect interview for this. You may think this fortune teller is responsible for half the deaths in Haven, but I don't.'

Counting to ten, Jennifer resisted the urge to tell DC Hardwick exactly what she thought of him, and left Will to argue it out. Signing her name on the scene log, she took some PVC gloves and placed overshoes on her heels, treading lightly to prevent puncture holes in the soft earth. Picking her way through the garden path, she tried to imagine the scene as the man fell to his death. She cast her eyes over the wooden ladder leading up to the weather-worn tree house. Why was he using two? She wanted to climb up and have a look at the view, but scenes of crime were already there taking photos, and would not appreciate the intrusion. She glanced over at Will and DC Hardwick, their heads bowed in heated discussion. She had muscled in on DC Hardwick's territory enough for one day. She stepped through the billowy grasses onto the broken paving stones to see the remains of the greenhouse. A light rain had diluted the blood clinging to the shards of glass, and Jennifer felt her stomach lurch as she inspected the grisly scene. Wide-eyed with shock, the man lay on his back among the debris, a shard of glass protruding from his thick neck. The metal ladder lay over his chest, his legs spread-eagled as he took the fall. Judging by the blood loss, Jennifer guessed he died upon impact. His heavy frame had demolished the roof, bringing it with him as he hit the plantless greenhouse floor. Jennifer looked back up at the tree house and frowned. His death may not have been exactly as the fortune teller described, but she had no doubt he was in some way involved. She stepped back to allow the crime scene investigators past, who were discussing covering the greenhouse with tarpaulin to preserve the scene.

Will made her jump as he crept up behind her, whispering so no one else could hear. 'Are you picking anything up?'

Jennifer clutched his arm as the paving stone wobbled under his weight. 'Oh, you gave me a fright. No, the only thing I'm picking up is that Hardwick can't get rid of us quick enough. He just wants to tie this up and get on with the rest of his work.'

'He's a knob. But from what I've seen, there's not a lot to go on, is there?'

Jennifer turned to Will. 'It's not over until the fat lady sings. Let's speak to his sister, see what she has to say.'

Geoffrey's sister Miss Pike lived just four doors down. A light mist of rain descended as they walked to the address, and Jennifer patted down the newly formed frizz in her hair. She had zoned out from Will moaning about DC Hardwick, grateful they had not far to walk. She didn't like him either, but she couldn't see the point in complaining all day long. People like DC Hardwick would never change, and it was best not to let them get under your skin. The doorbell of the two-storey house rang a cheery tune rang from inside the hall. A thickset woman answered the door. Jennifer's eyes were drawn to her short, permed, vibrant bottle-red hair.

'Hello, I'm DC Knight and this is my colleague DC Dunston. And you are Linda Pike, I take it?' Checking the identity of the homeowner was a given in their line of work. The last thing they wanted to do was to turn up to someone else's address to discuss a sudden death and discover they had the wrong person. The woman nodded, her red-rimmed eyes brimming over with tears.

'I'm so sorry for your loss, but could we speak to you for a few minutes?' Jennifer said, holding up her warrant card for reassurance. Linda nodded solemnly, waving them inside. Her skirt billowed as she walked, her wide hips waddling from side to side in an effort to carry her weight. A faint smell of chip fat hung in the air of the narrow hall, which was panelled with family photos either side. A freckle-faced girl stared back, teeth crooked, hands clasped awkwardly on her lap. Jennifer viewed the progression as the school photos evolved, another of the girl wearing braces, staring up from underneath her fringe. The last picture was the most magnificent. The young girl had bloomed into a swan; her eyes alight, displaying a perfect smile. Jennifer returned her attention to Linda as she showed them into a small living room, cluttered with newspapers and cabinets full of Wade collectables. A pair of budgies chattered and whistled in a gold-barred cage hung next to the window. Linda jabbed at the remote control until the television was silenced, and only spoke when Jennifer and Will were seated on the floral patterned sofa.

'Can I get you a drink? A cuppa perhaps?'

Jennifer raised her hands, detecting a slight accent, and she strained to pin down the origin.

'Oh no, not at all. I should be making one for you, it must have been a terrible shock, finding your brother like that.' It may have seemed a comical suggestion, offering to make someone tea the first time you stepped into their house, but both Jennifer and Will had done it many times when it came to sudden deaths. Shell-shocked relatives unable to comprehend the sudden loss of a loved one. Handing them a sweet cup of tea seemed the traditional British thing to do, and she had never been shooed out of anyone's kitchen yet.

Linda pulled a balled-up tissue from under her sleeve and dabbed her eyes. 'It was such a shock finding him like that. The police – are they finished now? I mean, have they taken him?'

'It won't be much longer. Linda, I know officers have already spoken to you, but do you mind me asking you a couple of questions? I just want to make sure we have covered everything.'

'Of course, but I don't see why the police are involved. It was his own fault, the daft bugger. I told him to stop going out spying on people, because it got him in so much trouble. I didn't mean he should take it up in his own back garden.' Linda sighed heavily, her shoulders drooping with the weight of her loss. 'He wasn't a bad man really. He told me he wanted to change, but he just couldn't help himself.'

Jennifer flipped back the pages of her pocket notebook and poised it on her lap. 'Was there anyone who held a grudge against your brother?'

'He never used to go out much, just to the chip shop for his tea, and sometimes a pint in the pub. Then he joined some online group, he used to go out every now and again to meet them, never said where it was.'

Jennifer's ears pricked up at the mention of an online group, and the pieces began clicking into place. Zoe had mentioned speaking to a Geoff in her report. He regularly flirted during their online messages, and had promised to invite her to the next meeting. But Linda was unable to come up with any satisfactory information on the group, and could only recall recent events.

'We hadn't seen each other in years, I left home at a young age while he stayed in Liverpool. He moved here so we could look out for each other in our old age.'

Jennifer nodded, her curiosity about Linda's underlying accent satisfied. 'You didn't see anyone suspicious hanging around?'

'No. I popped over most mornings.' Her face crumpled as a sob hit the back of her throat. 'I can't believe he's dead.'

Jennifer handed her a fresh tissue from the box on the coffee table. 'I'm sorry, I won't keep you much longer.' She waited a few seconds for Linda to compose herself before moving on. She hated questioning the recently bereaved, but it had to be done. The sooner she could end her questioning, the sooner she could leave the woman alone to grieve in peace. 'You mentioned when you called the police that your brother had a reading,' Jennifer said.

'Yeah, it was weird. He thought I knew the man through the spiritualist church. When I told him I didn't, Geoffrey was a bit shaken.'

'Shaken? Why?'

Linda sniffed loudly. 'The fortune teller said he would break his neck climbing down the tree house ladder. It was there when Geoff bought the place, left over from the last family. But it was falling apart, and the boards were loose. The man said that Geoffrey would come a cropper.'

Jennifer paused. 'So he climbed the tree using the wooden steps?'

'Usually, yes. But after the reading he said he would use the metal ladder. Of course he told me he was using it because he liked bird watching. The silly bugger, bird watching indeed!'

Jennifer turned it over in her mind. Geoffrey scuppered the prediction, but it happened another way. Had fate alone ensured his demise or had it received a helping hand?

With some disappointment, Jennifer realised her sense of foreboding had led to this moment. The tarot card reader had to be responsible, but why? Even if Geoffrey *was* connected to The Reborners, just what was the Raven getting out of these deaths? Was he a member? Acting purely as their judge, jury and executioner? Whatever the reason, people were dying, and the Raven was never far away.

CHAPTER FORTY-FIVE

What his sergeant called psychic instinct, Will called a gut feeling. He was proud of the fact he was the levelheaded one, with his feet planted firmly on the ground. But the more time he spent with Jennifer, the better a detective he became. Her passion for protecting the people of Haven had rubbed off on him, and the Raven played heavily on his mind. Today his investigative skills rewarded him richly.

Will slowed his car to a crawl down the narrow laneway, as his eyes fell on the orange VW van. Led by nothing but old fashioned detective work, Will allowed himself some pride in his achievement. And on his own too. Jennifer would kill him for keeping it from her, but he couldn't put her in the face of danger after her stunt in the woods. He pressed the side button of his radio to call for backup, before realising the battery was dead. He slid his mobile from his pocket and stared at the blank screen. Jennifer had warned him about this; close links to powerful psychic connection could zap batteries, give you headaches, blow light bulbs and shorten CCTV footage. It was all part of the strangeness he was being fed on a daily basis. But today she had been right. Will parked his car discreetly in the ditch. He should return to the nick and get backup, but if he left, the owner of the van would be free to drive away. That's if anyone was in it.

He rubbed his beard as he mulled it over. If the man was as old and frail as witnesses described, then he had nothing to worry about. As long as he didn't allow him to read his fortune, that was.

'Hello, can you open up?' Will said, tapping on the back doors of the van. A scuffling sound ensued within, rusted springs creaking as the occupant shifted their weight from one end of the van to the other.

'What do you want?' a frail scratchy voice said from within.

Will grew confident in his abilities to apprehend the owner of the voice. But he would need more than an old man in an ancient orange van to justify an arrest at this stage. He needed an identity.

'I'd like to have my fortune told,' Will said, hoping to pander to the man to effect an easy arrest. He slid a twenty-pound note from the folds of his wallet and held it out to the frail figure as he cautiously opened the back doors.

He was taller than Will, with gaunt features and dry flaky skin resting on the shoulders of his coat. His beady black eyes darted from side to side as he eyed Will suspiciously.

Will relaxed, finding it hard to believe that the man before him was capable of hurting anyone, let alone murder.

'I don't call them readings any more, they're prophecies, Mr …?' the man spoke, bent over as he shuffled out of his van and onto the dirt track of the isolated laneway.

Will slipped his warrant card from his jacket pocket and flashed it at the man as he spoke. 'Dunston. DC Dunston. And you are Bertram Bishop, I take it? Or should I call you "the Raven"?'

'Bertram means Raven,' the man said quietly, loosening his necktie.

'This is an informal visit,' Will said, hoping to put him at ease so he could persuade him to go for a ride in the police car.

'In that case you won't mind taking off your jacket and turning around. I don't wish to hear my own voice played in a court of law.'

'I'm not wearing any recorders. It's not CSI, you know,' Will said, removing his jacket and folding it over his arm.

'Turn around please.' Bert raised his hand and pointed his finger in a circular motion.

'Oh for God's sake,' Will said, raising his hands palms upwards and turning around.

He did not have time to register shock as the shovel came down on his head. He only experienced a flash of white-hot light, before his knees gave way and he hit the ground.

The floorboards of the darkened room pressed unforgivingly against Will's face as consciousness flooded in. Blinking to accustom his eyes, he emitted a moan of pain and confusion. Bound tightly, he lay on his side, fighting the sour taste from the oil-stained rag wound tightly against his mouth. Pain sliced through him as he jerked against his bindings. He was ensnared. Warm, sticky blood trickled from puncture wounds in his wrists and ankles, and he tried to breathe through the haze. The pain from his bindings competed only with the pounding of his head. With building dread, Will realised he was bound not with rope, but something much more vicious – spiked wire, which punctured his flesh every time he fought against it.

He strained to listen to the sounds around him as he tried to find his bearings. The muffled noise of a car engine revved in the distance, but the sign of life brought a little relief as hammer blows of pain rained through his skull. He groaned, feeling as if he was on a revolving floor. The room began to spin, searing pain bringing him to the edge of passing out. Nausea swept over him, and he fought to keep it down. Control. He needed to take control. Choking on his own vomit would kill him in seconds.

He blinked furiously in the dim light. All he could smell was the oil from the damn rag tied around his mouth, and wherever he was, it was as black as the night. If it *was* night. There was no way of telling what time it was. Just how long had he been here? Fear cranked up his heart, skipping beats as he tried to remember what happened.

The air was stifling, and beads of sweat broke out on his forehead as he choked a restricted cough. His head was pounding harder now, and he held his breath as a rasping noise broke out behind him. In the depths of darkness, he was not alone. Will stiffened for fear of further attack, his last memory turning around for the old man. He had become complacent, and dropped his guard. *Stupid … stupid … what a fucking stupid thing to do.* A crack of a match made him jerk, and he bit into his gag as the barbs cut further.

Bert sat before him, cross-legged on the floor. Will blinked as Bert's face danced before him, his button eyes black with intent, just like his namesake.

Shaking his fingers violently, his captor extinguished the match as it burnt the tips of his fingers. Another crack as a fresh match struck the edge of the box, and the smell of sulphur invaded Will's nostrils.

Bert dipped the match to the wick of the small candle, giving little light to the gloomy space. 'You shouldn't have turned your back. Appearances can be deceiving.'

Will tried to swallow, but his throat was too dry. He blinked at Bert, echoing his sentiments. How could he have been so stupid? The only comfort was that it was him, and not Jennifer. As if reading his mind, Bert spoke.

'It's barbed wire. I thought it was fitting, given that the police have been a thorn in my side. You should see what I have planned for Miss Knight. She *is* a special one, isn't she?'

Will responded with a muffled growl, chewing on the rag in an attempt to loosen it. The taste of engine oil, and the thoughts of being imprisoned by the madman before him made him retch.

'Shush, calm yourself, otherwise I'll have to put you asleep again. Your fate has not yet been sealed. Maybe you'll be lucky and the cards will set you free.'

Will thought that was unlikely, judging by the other victims who had met their grisly ends. He had to get himself out of this situation before he ended up like them. But how? Bert's yellowed teeth flashed in a manic smile, making Will's heart sink. He could not even reason with the lunatic before him. He wriggled his injured wrists, trying to work himself free from his bindings. His eyes danced around the room, seeing nothing but darkness. The tiny circular glow from the melted candle lit only inches before him. He could be anywhere. Will wriggled again, kicking out in an attempt to sit upwards. Like a dying fish he flopped around on the wooden floor, until Bert produced something from behind his back. The twelve-inch blade glinted against the flickering candlelight as he made his intentions clear.

'It would be a shame to kill you *before* the reading, but I will if I have to.'

The whites of Will's eyes widened with terror, and his nostrils flared to accommodate the breaths entering his body. Adrenalin flooded his system as his body fought for survival. All he could do was bite down on the gag.

'Sorry I couldn't find a clean cloth for you. I've had to be very inventive. Now let's get started. I'm so excited about your reading today I'm even doing it for free.'

It was only then that Will noticed the tarot cards spread out face down on the floor next to him. Three cards. This was not going to take very long. Will thought of Jennifer, his family, and all the things he wished he had said to them.

Bert turned over the first card, his eyes glazing over as he revealed Will's past. His happy childhood, his marriage, joining the police and meeting Jennifer. Bert shook his head in disgust as he conveyed how Will had made little effort to save his marriage.

'DC Knight turned your head, didn't she? If you'd minded your own business you wouldn't be here now. I had no quarrel with you, but you forced my hand.' Bert turned over the second card, revealing his present. His position in his job, his affair with Jennifer, everything was brought in front of him. Will wondered just how long the killer had been watching them to know so much. He was clearly insane, and his motive for the murders made him all the more unhinged.

'The prophecy cannot be stopped once it has commenced. As soon as I read your future, it will happen. Maybe now, maybe tomorrow. Who knows?' Bert cackled, his face set in a deadening grin.

Will conveyed his anger by shaking his head. But it was pointless. In the mind of a cold-blooded killer, everything is justified.

He blinked away his blurred vision. The shaking had subsided, and the only plan he could think of was to launch his body at the man if he came towards him. Slowly, he tried to wriggle out of the barbed wire, each movement bringing intense pain.

'I've wasted enough time. Now it is time for your future.' Bert rubbed his hands together before slowly turning the last card over, nodding and mumbling as he responded to the voices in his head. 'I am to do you a great service,' he said.

Will's heart leapt. Was he going to release him after all?

'You are to become acquainted with the blade of my knife, but it won't be a quick death. You have a whole day to make your peace with it, before your body expires.'

Will bellowed through the cloth in frustration, making Bert jump and topple the candle to its side, spilling hot wax on the dusty floorboards. Bert swore, patting his pockets for his matches. He shook the half-empty box before striking another, making it kiss the extinguished wick.

Bert's face darkened like thunder as he grabbed Will by the jawbone, his long nails digging into his skin. 'You shouldn't have done that.'

Unable to raise himself from the ground, Will bellowed for help, but was silenced by the tip of cold steel piercing his stomach. A trickle of warm blood ran down his side, and a fresh wave of nausea passed over him as he realised he had just been stabbed.

'The prophecy has been set in motion,' Bert said, transfixed by the bloody blade. 'Your body will sustain you until tomorrow, then you will die here, drained of blood.' Bert laid the bloodied knife on the floorboards behind him before stretching his limbs to walk away. 'So it will be done. You have twenty-four hours to live.'

Will sank into dark oblivion.

CHAPTER FORTY-SIX
Bert

He was getting stronger, he could feel it in his bones. Every cell was repairing, knitting together, expelling the sick, and cleansing his blood. The police officer may not have been part of his plan but he had come too far now, he could not risk getting caught. Now all he needed to complete his mission was to fulfil two more prophecies. The bound and gagged police officer was a good bargaining tool. If the homeless man did not bring Jennifer Knight to him, the death of her colleague would. He needed to arrange a meeting, and he needed her to come alone. This had to be personal, so personal that she would want him solely for herself. She was close. He could feel her energy reaching out to him, probing the darkness. It was all coming together, and he was ready.

Like a vampire, he would feed from the essence of her soul. Only then could he be free. Bert smiled as he watched in his rear view mirror of his mother's car. The ragged man slowly ambled up the road, his face wracked with discomfort as he clutched a rucksack over one shoulder, and his scruffy dog under his arm. A grey blanket enveloped the terrier's body, its small black nose peeping out from the layers. Bert pressed the brake, allowing the man to catch him up. The drizzly weather had kept people inside, and Bert felt his confidence in his mission grow. The car came to a slow halt as he unwound the dirt-streaked window, a spray of drizzle providing fresh vigour.

'Can I give you a lift?' Bert craned his neck to peer up at the man.

George pulled the scruffy terrier up under his right arm as he shuffled on the pavement towards town. He hunched his shoulders in a determined march, throwing a glance at the driver of the car crawling alongside the kerb. 'Do I know you?'

'Don't you remember? We shared a drink the other night. Can I give you a lift?' Bert tried to hide the glint of excitement in his eyes. Such enthusiasm tended to unsettle people, and although his prey may have overlooked it for the sake of a drink, in the empty streets with nothing but blackbirds circling overhead, he may not be as keen. He could also have been warned of a suspicious man in the area.

'I've got a little nip of something that should help warm you up,' Bert said, his patience running thin. His eyes flicked to the mirror to check the streets were clear. A knife lay hidden in the pocket of his door well. The dog could prove difficult, but if the old man didn't get in voluntarily, he would take him by force.

George came to a sudden halt, his dog shivering under his arm. Bert willed him to climb inside, wondering if the sight of rosary beads hanging from his mirror would give him some much needed reassurance.

George hoisted up the dog under his shoulder, his own discomfort evident by his pained expression. 'I need a lift to the vet's. Me dog is sick. I think he's caught a chill.'

Bert leaned across and pulled the passenger door handle. The bottom of the door scraped across the pavement and it protested with a loud creak. It hadn't been opened in years, and an earthen mossy odour escaped with a barely audible whoosh.

'Hop in,' Bert said, with his most reassuring smile.

George ducked his head as he climbed inside. 'Thanks very much, mister. Can ya drop me to the Haven Veterinary clinic on the far side of town? You'll have to turn around. Do ya want me to direct ya?'

Bert checked his mirrors as he pulled away from the kerb. 'No need. I know exactly where I need to go.'

George drew the seatbelt across his dog, strapping him onto his lap. Tinker blinked before narrowing his eyes at Bert, and a low rumble of a growl ensued.

'Tinker, stop that,' George said, stroking down the white hackles forming on the dog's back. The car veered left and began to gain speed as it took a country road out of town. 'You're going the wrong way, mister, the vet's back there.' George jabbed his thumb behind him.

Bert stared firmly ahead. 'In good time. There's a few loose ends to tie up first.'

George's straggly Adam's apple bobbed as he swallowed, his liver spotted hands shaking in tune with Tinker's nervous shiver. Probably desperate for a drink, Bert thought, knowing that would be the least of his worries soon. As if reading his thoughts, the dog gave a low growl, enough to tell him he was up to no good. Bert smiled in satisfaction. He had George exactly where he wanted him. There was no way he could get out of the car while it was moving so fast. The metal box shook as it hit the country lanes, the worn-out suspension making every bone in his body rattle.

'I don't have time for this,' George said, his teeth jarring as the car bounced out of another pothole. 'Just bring me back to where you found me and I'll be on my way.'

Bert tightened his fingers over the narrow steering wheel and threw George a poisonous look. 'You'll go when I say you can go. Now sit tight, this won't take very long.'

George's voice rose up a pitch. 'What do ya want with me? Sure I'm just an auld fella on the street. What interest do ya have in me or me dog?'

Bert shook his head. 'I saw your past, I read your cards. What's the saying? What comes around goes around. Well today destiny is paying out.'

'What?' George said, craning forward in his seat as the car slowed to a halt. As he gazed at the landscape ahead, it all became clear. The earlier drizzle began to thicken, as black clouds blotted the landscape. A low rumble of thunder echoed from far away.

'I'm not going in there,' George said, as Bert opened his passenger door from the outside.

Bert leaned across and clicked the stiffened seatbelt free, pulling back his hand from the snapping muzzle. 'Fine. Then we'll do this the hard way, because I always get what I want.'

Bert ripped the blanket from George's arms and threw it over the dog's head.

'What are ya doing to Tinker?' George yelped, slapping away his hands. 'Don't hurt me little dog.'

'I'm not going to hurt him, I'm just bringing him for a walk,' Bert said as a sheet of drizzle showered his face. Wrenching the dog from George's arms, he strode to the building ahead. George caterwauled in despair, shuffling and limping behind Bert, his black coat flapping in the rising wind. In the distance, a flash of light followed the boom of thunder.

The corners of Bert's mouth cranked upwards as a flock of ravens cut through the evening air. *One, two, three* ... there was no stopping the prophecy now.

CHAPTER FORTY-SEVEN

Jennifer nursed her cappuccino as she inhaled the delicious aroma of freshly ground coffee beans in the small cosy cafe. While most police officers frequented pubs in their leisure time, Jennifer could usually be found in one of Haven's coffee shops. Although she was not averse to going out for a drink, the smell of alcohol reminded her too much of her father, and the nights she had to pull on her coat to walk through the dimly lit streets to bring him home. Heads would turn as she entered each of the local boozers, full of drunken patrons elbowing each other to warn of the presence of a child. Their father had become an expert at dealing with the occasional visits from social services. Lying was a natural talent, and he used his charm to ease any lingering doubts.

Jennifer forced herself to snap out of it. Without work to occupy her, her thoughts often returned to the past. Only now could she comprehend how much danger she and Amy had been in. And yet her father was back, raking up old wounds.

She liked the coffee shop because she was always left alone to ponder. Nobody took your cup before you finished, or wiped your table to subtly pressure you into leaving. It was usually filled with young girls, admirers of the David Beckham lookalike barista who ran it. Jennifer turned her thoughts to Will, who had made the journey home to chat to his mum about their relationship. She didn't know what worried her the most, the fact he deemed their relationship serious enough to involve his parents, or their reaction when they found out how smitten he was. He didn't need to say he loved her, it was evident every moment they spent together. But it was no secret they wanted him to return to his remorseful wife, who was yet to sign the divorce papers citing her infidelities. Jennifer's fingers found the nape of her neck as a cold breeze danced on her skin. She shook off the feeling, telling herself she was being silly. But as she gripped her mug, a ball of dread dropped like a stone inside her.

Students giggled as they waited to be served, toddlers whined in their pushchairs, and the man across from her rustled the pages of the *Financial Times*. But it was all lost to Jennifer as she sat stiffly in her chair, oblivious to the outside world. Something was wrong. It chilled her bones and filled her soul with dread, detaching her from reality until the only sound she could hear was the beating of her own heart.

She jumped out of her trance as her telephone rang, bringing up her knee and spilling the contents of her coffee cup across the table. Jennifer mopped the cold liquid with serviettes. Just how long had she been sitting there? Grabbing her handbag she squeezed past a queue of customers to the front door. Of all the places for that to happen, she thought. I must have looked like a shop dummy sitting next to the window in a trance. But the feelings of misgivings had not relinquished their hold, and her heart skipped a beat as her phone rang a second time.

It was not Will's name that lit the screen but Christian's. 'Hello?' Jennifer whispered, fiddling with her car keys as she strode down the path.

Christian's voice was breathy. 'I'm glad I caught you. Bert's called my mobile. He said he was going to pay me a visit, but he had some business to take care of first. I've had a bad feeling all morning, I just knew something was going to happen.'

Jennifer's heart flickered. 'Did you hear any background noises? Anything to tell you his location?'

'He said something about being in the highest point in Haven. I could hear someone shouting in the background, something about letting go of a tinker. That's when the call ended. You need to arrest him, Jenny, please. I'm terrified he might come around and harm the children.'

Tinker? Jennifer searched the corridors of her brain as she tried to extract the information she needed. She stared at the cracks in the rain-dappled pavement, her forehead knotted in a frown. Tinker ... 'The voice, did it have an accent?'

'It wasn't local. He just kept shouting something about Tinker, and then the phone went dead. I didn't even know Bert *had* a phone.'

Jennifer nodded, even though Christian could not see her. 'OK. I'll call this through to control and send somebody over to keep an eye on the place. Keep the line free and call me if you hear any more.'

Jennifer tapped her fingers against her lips, pushing back her anxiety. The Raven must have taken George and his dog. But why would he want to hurt them? Membership of The Reborners came with a hefty price tag and Jennifer couldn't imagine him attending. And where the hell was the highest point in Haven? She alerted control to carry out a local search, and organised a unit to attend Christian's address for safeguarding. The wind whistled as the dark clouds whipped into a storm, sending loose leaves in a circular dance as the breeze picked up momentum.

The thoughts of the Raven hurting George filled her with trepid determination. She had to find the Raven before he killed again. A sense of déjà vu swept over her as she recalled her last big case, attending the boathouse to save her young nephew Joshua. In her eyes, George Butler was every bit as vulnerable. A small frail man with a trusting nature, she struggled to understand why the Raven would hurt him … unless it was solely to get to her. She thought of the last time they spoke, the raven glaring down at them from the branches of the tree. Was it an omen? Jennifer's heart pounded in her chest at the thought of George making his way to the highest point in Haven. But where was the bloody highest point? Haven was relatively flat. There was a river, woodlands, and acres of unkempt land, but no mountains or hills to be explored. Frustration pushed the breath out of her body and she fought to calm herself in short gasps. She couldn't keep driving aimlessly around, waiting for answers. She had to stop the prophecy.

She dialled her sergeant's number and patched it through to hands free. It was picked up on the first ring. 'Sarge, give me some answers please, where's the highest point in Haven?'

'I'm looking. There are several blocks of flats, or the radio station, but I don't think anyone can get in there. We don't even know if he means a building or land, do we?'

Jennifer could hear a keyboard tapping in the background. She was about to reply that she didn't know, when she was interrupted by Claire's voice.

'Hang on, I've got it on Google. The highest point in Haven is the radio station, it's located on the old industrial estate. I'll update control and get some units to meet you there. And Jennifer … you don't need to look for Bert's van. Officers picked it up down a side alley half an hour ago.'

The trees flashed past the window in a green blur as Jennifer drove towards Radio Haven. She glanced at her dashboard as the ding ding of her warning system alerted her she was low on petrol. Swearing under her breath, she gripped the steering wheel. It wasn't like her to be so disorganised, but with everything going on, her normally ordered lifestyle had been thrown into chaos.

Jennifer swung her car around and pushed her foot onto the accelerator as the engine roared into life. The Siri device on her phone obtained the number for the radio station and she punched it in.

'Come on, come on,' she growled as the slow tone rang out unanswered. Just what was she going to say if she got through anyway? Surely anyone trying to get access to their roof would be challenged, and if they'd seen anything suspicious they would call the police. She cancelled the call and concentrated on the road, wishing she had a blue light on the roof of her car.

Jennifer's car screeched up to the building, sending gravel skidding across the path as she yanked her handbrake. Pulling out her warrant card, she flashed it at the brunette on the reception desk.

'DC Knight. Has anyone suspicious come in this way? Any men you don't know?'

The brunette closed her magazine, a wad of chewing gum resting on her back teeth as she stared open-mouthed. 'No, nobody,' she squeaked in a small voice.

'How do you get access to the roof? Is it possible for someone to get on from outside?' Jennifer said, her heart pounding as precious seconds passed by.

The girl pointed at a set of double doors to the left of the building. 'There's a railing outside but it's safer in the lift. It'll bring you right up to the roof.'

'Thank you. We have concerns that an elderly homeless man may be trying to jump off a building today. If you see anyone matching this description on the premises then call the police.'

The girl chewed her gum a couple of times before answering, 'Sure, I will do.' But Jennifer had already left, and was hastily jabbing the buttons to call the lift.

She wrung her hands as the lift slowly ascended, the panelled numbers of each floor flashing red as they rolled across the glass screen, one … two … three … four … as if in slow motion. Jennifer's imagination went into overdrive, acting out every worst-case scenario. How terrified must George and Tinker be in the clutches of the madman? she thought, clenching her fists. She didn't trust the receptionist, who had been engrossed in her magazine when she burst through the double doors. They could have easily gotten past her and slipped into the lift. They could be up there right now. She envisioned them on the roof as the wind whipped around them. Bert standing behind George, his hands rough on his back. The skinny Irish man was skin and bone. It would only take a small push to send him over the edge. Clutching his little dog, he would either land on the concrete or on the roof of a car in the car park below. She willed the lift to move faster until finally it dinged.

A gust of cold fresh air invaded her space as the doors slid open. With slow, cautious steps Jennifer walked out onto the bleak flat roof. Thick blankets of clouds rolled overhead, carrying the guts of a storm, and loose wire cables whipped ominously against the tangled steel of a radio mast. Car doors slammed below, and the sound of heavy boots scrunching on gravel told her that her colleagues had arrived. But the roof was desolate, with no sign of the Raven or George. A gust of wind flapped her jacket open, and the reality that she had come to a dead end delivered with it a bolt of anger.

'Damn it!' she said, stepping back into the lift and pressing the button for the ground floor. Her colleagues were waiting for her as she got to ground level, and she shook her head as she stepped out. 'Sorry guys, it appears to be a false alarm. There's nobody up there.'

A ruddy-faced officer nodded. 'We've checked the ladder and the rear of the building. Reception will call us if anyone turns up. The PCSOs have checked the other high points, the tower block and the new church.'

It wasn't until Jennifer got in her car that the answer came to her. The Raven had been away from Haven for a long time, and his psychiatrist said he often lived in the past. His perception of the highest peak may not be the same as theirs. The radio station, the tower block and the new church were all built in the last few years since the expansion of the town. The officer's words filtered through her brain. They'd checked the *new* church. But not the old one. She opened her car door to alert her colleagues, then paused, allowing them to drive away. She could have been wrong, and the Raven may have been setting her up to look like a fool. But something in her gut told her she was on the right track. It was the same stubborn determination that made her want this arrest all to herself. Emily's little boy floated in her vision, starving and alone as his mother lay dead on the bed. She would be the one to bring the Raven in. She grabbed her shoulder harness from the back seat and pushed her arms through the loops. The weight of her baton, handcuffs, and CS incapacitant spray felt good as it nestled next to her ribs. She started her car and drove in the direction of the church. They had a bond, which would soon be broken. She was going to take the Raven down.

CHAPTER FORTY-EIGHT
Bert

'Please,' George said, his voice frail and broken. His tattered coat flapped mercilessly as he followed in Bert's wake across the open plains of the remote church land. 'Please, mister, just let me little dog go. He's not well.'

Bert strode in wide, dogged footsteps through the overgrown graveyard, squashing the growling terrier close to his chest. Moss-covered headstones slanted against the rushes trembling in the wind. The residents of this graveyard had little family left to mourn them, and as Bert stomped carelessly over their graves, his thoughts were focused only on reaching the bell tower. His mother used to say it was the highest point in Haven, and how once she had ventured up there after visiting Callum's grave. He knew then that she had considered jumping off. He often wondered what brought her back from the edge. It wasn't love, that much he knew. His twin's gravestone lay in the children's graveyard at the back of the church, and he recalled that a weeping stone angel stood guard over the young souls taken too soon. But none of that mattered, as Bert doggedly carried out his mission. All that was left was to carry out the final prophecies. A thin layer of sweat glistened on his forehead. The ravens above cawed and screeched their warnings, as ominous as the derelict church ahead. Time was running out. He didn't have a second to lose.

Bert pushed open the wooden door at the rear of the old stone-walled building, which had been there almost as long as Haven itself. Bats rustled overhead, disturbed by the footsteps echoing through the crumbling spiral steps to the belfry.

'Come along, I've got you a present,' Bert said, his words echoing as he climbed each step. George's terrier emitted soft muffled whimpers as he cried for his owner.

George wheezed as he forced his legs to climb the stone stairwell, Tinker's distress spurring him on. His neck craned upwards in the gloom, and he shouted a warning. 'I don't want yer fecking present. Now let us go or I'll call the guards on ya.'

Bert carried on climbing until he reached the bell tower, positioning himself perilously close to a windowless alcove.

'The guards?' Bert laughed, as George joined him, panting for breath. 'You're not in Ireland now, George. I've seen your past; I don't think you'd be welcome there again, do you?' Bert waited for the shock to register on George's face before carrying on. 'So take your present and be happy about it.' Wriggling in his arms, Tinker gave a threatening growl. Bert pulled back the blanket and slapped him on the muzzle.

George whimpered at the sight of his beloved pet being mistreated. 'Wait, I'm sorry, I'd love to see me present. Can't we go back down and take a look at it?'

Bert moved towards the shafts of light stabbing the gloom. 'There's no need, I have it here. Take a seat and I'll give it to you.'

George took one look at the madness dancing behind his eyes, and sat down before his legs gave way.

'Good,' Bert said, unceremoniously dropping the dog to the floor with a plop. Opening his rucksack, he pulled a long black cloth and shook it free of its creases before passing it to George. 'Put it on,' he said, a menacing tinge to his voice.

George said, 'What?'

'Don't play stupid with me. I said, put it on.'

George opened his mouth to speak, but instead was taken over by a series of spluttered coughs and wheezes. But there was little sympathy to be gained from Bert, who dumped the garment over his head and pulled his limp arms out either side.

'You don't know the lengths I had to go to, in order to get my hands on this.' Bert stood back and frowned. 'It's a bit big. Here, let me fasten these buttons.'

George's voice came in a throaty rasp. 'Please, no more. I'm not well.' He rubbed his tightening chest. His fingers touched the buttons of the cassock and his eyes grew wide as he realised the garments that had been bestowed upon him. 'What sort of tomfoolery is this?'

Bert widened his smile in mimicry as the lilt of an Irish accent passed his lips. 'Wat's going on? Ah sure I'm only an auld beggar man to be sure to be sure.'

Tinker barked weakly in the corner as George's trembling fingers worked to release the long line of buttons from the holes.

'Oh no you don't.' Bertram's long nails dug into George's scrawny wrists as he grabbed them tightly, causing him to cry out in pain. 'No you fucking don't, you hear me? Not unless you want to see flea-bag here bungee jumping without a rope.'

'What do ya want from me? Do I know you?'

'No but I know you, *Father Butler*. I've seen all your secrets. Did you really think you deserved a second chance?'

George's mouth dropped open, his eyes pleading with his captor. 'I … I haven't served as a priest for twenty years.'

Bert paced the narrow space. The wind screamed through the cracks in the walls while a sense of madness rose in the wild evening air. He stopped abruptly, smiling again. His moods changed by the second, and his unpredictability made him all the more dangerous.

A clap of thunder boomed in the evening sky, electrifying the air around them. Tinker looked sorrowfully at his master before lying down on the block floor. His teeth clacked together as he whimpered through his closed muzzle, his energy dissipating by the second. A flash of lightning drove a sudden shaft of light through the narrow space, and Bert stared at George with narrowed eyes. He could tell he desperately wanted to scoop up his dog and leave, but his heart was most likely beating at such a rapid pace it barely gave him enough strength to stand, never mind tackle him, whose determination had lent him strength unknown for a man his age.

Bert clapped his hands on both of George's shoulders, clattering his teeth as he forced him down. 'This will be your defining moment in the priesthood. Now what are we missing? Oh, of course, here it is,' Bert said, pulling out the white collar from his pocket. Bert's fingernails pressed into George's windpipe as he slid the collar through the cassock, then stepped back and admired his handiwork.

George gasped for breath, clawing his throat, which had been sorely deprived of oxygen seconds before. 'Please, are you finished? Can we go now?'

'We're finished. Yes,' Bert said, walking towards the terrier. 'Time to say goodbye.'

'No, please, you said you weren't going to hurt Tinker,' George said.

Bert smiled. 'Oh no, I would never hurt a dumb animal. It's *you* that's leaving. Don't forget, I've seen it all, Father Butler.' Bert waved his finger before tutting three times. 'What age was that girl again? Sixteen? Seventeen? You couldn't arrange that abortion quick enough, could you? And you, a man of the cloth!'

'She *wanted* to be with me, but I stopped it because it was wrong. She came to me distraught. I was just trying to right a wrong.'

'A wrong you've tried to forget ever since. You on your pulpit, preaching clean living, all the while arranging the murder of your unborn child.'

Guilty tears fell down George's weather-worn cheeks. 'Why do you think I live on the street? Because I know I don't deserve any better.'

'And yet you are still a coward, running away from me when I am here to deliver your prophecy. Surely you know that dying is the only way to receive absolution for your sins. I'm not completely heartless. If you really can't face dying alone, I'll let your dog go with you.' Bert reached for the dog's collar, and began to drag him to his feet.

'Bertram Bishop, I'm arresting you on suspicion of murder,' Jennifer said, her voice echoing as she rose from the stairwell.

Bert swung his head as Jennifer stepped into the bell tower, her baton extended in preparation to fight.

'What ... what are you doing here?' he stammered, holding Tinker mid-air by the collar. The helpless dog twisted under his grasp, his eyes bulging as he fought for breath.

Bert was so stunned by Jennifer's presence, he did not see George reach for the Swiss army knife in his right pocket. A gurgling scream passed his lips, as George plunged the extended fork into his hand.

Tinker wriggled free, finding a second wind as he bumbled down the stairs.

'Stand back!' Jennifer shouted to George, taking Bert's legs with her ASP as he lunged forward, pulling the knife from his pocket. The glint of the knife was her justification, and a crack of bone rang through the air as the metal baton took his shin in one precise hit.

Bert screamed as he rolled around the cold concrete clutching his leg. Jennifer pounced, pulling his arms roughly behind his back to lock the handcuffs in place. Indignant caws ruptured from the darkened sky, turning Jennifer's blood cold.

'You can't stop the prophecy,' Bert screamed, the words delivered in a maddening howl. The words had just left his lips when the rapid burst of a police siren pierced the air.

'Me dog!' George panted, as another roll of thunder boomed. 'They'll run over Tinker!' Stumbling towards the stairs, George called for his terrier as the siren grew louder, and as if in slow motion, Jennifer cried out for him to wait.

But George wasn't listening, and flailing both arms, his feet tangled in the long black material of the cassock as he went tumbling down the steps. Jennifer gasped in horror, leaning all her weight on Bert as she subdued him long enough to call out to George. But the bump bump bump of his body down winding steps silenced, and all Jennifer could hear was Tinker, fussing over his lifeless owner, lying bloodied and motionless on the bottom of the stairwell floor.

CHAPTER FORTY-NINE

Jennifer took the tissue from her sergeant and blew her nose. The two-bar heater had warmed the chill from her bones, which was brought on by more than the weather as Moonlight descended. Arresting Bert had given her little comfort. George's death struck deep, but her sergeant folded her arms, showing little emotion for the man she had helped over the year.

'I know it's sad, but you didn't really know George. You're best off forgetting about him.'

'That's a bit harsh, isn't it? He's barely cold,' Jennifer said, shocked by the chill in her words.

'If you knew the truth …' Claire paused, signalling at Jennifer to close the door '… You might not have given him the time of day.'

Jennifer leaned against the door and closed it without moving her gaze from Claire. 'Go on then, tell me.'

Claire sat on the edge of her desk, which was littered with overtime sheets and folders full of appraisals waiting to be completed. 'Did you know he used to be a priest?'

Jennifer's eyebrows shot up in surprise. 'No I didn't, but he was quite philosophical at times, I suppose. Is that why he was wearing the cassock?'

'I expect so. Father Butler served as a parish priest in Ireland for over twenty years until he left.'

Jennifer nodded. The idea of George holding regular sermons was not a far stretch of the imagination. 'A man of the cloth, eh? I wouldn't hold that against him.'

'You might feel differently when you hear his history. When he was thirty, he got a seventeen-year-old girl pregnant.'

Jennifer's hand touched her mouth. 'You're not serious.'

'That's not all. He arranged a secret abortion without the knowledge of her parents. It's outlawed in Ireland, so he would have had to pull out some stops.'

'That's awful ... but it *was* a long time ago, wasn't it?'

Claire nodded. 'And he's been paying for it ever since. It's why he *chose* to be homeless. George's loaded, but his guilt consumed him. He told me his story a while ago, and I promised to keep it to myself.'

'To think ...' Jennifer's eyes flared as her emotions tied themselves up in knots. 'To think I gave him soup!'

'It's a mind fuck all right. On one hand I feel sorry for him, spending all those years on the street, but then I think of what he did and he repulses me.'

Jennifer scrunched up her tissue and threw it in the bin. 'I guess you're right. I shouldn't waste my tears.'

'I think Bert wanted to make it look like George killed himself due to his guilt. That's probably why he dressed him up in the cassock,' Claire said, picking up her paperwork and throwing it down again.

Jennifer knew the feeling, her own paperwork demanded her attention, but the Raven case had knocked her out of sorts, and she found it hard to concentrate on anything else. 'Did George ever mention The Reborners to you? A vulnerable old man with money, sounds right up their street.'

'No, but it wouldn't surprise me if he was a member. But without Bert's testimony, who knows?'

Jennifer nodded mechanically, dropping her gaze to the floor. Claire's boots were scuffed with mud. 'Where's the dog?'

'My mum's keeping an eye on him at mine. Not many people want an old dog that howls for his master every night.'

Jennifer gave an involuntary shudder. 'I still can't believe it. I really liked him.'

Claire nodded, rubbing the tiredness from her eyes. 'As my old mum would say, "There's nowt so queer as folk."'

After five hours in custody, force medical examiners and the mental health team agreed Bert was unfit for interview. He had been taken back to The Rivers for assessment, but it was unlikely he would ever be released. Jennifer hated cases like that, and knew her unanswered questions would keep her awake for some time to come.

Arrests from The Reborners' raid had gained little information, other than a cult being led by a supreme leader whose name was known to very few. As far as Jennifer was concerned, the mysterious man behind the mask was Bertram Bishop, and she hoped that, one day, the mental health team would draw out some answers.

She checked her phone. A whole day had passed and Will had not called. She turned over in her bed, knowing she wouldn't sleep without finding out how things had gone with his parents. Putting the phone to her ear, she groaned as the robotic tones of his automatic voicemail played out. She hated leaving messages due to her tendency to waffle, so she terminated the call before she could be tempted to ask why the hell he hadn't rung. *As long as he's not having second thoughts about divorcing his wife.* Jennifer sighed as her mind grew fresh worries. As if she didn't have enough to keep her awake. But sleep came eventually, and as she turned and twisted, she was given an insight of nightmarish proportions.

It started much like many of her other nightmares, feeling lost in the darkness, alone and confused. Then she heard it. In a bleak confined space, an anguished moan. A clotted head wound, and beneath, a pool of congealed blood. Jennifer probed further and a man's wrists came into view. Bloodied and torn, they were tightly bound with barbed wire, clasped behind his back. Jennifer gasped as she recognised a silver ring edged with dry blood. Black wings flapped overhead, opening their talons to claim their prey. *Will!* Jennifer screamed, unable to reach him. The raven's eyes snapped towards hers as Jennifer's energy spiked in fear. Long talons reached into her consciousness, tugging on the tailcoat of her thoughts.

Morning light came to rest on Jennifer's face, and she wiped the sleep from her eyes, staring quizzically at the ruffled sheets and the pillows that had ended up on the floor. Recollection of the night before was hazy. She stared at the brightly lit screen of her iPhone, a sudden streak of terror running deep as the images in her nightmare began to filter through.

Jennifer held the phone tightly in her grip. The dark space, the sleeping man, and in the corner, a curled-up figure caked in blood.

'It's just a dream. It's just a dream,' she mumbled, over and over, under her breath, dialling Will's number with trembling hands. She paused over the connect button, scared of what she would find. 'Answer, please answer,' Jennifer whispered, pressing the green connect button and holding the phone to her ear. When she received no response, her fingers typed out a text: *WHERE ARE YOU?*

There was no time for a shower as she waited for a reply. She pulled back her hair into a bun and rushed around the room throwing clothes on the bed. She needed to get to work so they could triangulate the call. Should she call at Will's place first? Her mind raced. No, call her sergeant, give her an update, and then call into Will's flat, just in case he's at home. Tendrils of hair fell loose as Jennifer pulled the cashmere jumper over her head. Hastily pulling on her black leather boots, she took deep breaths to stop the tidal wave of fear that threatened to engulf her.

'If you can hear me,' Jennifer said, eyes turned to the ceiling, 'please, if anyone can hear me, please help Will. Please.' A sob escaped her lips and she swallowed hard. She would not allow herself to fall apart now. 'Please keep him safe, he's a good man. I can't do it without him.'

The journey to Will's house felt like an eternity as every learner driver in Haven seemed to clog the streets. The Fiat Punto in front of her stalled as the traffic lights turned green and Jennifer clenched the steering wheel as she growled in exasperation. Pulling her phone from her pocket, she patched in a call through her car, straight to the DI's mobile. After several rings it was answered by a surprised-sounding Ethan. 'Hello? Everything OK?'

Jennifer bit back the tears as she struggled to relay the words. 'It's Will. He's in trouble. I haven't been able to get a hold of him, and last night I sensed he was bound and gagged somewhere, with blood coming from his head. It's real. I know it is.' It sounded crazy, but Ethan picked up the worry in her voice and knew better than to dismiss it.

'It's not crazy, Jennifer. I … I was just about to ring you. We rushed through the forensics on the van. We've found traces of Will's blood.'

Jennifer gasped in horror as he delivered the words, her stomach clenching at the thoughts of her nightmare becoming a reality. She bit down hard on her lip, forcing herself to focus. She needed to be strong for Will, now was not the time to fall apart.

'Jennifer, are you there?' Ethan said, his voice sounding echoey and far away.

Jennifer took a deep breath. 'I'm OK. I'm almost at his flat. Can you look up his parents' phone number on the system and see if he's with them? He left two days ago to go to theirs but I haven't heard from him since.' She tried to work out a timeline. Bert must have kidnapped Will and then moved on to George. Traces of blood, the DI said, not pools. She clung to the hope it was not too late to save him. Had Bert given Will a reading? Just how did he overpower him? Questions came quick and fast as she realised the DI was still talking.

'Don't worry, Jennifer, Will's a tough nut, and I have everybody out looking for him. I'll contact his parents myself, and try to get a unit to meet you at his flat. God knows they're thin on the ground this morning. Keep me updated and don't send any texts or try to call him. I don't want anyone turning off the phone while we triangulate it.'

Jennifer nodded into the phone. At least triangulation would give them a rough idea of where he was, or rather where his phone was. Will never went anywhere without it. She thought of the dark space, the wire bindings, and the silent watcher. Will was bleeding and unconscious in her premonition. He was barely breathing but at least he was alive. But time was running out, and they needed to find him fast.

She wished she had accepted the offer of a key for his flat. But within minutes of talking to his neighbours she discovered he was not home, and nobody had seen him for a couple of days. His parents were on their way with a spare key, and her colleagues would search every inch of the place, but in her heart, Jennifer knew he was not there. Very gently, she closed her eyes and scoped the area with her mind. There was nothing. Standing outside, she searched the bushes for anything that may have been thrown away in haste if he had left in a hurry. The only thing she found were some strange looks from the PCSO that turned up to assist. Jennifer asked him to search the area for Will, but he was unconvinced there was anything to worry about.

'Will's always messing about, he's probably sleeping off a hangover somewhere,' the PCSO said jokily. He lived in the area himself, and had known Will for several years. He had only just come on duty, and had headed straight out after being notified of the search.

Jennifer updated him on the forensics, watching his eyes widen as he digested the news.

'Shit,' the young lad said, 'I've seen that Raven guy in all the briefings. If he's hurt Will … shit. He could be dead for all we know.' His pessimism was enough to tip Jennifer over the edge. She swallowed back the lump in her throat as she trotted back to her car. Turning up her police radio, she listened for updates as she drove to see Ethan

The CID office was bustling, the air filled with a sense of urgency as telephones rang and printers jammed. The doors between their office and Op Moonlight had been flung open, as both teams worked together to find their lost colleague. Jennifer collared Ethan as he rushed past, snapping at someone to turn off the radio in his wake. His shirt was stained with sweat, and she guessed he had not been to bed. She stood apprehensively at the door of his office as he went inside.

He waggled the mouse to awake his computer, his Outlook Express displaying virtual chaos as dozens of unread emails pinged up notifications. Ethan picked up a half-eaten ham sandwich from his desk, raising his eyebrows in Jennifer's direction as he chewed.

She hated when he was like this, uncharacteristically harried and stressed. She wanted to see him focused and hopeful. She'd known him long enough to know that snappy and tense meant he was worried. She began to wish she had troubled someone else for an update rather than relying on their friendship to provide her with answers. She desperately wanted to relay the strength of her intuition, but Ethan did not appear to be in a listening mood.

She took a deep breath. 'Have you managed to trace Will's phone yet?'

Ethan finished his sandwich and gulped back some cold coffee to wash it down. 'We're doing everything we can. His phone is dead, most likely battery failure. They've checked ANPR and his car hasn't left Haven, so he's most likely still about. The 'copter will be taking off as soon as weather permits. Now why don't you go home and let me get on with things. You're meant to be having a day off.'

Jennifer opened her mouth to protest and Ethan waved her down. 'We're doing everything we can to trace Will, now if you don't mind, I need to be getting on.'

The source of his irritation became clear as she caught a glimpse of an email from his superiors. It wasn't just Will's disappearance that was playing on Ethan's mind. She did not need psychic abilities to cotton on that he had received a rollicking for his run-in with the Lexton DCI. He picked up the phone to make a call, and looked at her as if to ask why she was still standing there.

Jennifer looked at him cagily. She was beginning to prefer the young and carefree Ethan, before he succumbed to the pressures of being her boss.

'With all respect, *sir*, this is my shift partner we're talking about, and he's in danger. I can't just go home and put on *Jeremy Kyle*.'

'Go home,' he mouthed, before speaking into the phone.

She nodded, tight-lipped, not trusting her response. But she was never one to do as she was told, and made herself a cup of coffee before checking her work emails in the empty office of Operation Moonlight. The budget only ran to one shift, but the sheer volume of mysterious cases hitting their desks dictated that soon the team would grow. She scanned through enquiries and responses to earlier emails, finding nothing of relevance surrounding Will's disappearance. Pulling on her jacket, she took to the streets in the hope of some insight. His car had to be in Haven, but where? Jennifer grasped for hope, unlikely tales spinning in her mind. Maybe he had come across the van and cut himself. Maybe he was away, chasing up leads, not knowing the Raven had been arrested. But why hadn't he been in touch? The same ugly answer resounded in her head: *Because he's dead.* Jennifer hit her steering wheel as the incessant thoughts drove her crazy. She couldn't face the answer that had been staring her in the face all along. It was why she felt Will's presence, breathing in the walls of her home. He had died, cold and alone, and had come back to be with her. Turning her car for home, she forced herself to face the truth. If she could not communicate with Will on an earthly plane, it was time to seek his presence on the other side.

CHAPTER FIFTY

Efforts to communicate with Will had proved fruitless, and Jennifer felt like banging her useless head against a wall. Not that the communication she desperately sought came from her head. No, it emanated from her soul, and for the hundredth time she wished it was something tangible she could physically control. Her eyes danced around her home, wishing she didn't feel his presence so strongly. It was her turn to call Christian for comfort, and she bit back her tears as she updated him on Will's disappearance. With the police failing to turn up any leads, he was her last port of call.

'Are you sure you want to do this?' Christian asked. 'Will's been gone some time, I may not give you the answers you're looking for.'

'I need to know where he is, dead or alive. I hate to ask so soon after Felicity's passing, but I don't know where else to turn.'

'I'm just dropping off the kids, I'll be with you in just over an hour. Together we may be able to pick up something.'

'Thank you,' Jennifer said, her voice barely a whisper.

'You're more than just colleagues, aren't you?' Christian said, his soothing voice relaying his empathy with ease.

Jennifer closed her eyes and squeezed the bridge of her nose. 'Yes. That's why I need to know.'

'Hold tight. I'll be there as soon as I can. If you hear anything in the meantime just call.'

Jennifer was no stranger to haunted homes, having researched them in her spare time. Sometimes people haunted buildings when they passed over, choosing to stay with their loved ones rather than explore what was waiting for them on the other side. The thought of Will being trapped in the walls of her home filled her with dread – and given the soft whispers that sometimes passed through her mind, he would not be alone. It was a thought she could not bear to entertain, and yet … She shivered. It was doing her no good sitting here, sick at the thought of losing the only man she had ever really loved.

Ethan rang to inform her that Will's parents were visiting the police station to speak to his colleagues. Jennifer apologised, saying she wasn't up to it. She recalled something Christian Bowes said after his fiancée died. *I know it sounds selfish but I just don't have time for anyone else's grief right now.* Had it really come to that? Jennifer pushed the thought away, muttering under her breath as she admonished herself for being so morose. But all the same, she knew what they would be thinking, that Will was fine until he met her, and if he had gotten back with his wife as they advised, he would be safe and well. Jennifer's stomach clenched, the small cramping sensations making her feel weak. She sat and wrapped her arms around her waist, leaning into the pain until it passed. She had experienced them when she was a child. Anxiety and hunger wrapped up in a painful little bow. Yet she welcomed it, because it was better than the deadening numbness inside.

Walking into the kitchen, she poured herself a glass of filtered water from the jug in the fridge. Closing her eyes, she stared inside the cool white box, inhaling the cold artificial air. The smell of cleaning fluid was barely discernible, and that unsettled her even more. She could clean it while she was waiting, use the extra thick bleach, then the kitchen cupboards …

'And what good is that going to do?' she moaned, closing the fridge door, pushing her forehead against the white sterile steel. It calmed her, making her think like a police officer instead of anxious ten-year-old Jenny who was lost and all alone.

She wanted to grill Bert, to demand he provide her with answers. He had to be responsible for Will's disappearance. But she was not going to be allowed anywhere near the suspect she had been thrilled to arrest. Never before had she felt such an anti-climax. Think, girl, think, she thought, gently tapping her forehead against the fridge door. She recalled her case the previous year, when she looked to the past for answers. Her knowledge of Bert's history was vague. He had lived between the mental institution and his home all his life. Officers had attended both addresses but it had not progressed their investigations. But they were level-headed men and women. They weren't like her. Pulling her bag from the counter, she headed for the door, car keys in hand. If she put her foot down she could make it to Bert's home and back in under an hour.

Satnavs weren't of any use when it came to finding Bert's address, so it was just as well she had scanned the police officers' statements at work, greedily taking in every last shred of evidence. His house was beyond Raven Woods, another quarter mile down the track where she had abandoned her car the day she was attacked by the ravens. An icy trickle of unease slid down her spine. It was the last place she wanted to be, and her sergeant would admonish her for attending when they had already conducted a search. But she had to try, and anything was better than sitting alone, with the feel of Will all around her.

The journey to Bert's home was easier than she thought, as she followed the tyre tracks from the police 4x4 dug into the soft soil of the narrow laneway. Jennifer stared straight ahead, her fingers gripping the moulded grooves of her steering wheel. She didn't want to see the woodlands, much less the flocks of ravens overhead. A tiny voice told her to stop and call for backup. Jennifer pressed the accelerator as her internal monologue argued the toss. She couldn't waste another minute. Will was hurt, or worse. If she found anything *then* she would call for help. She sighed. One side of her desperately wanted to find him, while another wanted to live in the moment of hope and possibilities. What if he was dead? Will was the kindest, most thoughtful man she knew. He didn't deserve this. Just how would she cope without him in her life? Jennifer's heart felt like it was being squeezed by an ice-cold grip. Taking slow, steady breaths, she eased the car up the leaf-strewn gravel driveway of Bert's home.

The gloomy building was bigger than she imagined, and in a state of total decay. Half-drawn graffiti was daubed on the side of the home, discarded cans of paint thrown on the ground. Like many places on that side of Haven, visitors did not stay very long before beating a hasty exit. There was no beauty to be found in the grounds either. It no longer lay in the dying flowerbeds, choked by the weeds taking dominance over the soil. Rotting brickwork glistened with torn cobwebs, dancing mournfully in the breeze like silken fingers pointing, *go back, go back*. It was the same breeze that carried the sour smell of the woods. A crow's caws echoed in the distance. Jennifer quickened her steps towards the crumbling building; Will's life was at stake and she had to make the most of the fading light.

A thought occurred as she reached the unsecured front door. Dr Carter had said that Bert sometimes imagined his mother was still alive. What if her spirit still clung to the land? What if she was still here, imprisoned by the house which encompassed so much misery? The front door emitted a rusty screech as Jennifer pushed it open, wishing it was a little brighter inside. As soon as she stepped in the hall she felt like an imposter, and it took all her strength not to turn around. Her eyes flicked up to the cobwebbed ceiling, and a wide-legged spider retreated into its web. Jennifer stiffened, reaching for the door handle of the room on the right. As she twisted the cold metal doorknob, she focused on the energies in the house, stepping back to a time when it was infused with life. As she pushed open the door, her eyes were drawn to a wide stone fireplace, blazing with a fire radiating a yesteryear heat. It was then that Jennifer saw her first embodiment, and froze to the spot. It should not have come as such a surprise, given her previous encounters with the supernatural. She was used to picking up voices, like an old radio channel filtering through her mind. But a real-life ghost? She looked just like a normal person, rocking in her chair. It was Bert's mother; the grief lining her face told Jennifer all she needed to know. Her hair was scraped back in a bun, and her pallid flesh encased a withered body frozen in time. She wore a long black skirt that brushed the ground each time her rocking chair bowed forward. Yet Jennifer knew from the glazed expression and listless energy she was a shadow of the past. The ghostly apparition could not cause her harm, but just like in her dreams, her body perceived the situation as a threat, and Jennifer's heart thundered in her ears as she forced herself to stand her ground.

The room dimmed as Bert's elderly mother curled her arthritic fingers around the arms of the wooden chair and set it to a halt. The corners of her mouth turned downwards as she craned her head in Jennifer's direction, raising a bony finger in the air.

'Get. Out. Of. My. House.'

Jennifer's heart felt as if it was going to beat out of her chest as she faced the shadow of what once was. The room temperature dropped steadily until it was icy cold. Jennifer's words carried on frosted breath as she uttered the words, 'Mrs Bishop, I need your help. It's about Bertram.'

The woman's eyes blazed at the mention of Bert's name. 'What do you want with him?'

Jennifer tugged her jacket around her shivering body. 'I'm looking for my friend Will, and I think Bert may know where he is. Has he brought anyone here?'

Bert's mother relaxed into her rocker, setting it back in motion. 'I'm waiting for Callum. He'll be home soon. Bert's in bed. He's a sickly child.'

Jennifer sighed. She was not going to get any assistance from a dead woman's ghost and it was time to move on. 'Mrs Bishop, I don't think it's good for you to stay here.'

'I'm waiting for Callum.'

'*He's* waiting for *you*, Mrs Bishop. He's been waiting a very long time. Don't you want to go to him?' Jennifer swallowed, mystified at the words leaving her mouth. It was not the first time she found herself uttering words she did not understand, but if they provided comfort then she was happy to continue.

The woman's face clouded over, the frailty of her soul laid bare. 'I ... I can't leave the house.'

'Yes you can. You don't need it any more. Let it go. When you feel Callum's presence, step up and take his hand. But you don't need to stay here. There is so much more for you, if you can find the strength to leave.'

But she wouldn't. At least not yet, and she returned her gaze to the fire as it hissed and spat orange sparks that went nowhere, delivering heat that could not be felt. Slowly Jennifer left the sad figure, and wandered through the rest of the house, her ear sharply attuned to the flapping of the ravens gathering on the fence outside. She rubbed the back of her hand. It had healed well, but the small scar would serve as a reminder of her stubbornness, and inability to ask for help for fear of looking like a fool. She checked her mobile phone, the absence of calls a painful reminder that time was running out. Five minutes. She would give herself five minutes and leave.

Every room door was ajar and she was relieved to see the loft hatch gaping open, its mouth an empty chasm as sharp-clawed rodents scurried overhead. Officers would have already searched the gloomy space, which meant she didn't need to. The oppression in the house grew with every second that passed, until the derelict building took on a life of its own. I shouldn't be here, she thought. Not only was she under a ceiling that may well give way, her presence was most unwelcome, and the birds that had swooped to attack her were now gathering outside.

Jennifer ventured into the kitchen as the building groaned above her. Small black pebbles of droppings littered every counter, and in the absence of food, there lay empty bread wrappers, chewed by rodent teeth. It felt as if a hundred sets of eyes were beating down on her back. She wondered if the attending officers had felt it when they conducted the search. She turned to leave, passing each ramshackle room until she came to the largest bedroom. Like the rest of the house, it was caked in a layer of dust. The peeling sash window allowed generous light to flood over the rusted metal bedstead, and she guessed it was Bert's room. Her heels echoed as she walked across the cold wooden floor, and she imagined a small hungry boy, lying on the sunken mattress as he stared at the oak tree outside. She pulled back the damp mouldy blankets and lingered long enough only to check under the bed. Another wave of despair passed over her. Will was not there. He never had been.

She turned on her heel and made her way to the hall, but the noise of the ravens suggested there were more than one or two waiting for her exit. She peered through the gap in the door, catching her breath as she caught sight of the black feathered sentries gathered on the fence. A horrifying sense of dread enveloped her as she realised she would have to pass them on her way out. Why didn't I park the car nearer? she thought. If the birds attacked, they could do a lot of harm in the precious minutes it would take her to reach it. Tapping her fingers against her bottom lip, she formulated a plan. She picked up an empty milk bottle from the floor and pressed the central locking button through the gap in the door. A chorus of excited caws ensued as her car beeped in response, and they flapped and danced on the fence in preparation for their prey. They'll rip me to shreds, Jennifer whispered as she backed away. She would get only one chance. She had to be quick or she would pay the consequences.

She returned to the kitchen, holding her breath as she slowly turned the handle of the back door. Relief flooded through her as it opened, and she tentatively slid out, tiptoeing through the undergrowth at the side of the house. The front of the house was black with ravens, their beady eyes focused on the front door. She flung the milk bottle, sending it rebounding on the front porch, startling the ravens long enough to race to her car. Soon she was safely inside, sending gravel shooting in her wake as she raced down the driveway for home.

Jennifer dropped her car keys onto the hall dresser. Her stomach growled to remind her she had not yet eaten, having been sick with stress all day. She opened the fridge door, gulping back the last of her mineral water. Pulling out a block of cheese, she laid it on the chopping board next to a chunk of bread. She checked her watch. It granted her enough time for a quick shower before Christian came around. She needed to wash away the dark barbs that clung from the horrors of the day. But the feeling of Will's presence had grown stronger since she came home, each step inside telling her she was missing something, something she should have known. She tore off some bread and nibbled on enough cheese to silence her rumbling stomach. Hopping up the stairs, she turned the shower to the hottest setting and slipped off her clothes. A creeping sensation on the nape of her neck made her whirl around, a shriek emitted through her lips as she faced the steamed-up mirror. There, in the midst of her distress, the answer came. She knew where Will was. It had been staring her in the face all along.

CHAPTER FIFTY-ONE

In the mirror, daubed in ghostly fingerprints, were the scrawled words 'LOOK UP'. Jennifer froze, her heart pounding as she steadied herself against the ceramic sink. Her eyes darted around the steaming bathroom, as she hastily pulled on her shirt and trousers, unable to take her eyes off the fogged writing. It was the only morning she had not showered. Just how long had those words been written on the mirror? And who put them there?

A frown burrowed its way into her forehead, and she stared up at the ceiling spotlights for answers. What does it mean, look up? she thought, her heart picking up a beat.

The extractor fan kicked in, fading the words as it sucked the steam from the room. She squeezed her damp feet back inside her boots, her flesh pinching against the taut black leather. The answer came to her like a bolt of lightning. The loft! He's in the loft! The realisation invoked a fluttery, breathless feeling upon her. All thoughts of Christian's visit were forgotten as she dragged the vanity chair to the landing, her mind flooded with thoughts of Will. Her nightmare showed him in a dark space, warm and heady … just like her loft. The moans she heard in her sleep – had they been real? Had he been calling for help? Had Will been lying in agony as she slept in her soft warm bed below? And if so, who put him there? Had the Raven been above her head all along? Had he crept into the loft while she was asleep? Surely she would have known. The thoughts lingered as she pulled down the extendable silver ladder, allowing it to clank against the soft woollen carpet below. A wave of sickness descended on her as fear ran riot with her imagination. She steeled herself as she gripped the cold aluminium, trying not to think the worst. How on earth could Will have ended up in her home? Cobwebs lingered along the edges of the dark space. It was the one room she could not bear to clean. But cobwebs and spiders were the least of her worries as she entered the attic. She inhaled through her nostrils, praying she would not be greeted by the scent of death.

Adjusting her eyes to the dark, her hands grasped blindly for the nylon string to activate the single light bulb hanging from the ceiling. She swallowed back the dryness in her throat as dread flooded her system. Stale heat cloaked a musky smell, which hung heavily in the air. She whispered a quick, silent plea for help before calling Will's name. Her right hand grasped in the dark air as her left clung onto the cold metal steps. The long nylon string teased her palm and she grasped it quickly, tugging hard until it lit the loft with a sharp click. Her eyes darted around the shadows and settled in the corner, focusing on a body.

The figure of a man lay on its side, bathed by the shadows of the dim light.

'Will? Is that you?' Jennifer said, wobbling as she hoisted herself onto the thin wooden floor. Her heart was pounding faster now, and she prayed for signs of life. Crouching under the slanted ceiling rafters she crept over, trying to accustom her eyes to the faint light. A sharp intake of breath passed her lips as she recognised Will's suit. It was just like in her dream. He was on his side, facing away, his legs bent up to his chest, his bloodied hands bound behind his back.

Jennifer inched forward, blinking away the tears pricking her eyes. 'Will,' she said, 'please Will, say something.' The silence was deafening. Fumbling in the shadows, her legs became weak, and she stumbled onto her knees as the loft walls began to close in on her. 'What the hell is wrong with me?' she slurred, clambering over to Will. Anguish and torment stabbed her heart as a dark pool of blood soaked into the knees of her trousers.

'Will!' she cried, her voice piercing through the stifling air. With shaking fingers she tentatively reached out to touch his cheekbone, whimpering *'Please be OK, please be OK.'* She could not bear the thought of touching his cold dead body. Relief flooded through her as she felt life in his clammy skin. Tears sprang to her eyes at the sight of Will reduced to such a pitiful state. Cradling his head, she called his name, lightly tapping his cheek. But it made little difference as he lay lifeless and gaunt under the light of the single bulb.

She shook her head, trying to ward off the drunkenness invading her body. She was sick, but could not understand why. Could there be a gas leak? Carbon monoxide? she thought, feeling like she was on a carousel. She needed to get out of the loft before she passed out, or they would both be in mortal danger. Shuffling over to some boxes, she tipped over the one containing the blankets and sheets she had been saving for the dogs' home. She worked swiftly, placing a folded blanket underneath Will's head, and covering him with the other. She winced as she pulled back the blanket to inspect his bindings.

'Sick bastard,' Jennifer said out loud. It was the Raven's handiwork. And she had been next. She needed to get help, but couldn't leave him either. Pulling her sleeves down over her fingers, she unwound the wire around his wrists and ankles as gently as she could. The barbs prodded into her skin, intermingling her blood with Will's, another wave of dizziness overcoming her as she laid him in the recovery position. But even the movement was not enough to bring him around. She quickly scanned his body, each injury stabbing her heart. His shirt was damp with the blood pooling on the floor, and she nimbly opened the buttons to discover the small knife wound to the right of his stomach. Grasping the edge of a sheet, she ripped enough padding to press against the wound, holding it in place with the waistband of his trousers. She touched his face, promising to return. If she passed out here, it could be days before anyone found them, and by then it would be too late. Feeling drunk, she clung to the ladder like it was a lifeboat, clambering down the stairs to search for her phone. But her mind was foggy and she could not remember where she left it. The doorbell rang, and she swung it back, virtually running into Christian, who looked as shocked as she was.

'Jennifer, are you OK? Oh my God, is that blood ?'

'I need a phone ... call for help,' she said, concentrating hard on her words. 'Will's in the loft. He's hurt. I need ... ambulance.'

'What! Are you OK?'

'I ... I don't know,' she gasped, hanging onto the banisters for support. 'I don't feel so good. I'll explain later. Please, call them.'

Christian's blond quiff bounced as he nodded ferociously. 'Of course. You go inside, I've got my phone in the car, I'll call them straight away.'

Satisfied, Jennifer turned and headed back upstairs, her legs feeling like lead as she forced them up each step. Half way up she heard a car door slam. At least help was on its way. Just how long had Will been up there? He must be dehydrated and in need of food, but moving him would only exacerbate his blood loss further. The way she was feeling, she could barely make her way upstairs.

She gritted her teeth in determination as she mounted the stepladder and hoisted herself into the loft. 'It's OK, Will ... help is on its way,' she said breathlessly as her heart pounded like a jackhammer.

Someone shuffled in the kitchen downstairs. It must be Christian waiting for the ambulance, Jennifer thought. She touched Will's face, cursing herself for not bringing water up with her.

'Will, if you can hear me, just hang in there. Help is coming. I'm so sorry. I'm sorry I didn't find you sooner.' Jennifer shuffled over to the tiny loft window, one of the original features of the Victorian home. It offered a view of the streets below, and she peered out through the glass, praying for an ambulance to arrive. But there was no ambulance. What she did see chilled her to the core.

CHAPTER FIFTY-TWO

Jennifer's stomach lurched as footsteps creaked on the loft ladder. She needed to get back to Will, but her sickness was coming in waves, weakening her legs, and blurring her vision.

Christian appeared through the hatch, his expression blank. 'The ambulance will be here soon. Is he still breathing?'

Jennifer nodded, taking small, quick breaths as the room began to swim. She strained to listen for sirens, but silence was returned. Christian took another step up the ladder, and her body stiffened in his presence. She locked her eyes on his, stunned by his betrayal.

'There's no ambulance is there, Christian? Or should I call you leader?'

His mouth twisted in a sneer as he clapped, the palms of his hands striking together in three slow, forceful beats.

'Well done, detective, you got there at last. Tell me, what part of my award-winning performance didn't ring true?'

Jennifer pointed to the window. 'The chalk … from the quarry. It's all over your tyres,' she paused to look him in the eye, barely believing her own words 'It was you all along.'

'I can't take all the credit, darling, Cousin Bert had his role to play too. Such a shame you had to interfere. Still, I'm sure we can rectify that.'

'You … you helped him?' Jennifer said, the weight of betrayal falling heavily.

Christian climbed off the ladder and sat on the loft entrance, his legs dangling down. 'Darling, I didn't help him, I *orchestrated* him. That's what made it all so perfect. There's nothing to trace the murders back to me.'

Will stirred in the corner, a small moan escaping his lips.

A cold sweat ran down Jennifer's back. The answer had been staring her in the face all along. She needed to buy some time while she worked out a course of action. There were two things Christian loved most in the world: a captive audience, and the sound of his own voice. She relied on him not being able to pass up the opportunity for either.

'Why?' Jennifer said, knowing that even if she was able to get past Christian and make it downstairs, she could never leave Will at his mercy.

'I'm here to finish what Bert started. He's always idolised me, you see,' Christian sighed dramatically. 'It used to be such a pain, until I found good use for him.'

'I don't understand,' Jennifer said. She mentally assessed his strength. He was slim but toned and completely blocking her exit from the loft. She, on the other hand, was sick and groggy, while Will was unconscious and bleeding out. The odds were not in her favour. She tuned in to his voice as he revealed the truth.

'It all started with Felicity. The engagement was all her idea, and I couldn't dump her after she appeared on that reality TV show. Our relationship boosted my ratings, and I knew the press would turn against me if I broke off the engagement. Next thing I know, she's arranging the wedding and talking about kids. I mean really? As if I'd want to spend the rest of my life with *that*. So I did the only thing I could do, I found someone pliable, someone whose life meant nothing, and used it to my advantage. Bert had told me how he'd used the cards to kill people in the past, so I decided to test him out on Alan Price. All I had to do was plant the seed in Bert's brain and let him think it was all his idea.' Christian smiled at his ingenuity, the light from downstairs casting his face in a ghoulish glow.

Jennifer was sitting now, shifting slowly backwards, her hands silently groping the floor, for something, anything she could use to defend herself. 'But you reported Bert for harassment,' she said, needing to keep his focus turned inwards.

Christian flapped a well-manicured hand. 'Oh that? It was just a cover, something to make me the victim. It was me calling him. Sometimes he'd tune out, but I knew a part of him was always listening.'

'You were so bereft,' Jennifer said, fighting the rising nausea. Mind over matter, she thought, taking slow deep breaths to work through the sickness and build her strength. But she needed more time. Time Will couldn't afford.

Christian beamed a smile, revealing perfect white showbiz teeth. 'I know, and to think they said I couldn't act! I even managed to get a couple of newspaper interviews about my tragic loss, as I waited for the insurance policy to come in. God knows I needed to bolster my show ratings. Felicity and that silly cow of an ex-wife of mine bled me dry. My livelihood, my home, everything was at risk. The network had been threatening to drop the series. Don't you see? I had to do something.'

'But murder?' Jennifer said, fighting to steady herself. 'You were making money from the cult. Why resort to murder?'

'I didn't set up The Reborners', I managed it. They needed someone intelligent, who could launder the money and control the members. But drugs aren't my scene, and it became too big for me to handle.'

'Mike Stone,' Jennifer said, her voice a whisper. Everything drug related in Haven came back to him.

Christian nodded. 'Alan Price was one of the few people who knew of my identity. When I confided in him about my association with Stone, he started calling me a fraud and threatened to go to the papers. Then he blabbed to Emily and Geoffrey, and they tried to blackmail me for money.' Christian rolled his eyes at the audacity. 'They soon shut up when Price died. With each death, Bert became more hands on. It was fascinating to watch his confidence grow.' Christian chuckled. 'So I whispered some more, and allowed your little priest friend to get his comeuppance. I made Bert think it was all part of some big prophecy. He actually believed that if he didn't go through with it, something terrible would happen to him.'

'Why did you warn me about George?' Jennifer said, trying to distract Christian as she kept her focus on Will's faint breath.

Christian blinked in the dim light. 'The same reason I sent you those letters: to implicate Bert and stop him going too far. He's completely mad.'

'And Will? Was he part of your plan?'

Christian crouched as he approached her. 'He should never have interfered. I figured you could find Will dead and blame it all on Bert. But then I knew. You'd chip away until you pointed it all back at me. And what if Will survived? I couldn't stop now, not when I'd come so far. Can you imagine what they'd do to me in prison?'

Jennifer opened her mouth to respond, but another wave of sickness fell over her, and she leaned on her hands to catch her breath.

'Ah good. The drugs have taken hold. I was worried you'd taste them in the water.'

Jennifer had already guessed her drinking water had been drugged. She tried to cast her mind back to when she came home; just how much had she consumed?

The bulb flickered overhead as loud scratching noises echoed from the darkened corners of the room. Christian sneered in the erratic light as he loomed over her. 'It sounds like your boyfriend has woken up. Best you say your goodbyes. If it's any consolation, I'll make it quick.'

Christian clenched his jaw in frightening determination as he straddled her body. She struggled under his weight, gurgling a scream as her body betrayed her, a limp and lifeless rag doll.

Clamping his hands over her mouth, he sealed her last breath as she weakly kicked and bucked underneath him. Her muffled screams petered out, her lungs burning as she lost the air to accommodate them. In a flash she saw her death, then Will's; dying next to her as red blossomed around him, seeping through the floor, to be found as a scarlet bloom soaking through to the ceiling below. Horrified officers would climb the loft and find two of their colleagues dead. One murdered, one suicide.

NO! she screamed inside her head. I'm not fulfilling any prophecy. She dug her nails into Christian's wrists in an attempt to aid her survival. He groaned, his breath coming in gasps. A bead of sweat rolled off his forehead, then onto the tip of his nose, before dripping onto her shirt.

Sweat dampened the roots of Jennifer's hair as he pushed her head back on the hard wooden floor. She dug her nails in harder, dragging precious forensics behind her nails. He would not get away with her murder, she thought as stars blinked in her vision. But what about Will? A thump from behind caused momentary relief as a book came whizzing out of the darkness, making Christian yelp as it hit him squarely in the head.

Jennifer leapt on the distraction, and sank her teeth into the back of his hand.

Shaking his hand, Christian stared in disbelief. 'You bitch!'

Using every ounce of strength, Jennifer scurried forwards on her hands and knees towards Will, grasping, reaching out for something, anything to help her fight. She gasped in disbelief as her fingers wrapped around a thick-handled knife, and a flash of realisation clawed its way into her brain. The knife was Bert's, left behind after he stabbed Will. Christian had seen it too, and he launched himself upon her, clawing at the weapon. It sat in the small gap between the heat of their bodies, and a shocked gasp escaped Jennifer's lips as it turned. The knife met flesh and plunged. It clanged against the floor and they both collapsed, heaving for breath. Jennifer's fingers traced the warm blood dampening her shirt. Anxiously she traced the skin underneath, to the backdrop of Christian's breaths, now coming in whistles and frothy bubbles. It was not her blood. It was his. He clasped his hands to his chest, until they slid down to his side, and his eyes became vacant.

Rifling through his pockets, she found his mobile and dialled 999. Perhaps later she would feel sorrow for Christian, but for now, her only concern was saving Will's life.

CHAPTER FIFTY-THREE

Jennifer felt relief that Christian survived, not due to any concern for him, but because she did not want to be responsible for his murder. Facing charges for kidnapping, attempting to pervert the course of justice, witness intimidation and attempted murder, he was not going anywhere soon. But first, he had to recover from his punctured lung. It came as little surprise that Bert had fallen into decline and would spend the remainder of his life in an institution.

It was the topic of the office as Jennifer returned to work, having used up all her leave to care for Will, who was steadily recovering from his injuries. Leaving him in his mother's care, Jennifer was keen to discover the full extent of the investigation.

'So how's Will?' DI Ethan Cole said from behind his desk. He seemed to be getting a grip of his role, having almost lost two of his best officers. Her eyes fell on his desk in admiration as she noticed his sharpened pencils lined up neatly in row. She smiled at her superior, grateful for the opportunity to mull things over.

'He's champing at the bit to get back to work. His mum is so cute, she won't let him outside until the doctors give him the all clear.' Jennifer smiled. She had gotten on famously with Will's mother since the incident. Rather than blame Jennifer for her son's injuries, she was full of praise for her 'brave actions' –

staying with Will, when others may have left him to fend for himself.

Ethan looked at her thoughtfully, as if reading her mind. 'He's very lucky. It could have been a whole lot worse, for both of you.'

Jennifer recalled the small scars dotted around Will's wrists. The dehydration was almost as harmful as the knife injury, and they both carried guilt for not noticing the criminal right under their nose.

'Thankfully there's been no permanent damage. Still, it sticks in my gut to think Will was in my house the whole time we were looking for him.'

Ethan blew out a gasp of exasperation. 'I've never met anyone like you before. There were teams of police officers looking for Will, but you sensed he was in your home. Something drew you back there, and you saved his life because of it. It's a good thing Christian is as crap at dispensing drugs as he is at telling fortunes, otherwise you could have died. So give yourself a break, eh?'

Jennifer shrugged off the compliment. Everyone knew the story of how Will found the Raven, and no doubt Ethan would give him a telling-off for going it alone instead of bringing in his colleagues. It all came back to their visit to Christian. As the crocodile tears flowed, Will had noticed the white bonded notepaper on the dresser; the same notepaper used to send Jennifer the letters. It led him to seize the phone records from The Rivers mental health institution, which listed hundreds of *inbound* calls to Bert. Jennifer was furious at her incompetency. Having had so much on her mind, she had been in no hurry to seize the phone records, and believed Christian when he said the harassing calls had been made to him. After finding out about the insurance claim on Felicity's life, Will took the details of the CCTV company outside Christian's home. A security system recently installed in the periphery of

Christian's garden led Will to finding Bert parked under the cover of private wooded land. But Will's curiosity had not gone unnoticed, and Christian had already wormed his way into Bert's consciousness, advising him that Will was a danger to his bigger plan.

Jennifer reminded Ethan that hindsight was a wonderful thing, and sometimes hunches or suspicions were not enough to call in the cavalry and risk looking like a fool.

Ethan broke into her thoughts. 'They've taken Christian's show off the air. His ex-wife was offered a nice payout for that story they ran in the Sunday paper.'

Jennifer smiled. 'I wasn't entirely surprised. It was only a matter of time before the media turned on him.'

Ethan gave a bemused smirk. 'He's certainly the villain of the piece now. I don't think they'll give him an easy time of it in prison.'

Jennifer shook her head. Her disgust at Christian's betrayal left a bitter aftertaste. She gave her trust to so few people, and he had let her down. She thought of how he had sympathised with her about her tough upbringing. His whole career was based on taking advantage of people in their grief, and he had become a master at it.

'It's all such a waste of life. And for what?' Jennifer said, imagining the ghost of Bert's mother waiting for her son to come home. Her feelings about the Raven were mixed. Since being institutionalised, he had reverted back to his previous state, with no recollection of his time outside the institution. It was hard to stay angry with someone who was being used as a pawn to commit evil deeds. The thought struck deep within her, although she could not fully understand why. She shuddered, feeling as if someone had walked over her grave.

Ethan touched the pencils on his desk, aligning them for a second time. 'That Bert gave me the creeps. When they brought him into custody ... those big black crows ... the rear yard was swarming with them. Three of them slammed against the window of the SERCO van when they took him away.'

Jennifer vaguely remembered picking up the dead raven outside her home. The nightmares that followed, being attacked in the woods, she would never quite feel at ease with ravens again. She nodded, keeping the information to herself. 'His readings, apparently they were very accurate.'

'Yes, but sometimes he helped them to come true. All the same, I wouldn't want to be on the receiving end of one of his predictions.'

'You know what I think? Leading The Reborners was a massive power trip for Christian. I'm not convinced that Geoffrey or Emily tried to blackmail him. Running the cult made him feel godlike, choosing who deserved a second chance and who didn't. His ratings were flagging because of his rubbish predictions, and the public was fickle, only loving him for his fiancée, not for himself. He involved Bert because he was jealous of his psychic powers, and maybe even mine.' Jennifer stared through the office window, thankful for clear blue skies. The more she spoke, the closer she came to believing her own theory. 'Christian wanted Bert to get his comeuppance, just like the others, but the power of Bert's convictions scared him, and that's why he always kept us one step behind, in case he needed us to bail him out. We found other letters in his home, one for Geoffrey, and one for George. I guess it became too risky to deliver them, with all the police on the streets.'

Ethan swivelled his chair to face her. 'The main thing is that you and Will came through it in one piece. If you ever need to speak to anyone, my door is always open.'

'Don't worry about me, I'm like a rubber ball,' Jennifer said, wearing her most convincing smile. She was glad of the distraction of staying at Will's while he recovered, and did not relish the thoughts of going home alone. The adjoining loft to the empty flat next door had been sealed up, but she still felt ill at ease in her home. Will had denied making any noises in the loft, much less throwing the items that distracted Christian long enough for her to fight back. He had looked at her blankly, when she put it to him. His only memory was being held captive by Bert, and passing out as he inched the knife into his stomach.

Christian had given his interviewing officer the same blank look when questioned about writing on her bathroom mirror, with the words 'LOOK UP'. He actually had the cheek to send his apologies, and planned to write a book of his experiences. The news of his denial provided her with comfort. Whatever was in the walls of her home had tried to help her, and she would not question it further. Perhaps it was George who had come back to right a wrong, or the written warning had come from older souls, who had inhabited the space long before. Whatever the reason, such occurrences were woven into the very fabric of her life, and impossible to escape. The best news came in the form of George's dog, Tinker. Having heard the story of the pining pet, Will persuaded his parents to take him in. It may not have been the grandchild they wished for, but being the focus of their adoration helped the little dog settle in quicker than any of them dared hope for.

Ethan's voice broke into her thoughts as she rose to leave. 'Hang on, Jennifer, I have a proposition to put to you.'

'Go on,' Jennifer said, eyeing him warily. It was no secret she was with Will, and she tried to contain the blush spreading to her cheeks as she wondered what he was going to say.

He slid a manila folder from his neatly stacked pile. 'How do you feel about doing a little family liaison work for a couple of weeks? It's day shifts, and would give you a bit more time with Will.'

Jennifer frowned. She had trained as a FLO before joining Operation Moonlight in the hope of being given some better jobs. It hardly seemed to matter now. 'What's it all about?'

Ethan flipped open the folder and handed her some copies of the enquiry log. 'It's Sergeant Duncan from Lexton MIT. You may have heard that one of his twins went missing … The press is going to be all over this and we need one of our best officers supporting the parents. Are you up for it?'

'That's awful,' Jennifer said, reading through the paperwork. A photo of the identical blonde girls caught her eye. Both wearing the same colourful dresses, the children smiled brightly for the camera. She read the names, Abigail and Olivia. They weren't much older than her nephew Joshua. A pang of sadness drove through her chest as she wondered which girl had disappeared. But she couldn't bring herself to take it on. Her emotional involvement would only serve to hinder the case. It only took seconds to decide against it.

'I appreciate you thinking of me, boss, but I'm not sure I'm the right person for this family. After all, I've just joined Op Moonlight, and Claire needs me.'

'Your sergeant suggested you for it. This is far from straightforward, Jennifer; there's been some strange goings-on with the other twin,' Ethan said.

Jennifer eased herself back into her chair, her interest piqued. 'Really? What sort of things?'

Ethan gave her a knowing smile. 'Enough to make the current FLO walk out on the family. Let's just say we need someone with your *skills* to handle the case.'

Jennifer slowly nodded, a flutter of excitement awakening inside as the meaning behind his words took hold. 'In that case, count me in.'

LETTER FROM CAROLINE

Releasing my first fiction novel, *Don't Turn Around* was a nerve-wracking experience. I wondered if readers would suspend their beliefs long enough to take DC Jennifer Knight into their hearts. An ordinary detective dealing with the extra ordinary took on a whole new level when I introduced Frank Foster AKA 'The Grim Reaper' to the scene.

Nothing could have prepared me for the amount of support I received upon release. I was literally moved to tears. Many of you will know my own story, and of my personal experiences with a paranormal entity in my home. During those difficult years when the activity was at its worst, my family and I felt very alone. My writing career is the silver lining, which has blossomed from those dark days, and using my personal experiences in both the police and the paranormal has helped me develop immensely as an author.

Thank you to everyone who has promoted my work through word of mouth or by social media. Every tweet, share, review and recommendation really does matter, and I am so very grateful. I have been fortunate enough to meet many new friends in the form of authors, industry professionals, book bloggers, and readers since joining Bookouture, and I value your support dearly.

www.caroline-writes.com

Facebook.com/paranormalintruder

Twitter.com/Caroline_writes